GOSHAWK

Also by R. Douglas McPheters

My Dream or Yours

GOSHAWK

DOUG McPHETERS

Goshawk

iUniverse books may be ordered through booksellers or by contacting:

iUniverse
1663 Liberty Drive
Bloomington, IN 47403
www.iuniverse.com
1-800-Authors (1-800-288-4677)

ISBN: 978-1-4759-8115-5 (sc)
ISBN: 978-1-4759-8116-2 (ebk)

Library of Congress Control Number: 2013906681

Printed in the United States of America

iUniverse rev. date: 04/24/2013

Author photo by Dennis Hyde

DEDICATION

Absent the zeal of the staff of the Division of Investment Management of the US Securities and Exchange Commission in flyspecking an application to list the securities of a company on NASDAQ, the adventures and discoveries revealed in this work of fiction might never have seen the light of day.

People who carry knives are not necessarily cooks—Russian proverb

PROLOGUE

Like a grotesque nightmare, a silent slide show of horrors cycled through Layla's exhausted brain. She relived pushing her younger brother, Sami, on an old tire hanging from a frayed rope behind Liberate Delta Secondary School in Basra. The first sign of trouble was reflected in his eyes—men in work clothes running toward them. Layla could still feel callused hands grabbing her arms and legs, holding her down, tearing at her robe. First, one forcing himself on her while others cheered, then another and another. Then just a boy wearing a T-shirt with a picture of five colored rings and the words "MOSCOW 1980" in big, dirty letters. At last, she slipped into blessed unconsciousness, but the possibility of her own children had been torn from her insides that afternoon.

The only sound in Layla's nightmare was her mother's calm voice: "come and have some hot mint tea, Layla, dear. You'll feel so much better if you relax and try not to think about the school yard and the shame of what they did to you."

A loud, wooden thump jarred Layla out of the fog of the last afternoon of her life. She was disoriented and fearful, suspended in half-awake, patting herself in search of a weapon without success.

Then Layla popped to the surface of where she was and what she was supposed to be doing. A mound of the equipment lay on the rocky ground between her dark winter boots—two pair of gold, anodized aluminum tree spurs, dual coils of twelve-ply nylon rope, and six extra magazines of dum-dum bullets for both AK-47s, which all reminded her of the challenge ahead.

Glancing over the desolate landscape, Layla remembered only she and pudgy Fatima from the original team had survived the trip.

She growled impatiently at Fatima, "you empty boat?"

Layla looked over at the carvel-built Pearson 24 inboard rocking in the heavy chop, its bow knocking repeatedly against a nearby granite finger jutting out into the nearly frozen fresh water. She watched the burly pilot who had ferried them to this desolate part of the lake country of Finland as he busied himself about the boat's cockpit. Layla could tell from the way he pretended to ignore the two Iraqi women that the pilot felt shamed by the very idea of sending mere women on this important mission. All the while, the pilot puffed furiously on his treat of the chocolaty taste of a Turkish cigarette of Diyarbakir tobacco clenched between richly stained teeth. With little success, he kept trying to ward off the wintry wind by drawing a cheap plastic raincoat close about his ample frame.

Finally acknowledging Layla's dismissive flick of the fingers of her good left hand, the shivering pilot tossed the butt of his glowing cigarette into the darkening waves and watched it hiss out. He motioned for Fatima, Layla's ungainly helper, to push the boat's bow away from shore then engaged its clutch and grumbled the wooden craft slowly backward, churning toward deeper water. His twirl of its small aluminum steering wheel pointed the powerboat's bow southwest, toward the last faint glow of afternoon light. Grinding its clutch again, he revved its sputtering engine as the single propeller bit into the dark blue water, pushing the boat forward with slowly increasing speed.

Layla again wearily surveyed the pile of supplies on the frozen ground in front of her, which included a small, waterproof black plastic pouch of emergency rations, a larger canvas bag, and her own AK-47. The weapon leaned on the stack of six spare magazines of bullets for the automatic weapons, each slug with an *X* carved into its tip so it would fracture into many tumbling shards at first impact, enhancing damage. There were also four hand grenades, Fatima's coil of blue-and-white nylon rope, Fatima's Chinese-made AK-47, and two pair of tree spurs for climbing telephone poles and trees. Her own climbing rope was slung over the shoulder of her own Gore-Tex jumpsuit. Nothing missing!

She poked Fatima in the shoulder. Once the subordinate finally turned to face her, Layla drew her left index finger sharply across her own throat.

Fatima looked anxiously from the mound of equipment to the rapidly receding motorboat, then to Layla and back to the increasingly distant craft. The younger woman kept gnawing the knuckle of her right index finger, looking back and forth from boat to shore.

"Now, FATima! Finish it NOW, RIGHT NOW!"

"Where is thing?"

"Worthless bitch," Layla muttered, ignoring the question, as she jerked a tiny black box from a single waterproof pocket inside the larger canvas bag and pointed it toward the slowly accelerating powerboat. Without hesitation, she squeezed the solitary red button atop the black plastic box. A bright flash blossomed under the retreating boat's cowling, silencing its engine. Then a slight grumble reached the women's ears as a burst of orange fire swallowed up the small craft, engulfing its cockpit and the hapless pilot. Layla and Fatima could see his arms flailing frantically in terror above the fierce blaze. Feverishly slapping at himself to put out his burning clothes, he leaped into the choppy water. Struggling ever slower near the rapidly disintegrating boat, he screamed in a language neither Layla nor her accomplice could understand as he sank deeper into the nearly black water. Even a competent swimmer would have been dragged down by his sodden winter clothing and rapidly swallowed by hypothermia in this frigid water. This Kurdish refugee probably couldn't even swim. Soon there was only the lap, lap, lapping of waves against the shore.

Where the Pearson 24 had been, just a charred and shriveled black plastic raincoat floated on the rippling surface.

Once again, Layla scanned row after row of red cedars on the lake's far shoreline with her binoculars, methodically covering it in two-degree increments. Hopefully her peripheral vision would spot any possible threat that normal but tired search might miss. From medieval cylindrical, yellow-stoned watchtowers dotting thick fortress walls outside Savonlinna, Finland, at the water's southern edge to the target's house overlooking its northern shore, the darkly clad young woman carefully inspected every tree and rock in sight again and again. She could find no sign anyone had noticed the explosion. A thin wisp of fog oozed over the dark water's surface.

Layla pursed her lips and exhaled on the barrel of her weapon. As her moist breath condensed briefly on its shiny metal, she firmly pressed her right index finger into the foggy place.

No fingerprint, she thought to herself, *all thanks to butchery of Surgeon Captain Iqbal, and his methodical eradication of my fingerprints. "For protection," he said. Whose protection? Maybe the big man's nephew, Tariq al-Tikriti. But I'm just a poor southerner, doing what I'm told. Will lack of fingerprints help me? Not very likely. If something happens to me, Boss and his people can claim I was working for Hamas, Hezbollah, or maybe bin-Laden.*

While Layla's attention wandered elsewhere, a small red squirrel had ventured close, its tiny black nose twitching furiously. The furry animal crouched on its hind legs, trying to figure out what to make of the slowly moving gun barrel and the woman holding it.

Beat, beat, glide. Beat, beat, gliiiiide. Another pair of eyes was watching Layla, searching for something juicy to eat. Had Layla been looking up, she might have seen its gray-and-white striped wing feathers and its long, slate-colored tail, or perhaps some nearly dried blood on its beak from the small Pomeranian the bird had almost dragged away from its owner in the small, lake-country village nearby. The male raptor's keen eyes, which glowed the same malignant red-yellow color of poisonous nightshade berries, spotted the squirrel's jerky movements on the snowy ground beside Layla.

"Kak! Kak! Kak! Kak!" shrieked the diving bird, swooping toward Layla, beating toward the shivering young woman with its powerful wings, its corn-colored feet and curved ebony talons stabbing for the frightened squirrel.

Startled by the huge bird's sudden attack, Layla instinctively tried to swat it away. For her trouble, the goshawk sank its hooked beak deeply into the back of her right hand, and grabbed at her wrist with both claws.

"Leave me alone, you vulture! Get away!" she screamed, flailing at the bird, first with her arm and then swinging her AK-47 like a powerful whip.

In the confusion, the black-eared red squirrel had taken refuge between Layla's insulated military boots.

Faster than the eye could follow, Layla grabbed the squirrel's jerking tail and smashed the helpless animal hard against a large boulder, crushing its skull. The frozen surprise on the dead creature's face looked almost human.

"Disgusting little rodent," she muttered, contemptuously tossing the quivering carcass into the bushes.

Layla looked around for the horrible bird, but he was already flying away, low over the lake's surface, heading toward distant red cedars and beyond in search of less combative prey.

Cold and beyond bone-tired, the Iraqi assassin stomped her feet impatiently on the frozen ground, making tight, little squeaking sounds on the narrow strip of packed snow and gravel. Her tongue worried the stump of a shattered incisor and the adjoining bloody socket. Each breath of cold air felt like a rusty dental pick jammed deep into the gaping hole. Only Layla's confidence in her ability to cause the miserable harlot's coming death kept her attention regularly coming back to the task ahead.

Bitch, Layla thought. *Lazy, stupid, bitch Fatima! Tripped me with pile of climbing rope dumped where she knew I'd jump out of boat. I never saw sharp piece of granite until was too late! If she coiled up rope like I told her, wouldn't be drooling blood in snow right now.*

Trying her best to ignore the deep throbbing inside her jaw, Layla again sighted down the barrel of her Bulgarian-made AK-47, checking every tree and shrub across the frigid isthmus and up and down both sides of the rocky shore where she stood.

"Layla! Answer me!" Fatima whined.

"Shush!" Layla hissed through clenched teeth. She tried warming the index and second fingers of her right hand with her long pink tongue. They still hurt from her surgery. The coming Finnish winter in the air made them throb, almost as much as her broken tooth.

Am I to die in this godforsaken place because some Revolutionary Guard's wet dream needed job? How could they expect me to carry out difficult mission and then saddle me with such a useless, sniveling malingerer when I need some real help? God willing, I'll keep her from ruining operation.

Layla softly rubbed her right eye, trying to soothe away some of the tiredness that was sapping her will to continue. All along the trip from the assembly camp—stops, starts, hiding during the day, nowhere decent to sleep, two others arrested by border guards—Layla's fingers burned from the results of the operation that removed all of the fingerprints on her right hand, the one Surgeon Captain Iqbal thought she normally favored. It was too soon after her surgery to launch the operation, but instructions had come down, supposedly from Fearless Leader's nephew himself. Layla tried not to think about the danger to herself in this mission, and what little personal risk her handlers faced as a result of what she had been ordered to do. Fortunately, she'd bribed the butchers into leaving her left hand alone. One mutilated hand was bothersome but two would have been almost impossible. But then, eradicating her fingerprints wasn't for

HER protection. No loose ends, they'd made her promise, and, Layla would not allow Fatima to become a loose end!

"Layla! What should I do next?" Fatima's whining continued, grating on Layla's nerves like a shot of compressed air directly into her empty tooth socket.

Ignoring her own anger, Layla silently implored the darkening skies: *what did I do to deserve this stupid tub of lard?* Allowing a long, weary sigh to slip out, she turned her right hand palm down, so the results of her operation would be hidden from her eyes for at least a moment or two.

Moon's becoming too bright, Layla admitted to herself, her stomach muscles tightening involuntarily. Despite the plunging outside temperature, her palms began to sweat—weakness in herself she hated.

Thinking ahead to the final steps of their assignment, a small shiver of excitement surprised her. *At last,* she thought, *revenge for her father and safety for her mother and her brother, Sami.*

Layla watched as the silvery half-moon disappeared behind a swiftly moving patch of storm clouds and wondered how this change in weather would affect their chances for a successful mission.

Her eyes downcast, Fatima turned to Layla. "Let's get on with it! I know you don't think I can do it, but I can."

Layla pointed toward an angular multistoried home crowning a steep but narrow hill beyond the next cove, peeking through a stand of ubiquitous red cedars. Cozy, yellow lights beckoned invitingly from a grand front room's floor-to-ceiling windows. Through her night-vision binoculars, Layla could see a brace of lighted candles flickering softly in front of a blazing fireplace and a heavily laden dinner table in the foreground. As the breeze off the lake stopped for an instant, the harmonies of Ottorino Respigi's "Fountains of Rome," probably the movement known as "Villa Medici Fountain at Sunset," greeted their Iraqi ears from the direction of the harlot's mansion on the hill.

Layla counted out the magazines of extra bullets for both weapons, making sure each was fully loaded. She took four magazines for herself and handed two to Fatima. "This ought to be more than enough to get the job done," she whispered quietly to no one in particular. Then Layla removed two documents from the inner lining of her jumpsuit—a Pakistani passport for herself and a Palestinian identity card for the Revolutionary Guard's spawn. Hopefully no Finn could tell the difference between an Iraqi and a Pakistani or Palestinian. *Praise Allah, the merciful and mighty, their escape would go smoothly.*

These two young women, now old beyond their years, had been selected for this dangerous mission in part because security screeners in Northern Europe assume women pose no threats and are more likely to complain of sexual harassment if challenged.

The two Iraqis shouldered their packs, raised their automatic weapons briefly overhead in a weary gesture of defiance and stepped through the dense underbrush crowding the water's edge. Layla led the way while Fatima dejectedly stumbled along behind.

Bent under the weight of their packs, the pair slowly trudged along the jagged shoreline toward their target in the distance, weaving through boulders and thick foliage and around tree stumps.

"Just one foot in front of the other," Layla said sleepily. "Left, right. Keep my eyes on the house up there and try not to stumble. Slowly around this next corner, swing over that fallen log, up that hill. Left, right, left, right. If only I could sleep just a bit."

As fine particles of new snow began to swirl about them, the two women quietly used razor-sharp tree spurs strapped to the insteps of each military boot to climb high into the bushy branches of a giant fir tree hanging over the house's second story. Swaddled in black industrial-grade winter gear from head to toe, the two assassins settled in among the sheltering branches to wait as long as necessary, birds of prey poised to swoop down and choke all life from something warm.

Layla scowled at the half-moon that occasionally peeked faintly through the cloud of tiny snowflakes spinning around her, as if it might expose their lair. Through a pair of night-vision binoculars and her own drowsiness, she watched dancing infrared images of dim lights and the red heat of a glowing wood stove topped by lava rocks in a rustic sauna cabin perched beside yet another rocky finger of the long lake, down a broad flagstone path from the home's rear entrance.

She involuntarily drew a sharp breath as the back door squeaked open, pointedly reminding her of the broken tooth. A man's strawberry blond head peered around the massive oak door frame. He looked up at the swirling mix of snow with a bulky cellular phone pressed tightly to his ear, checking in with his sons, Peter and Will, ages eleven and eight, at their mother's home in Manhattan.

"No, Peter, sorry I can't have dinner with you and Will tonight. I'm just finishing up some business here in Finland. You know I miss both of you. Just called to see what's going on before you left for hockey practice. It's pretty late here in Savonlinna. I'll check in with you tomorrow at the beginning of your day. Please tell Will I called but that I can't be there for his school play tomorrow morning. Love you!"

He squeezed the blinking button, ending the call, and dropped the bulky phone into a patch pocket on the left hip of his plush navy terrycloth robe. Surveying the rows of dark tree trunks already lightly dusted with moist new snow, lost in thought, David Garvey took a deep breath of cold night air and cinched the sash of his robe tightly around his naked waist.

"C'mon, Marja. This is what I came all the way to Finland for," he yelled into the house. "Can't wait to get into the sauna and into you later!"

A lithe blonde slipped through the open door behind him. Soft light from inside the house revealed the silhouette of her hard nipples and flat stomach through a sheer cranberry chemise. The screen door banged shut behind her. Though smiling faintly, she shook her head.

"I can't wait either. You just don't have to talk about sex so much. It's natural for us, you know, going to sauna and making love, especially with you, my crass American! And you know, David, I have surprise for you."

He grabbed playfully at the hem of her flimsy garment. To his surprise and delight, she wiggled out of it and stood defiantly before him, hands on her hips, tiny snowflakes dancing around them, blurring her nakedness. Her outrageous pink tongue teased vibrant, cherry lips. As he rushed toward her welcoming warmth, the cranberry chemise tripped him up and he stumbled heavily onto the low, broad-plank porch. She scampered away toward the sauna, squealing excitedly.

"If I can catch you, I'll nibble your luscious ass!" he shouted after her, taking up the chase.

The two lovers disappeared through another creaky door into the warmly glowing sauna.

Brazen harlot, Layla thought to herself, squirming uncomfortably, her face growing flushed despite the cold. *What kind of a mother would that whore be, cavorting around naked in the snow like some hungry prostitute?*

Layla tried to forget how much she had wanted children, her own children. At least, Layla tried to comfort herself, she would never have acted like such a slut as this blonde Finnish whore! *May Allah curse this harlot and all she touches!*

Quiet descended on the Finnish lake country, broken only by the occasional faint cooing of an Eurasian pigmy owl and the light tic, tic of snow through the nest of branches surrounding the two waiting Iraqis as they tried desperately to stay awake.

Dawn Falls

"Nothing's more erotic than sitting cheek to thigh with you in the sauna, unless it's having your head on my shoulder and listening to your heart beat in this luxurious bed, under our own fluffy down quilt. Just the two of us!" he whispered, kneading the knots of muscles behind Marja's long, slender neck and under her deeply tanned shoulder blades. She seemed to almost purr under his caring touch.

"You know, David," she observed dreamily, "I have something very happy for you." Marja raised herself up on one elbow and, in one fluid motion, slowly turned her glowing body toward him while sliding an inquiring toe up along the inside of his thigh. Even though she had deeply satisfied him just a few moments earlier, his heart skipped a beat as he slowly marveled over the halo of her flaxen hair, firm breasts rising up sharply to meet him, and then the faintest hint of blonde fineness below her navel that drew his gaze toward the pelt of rusty curls below.

"And what might that be, my darling?" he gasped, looking directly into her piercing blue eyes as he caressed the palm of her outstretched left hand.

"You know when I went into town this morning? Well, I went to see doctor. To make short story, as you say, I am having baby, our baby."

"Wonderful!" David exclaimed. "I can't think of anyone more worthy of being reproduced than you. And to think I had so much fun getting it started. Peter and Will always wanted a younger sibling. When's the baby due? Boy or girl?"

"There are many, many times for all your questions, my love. But now, I am being so very tired. I am just about drifting off."

David continued to gently massage Marja's left palm and wrist, passing lightly over the simple, lime jade ring he had just given her. She quickly fell into a deep sleep.

The half-moon's glow through the skylight cast a faint shadow on the bedclothes over her sleeping profile. He quietly basked in the gentle curve of her slender neck against the starched white pillowcase. She was his every hope and dream. David wanted very much to touch her again, to tell her more plainly than ever before how much she meant to him. He leaned over to gently caress the line of her chin but couldn't bring himself to disturb her slumber.

Then David quietly eased himself out of their bed and tiptoed across a narrow patch of polished birch tiles toward the stairs and down into the den below, slipping into his navy robe along the way. Once downstairs, he curled up in his favorite overstuffed chair in front of the raging fire. He was much too excited to sleep.

A baby! He never imagined he'd want another child after the unpleasant divorce. *All that mess. Doesn't seem to have affected Peter and Will very much, but how to tell?* he thought to himself. *This one will be different! I'll avoid the old mistakes.*

The brightly burning fire atop a pair of rugged andirons in the fireplace reminded him of his mother and those times after school when he was growing up in eastern Maine. David ran home from school every day, down the muddy hill and through the Johnsons' raspberry patch, to tell his mother about everything that had happened in second grade homeroom. She would be sitting at the kitchen table, deeply inhaling her Virginia Slims ever so elegantly, a slender glass of domestic white wine on the table next to an overflowing ashtray. From what now seemed like a very great distance, he watched as his mother leafed methodically through a thick stack of glossy fashion magazines. David remembered looking up at his mother, asking her questions, and trying to get her to listen to him. Although she moved her mouth and words came out, she really wasn't hearing him, much less responding. It had taken David all these years to figure that out! Now, he felt connected to Marja, like no one before. She made him feel so very warm and comfortable. At last, David slipped deeper and deeper into his memories.

A wave of shattering glass roused David from his fitful slumber. Smaller glass breaking followed several bulky thumps. Marja's shrieks made the hair on the back of his neck stand up!

"David! Daaavid, where are you? Help me! Daaaavid!"

A single automatic weapon chuttered three times. He heard more glass breaking, wood smashing. Light running footsteps crossed the bedroom floor and plunged toward him through the carpeted stairwell. David was momentarily paralyzed by his fear then immediately jump-started by a fiery dose of adrenalin.

He kicked the wheeled Ottoman toward the base of the stairs and groped frantically in the darkness for something, anything to protect himself. A lone shadowy figure hurtled over the bottom steps, coming down hard on the Ottoman. Together, the darkly clad woman and the Ottoman wobbled heavily over the uneven floor slates toward the cold fireplace. Both woman and Ottoman jerked to a stop at the edge of the deep gray wool carpet. A long gun slipped from her grasp and clattered across the fireplace hearth as she tumbled onto the floor, lunging for the weapon.

David's left hand found the handle of that curious fireplace tool Marja had insisted on buying him for Christmas—a porous stone orb mounted on a sturdy brass shaft which rested in a bronze kettle of liquid fire starter. His first quick chop smashed the woman's slender, outstretched fingers against the lattice of bricks cemented around the fireplace before they could reach the automatic weapon.

David could hear Marja's moaning in the bedroom, calling him. Tears clouded his eyes, but he swung what had become a weapon

3

overhead with both hands, a sledgehammer speeding toward an anvil. In the fevered beginnings of dawn, the speeding stone ball extinguished Layla's glaring dark eyes, as it crushed her skull. The ruptured olive balloon hissed, "Inshallaaahh . . ." and fell silent. Her right leg twitched once and then her entire body sagged, a marionette with its strings cut.

As Layla's life began to slip away, she imagined her mother standing beside her. *"Time to rest, Layla,"* her mother whispered. *"You've done your very best. Sami and I are so very proud of you, and I know Father would be too."*

"My hand, Mother," Layla muttered. *"Vulture bit my hand! So cold and tired, soooo tired . . ."*

David bounded up the stairwell three steps at a time, his heart in his throat. Marja lay in the middle of bed, their bed, her right arm cocked awkwardly behind her back, ruby life gushing away. He tried furiously to staunch the flow of her blood with his hands, with quickly torn sheets and pillows, but she weakly touched his ear and pulled him toward her faintly moving lips.

"It's no good, you know," she whispered hoarsely, "sauna rocks . . . they told me it might be time . . . please hold me close, David. They are now coming back to finish off job," she coughed weakly.

"Don't worry. I'll save you!" David prayed.

He cradled Marja's head in his lap, rocking slowly back and forth on the edge of their bed, his tears kissing her lifeless fingers.

David didn't hear Ilka, the Finnish caretaker, break open the back door. Ilka stopped to inspect the black-clad corpse in front of the downstairs fireplace.

"David, where are you?" Ilka called out. "What happened? You OK?"

The caretaker feverishly searched all nine first floor rooms of David's lake country retreat. Finding nothing out of ordinary there, he scampered upstairs. Momentarily stunned by the carnage, he hung back in the doorway.

"David, you are OK?"

Tiptoeing hesitantly across lightly polished birch tiles, now sullied with Marja's blood, Ilka touched David's shoulder and whispered softly in his ear.

"Should I call doctor? You want me to call police? What you want me to do?"

He leaned past David to gently put his right index and second fingers deep under Marja's jaw, feeling for a pulse in her carotid artery, all the while trying to avoid her vacant stare and bloody gaping mouth. Nothing.

"David! My God, she's dead! What you want me to do?"

Ilka grabbed David and shook him roughly by both shoulders.

"They came for me. Got her by mistake," David offered.

Eight somber, throaty tones of an antique grandfather clock in the living room below at last called David Garvey reluctantly back toward the world of the living.

"Have the police come look at the dead woman downstairs," he said. "There's another one impaled on that wrought iron lamppost over behind the sofa. Looks like she landed on it after jumping through the skylight. Marja's beyond help. I'll clean up. Please call me a taxi in twenty minutes. I have to get to the airport."

Jumping to his feet, David looked quickly around as if the cold hand of death had touched him from behind.

"I've got to get out of here!"

"Won't police want to talk to you?" Ilka asked.

"Yeah, but I won't want to talk to them. I've got to leave you in charge, Ilka. My boys may be in danger. I—"

David turned and stumbled blindly into the nearby *en suite* bathroom, oblivious to almost everything around him. Thick clots of blood, Marja's blood, pasted the navy robe to his heaving chest. Leaning on the gray marble double sink for support, despair gnawing at his very soul, he collapsed on the floor, sobbing uncontrollably. As his weeping began to subside, David rummaged in the pocket of his robe for a handkerchief. Instead, he chanced upon the tiny computer disc Marja had pressed into his hand at the very end—just made him take it. Through tear-filled eyes, David looked intently at the tiny bit of computer memory. Anxious for something, anything, to distract him from the nearby horror, David popped the disk into his mouth for a moment, wiped it clean with one of Marja's monogrammed linen face towels and slipped it into the external drive recessed into the wall beside the bathroom double sink. Next, he turned with a vengeance toward the task of expunging all evidence of the recent carnage from his body.

Pinpoint streams from the conical chrome showerhead assaulted his weary body as a flood of deeply then faintly crimson water cascaded over the polished Italian tiles at his feet and quickly disappeared down the drain. Over the steamy hiss of the water, David heard loud, guttural voices coming from the view screen. He peeked out of the fogged glass shower door, ignoring the deluge of soapy water running out onto the floor.

On the nearby wall-screen, David saw an elegantly dressed young fellow, probably an Arab. He was sitting on a low couch in a windowless room, opposite a hulking and obviously very angry older man, whose face seemed vaguely familiar—wavy dark hair and eyes, thick black mustache, rows and rows of medals and ribbons on his military uniform. At first, David couldn't hear what they were talking about; as he moved closer and stabbed at the holographic control to increase the volume, what he heard and saw made his blood run cold.

Slowly patting himself dry with a bedsheet-sized fluffy cotton towel, David touched glowing numbers floating in the air in front of his holographic access control panel to open a locked steel case built into the wall at the right of the fogged bathroom mirror.

Who should I be today? he wondered to himself, carefully inspecting several pairs of contact lens cases, each marked with a different color—light blue, dark blue, hazel, green. If I want to get out of Vantaa International Airport alive, my Swedish disguise would probably arouse the least suspicion. David selected the pair of light blue contact lenses, irrigated each eye with saline solution, and expertly popping them in place.

Next, he removed a nondescript gray winter suit from a rack in the walk-in closet. Selecting a long, utilitarian necktie from a concealed tie rack, David bent over to grab a pair of scuffed brown work shoes. Once again in front of the mirror, he waved a finger through similar glowing holographic images to open a larger locked cabinet under the sink, revealing several wigs.

"Must pick one that works with my skin color," David mused, "as so many of the bad rugs do not." He used two of Marja's clips to pin back his own hair, accommodating a wig of only slightly lighter color than his own hair and stepped back to examine himself in the mirror.

*   *   *

The heavy trunk lid slammed shut, jarring David Garvey from his nightmare. His heart was pounding. He was afraid the terror had only begun. Someone was trying to kill him. They had very nearly succeeded! David continued to tear at the cuticle of his right index finger and tasted the scant remains of dried blood under his fingernails. He knew it had not been just a hideous dream.

The burly Finnish taxi driver barked at David through the fogged rear window, "wake up! I am now being late!"

David fumbled with the door handle and lurched unsteadily out onto the icy pavement, stepping on his smaller bag in the process. Something crunched. David groped inside the green nylon bag for a picture of his family that had been taken several lifetimes ago on a beach in South Carolina when both boys were still blond, a beaming portrait of domestic tranquility. The glass in the bent picture frame was shattered, just like his marriage. He was alone in the windy parking lot and very frightened.

David dug into the money belt inside his dress shirt and let the taxi driver charge euros for the lengthy ride to a credit card stolen only a few days earlier, owned by an actual person in New South Wales. Whatever the driver grumbled in Finnish was lost in the deafening roar of a descending Kazahkair passenger jumbo passing close overhead on final approach to Helsinki's Vantaa International. The driver slammed the cab door and shook his head in David's direction. Then the battered Saab taxi slid sideways across the icy lot before pulling slowly out into the growing stream of airport traffic. Its ruby taillights disappeared toward the main terminal into a cloud of swirling snowflakes, leaving David Garvey alone in his private hell.

Lighting up a double-dose Marlboro, the taxi driver inhaled deeply and turned up the volume on the local classical station. *Strange job*, he thought to himself. *I pick up this foreigner on radio call. He is then staring at floor entire trip down from Savonlinna. He never said nothing. Then just went to sleep.*

Back in the windy parking lot, David was shivering almost uncontrollably. He shuddered inwardly, just thinking about what dangers might be lurking between here and the outpost in Königsberg. If he could just get out of Finland and survive the Baltic crossing, maybe he could figure out what had gone so horribly wrong with his apparently innocuous plan to harvest cash from the economic chaos in Central Europe, a scheme that now seemed to jeopardize his life and family. Why hadn't he been satisfied with growing his international law practice in Manhattan?

David's tense fingers absently worried the tiny black disc Marja had pressed into his hand just before she slipped away. He held it tenderly, deep in a warm inner pocket of his Arctic parka, as if he were guarding Marja's soul. Even the crude bandages protecting his left hand could not isolate its highly polished surface from David's tentative touch. He wanted to remember that someone else had ripped those bloody bedsheets into narrow strips back in the depths of the snowy forest to try to staunch her mortal wounds. At least for now, David needed to turn a blind eye to the horror of what had just happened. But the smoothness of the tiny black chip seemed to call out to him, even though he knew from watching it that it contained the first evidence of the terror's malignant birth. He wondered how Marja could have come by that disc. Now it was too late to ask her.

As he ducked beneath the bone-shaking roar of another descending jet, David could again see those stark images flicker before his tired eyes—an ominous tale recorded by a concealed camera. It had undoubtedly been inspired by the Fearless Leader's well-known paranoia and was now captured on the innocent little disc David was slowly rubbing like it was a magic lamp as if its luster might somehow bring Marja back to him.

Incubation

Tariq al-Tikriti admired himself in the shiny wall panel and tapped the elegant new white porcelain cap on his left front tooth with the manicured tip of his right index finger. "Just right," he noted with evident satisfaction.

Tariq opened his mouth just wide enough to inspect yet again the recently acquired brilliant white porcelain caps on each of his molars and incisors. Enthralled with their uniformly creamy appearance, he carefully adjusted the four-in-hand knot of his emerald silk French tie and checked to make sure that both gold, diamond-studded cufflinks in his heavily starched white 500 thread count Egyptian cotton dress shirt were arranged in precisely the most pleasing manner. Equally satisfied with the knife-like crease in his silk trousers, Tariq imitated the casual stroll he had affected in crossing the stage to accept his Business School diploma from the President of Harvard University, enjoying his own smooth mannerisms, reflected in the shiny surface before him.

Perhaps he should have been exhausted after the overnight flight from Boston's Logan Airport to Istanbul then on to Amman, followed by the long, dusty drive to Baghdad, but he was still on an emotional high from his graduation from the B-School, not quite two days ago. Not to even mention the almost unbearable rush from locking himself in the jumbo's first-class lavatory with that frisky blonde stewardess high over the Atlantic just before sunrise that morning, after just the smallest sample of nose candy.

Several floors above where Tariq was reveling in the spoils of his professional and extra-curricular activities in Cambridge, Massachusetts, and the New York financial world, his powerful uncle had surveyed the skyline of Iraq's noisy capital, secure in his power.

Just before Tariq's appointment, Fearless Leader had answered a small tug on his uniform trousers by bending down to meet the sparkling dark eyes of his youngest granddaughter, Rana. Burying his nose in the youngster's curly mop of hennaed hair, this self-appointed guardian of Iraq's ambitions and defiance was reminded of his humble beginnings and the quiet family life of Tikrit, now protected by his forceful leadership.

Praise God, the military man mused. *This bubbly child evoked memories of my own mother. If she had lived to see how far I have come. Now I must meet with the nephew so many depend on, even though no one else in the family really understands that. This young man might be the only thing keeping his family from oblivion. But such a dandy, that's the right word!*

It seemed like only yesterday Tariq's mother and three sisters had kissed him good-bye in the courtyard of the family's modest, shaded compound, not far from the marketplace in the center of Tikrit. First by rickety bus to Baghdad, then on to Amman, all during the scorching heat of an Iraqi July, he had begun his journey out into sophistication of the despised Western world. Then, his first airplane ride ever, from Amman to Istanbul in time for an afternoon Turkish Air flight to New York's John F. Kennedy Airport. More buses, a train and finally another bus finally deposited him at Hamilton College in Clinton, New York, well south of the dormant factories and industrial detritus of Utica, New York, and other urban graveyards in the struggling Mohawk Valley.

Four cold and desolate but challenging years in upstate New York had led Tariq to the Dean's good list and ultimately a Phi Beta

Kappa Key in his senior year. Not bad for a poor boy from Tikrit. And some creativity along the way earned him a full scholarship. He didn't even mind several part-time jobs to feed his fantasies and vices. Then immediately after receiving high honors at his Hamilton College graduation, he took a leap into the trainee pit at Dubinsky Brothers, the most aggressive and creative investment banking firm in Manhattan. Once he had proven himself there, al-Tikriti applied to Harvard B-School, starting not quite two years ago. During his stint in Cambridge, Massachusetts, he'd kept a floating position at Dubinsky Brothers over vacations, summers and holidays to supplement his other income.

The young Iraqi had been awed by the pageantry of formation in the wide variety of academic dress in Sever Quadrangle at Harvard and then even greater swirling bustle of elaborate gowns and stoles in the Harvard Yard during the parade of academics that kicked off commencement ceremonies in Cambridge. Yet he particularly relished hearing his very own name read in the list of Baker Scholars, with High Distinction no less, the *crème de la crème* of the Harvard B-School. Never mind if his financial resources had facilitated a few fingers on the scales of justice at opportune times. And he was actually receiving his diploma from the female President of Harvard. If only his mother and sisters had been allowed to leave Iraq to be in Cambridge to share his honor and pride.

Later that night, strolling through the cobblestone streets of Boston's Little Italy after dinner with his B-School friends, people he would probably never see again, Tariq couldn't contain his pride and happiness. He wallowed in these warm feelings as he waited for his uncle and wondered why he had been summoned home to Baghdad on such short notice, without even the chance to call or visit his family in Tikrit.

The single heavy metal door slammed roughly against bunker's concrete wall. His uncle strode into the stuffy compartment, trailing two armed guards dressed in dark green uniforms of the Palace Guard.

Tariq leaped from the low couch and bounded toward his only uncle, unconsciously primping his hair and straightening his tie yet again.

"Honored Uncle. How good to see you after these many long years!" Tariq beamed with some difficulty.

"Sit down, my sister's golden son. You are tired from your trip?"

"No, Uncle, not too tired so far. I'm excited to be back home! Is there something I can help you with?"

"Good! Let's get started. We have much to cover. Later, we can have some entertainment, perhaps, and a meal."

The two Iraqis sat on separate couches at right angles to each other in the small, windowless room entirely bereft of any decoration. The men were alone except for two guards rooted on either side of the only door, near the right rim of the wide-angle camera's field of vision from behind what appeared to the uninitiated to be a mirror. First looking confidently into the camera's eye, the old warrior slowly surveyed the sparse space around him and then imperiously flicked an imaginary bit of dust from the gold-encrusted medals crowding his uniform blouse; by contrast, the younger man, though elegantly dressed, looked about furtively—the lion and a ferret.

"Tell me! What did you learn about buying companies at your Jewish bank in New York?"

The one David now knew from his assiduous research as Tariq al-Tikriti stared for some time at his uncle's impassive expression before trying to answer such an open-ended vague question, looking in vain for some guidance in the Leader's implacable demeanor. Even in this private, calculatedly comfortable setting, Tariq's most famous relative exuded raw power and intimidation from the bright gloss of his military boots past the unfastened but bulging holster to the rows of decorations under a circle of gold stars on each shoulder. Tariq must have felt like a bug under a powerful microscope. On one hand, Fearless Leader could be his key to great wealth, power, and the well-being and protection of his family. On the other hand, Uncle Saddam could become his personal Satan and wipe him and all of his relatives from the face of the Earth without hesitation or so much as a trace.

A story he'd heard about Ivan the Terrible focused Tariq's thoughts. Following the completion of St. Basil's Cathedral in Moscow, the Russian despot had asked its builders whether they could duplicate that feat. When they enthusiastically assured him that would be entirely possible, he had them both blinded on the spot so no other edifice could ever rival St. Basil's unique beauty.

Just the atrocities known to the general public, which were attributable to his uncle's personal instructions, were enough to make even a close relative like Tariq extremely cautious in dealing with him. Even closer to home, everyone was keenly aware of what had happened to the two el-Majid brothers after their defection to Jordan and their groveling return to the fold, despite the fact they'd been married to respected Uncle's daughters until just before their bloody extermination. Surely Tariq couldn't seem less than eager in answering the Leader's questions, much less refuse to enthusiastically carry out whatever instructions he might be given. Still, it was plain from his anxious glances about the room that Tariq had no idea why his mother's brother had summoned him to this cramped, stuffy dungeon below Baghdad's central hospital.

"Well, I learned how to buy Western companies, praise God, but perhaps you could please tell me what interests you," Tariq ventured.

"Why do you think you were allowed to study abroad? We have serious problems here at home! While you were enjoying the good life in America's den of harlots and thieves, your people were starving because of the filthy UN embargo. You must be part of the solution!"

"What do you mean, revered Uncle?"

"I mean women and children are dying because the Americans keep the UN from lifting its embargo. I can only feed so many mouths personally, like your mother and sisters who are now living under my protection in one of my palaces."

Tariq's warning radar blinked on, perhaps a year or two late. *Why was his family living with this terrible man? Were his mother and sisters hostages to insure his own fidelity and performance? Great care was needed.*

"How are my mother and sisters?" he asked. "I have not seen them in nearly eight years."

"They are just fine. We are considering a marriage proposal directed toward Aisha. You should become involved in those discussions, as the man of the family. Soon we can go out to visit them. But, for the moment, let's get to work!"

Tariq teetered on the edge of a precipice, as if the plush Oriental rug under his feet and the floor beneath were evaporating into thin air. He couldn't figure out what his uncle was after. Jet lag was starting to creep over him. He sipped deeply from his tiny cup of turgid coffee, hoping against hope to find some insight among the muddy dregs. He kept both eyes riveted on his uncle's rigid torso, noting the way his muscular hands gripped the arms of his sofa so tightly at times that his uncle's knuckles turned white. What was really on the Leader's mind?

"We're kept in chains by that camel dung American President and her lackeys in Europe, all puppets of the Zionists! After all these years, there's still no end of the wretched embargo in sight. Once we loosened its grip, when we pretended to allow those evil inspectors to nose about our homeland. But that was before the inspectors discovered our cache of anthrax and VX missiles," the Leader continued.

"I know, Uncle. I have followed those events closely on CNN and in the American papers, biased against our country—"

Ignoring his nephew, the dictator interrupted, "We have money hidden in many places but nowhere to spend it while those UN clerks are trying to run our country from little pissant offices at our borders and here in Baghdad. Every week Al Qadissiya reports some new examples of foreign attempts to castrate our nation."

15

"Surely we are more cunning than those UN bureaucrats!" Tariq added. "Sometimes even the Western press reports how silly we make them look."

"God willing, that is true, but we can't escape the embargo without surrendering all of the military and economic independence we've worked so hard for these many long years. How can we remove the UN's grasping fingers from our nation's throat?"

His bemedalled uncle looked away, carefully scrutinizing each of the guards. Then, he turned his attention to his nephew, softening a bit.

"My usual advisors are either too old or too timid. You're family. I can count on you to share your private thoughts with me."

Tariq's faint shudder was not lost on the camera's cold eye. Perhaps he was imagining cousin Ahmed having the same sort of intimate conversation with the Fearless Leader. Ahmed's family had all been murdered after he crossed the Leader during the weeks immediately before the Gulf War. Rumor had it respected Uncle had personally strangled his own nephew with his bare hands!

"I'm just a young man, revered Leader. My knowledge of military things is somewhat limited. Perhaps you would consider buying more missiles and chemical weapons from our friends the Chinese? For myself, I'd poison the upstate reservoirs—"

"Enough! I didn't summon you here to babble about things my generals have spent their worthless lives trying to learn. Unlike our country, praise God, the West lives on business, money, cash. How do we get our hands into their businesses, their bank accounts?"

Tariq brightened visibly as if suddenly connecting the dots of his present predicament with some recent events.

"You are perhaps thinking of increasing our country's commercial presence in America and England?"

"You are at least thinking in the right direction. You have no doubt read about our purchase of Matrix Churchill in Cleveland, Michigan? We used a foreign company to buy Matrix Churchill to employ its machine tool business to make our defense capacity even stronger. We avoided American restrictions on the purchase, but the Americans stole it anyway after we liberated Kuwait. More bureaucratic strangulation of our legitimate aspirations."

Tariq ventured a look directly into his uncle's eyes, now roiling, ebony pools of hatred. His tongue suddenly felt very heavy, frozen. For a moment, the young Iraqi couldn't speak.

Respected Leader paused for an instant, then continued his diatribe. "Even if we could move money around those despicable United Nations sanctions, if even a scent of our activities reaches the cutthroat, rumor-mongering American press, nothing is possible. No, my nephew, we will not be putting more money into the United States or even England."

An ever so faint glimmer of pleasure crossed Tariq's moisturized and lightly powdered face, perhaps a memory of some dalliance in Paris or one of the other founts of sensuous conquest on the European continent, a most welcome way to serve his puritanical country. Some tangible cause for zealous devotion!

Without thinking, Tariq licked his lips before speaking. "The depressed economy in Europe presents many bargains, France and Italy, in particular—"

"Decadent! Those duplicitous French! By the beard of Allah, they never help anyone but themselves and are so arrogant and difficult to deal with."

A telephone at revered Uncle's right hand buzzed twice. He picked up the receiver, listened intently, muttered a single syllable, and then returned the instrument to its resting place. Tariq wondered whose fate had been determined by that brief interchange.

"Those Italians are even worse! You know there was even a whore elected to the Italian Parliament? No, we need investments that will get the attention of the right politicians and help get us out from under the embargo and other American attempts to interfere with our lives. No more Iraqi dollars, francs, or lira for France or Italy."

"What about Sweden, Denmark, and Norway?"

Given his extensive European travels and expensive tastes, Tariq had many friends in Köbenhaven and Stockholm, slender attractive young women with sparkling blue eyes, skimpy bikinis, and great eagerness to please. There could be many worse places in the world to live, work, play, and party, party, party. But he still couldn't figure out what the Leader wanted. Maybe his uncle didn't even know what he wanted. But then, revered Uncle was not famous for his interest in lively discussion. He permitted none of the sort of give and take Tariq remembered from his early stint on the trading floor at Dubinsky Brothers and later on while working around the clock on the firm's foreign acquisition teams. He suspected his uncle had already made up his mind and was merely expecting him to present the desired conclusion. It was so hard to read the Leader's thoughts!

"Have you thought about Scandinavia, Uncle? Those countries look very favorably on any type of significant investment. But, it might be very hard to import any significant—"

"RIDICULOUS! None of the Northern countries would officially permit the sort of investment or influence we must achieve in order to succeed. Further east!"

Further East? There was nothing east of Scandinavia except . . . surely not! Tariq blanched. *Could his uncle be thinking of that locust horde of hungry mouths, the idle factories and cesspools of pollution in what was left over from the breakup of the Soviet Union? The grey death?*

"Perhaps my treasured mother's brother has in mind Greece and Turkey—"

"NO! Our opportunity lies in the lands of our former arms supplier. One moment a respected military power of the first order, willing to share its resources with our country; only a few months later like a pack of quarreling school children. Something we would never permit here. Lacks strong and effective leadership!" the dictator sniffed.

"But, Excellency, there are sooo many problems in Eastern Europe. No one knows who really owns the factories. The workers are worse than lazy. Local economies—"

"Perhaps someone made a mistake in sending my little nephew into the Western den of Jewish thieves. You sound like the whining lawyers our agents tried to hire in America after that traitorous, lying, deceitful George Herbert Walker Bush first began to isolate our nation from its rightful place on the world stage. We need someone to work around obstacles and get the job done."

The Leader cleared his throat loudly and started again.

"You must keep in mind what we have achieved here at home with so little! How have we grown stronger after a war that sniveling little harlot the Americans now call a president gloats over endlessly? Discipline, hard work, and good leadership!"

"All true, praise God, thanks to our prudent and effective leadership, but the remnants of the Soviet Union are like some Kurds, Hamas, and the Israelis, all trying to manage the same apartment building, with some Nigerians and Koreans thrown in for good measure."

"Exactly! We bought several senior nuclear scientists from idle Russian defense plants for the price of some blood-sucking bank clerks in Amman. Even if Russian factories are old and badly maintained, we could obtain entire facilities at bargain prices, and our money would be appreciated. If no one in Tikrit had a job, would we insult someone who wanted to reopen an idle factory and pay salaries by asking many embarrassing questions? I don't think so!"

Tariq could sense the basic melody of his uncle's song but the lyrics were somewhat garbled. The Leader evidently remained confident in Russian technological prowess and did not share the widespread Western view that little of use remained in the shards of the Soviet Union besides raw materials and some primary production capacity. Apparently the enlightened Leader's idea would be to buy companies employing large numbers of people to achieve maximum leverage with the politicians, regardless of who was in power.

"That's an excellent idea, my uncle. May I perhaps ask about some of the details? I might need to know about this information if I might be so fortunate as to be asked to assist in implementing your insightful plan."

"Of course, my nephew, anything you like."

The sour expression on his uncle's scowling face reminded him not to prolong this discussion, that his invitation probably meant "don't ask."

"Well," Tariq began, "buying companies requires the full-time efforts of many experienced people—accountants, financial analysts, engineers, and lawyers—"

"NO EXCUSES! You have all that fancy Western education and training! Why do think you were sent to the Harvard Commerce School? And, how do you suppose that plum of a position in that Jewish bank just dropped into your lap? You think of something. Quickly! Our family's survival is depending on it!"

The young Iraqi's brain was racing, grasping at straws—anything to get out of this dungeon. He must play for time.

His mental frenzy was interrupted by a throaty growl. The Leader sprang from his seat and grabbed the younger guard's throat with his left hand.

"WHAT IS IN YOUR POCKET?" revered Uncle bellowed, standing nose to nose with the pudgy sergeant. "Show me every last thing in your pocket! NOW!"

Sheepishly presenting some keys, a comb, and a small handgun for inspection, the sentinel tried to explain.

"I need this pistol to better defend you, Excellency, I am afraid for your—"

Tariq watched in horror as his uncle whipped the .45 automatic pistol from his hip holster, jammed it into the rigid guard's forehead between his gray green eyes, and pulled the trigger before the doomed man could finish his sentence. The soldier's skull recoiled sharply against the gray cement block wall, splattering it with a gory circle of bits of brain and blood. Then his corpse slid slowly down the rough concrete face and collapsed into a lifeless heap beside the other guard's blood-spattered boots.

The Leader casually wiped the smoking gun barrel on his uniform sleeve and returned the weapon to its holster.

"Assassin! No one . . . NO ONE is permitted any weapon in my presence! The fate of our nation is too perilous to allow any of our enemies the slightest opportunity to destroy our country's leadership. Probably a Zionist agent! He might have silenced me if I had not detected and exposed his treachery. Praise God, I am vigilant."

Without so much as a glance toward the cooling corpse on the floor, respected Uncle returned to his place on the couch and turned to Tariq as calmly as if he had only paused for a moment to blow his nose.

"You were beginning to tell me how you plan to achieve a foothold in Russia and its former colonies without the lengthy delay and huge manpower requirements you described. Continue."

Tariq was at once frightened and relaxed. He was beyond terrified by the raw brutality he had just witnessed, by the instant death that had leaped from near him on the couch and now sat quietly next to him once again. And yet he was somehow soothed by the overwhelming helplessness of his position. Tariq now understood that his fate was almost surely beyond his own control and unexpectedly drew a comforting dose of solace from his inability to affect his own future. He would do the best he could, but, after that, it was completely out of his hands. Only Allah knew the outcome.

"Our problem, respected Uncle, is that we don't have enough experienced people or time to quickly—"

"NONSENSE! What does that mean? Don't confuse me with riddles! Get to the point! Our nation is dying. No time for word games!"

"What I mean is that we need someone to do our work for us. We have to find a way to bypass the normal, time-consuming negotiation and acquisition process to give us power over important companies without the need to deal directly with all those Russian, Moldovan, and Belarusan bureaucrats until my unborn children have grown old and all of my teeth have fallen out."

Faced with this apparently overwhelming task, Tariq must have felt fatigue creeping over him like a heavy wet blanket.

"I beg you, Excellency, let me have some rest. I haven't even slept in two days. I'll report to you in a short time, after I have considered your ideas and suggestions further and reviewed once more the documents concerning our nation's foreign holdings. You'll get a plan to approve as soon as possible."

His uncle stood up abruptly.

"You have until next Sunday, not a day longer! You'll be summoned to explain your plan to me in detail. In the meantime, you may sample my Finnish houry."

He stood up and motioned the remaining guard to open the door. Tariq jumped to his feet respectfully, as if on command. Without another word, the Fearless Leader strode confidently out into the dimly lit corridor, followed by the corporal three paces behind, eyes to the ground. As revered Uncle disappeared around the corridor, Tariq heard him clap his hands sharply twice. With that, the faintly whirring video camera fell silent.

Tariq collapsed onto the sofa, his knees weak. How could he produce what must be a very complicated and creative plan in fewer than seven days? Although his uncle probably didn't understand it, the Iraqi leader expected his nephew to quickly accomplish many diverse objectives and didn't want to hear about any of the steps needed to accomplish his diffuse goals, both articulated and implied at the same time. Sad, but true, his country was very thin in management talent. Although the Leader would not hear of it, the idea of a group of Iraqis mounting any kind of an acquisition was almost silly. The project his uncle had described would daunt most investment bankers. Even if a loophole could be found in the embargo that would permit Dubinsky Brothers to help, his parsimonious uncle would surely hyperventilate if the size of their fees was even mentioned. How could he be expected to satisfy honored Uncle's whims, save his own skin and perhaps get rich along the way? Tariq decided right then he would focus his efforts not on how to develop nonexistent Iraqi business and financial expertise but on ways of giving birth to Trojan horses. He smiled faintly, recalling some useful advice given him by an ex-military type he had worked for at Dubinsky Brothers: "Leadership is the art of getting someone else to do your work!"

The bunker door swung open slowly. A slim, blonde young woman stepped disdainfully over the sergeant's corpse and walked straight toward Tariq, her head high. He preferred reticent, submissive women. The assertive manner of this foreigner, who obviously had some connection with his powerful uncle, already shamed him and questioned his manhood. Her warm breath on his forehead embarrassed him, underlining his diminutive stature even before she uttered a word.

"It's better if you don't know my name," she announced, looking directly into his averted eyes. "Your uncle says you're very shy. Well, I'm not!"

As if for emphasis, she felt al-Tikriti through his expensive silk French trousers.

"Respected Uncle mentioned I might meet one of his, er, ah, colleagues," Tariq squeaked. "I'm very pleased to meet you, but I really must be going. Uncle has called on me to attend to some very important matters for him. There is a very tight time schedule—"

"You don't understand! He gives orders and I do what I'm told. That is very good for my bank account in Liechtenstein. I don't want to end up like that!" she spit out disdainfully, gesturing dismissively toward the crumpled carcass on the floor.

"Surely my uncle would not arrange such things without informing me. I mean this really is not how things are done by the Leader—"

She hooked her strong index fingers into belt loops at each of his hips, pulling him close so quickly he was nearly smothered by her firm breasts, free beneath a sheer amber silk blouse. He could no longer avoid looking up at her. A slight scar ran diagonally across the right side of the beautiful young woman's nose, almost hidden by her dark glasses. She removed the glasses and dropped them into a pocket in her billowing skirt, then teased her upper lip with the tip of a moist index finger. Suddenly, she grabbed al-Tikriti firmly about the ears with both hands and probed his mouth deeply with her tongue.

Although Tariq thought he might resist, he found himself coming alive. He reached over to steady himself on an arm of the sofa, but something caught his right foot and tripped him! He sprawled backward into the soft cushions, his heart pounding. Her skirt and blouse were lying on the grey carpet. She was standing over him, hands defiantly on her hips. Her long legs straddled his thighs as she bent over to unbutton him. Looming over him, she pulled his gaping mouth to one of her stiff nipples and then tore open his pants before swallowing him up in her warmth. He gasped and dug his nails into her heaving shoulders.

Although the lusty blonde was already on top of him, Tariq grabbed her left knee and flipped her over onto the sofa.

"Not so fast!" he barked.

A Horse Is Born

Diether Kreuz tenderly shifted his weight to his left foot before carefully stepping down the last steps of the wheezing Romanian-built bus. He turned stiffly to look down the nearest row of dingy tenements toward a Soviet-style office building situated on the south side of Lübecker Straße. The structure's squat ugliness crowded what had once been an airy, linden-lined boulevard in the heart of Schwerin, Germany, the capital of Mecklenburg-Vorpommern, after the Berlin Wall came down as during the hold of the Deutsche Demokratische Republik (DDR in daily use) over East Germany.

Once more, he checked the battered Casio watch dangling from a loose, black plastic strap on his bony wrist—still late. Kreuz's shoulders ached from a cramped night beside a squalling baby in economy class on the overcrowded Lufthansa flight and the pinched nerve in his right hip was acting up again. Since hurrying out of the offices of Neu Ost Bank (commonly known as NeuBank) on Manhattan's Park Avenue in late afternoon of the previous day, the elderly German had suffered through a delayed and exhausting trip from New York, despite the highly overrated German efficiency at managing transatlantic crossings.

First, out over the North Atlantic to Berlin after what seemed like an interminable wait on the tarmac at JFK for a departure slot. Following a heavy German breakfast of *Harzer* cheese, *Schinken,* and *Schwarzbrot* in an antiseptic cafeteria down one wing of Brandenburg

25

International Airport, the next leg of his trip involved a short hop by feeder jet to Schwerin. Finally, he bumped along in a ramshackle bus through nearly horizontal sleet into the old, dilapidated city. *So much for taking care of the Östies*, he thought.

He had traveled so far, all this way sitting up with a bad back and changing time zones so many times without the comforting sleep that always seemed to elude him on airplanes. Kreuz was normally wary. His customary anxiety had been heightened by this unexpected summons to NeuBank's head offices. His paranoia was sharpened by the unwillingness of his superiors to give any reason for having to return to Germany on such short notice. There hadn't even been time to stop by his modest two-bedroom ranch house in Mamaroneck to pack a suitcase or even a toothbrush before racing to the airport. Just a moment to call his wife and speak with his two daughters before picking his way down cracked concrete steps into a tunnel to find the subway bound for Kennedy Airport.

So now Kreuz hobbled down the rainy street past several prewar buildings, each badly in need of repair and charcoal brown from the driving sleet on this dreary autumn afternoon. Even though he had grown up in Schwerin's suburbs and his family had lived in the area for generations, Kreuz preferred to forget the crumbling city was the headquarters of his recycled bank, now named Neu Ost Bank, the place to which he was always supposed to return. Kreuz had held on by his fingernails throughout the long grayness of the German Democratic Republic of Workers and Peasants, had even somehow survived the cold plunge into the German-style free market conditions imposed on the East after the Wall came down and Germany became one again. But Kreuz had been a faithful, unquestioning public servant for a very long time. He was weary, bone-tired.

Beyond waiting out the waning years of his professional life in the relative comfort of NeuBank's New York office and hoping to see both his daughters marry well, he had few ambitions, and no longer any dreams. So, on this soggy fall afternoon, he limped mechanically along the sleet-swept sidewalks, clutching his sodden briefcase. His umbrella had been confiscated by overeager airport security cadre in New York. He headed toward the brooding archway just ahead, its keystone bearing a somewhat dated rendering of NeuBank's emblematic black bull.

Having subsisted for years under the DDR's system of informants, neighborhood monitors, and office spies, Kreuz was thoroughly pessimistic about possible reasons for his trip. Perhaps the Bank's Directors had yanked him back from New York so unceremoniously to put him out to pasture or make him redundant, as the English so artfully put it, now that the central government bureaucrats in Berlin had pretty much eviscerated the country's traditionally extravagant severance and retirement benefits. Or, worse yet, perhaps they were making him return to this headquarters tomb to wait for his struggling career to gasp its last.

Swallowing his pride, Kreuz meekly pushed open the shiny glass door on General Tanz Straße leading into the stark lobby of NeuBank's home office, as if hoping to escape notice. From behind a low slab of granite, a nondescript but ancient gray-suited porter struggled to his feet, bowing ever so slightly.

"Welcome in Schwerin, Herr Doktor Kreuz! The Directors are all waiting for you in the main conference room. May I take your bags?"

"As you can plainly see, I have no luggage. Show me where the toilet is on the way to the meeting and be quick about it!" he barked, surprising even himself.

Hair combed, mouth rinsed out, and his more immediate needs satisfied for the time being, Kreuz allowed himself to be ushered into a decidedly modern meeting room looking out onto an interior rock garden, softened with new wet snow. Six pairs of inquiring eyes met his own.

He quickly inventoried the seats around the rectangular oak table and made a careful mental note of who was sitting in each one, shaking hands with each Director in turn, in order of rank. Eight chairs, three places on one side, a vacant chair to the left of the head of the table. First the Austrian, Heinrich Lindner, Managing Director for Administration, then Karl Doppelt, one of two Managing Directors for the Middle East. At the lowest end of the pecking order, Frau Frederika Bockmann, the newly appointed Director of Credit Analysis. Continuing his ritual greeting of the assembled senior management of the Bank, Kreuz first recognized Gausmann the younger, in charge of Eastern development at last report; then the old warhorse, Bruno Kopke, the only other remaining holdover from the Communist gang; and finally his childhood comrade, Uwe Scharnhorst, now Managing Director of Corporate Lending, standing in front of the seat just next to an empty chair at the right of the more ornate vacant seat at the head of the long, highly polished table.

"Please come in, Herr Kreuz, and take a seat. You must be exhausted from your long journey," Uwe Scharnhorst said. His old friend clapped him warmly on the shoulder and gently maneuvered the new arrival around the empty head chair toward the only remaining vacant armless chair, at the left of the seat of power.

Kreuz leaned close to whisper in his friend's ear, "Can you tell me what's going on?"

"Would you take some coffee?" Scharnhorst asked in response.

Kreuz was again off balance. Expecting to encounter something terrible, he couldn't now fathom why everyone around the huge table was watching so intently as he padded across the heavy carpet to what seemed to be his assigned seat. The presence of a black wreath in the armchair at the head of the conference table unnerved him. He nodded to each of the other officers around the table and then paused to drink from the heavy cup of steaming black coffee that appeared before him, wondering what might come next and still expecting the worst.

As the liquid warmth spread throughout his weary body, Diether Kreuz cleared his throat softly and turned his attention again to the silent group of executives.

"As soon as our Chairman, Herr Gausmann, arrives, I shall be prepared to present my report concerning the status of our New York operations."

"I'm afraid that will not be possible, Herr Kreuz," Scharnhorst ventured in a subdued voice.

"But what do you mean, Herr Scharnhorst? I am totally aware of every detail of the Bank's New York activities as well as its booking operation in the Bahamas. We can begin at any moment. And I have asked my deputy to transmit the written version of my report so that it should be arriving near the end of the day here in Schwerin."

Scharnhorst slowly looked around the group of bank officers. Kreuz noticed that each of the Managing Directors now seemed to avoid his friend's gaze. Again, Scharnhorst's attention turned to the recent arrival from New York.

"You see, Herr Kreuz, we have here in Schwerin a terrible and complicated problem. And very soon that problem will undoubtedly touch our operations in New York. Our beloved Chairman, Herr Gausmann, and his loyal wife, Frieda, perished just two days ago. Their little house by the shore of Schweriner See exploded in the early hours of the morning."

Kreuz couldn't believe his ears. He looked around the table of assembled bank executives for some explanation. Not one of his colleagues would look at him directly.

Scharnhorst continued. "No witnesses and not even much wreckage. Just a big BOOM and very many little pieces. The police are officially speaking about a gas leak, but those of us here in this room think it has something to do with our new investor and some of the new investor's proposals about the business of the Bank. Are you familiar with the report we sent you last month about this new investor?"

"Why, ja, of course, I read that report with much interest, but what does that have to do with the untimely deaths of Herr Gausmann and his wife and our office in Manhattan?"

29

"I believe that will soon become clear, Herr Kreuz."

Kreuz frantically continued trying to think of ways to address the question he had not yet been asked.

Scharnhorst continued. "The report mentioned the very large amount of subordinated equity contributed to the capital of the Bank by a corporation with headquarters in Cyprus. I well knew that when the central authorities reorganized the institution that is now NeuBank after reunification, no one could imagine that the funds promised by Berlin would not be forthcoming. I was as shocked and surprised as you undoubtedly were to find our colleagues in the Ministry of Finance pretending that no commitment had ever been made."

Looking carefully around the room, Scharnhorst turned pointedly to the Bank's Director of Administration.

"Please tell me, Herr Lindner, has this room been today swept for electronic eavesdropping devices?"

"Ja, but of course, Herr Scharnhorst. We are each day checking this room and all important offices as well as the officers' toilet since Herr Gausmann and his wife were killed. Nothing to report since the first time. And we will be each day checking these rooms as long as the problem persists."

"Forgive me, Herr Scharnhorst, but I do not understand what this has to do with either the new investor or my responsibilities in New York," Kreuz noted.

"I will speak to that presently," Scharnhorst said. "Of course, if either other sector directly affected has anything to add, whatever is appropriate should be brought to our attention," the Managing Director of Corporate Lending added, looking directly at Karl Doppelt and Heinz Gausmann.

"Well, here it is in a nutshell," Scharnhorst began to explain. "Our new Cypriot investor, known as LIFT Corporation, invested 1.2 billion euros in the Bank's subordinated capital account without precondition. Most unusual, however well we could use the funds.

Yet, exactly three months after that capital injection, Herr Doppelt received a formal visit from the President of LIFT Corporation, one Tariq al-Tikriti."

"Could I ask you to please repeat that name, Herr Scharnhorst? It is unfamiliar to me."

"al-Tikriti. I understand he carries an Iraqi passport, although, at that time, he presented Cypriot documents. He suggested to Herr Doppelt that the Bank should back one of the funds that is now investing in various areas of what used to be the Eastern Bloc, the Königsberg Fund, a hard money lender operating from somewhere in Kaliningrad, apparently run by a very aggressive American lawyer who works mainly in Manhattan."

"Pardon me, but I still do not see what all this has to do with our operations in New York," Kreuz interjected.

"Be patient! You soon enough will learn that, Herr Kreuz. According to the information provided by the Iraqi, the Königsberg Fund lends fully convertible currencies to local clients at excessive interest rates on security of real estate or shares of recently privatized companies. Apparently quite profitable but also very risky. Herr Doppelt properly reported the young man's visit to me, and I passed the information to our Chairman as required by our procedures. Because the project was very much too risky for our portfolio, nothing further was done, and a memo was placed in the appropriate file."

"Surely that was the end of the matter," Kreuz observed.

"Not exactly. Precisely six weeks later, Herr al-Tikriti arranged an appointment with Herr Doppelt, myself, and our late Chairman, Herr Gausmann, which the Iraqi requested for the purpose of discussing his 'proposal' concerning the Königsberg Fund. Although this was most irregular, we reluctantly agreed to meet with him. After all, it would be impolite to ignore such a large investor in the Bank, ja? Perhaps I should let someone else at that meeting describe what happened. Would you please fill in the details for our colleagues, Herr Doppelt?"

Scharnhorst turned his attention to a rotund, red-faced executive shuffling quickly through a messy stack of papers on the table before him as if trying to find something he had misplaced.

"Ja, of course. Thank you, Herr Scharnhorst. Herr Scharnhorst and Herr Gausmann, the younger, of course, who was also present at that meeting, could confirm what I am about to tell you," Doppelt began.

He glanced furtively around the circle of bankers seated around the conference table before continuing.

"This will be of great interest to you, Herr Kreuz, because this operation will be directly involving you and our other colleagues in New York. Our meeting with Herr al-Tikriti was very short. He asked how we were progressing on his proposal for lending to the Königsberg Fund. He was angry to learn that we had not taken any action with respect to his proposal. Herr al-Tikriti informed us that the Königsberg Fund was seeking bids from several banks to obtain US$150 million or its equivalent in another fully convertible currency to finance ongoing operations."

He paused to let the significance of the proposed transaction sink into Kreuz's tired brain.

Doppelt continued. "Our late Chairman observed that amount was simply out of the question. At that point, the conversation became somewhat heated. Herr Gausmann said that the meeting was over. Herr al-Tikriti simply smirked and said that Herr Gausmann should carefully reconsider his proposal. Then he demanded a final response within two business days. Herr Gausmann, barely able to contain his rage, tossed just one word over his shoulder as he stormed out of the meeting: '*ausgeschlossen!*' You know, out of the question."

Scharnhorst then nodded to Gausmann, the younger, who began speaking rapidly, first in a hushed tone.

"My wife and I thank each of you for all your expressions of condolences on the unfortunate deaths of my mother and father. As Maria and I were nearing our car after the funeral of my parents, a large gray Mercedes sedan with dark windows stopped beside us in the street. Herr al-Tikriti leaned out. All he said was: 'Now you will make the loan to the Königsberg Fund. The bids are due in ten days. You will receive the details electronically tomorrow. Don't endanger yourself by yet again ignoring this request.'"

The young executive paused for a moment, struggling to control his emotions.

"You are still no doubt wondering, Herr Kreuz, what this has to do with you," he continued. "Well, the Königsberg Fund is operated from New York by its American founder, a lawyer named David Garvey. Herr al-Tikriti has directed that the loan be made from our New York Branch, Herr Kreuz. As you can see, our fate is in your hands."

Now Diether Kreuz understood why he had been summoned without notice to Schwerin. A sinking feeling filled the pit of his stomach.

WHEELS UP

The muscular security guard watched David closely as he slipped through a narrow gap in the shoulder-high chain-link fence. Barely moving his lips, he muttered into his partially opened desk drawer, "Get ready! He is now coming."

The guard knew David Garvey only as a foreign businessman who usually spoke to him in halting Swedish. He resented the odd jobs David tried to hire him to do, as if a few euros could buy his approval. He recoiled at the brash foreigner's inappropriate familiarity; it felt like he was trying too hard to be friendly. He saw David zip up his parka and warily inspect the building's entrance as well as two empty cars covered with snow parked nearby. What the guard couldn't see, as David turned his head away to look once more down the row of hangars, was that he inserted a tiny plug from inside his parka collar into his right ear.

David pushed open the green-tinted glass door, losing his footing for a moment on the hard-packed snow. He forced a smile for the first time that day; the security guard was a friend of his. *What a stroke of luck*, David thought.

The guard tried hard to look bored and tired, apparently engrossed in a ménage à trois in the centerfold of the lurid Hungarian skin magazine in his lap. David stepped tentatively in front of the raised desk, letting the green glass door behind him swing quietly shut with a slight hiss.

Once inside the low, rambling building, David felt almost instantly warmed by the familiar aroma of metal, machine oil, and drying paint, more comforting than the dry, frigid air outside. And being inside felt safer from predators of the two-legged variety than standing alone in the vast frozen parking lot. Eager to please, David greeted the hangar watchman in Swedish.

"So, Ari, get any ice time this weekend?"

"Yaaw, Mr. Ekblom, I played down to Espo, and my boys did too. And how was your weekend?"

"Yuust fine, Ari."

The guard waved David through into the main building without evident interest, recording the foreigner's arrival with a worn wooden pencil on a nearly empty log sheet. The watchman, an ethnic Finn, knew so little Swedish David hoped his lack of fluency might go unnoticed and that his cover as a traveling businessman from the west coast of Sweden would be transparent. David had spent long enough in Finland to understand many ethnic Finns were not really fluent in Swedish, the country's other official language. He took advantage of that disparity whenever possible. David's Swedish was only passable but hopefully smooth enough for the immediate task at hand. Fortunately, David thought, the hulking guard seemed more interested in his magazine than him. He breathed a faint sigh of relief and escaped through the only interior door with a perfunctory wave to his friend.

David scurried quickly down a narrow corridor lined on one side with the blank stares of darkened office windows and on the other side closed storage locker doors. He suddenly sensed movement to his right and turned toward it quickly, left hand clawing at the plastic stock of his Glock 19 sticking out of its shoulder holster under his right armpit. It was only a scrawny calico cat.

Flushed with adrenaline, David hesitated for what seemed like an eternity to look cautiously up and down the long hall and listen, and then listen some more before continuing. Convinced he was alone,

David stepped sidewise through another doorway looking out over a vast, open hangar where eight small planes and two helicopters were parked, two partly encased in portable aluminum scaffolding. Chocked aircraft looked strangely abandoned in the gathering gloom. The hangar's long, hazy tube stretched toward a 40-degree opening to a wide, snowy landing field dotted with glowing, blue runway beacons with a backdrop of rows of pointed evergreens stretching as far as the eye could see. David's own plane languished closest to the runways, just inside the hangar's maw but more than 50 yards from where he stood. Two men in greasy coveralls were working under the tail section of a dark olive helicopter, tools scattered around them on a torn canvas tarpaulin. Only the occasional crackling arc of their welding torch interfered with David's view of his plane in the half darkness.

David slowly pulled the zipper of his bulletproof jacket up tight and methodically coaxed a supple black leather glove over the knuckles of each hand, a somewhat calming procedure. *Only a few more yards to safety*, he thought to himself. He reminded himself again to just take it slow and easy, one careful step at a time.

Just as David stepped lightly down the lime-colored utility mats covering each of seven corrugated aluminum steps leading to the hangar floor below, a hairy hand snagged his right boot! He reeled forward, bags tumbling away, and caught himself with both hands on the railing just in time to bring his feet sharply together. Quickly sliding his hands apart on the smooth iron railing, David arched his back and snapped the toes of both steel-shank boots into the left temple of a thin man now crouching near the right side of the steps. His swarthy assailant slumped to the concrete, as a stiletto clinked to the cold floor. Fearing one of the workmen had noticed or heard something, David Garvey held his breath, but the welding continued unabated.

Already beyond distress, David dropped to his knees beside the prone body, shaking. Reaching into the side pocket of his duffel bag, he removed two bulky foil packets, ripped open their seals, and poured two mounds of glistening finger-sized cords on the gray concrete beside his unconscious attacker. The white plastic worms wriggled as if newly born.

He rolled the inert man over onto his stomach, then wrapped one fleshy cord tightly four times around each ankle and three more times around both ankles together. He used the second coil of the moist thongs to bind both wrists in similar fashion behind the waist of the man's grimy gray jump suit. After counting silently to fifteen, David bent down and removed his left glove to snap the now nearly opaque bonds with the nail of his left index finger—click, click. Already they were taut and stiff.

Next, David unfolded a soft, dusky patch of fabric from the same pocket of his larger bag and used it to tape the assailant's jaw shut, leaving an ample breathing hole. As an added precaution against further interference, David unscrewed the cap of a tiny glass vial and removed a dropper filled with pomegranate-colored liquid. He squeezed three drops into the man's upturned ear. A slight shudder from the coldness of the liquid's intrusion shook the man's shoulders. Once the dark red liquid reached his inner ear, he would have no sense of balance at all for at least an hour.

David quietly folded the inert body into a fetal position and pushed it out of sight in a pool of shadows under the aluminum stairs.

During the attack, the long hangar had grown even gloomier, as late afternoon shadows continued to lengthen.

David stole furtively down along the hangar's right outer wall, giving the welders' bright crackling a wide berth, his heart racing from a combination of fear and hope. And then, there it was at last, his way out of this carnage.

His ebony Goshawk 93A-X was poised near the hangar's corrugated right wall, as if straining to escape into the gathering dusk; its dormant pair of jet turbines spinning slowly from the stiff breeze.

David quickly scanned the area nearby but couldn't see anyone except the two busy welders far on the other side of the hangar. He dropped to the floor and crawled on all fours toward his sleek jet aircraft from the side farthest from the workers, seeking the shelter of the darkness under its low fuselage.

As he crawled forward, David's outstretched left hand recoiled from touching an unexpected hard object. After some reflection, he concluded it was the sole and heel of a large steel-toed boot, toe pointing skyward. Then the leg of a pair of industrial trousers. Another body. Investigating further, while glancing quickly around for others, David checked for a pulse. None! The breeze from the snowy plain outside the hangar brought David Garvey a slightly charred smell, mixed with the kind of electrical odor that lingers in the summer breeze after the crash of a bolt of lightning. Quickly figuring out what had happened, he crawled quickly past the corpse and cautiously stood up in front of Goshawk's cockpit door.

Looking nervously over his shoulder, David poked a small metal spike from the lower hem of his parka into the second of three chrome sockets near the right side of the aircraft's only door. He swept his right palm quickly over the right cockpit door seam. Inside the plane something clicked and began to hum faintly. At the same time, David put his left index finger into a small hole outlined faintly in red in the fuselage just above his left shoulder. He noticed some crispy debris around the circumference of the opening. As he passed his hand over the door seam, Goshawk's onboard computer had read an RFID chip embedded under the skin of David's right wrist.

The computer hardware scanned the implanted chip and announced brightly in David's right ear:

"David Garvey. Born 31 October 1943. American Passport Number 0970239256. Bloods Type A Negative. Divorced, two children. Weight: 71.5 Kilos. Please wait for checking of fingerprint."

Although he had personally designed Goshawk's security system to foil intruders, this verification process seemed horribly mechanical, as if he could somehow be adequately described by only a few bytes of data. But no data on that tiny chip could adequately convey how desperate being hunted made him feel.

In theory, David's data chip could perhaps be surgically removed from his wrist and used by someone else, but also putting his left index finger into the small aperture in Goshawk's fuselage allowed two additional identity checks. First, his fingerprint could be compared with the sample residing in Goshawk's computer files. And, because David was double-jointed, he could insert just the tip of his index finger into the small hole without touching its sides, simply by bending only the first joint. That was something few others would think of, much less be able to do; the dead man at his feet had obviously either not discovered that trick or failed to do properly.

During what might have been a pause between measures of the melody of Goshawk's onboard computer's surveying the chip's data to finish evaluating the information presented by David's body, Marja's voice, the human voice David had engineered into his creation, continued.

"Your bloods pressure is a bit high, David. I hope that is from some fun we had together, you know. You have two messages. We go on scrambled uplink after cruising level to retrieve them."

Had David's identity not been verified by the plane's database, the small hole would have closed tightly around his left index finger. Then Goshawk's emergency battery pack would have shorted across the path between his left index finger and the grounded steel disk in the hangar floor beneath his feet. That burst of electrical current would have passed directly through his heart, causing immediate cardiac arrest. He would have died instantly. Somehow the corpse under Goshawk had known enough about the aircraft's security system to get through at least part of the screening. But luckily for David, one of the last few checks had shut down this unfortunate intruder for good.

The cockpit door hissed open to reveal the faint orange glow of Goshawk's awakening instrument package. A clear plastic bag of pistachios waited in a small, mesh pouch dangling from a sturdy plastic hook on the bulkhead inside. David tossed his duffel bags into the waiting bin and scooped up a handful of nuts on his way into Goshawk's cramped cabin. David winked wearily toward recent pictures of his two growing sons mounted under the lip of the plane's dashboard, a glimpse of sanity in this vortex of unending terror.

Since David always flew alone, he needed an electronic partner, an active voice, to help with preflight checks, takeoffs, landings, and navigation, not to mention provide some company along the way when boredom and lack of attention could be fatal. And David was more likely to pay attention to Marja's warning messages than some impersonal twang of a faceless, computer-generated voice. In a way, Marja could always be with him, even on these dangerous missions. But now, hearing her speak submerged him in sadness. No one would ever hear Marja's real voice again. Her closeness to David had taken her from him forever.

The cockpit door whispered shut behind him, blocking out distant crackling of the welding torches as well as all other background noises, and wrapping David in the faint hum of Goshawk's computer installation and navigation package. Collapsing into the single pilot's seat, David was automatically embraced with his seatbelt and shoulder harnesses. He sank into the pillow of soft leather cushions, allowing himself to believe, for just a brief refreshing moment, there really might actually be some way out of this horrible mess.

From his low chair, David could clearly see the smooth, painted floor of the hangar in front of Goshawk's nose wheel and reach the throttles, instruments, and yoke without even the slightest stretch. But already crowded by the wraparound cockpit, David became impatient.

"Punch up Vantaa ground control, Marja, if you please."

Instantly, 118.125 megahertz flowed into the tiny LCD transceiver screen near his left cheek. Clearing his throat to test the transmitter's voice activated switch, David announced, "Vantaa ground control, here is Polish Postal 261 first inside Hangar 25E. Please send us mule and give us stand for preflight."

"Polish Postal, mule on the way. Your spot Stand 46."

For the first leg of his journey, David adopted the guttural patois of a Polish pilot known to Vantaa International's local air controllers as Tadeusz Biełecki, a native of Białystock in eastern Poland, to substantiate his impersonation of a pilot for the privatized Polish Postal Agency.

Shortly, a yellow, battery-operated cart driven by a slender young woman seemingly painted with a tight blue jumpsuit whizzed through the open end of the hangar bay and hummed toward Goshawk. Her flowing flaxen hair caressed a pair of green sound suppressors jiggling around her bare neck. Once close enough, she spun the cart sharply away from Goshawk and squeaked to a stop. Then she quickly whined the battery-powered vehicle toward Goshawk's nose gear, attached her tow bar to the single eye in the plane's nose wheel strut, and jumped down from her bench to jerk away all three of Goshawk's wheel chocks.

David looked away just long enough to reach over and release Goshawk's wheel brakes. Its electric motors humming smoothly, the mule maneuvered the silent Goshawk serenely out through the hangar's wide bay to the jet's assigned spot on the concrete apron. Pointing Goshawk's nose toward the southwest, the shapely blue jumpsuit kicked off the tow bar. The cart hummed away toward Vantaa's cargo terminal. The buxom blonde turned to wave in David's direction from the far edge of the tarmac. He wistfully imagined she was probably married with four kids and a devoted husband.

He cracked open several pistachios and chewed them thoughtfully. David wondered when the monster he had created would rear its ugly head in the Americas. Putting worry aside for the moment, he pulled three navigational charts for the outbound flight from a slot in the side of his couch and spread them out within easy reach. As if on cue, Marja initiated their duet of pre-flight checks.

"Engage navigational console. Check latitude N60° 18.9'. Check longitude E024° 57.8'. Check altimeter 179 feet."

"Navigational console engaged," David responded. "Latitude checks N60° 18'54. Longitude checks E024° 57'55. Altimeter indicates 176 feet. Correcting."

"Check main hydraulic pressure normal," Marja's voice continued.

"Main hydraulic pressure checks normal," David answered.

This indispensable routine was so repetitious and tedious David couldn't keep his mind from wandering, and blissfully slipped away into the comforting glow of his short life with Marja.

Marja Kapivari was the manager assigned to his Königsberg project by AB Kangaslampi Oy, a leading Finnish construction company with long experience building difficult projects in the Soviet Union. Her twinkling sapphire eyes and quick smile camouflaged a persistence fostered by nearly crushing personal adversity, a common bond she and David shared from the beginning. Marja once told him that her naval engineer husband had been suffocated by lethal gases collected in the lower levels of the hull of a merchant vessel he was inspecting shortly before construction of the Königsberg Fund's outpost began in earnest.

Marja's quiet efficiency in managing the project gradually overcame David's reluctance to rely on anyone, driving the planning and initial construction of the outpost off dead center, in the face of apparently insurmountable obstacles, while Balts, Russians, and Ukrainians celebrated the demise of Communism and the collapse of the Soviet Union. She nurtured the outpost and made it quietly bloom in calculated obscurity on the banks of the Pegel River. Along the way, her warmth melted some of David's defenses. He found himself beginning to daydream, slipping back into happier times.

Last rays of an autumn sunset had just slipped behind a stand of evergreens across the lake. A glowing heap of sauna rocks atop the bulky iron woodstove brightened the small pine cabin's rustic interior. The double-diamond deck-plate stove's aluminum tank had already given up its treasure of steaming lake water to rough birch buckets David and Marja had used to thoroughly soap and rinse each other in the warming room outside. Inside the sauna, a *Rovaniemi* beer thermometer hovered at 96ºC, warmer than many Finns prefer. Nearly suffocating dry heat pushed aside all other thoughts and worries. Now it was time to listen to the rocks.

"You are ready for some real heat, David? I will be putting water on rocks," Marja announced.

Without waiting for his answer, she deftly tossed a wooden ladle of icy lake water toward the glowing lava rocks filling a metal box that formed the top of the metal wood stove. The splash of cold water momentarily cut the gleam those rocks cast on David's glistening cheekbone beside Marja's naked thigh. She was reclining on the slatted upper bench to take full advantage of the sauna's searing heat. A long hiss of flash evaporation preceded the invisible hammer of steam.

"Pour some over my head! I've gotten out of practice. What do the rocks say? You know I don't understand the old Finnish they speak," David ventured, humoring his lover's pantheistic superstitions.

"Well, rocks they say you have been away too long. You forgot them. You are not listening to what they say."

"How can you tell that?"

"I've been listening to rocks since I was only little girl, first going to sauna with family," Marja explained. "Another ladle for rocks?"

A blanket of nearly liquid warmth smothered David and seared his ears. He splashed a double handful of water over his face and shoulders—relief, at least for a moment.

"What do the rocks, what do they say now?" he asked again.

Marja had peered intently into the liquid fire, her eyes glistening brightly. Faint wisps of vapor made the sauna rocks and the forest disappearing into shadow across the lake appear to shimmer and weave in the faint evening light. At last, crackling of the rocks bubbled away, replaced by faint hissing. Sighing sadly, she whispered, "I can't really hear them. Come now, into lake, my love."

Every hurried step they took left moist footprints in a light dusting of new snow on the dock's broad planks. The sauna's extreme heat had so confused David's senses that the Aurora Borealis seemed to pirouette overhead as if dancing through the blur of a summer evening. David and Marja didn't notice that the air temperature outside was already well below freezing. One airborne pause out over the deep water, then plunging through a tinsel shell of fresh ice, David and Marja were both swallowed up in a dark vice of intense cold that squeezed them mercilessly in its frigid grip. Marja squeezed David's arm when the lake stole their breath away and blocked out all of their cares.

Later she looked down into David's eyes in the flickering half darkness. He reached up to tenderly trace the outline of her ears, at once struck by Marja's calm beauty and haunted by her eyes, half hidden in the shadows. David briefly savored her moist curls before his fingertips touched lightly behind her back, coaxing her even closer. He was nearly overcome by her taste of birch smoke and the coming winter. They flowed together into another warmth, gentle at first and then more insistent, eclipsing the fading firelight.

Once more the shattering of glass tore at David's heart. He was alone in the winter darkness and so terribly afraid. Marja was calling for help, but David couldn't move from his chair beside the stairs, as if his arms and legs were frozen solid. He felt tied to his seat!

Persistent buzzing brought David back to Goshawk and the litany of preflight checks.

"Ground Control, Polish Postal 261, request takeoff clearance," David transmitted.

"Polish Postal 261, you are cleared for Runway Two Romeo. Proceed Runway Two Romeo by taxiways Uniform, Golf and One to holding position. Switch to ATIS," an air controller responded.

"Roger, Runway Two Romeo. *Gittos*, Ground Control. Switching ATIS."

David pried open two more pistachios, popped the nutmeats into his mouth, and reached over to select 114.2 MHz on his transceiver. He released Goshawk's brakes and gave her some throttle, a bit more with the left engine to nudge her slowly off Stand 46. Goshawk edged slowly to the right to point at the intersection of Taxiways G and 1. Rows of tall spruces stood silent watch behind Runway 4L/22R. Once at that intersection, David would guide Goshawk to the left, parallel to the main runaway, until it was his turn to take off.

"ATC, Polish Postal 261, proceeding Runway Two Romeo for takeoff," David reported.

"Roger, Polish Postal, proceed Runway Two Romeo. You are number three in line. Hold Cat III 'til further clearance."

David nursed Goshawk down Taxiway 1, past the bright lights of the passenger terminal on his left and the crowded revolving restaurant crowning its peak. He crossed Taxiway 2 and pulled up short in front of Runway 4R/22L with a squeak of Goshawk's tires. A white-and-blue striped windsock flapping above the field of withered grass and small bushes showed a stiff breeze out of the northeast, opposite from the southwest where a faint, pink patch of the day's fading light still lingered.

"ATC, Polish Postal 261, request clearance to cross Runway Four Romeo/Twenty-Two Lima and hold at Cat III."

"Roger, Polish Postal, proceed Cat III Runway Two Romeo. Switch to Tower at Cat III," the tower acknowledged.

"Roger, ATC, proceeding Cat III Runway Two Two, switching to Tower. *Gittos*, ATC," David confirmed.

Pushing her linked throttles forward, David powered Goshawk ahead smoothly, putting the lights of the terminal farther behind him. Wishing that his personal nightmare would also fade away the same way, David felt very much alone in Goshawk's cockpit, with only the orange glow of her instrument panels and the pulsing belly lights of the plane immediately ahead for company. He pulled up short at Cat III and switched to the published tower frequency, 118.6.

In front of him, an enormous 789 turned slowly to the left and lumbered out onto the main runway. The jumbo jet sported a lit tail emblazoned with a blue gazelle bounding through an orange circle. The pilot's banter with Vantaa International's tower revealed many lands and times: Afrikaans-flavored English answering English spoken by a Finn whose native tongue was probably Swedish. Even inside Goshawk's sealed cabin, pulsing turbine thunder riveted David's attention on the South African heavy as it surged toward peak power before beginning its takeoff roll.

"Tower, Polish Postal 261, holding Cat III, request takeoff clearance Runway Two Romeo."

"Roger, Polish Postal. Cleared for takeoff runway Two Romeo. How do you copy, over?"

"Roger, Tower, copy cleared takeoff runway Two Romeo."

Again pushing her throttle yoke forward slightly and giving her right engine slightly more juice, David coaxed Goshawk to the left and out onto Runway 2R, feeling the seam of the concrete pavement thump under her rubber tires. Together, David and Marja quickly finished the remainder of their checklist, an ever so faint duet on the near edge of darkness.

"Cycle slats!" Marja ordered

"Check slats cycled and extended," David confirmed.

"Full throttle both engines!" Marja demanded.

"Indicates FIREWALL throttles," David replied doggedly, jamming both throttle levers past their normal full-power range into their forward stops. With a sense of growing excitement, he watched both engine tachometers lurch into the red danger zone. His life on the line, David knew there was no reason to be timid any longer. He had to reclaim the initiative.

Goshawk's nose yawed under the strain of her screeching jet engines, beyond their limits.

"Release brakes! We are going!" Marja squealed gaily.

"Brakes released."

Goshawk slipped her leash and bounded down the oil-spotted tarmac, pushing David sharply back into his seat. Rows of purple lights recessed into the runway's surface began to rush, then flutter, past. Goshawk accelerated quickly, like a smooth, dark stone skipping across the glittering snowfield toward night's enveloping blackness. Even in the depths of his sadness, David couldn't contain his exhilaration. He was tired of being a punching bag.

"Mark 80 knots!" Marja's voice called out. "108 knots, here comes V1. Mark V1. Point of no return. We must now take off. Coming up on V2. Mark V2, 121 knots. We are ready to takeoff, David."

"Rotating," he responded, pulling back ever so slightly on the yoke between his knees. The lavender blur of lights imbedded in the runway beneath Goshawk began to sink slowly into an inky pool of darkness, stayed for only a fleeting moment by the solar pulse of her underbelly beacon.

"Wheels up!" Marja directed.

"Wheels coming up," David confirmed, his remark punctuated by a loud clunk. "Wheels up and locked."

"Polish Postal 261, Vantaa Tower, come left to 159º. Switch to Helsinki approach frequency. Proceed 22,000 feet. Acknowledge, over."

"Roger, Tower, Polish Postal 261, coming left to 159º, proceeding 22,000 feet on flight plan to Gdansk. Switching to Helsinki approach frequency. *Tak*, Vantaa."

David dutifully switched to 119.1 MHz and checked in with Helsinki approach. Following his flight plan, Helsinki air traffic controllers directed him to proceed over the island of Balti, at N59º 54.1', E025º 12.4', and then come right to 198º to follow route A22 over Tallinn, Estonia. Gdansk on the north coast of Poland was the destination David had designated in his flight plan, because the airport in Gdansk was officially closed outside normal Polish business hours, an extremely flexible concept. David had actually never been to Gdansk in all these trips and never expected to set foot there, ever. The success of his scheme depended upon this sort of detail regularly falling through the cracks in the cumbersome and overburdened air traffic control system over Finland, Estonia, Latvia, Lithuania, and points east.

Passing through 6,000 feet, David reached over to calibrate the barometric pressure setting of his altimeter at 29.92.

". . . shift . . . auto . . . pilot."

"Autopilot engaged," David answered, jiggling the speaker's toggle switch.

". . . love me? . . . love? David . . . getting cold—"

David hammered the tiny computer cabinet in frustration but Marja's faltering voice disappeared into a cloud of static. He anxiously rebooted the voice-activated computer and leaned close to its speaker:

"You there, Marja? Can you hear me? Don't leave me now! I don't know if I can make it without you."

Desperately, David looked around Goshawk's compact cockpit for some way to bring her back. But hopelessness gnawed at his resolve as he relived the sights and sounds of Marja's death in his arms. He looked out into the night sky, seeing nothing. Marja would never be beyond his thoughts.

IN TRANSIT

An insistent bell tinkled at David's elbow. He wiped the warm tears from his weary eyes. Then he clicked the incoming call into his headset, hoping without reason it might be Marja.

"Yes?"

"That you, David?"

"Who wants to know?"

"It's Ani, David. We have big problem. So I'm now calling at your office to tell you."

"I'm not in the office, but my calls follow me. You passed the voice scan, Ani. What's the problem? You're on my scrambler."

"I just got report of last week's loan collections," Agnieszczka Czarnocki, David's on-site manager, continued. "Way down! Some customers say German bank told 'em not to pay. At this rate, we are going out of business in month. What you think we should do?"

"Where are you, Ani?"

"At outpost," the young woman said. "And, ah, one of our collectors surprised German banker with one of our customers. She's downstairs in quiet room, ah, waiting to speak with you."

"Don't be surprised if you see me soon. Any security problems right now?" David asked.

"Seems pretty quiet. But be careful!"

"Please tweak up the perimeter sensors. Out!"

David Garvey looked over the faintly glowing orange instrument panel into the soupy darkness surrounding Goshawk. He vowed never to rest until Marja's death was avenged.

With just the slightest pressure on the yoke, David overrode Goshawk's autopilot and smoothly changed her course toward the right, to 215°, bringing her flight path parallel to the ocean shipping lanes outbound through the Baltic toward the North Sea.

Although David Garvey had never personally sailed in Baltic waters while a US Navy submarine officer, he was quite familiar with its shipping lanes from pouring over navigational charts squirreled away in his boat's locked collection of classified documents with instructions on "what to do if the balloon goes up." He could imagine himself commanding a freighter loaded with perlite outbound from St. Petersburg plying the gray waves far beneath Goshawk's slender wings. The heavily laden vessel would have soon passed south of Espoo, where the treacherous hangar guard had supposedly played hockey with his children then left the beacon of the Porkkala light abeam to starboard. Continuing in the darkness through choppy swells, the freighter might have wallowed past the tiny ferry terminal in nearby Hanko.

David remembered with some new fondness the regularity of shipboard life: working, eating and sleeping in the four-hour pieces of each day—life to the tune of eight bells. And yet, once the boat's last line had been taken in and officers and men had sailed with the tide, a whole host of personal problems went into the deep freeze until return to port, silencing the bill collectors, ex-wives, children, girlfriends, insurance salesmen, and mothers.

But David was in serious jeopardy without Marja's navigating skills. Now there was no one to talk him through the intricate flight to the outpost. To escape detection, David would need to fly at top speed and almost no altitude, while turning on a dime whenever confronted with any sort of obstacle. Without her help, he would have no choice but to try it alone. David checked the settings of Goshawk's autopilot. Then, as protection against his own growing excitement, he very deliberately confirmed each reading again. Next, David energized Goshawk's masker equipment, which electronically produced an image of each sound of her turbines and associated auxiliary equipment, a rich mix of tones and volumes, but a mirror image of each of the originals. Masker's second stage emitted a collection of sounds representing each of those mirror images, designed to cancel the real equipment noises.

As David carefully adjusted the amplitude settings, Goshawk's propulsion noises seemed to fade away. The silence was so sudden and complete that it reminded him of the momentary deafness following loss of cabin pressure during a commercial flight, but without the accompanying drop in temperature. Then David connected the masker's controls to Goshawk's throttles. From now on, every change in Goshawk's machinery noises would be matched by a corresponding change in the masker's countervailing noise output. By introducing into Goshawk's slipstream noises opposite to those of its engines and other equipment, the masker's output canceled the din gushing from her propulsion system. David hoped his flight from here to the safety of the Königsberg outpost would arouse no more interest in the ears of those below than a faint whisper in the wind.

For as long as he could remember, David Garvey had dreamed of flying—not just sneaking down to the local airport to beg a ride kind of flying, but actually flying himself. In that lightness of almost asleep, David imagined scampering through moist evening grass in his bare feet, spreading his arms to soar over the hedge beside the gravel driveway, climbing up over the Robinsons' house next door to watch the sun set behind the black-shingled steeple of the Congregational Church on Buck Street. And then silently floating over darkening homes below and watching streetlights and porch lights flicker on, he would effortlessly roll over to watch the stars come out around him, keeping his speed and altitude by swimming through this flowing freedom of his endless young summer. At other times, David would dream of flying high above the flowing Penobscot River until it reached the sea and then far out over the ocean, high above the waves on his way to a glistening somewhere beyond the night horizon.

Back in the airport hangar, David had put on a black body suit, just in case. As he plugged the suit's trailing cables into the Peregrine console, its faint blue-green glow of its four screens beckoned to him seductively. Next, David slipped a soft black boot over each bare foot and snapped a pair of electronic connectors between each boot and the legs of his flying suit. David slowly curled and uncurled the toes of his right foot and watched the fan-like movement of Goshawk's gray-and-white tail feathers flow back and forth across the lower right screen. Peregrine's video presentation of those movements reversed the lengths of the joints of that foot to conform to the configuration of his apparent tail feathers. Satisfied with the results, he completed the same procedure with his left foot, getting ready to fly.

The cabin's video recorder witnessed David half standing in the cramped space, then bending to lower the back of his seat and fold out an armrest on each of its sides, each with a bulky glove built into the end, resulting in a flat, cross-like surface. Plugging two jacks from each glove into the wristbands of his body suit, David knelt to slip his left hand into its own fixed glove.

At first, he inspected the intricate unfurling of the array of feathers representing his left wing. Testing the right glove's responsiveness and control in the same fashion, David marveled at the way his apparent wings reacted in exquisite detail to each puff of wind or tiny movement of each finger, feathers first reaching forward, then smoothly pulling back as he tested the marriage of his wings to Goshawk's throttles and control surfaces.

Goshawk's Peregrine computer allowed David and the aircraft to become one. Working as an inseparable being, the computer and the no-longer-young pilot duplicated the swift diving and climbing of her namesake, a powerful hawk, by fusing an overlay of his body movements with the jet's control circuits. David's arms became Goshawk's wings, the movement of his arms and fingers, her wings and their feathers, all translated into thrust and lift. His feet, now Goshawk's oversized tail feathers and sharp talons, became functionally inseparable from Goshawk's tail assembly and landing gear.

David and Goshawk soared as one, with more precision than could ever be achieved with ordinary instrument flight—a man's brain with a raptor's speed and agility. After the Peregrine computer and David became connected, each change in Goshawk's control surfaces came from a movement, however slight, of some part of David's body. His ability to fly and revel in every sensation of flying was magnified by wind, temperature, and pressure felt through sensors in Goshawk's skin, bathing David in rain, wind, or sun outside Goshawk. This exquisite combination of body and technology also enabled David to steal into forbidden territory and land in remote areas without a runway, but it might be impossible without Marja's companionship and navigation.

For David, these dizzying technical achievements paled before his sheer joy at flying in a way never even imaginable from the stodgy confines of an ordinary pilot's chair, however fast or maneuverable the plane. While piloting a versatile, high-performance jet aircraft, he could experience all the sensations of personal flight. Now David could soar and dive, fast and free.

Before lying face down and finally putting both hands in the attached gloves, David clicked the leads to his headgear. But he hesitated. A leap of faith was needed to don the helmet, because putting it on would blind him to all of the cockpit instruments. Instead, he would have to rely only on the image of an altimeter in the lower corner of his right field of vision and the image of a compass heading in the corner of the other eye. When necessary, Goshawk would hopefully warn him about low altitude or anything that came too close, all soft words of encouragement from Marja.

David hesitated, almost confronting his longing and self-deception. He had to try. Too many people were depending on him. David gulped, said a short prayer, and quickly pulled the electronic headdress over his head, adjusted the necklet, and leaped onto the couch.

As windswept sea yawned away beneath his wings, the pit of David's stomach told him he might fall. The single white masthead light of a small trawler nearly hull down on the horizon bobbed among long, wind-laced swells. David searched the vastness below with the keen vision of a ravenous hawk looking for something to eat—any warm, living thing.

Once each hand was in its glove and both feet were in their stirrups, Goshawk's couch smoothly but firmly clasped his arms, legs, shoulders, and waist. David fluttered free. He pulled his claws close, lowered his wings, then dipped his head and plummeted toward the murky sea, the tear of his altimeter blurring, both wings pressed tightly to his sides. Time seemed to stop as he fell toward the water like a stone. Just in time, David's wing tips strained for the heavens, quickly high up and back, his talons swinging forward, dancing lightly over crests of foamy breakers.

With powerful overhead strokes from both wings, full afterburner, punching through a bright window in the cumulus and altimeter flowing, David burst into the starry heavens. He soared up and over the highest loop of the roller coaster, escaping the chains of gravity for just a few heartbeats. Momentarily comfortable with his control of the situation, David began a leisurely wingover to the right. As he slowly scanned the eastern horizon and spotted the faint lights of Tallinn in the distance, David drank in the silver sheen of that fateful half-moon, then a translucent climate control panel outside the atmosphere blocking several stars and the ruby wing light of a jumbo jet inbound to Helsinki's Vantaa International airport. Patches of the dark ocean below rolled slowly into view once again through gaps in the slate cloud cover. With his head cleared and senses heightened,

David slipped sideways toward the grim surface spread out beneath him, building his speed as he swooped through the ominous bank of clouds. His earphones crackled noisily. He was startled and pleased to hear Marja whispering to him:

"We are 248 kilometers out of Vantaa, David. Five seconds to turning point, 58°N, 21°E. Mark, turning point. Come left to 180°."

David obediently raised his right wing tip. His heading precessed slowly to the left: 210°, 200°, 190°, 180°, 176°. At first, he leveled his wings but then raised his left wing a bit before settling on 180°, due south. A stiff breeze out of the southwest required him to occasionally raise his right wing for correction in order to proceed down the line of 21° East longitude. He planned to fly some 260 kilometers farther to be abreast of Klaipėda, a port city on the western coast of Lithuania. Known as Memel to Germans, Klaipėda is Lithuania's only seaport, situated at the head of the Curonian Lagoon, which drains into the Baltic Sea.

"What happened back there, Marja?" David asked.

"It was so cold, like too long in lake after sauna. I could hear you, but my mouth did not answer."

"I'm glad you're back! Are you OK?

"Still very cold. Hard to stay awake. But I try to get you to outpost. Then sleep."

Through Goshawk's piercing night vision, David could examine in minute detail every feature of the ocean's surface and, later during his journey over land, the land below, but without the dangers and limitations of earlier night vision technology. His familiarity with every aspect of each hill, wood lot, and body of water on the way to the outpost had been sharpened by studying nearly microscopic videos recorded by Goshawk's belly cameras on each previous run between Helsinki and the outpost in Königsberg.

"Klaipėda, David, passing in five seconds!" Marja reported.

David locked on an occulting green light from a navigational beacon above the thin strip of sand on shore near Meinragé, just north of Klaipeda, a light industrial city on the water some 175 kilometers northwest of Kaunas. One click of the button above David's left thumb entered the precise bearing of that light into Goshawk's navigational computer. He had engineered this detail himself to avoid entering erroneous information from squeezing the glove during times of stress. Now, little more than a fleeting shadow just above the surface of the cloud covered sea, David sped over the Kurskaya spit, too close to the Nida beacon atop its red-and-white candy-striped tower, its intense red light blinking twice every nine seconds. Its brightness hurt his keen raptor eyes. So close, he could clearly make out the individual parts of the huge lamp's filament.

AN DEN PEGEL

Night flowed pleasantly through David's wing feathers. An ancient Trabant rattled past a clump of low, scrubby berry bushes alongside the narrow dirt road below as it sputtered around a sharp curve. Its headlights jiggling from the effects of a deep pothole, the old East German car clattered over a rickety steel bridge. One of two men fishing over the bridge's corroded iron railing inhaled deeply on a cigarette, its orange glow spreading over his craggy face, emphasizing his prominent eyebrows. His companion carefully placed a large, dark-colored bottle against a concrete bridge abutment and turned away to face into the bushes.

Trying to reduce the possibility of detection as much as possible, David flew even closer to the glassy surface of Kurskiyj Bay. The few waves on the shallow Baltic itself near shore were blocked out entirely by the low spit of land he had just crossed. Only seconds from real landfall, David left immediately to his right the slowly blinking signal atop a decrepit water tower near Rybachjiy. Whispering close over the rambling second growth of wooded shoreline, David spotted a gray patch under a spreading birch at the edge of an almost invisible stony path. Suddenly, what now appeared to be a rough gray wool blanket moved, exposing a pair of upturned bare toes. Between those upturned toes, two bare heels rocked insistently back and forth, a thrusting motion that made David snicker.

"Coming up on Zjeljenogradsk, David, better slow down to test hover," Marja interjected.

Although David Garvey used a number of different routes to the outpost, for variety as well as to avoid detection, tonight he would cross over the south shore of Kurskjiy Zaliv, continue west-southwest to Yantarnjiy on the western tip of what used to be Kaliningrad Oblast and circle quietly to wait for the evening freight train bound for Gvardeysk, a small city at the intersection of E77 and P512, due west of Königsberg, most recently Kaliningrad—old places, old names now new names. In his musings, David could see his Holo's projecting the ebb and flow of interactive maps of Polish, German, Ukrainian, Russian, Swedish, and Baltic sovereignty over this region during the course of the last two hundred years. Much German influence, strong Russian imprint since the end of World War II and now almost a vacuum, with at least some of the German names and influences beginning to return, like particularly persistent perennials.

David hoped that a rumbling freight train would cover whatever noise might be leaking around the masker or at least make someone on the ground this time of night less likely to look up while David was gliding through the damp night air overhead. He knew every hillock, swamp, and road along the way and could almost find his way by touching the rooftops and trees. Unfortunately, train schedules in this part of the world were often a sometime thing. But this lawyer didn't mind the chance to dawdle quietly through the nearly liquid darkness, waiting for his cover to come screeching slowly along the Russian gage track stretching crookedly out into the distance.

After the swift demise of Communism and the dramatic weakening of the Russian grip that swiftly followed, Kaliningrad had been isolated from the bits and pieces of the Soviet Union by a fiercely independent Lithuania. As Kaliningrad was pretty much left to its own devices, former Soviet military facilities in Kaliningrad had withered even before its old German name crept back into use. Effective rule from Moscow, the capital of the Russian Federation, being conspicuously absent, there was little local interest in activities that might seem threatening elsewhere. With comparatively easy access by road to Poland, the Baltics, Belarus, Ukraine, and western Russia, all important in building the Königsberg Fund's assets, Marja had easily convinced David to hide the outpost in Königsberg, as Kaliningrad was coming to be known again.

David's overall plan had nearly been stymied by some very basic problems, such as how to obtain dependable electrical service for indispensable banks of computers and their satellite feeds to the New York base, given Kaliningrad's faltering infrastructure. Marja had solved that one by tapping into three separate electrical grids, all surreptitiously and without compromising the outpost's existence, backed by a remarkably reliable switching mechanism designed to nimbly abandon any failing source in favor of another. Several tons of nickel-cadmium submarine batteries stood in additional last reserve. David still hadn't figured out how Marja had managed to make those very heavy and bulky items appear almost magically in the outpost's subterranean levels—all fully charged at that!

Another puzzle had been how to dress up the building so no one would even think about trying to break in while it was unattended, as it would often be the case. Marja had creatively addressed this particular challenge by choosing an abandoned chemical factory site, quietly completing all construction without altering any part of the exterior, then posting huge signs outside the building in block letters and several languages announcing its designation as a virulent toxic waste site, subject to the long-term supervision of a nonexistent foreign waste disposal conglomerate.

A grumbling line of boxcars clanked out of a pool of shadows behind the starkly lit freight yards at Primorsk. An ear-splitting screech assaulted David's ears as the train slowed only briefly before jolting through a series of track switches leading into the main rail line toward Königsberg running parallel to Secondary Highway E193. Positioning himself over the far side of the train, away from the highway, David slowed to nearly hover speed so as to match its jerky progress east as nearly as possible. Looking down the two pair of rails ahead, all David could see was inky black, an occasional dimly lit track signal and the intensely focused headlight of the decrepit electric engine.

David's delicate task during this part of the flight would be to shadow the string of lumbering freight cars but not so closely as to get snagged in its overhead electric power supply or scooped up by a railway tunnel along the route. Traffic on the nearby motorway being mercifully scant, David flew on through the darkness toward Königsberg itself, just 38 kilometers farther east.

In ordinary circumstances, David preferred to approach the outpost from over the Baltic itself, if only because the final leg of that route allowed him to pass eastbound near Yantarnyi, a small town near the coast, instead of from the West as he had done during this transit. Yantarj is the Russian word for amber, one of the more lucrative hard currency exports of the eastern Baltic. Sometimes made into jewelry, these tiny time capsules, the color of strong tea, often holding insects or tiny plants from eons ago in their frozen syrupy grasp, fascinated David.

Now running alongside the tracks carrying David's cover of the noisy train, the main highway disappeared ahead, tunneling under a railroad bridge from a feeder rail line before entering the outskirts of Königsberg. David swooped slowly to the right, over a twenty-four wheeler heavily loaded with rusty earth-moving equipment, taking him toward the north. He took his bearings from a pair of concrete electrical pylons just ahead and slipped easily to his right.

"Coming home, David. I lit them for you," Marja noted.

David spotted three beacons faintly pulsing blue around the outline of a nondescript patch of scraggly grass in front of the outpost. Before landing, he made a tight turn around the entire complex to make sure there were no unwelcome visitors. While David completed his prelanding checks, Peregrine interrogated the outpost's console to verify perimeter integrity.

Slipping silently toward his destination, David lowered his talons to skim the overgrown weeds, cold and wet from the remains of that afternoon's snow. As Goshawk slowly rolled toward what was left of the old factory until her nose nearly touched what seemed to be boarded-up windows, all of the blue landing beacons winked out in unison. Slipping from the couch's seductive embrace and pulling off his helmet, David Garvey shut down Goshawk's propulsion system with the click of a switch, jumped down from the plane and hurried up to the blank wall in front of him.

A counterclockwise turn of a badly corroded light fixture and the entire near side of the building rolled silently to the right, revealing the warm glow of Goshawk's hangar. Three hydraulic arms shot silently out of the shadows of the outpost's bay toward the waiting aircraft. David bent down to attach the middle arm to a heavy eye just above Goshawk's nose wheel. Without any further direction from David, the two remaining hydraulic arms clasped similar eyes above Goshawk's two main landing wheels. Goshawk was drawn noiselessly into the cavern as David jogged along alongside, ready for anything. The masonry wall slid quietly back into place, allowing the outpost's 36 tons of air conditioning to replace the cold night air with the even climate of an office building. From the outside, it looked like nothing much had changed since the end of World War II.

The electronic message board on the outpost's console was blinking rapidly. Ani ran up to him, babbling excitedly in Polish and pointing toward the stairwell into the outpost's lower levels.

Out of the shooting gallery, into the cauldron.

A Glimpse of the Plan

Once the lithe and luscious Polish blonde he later knew as Agniesczka Czarnocki caught David's attention during his summer trek through Eastern Europe, the trip became much more fun. Falling for this perky illegal currency trader as he watched her conduct business in Krakow's main square was probably the most irresponsible thing he'd ever done. And it must have felt like a warm spring day. So what if his instant infatuation with Ani might have been a reaction to getting thrown out of his home and the beginning of his nasty divorce, with all the accusations, threats and pain? Maybe the precipitous departure of his partner, Gideon Stahl, to become Ambassador to Namibia, leaving David to clean up the financial mess had made him do it. Or maybe his difficult childhood or the Devil made him do it. Right!

Truthfully, Ani was new and different; she fascinated him, heightened his senses, and teased him. And he was really intrigued by the way her illegal business worked.

With a final twist of the leather-covered steering wheel of his BMW, David Garvey had squeezed his racy convertible tightly into the narrow space between a bubbling stone watering trough and a yellow mailbox on a cobbled back street just off the square in Krakow's Old Town, trying to minimize his chance of getting towed. Pressing a tiny red button on his key ring to click the car's doors locked in front of what seemed to be a clock repair shop, he remembered that this wasn't New York City. *Give it a rest*, the young lawyer thought to himself, "*you're on vacation*. Then David Garvey felt someone tugging at his arm, a skinny young boy wearing grimy khaki shorts and a pair of bedraggled sandals looking up at him with beseeching eyes.

"You want my mother?" the lad asked. "She virgin."

He'd traveled all the way to southeastern Poland to find a comedian. "Shouldn't you be in school, kid?"

"Got your attention. Right, Meester?"

"So how'd you know I speak English? Don't I look German? German car, German plates."

"But American shoes. And American haircut. East Coast?"

"Smart kid. What you really want?"

"Change money? Best deal outside Warshava," the youngster claimed.

"Show me what you got, but make it quick," David directed. "I've got tickets to a chamber music concert, in a church behind the square."

"Follow me, boss."

Dragged along by the young entrepreneur, David followed him along the narrow, twisting street until it turned into the wide, open square across from Krakow's famous watchtower. The broad plaza was bustling with tourists leavened by the occasional Polish businessman hurrying home from work. Pointing toward a pair of overweight men in loud Hawaiian shirts, one with an elaborate Japanese camera sporting a long telephoto lens bargaining furiously with an animated young woman, the boy pulled David toward the trio. As David drew closer, he could begin to make out their back and forth above the clump, clump, clumping of shoe heels over the square's uneven cobblestones.

"You want to change 200 US? I give 94 euros," the young woman announced.

"Listen and learn, Jerry! I didn' spend thirty years in the jewelry business on 47th Street for nothin'. You ain't seen hondling yet," the

American tourist with the very long camera lens smirked, taking a deep drag on his double-dose Marlboro. "103!"

"How about 92?" the trader ventured, caressing the entire length of her right index finger with the tip of her long, pink tongue, eyeing David in the process.

"Some hondling, Herbie. She's goin' in the wrong direction. Probably doesn't understan' English," his companion observed, reaching into his bright red and yellow open-necked shirt to scratch a hairy armpit while noting the time on his oversized Rolex. "My prostate—gotta take another leak, Herbie. We don't have time for this shit."

"The Ladies' Man here says she's really hot, Jerry. She's got that look in her eye. I can get more than euros outta her! I could sure use a hummer. How 'bout choo? Betcha a hunerd I can convert this one into a hummer. You in?"

"I'll do ya one better. Two hunerd! Bet you can't even cop a feel!"

Apparently oblivious to their banter, Agnieszcka Czarnocki smoothly fanned a collection of folded euro and *złoty* bills, grouped according to denomination, between the fingers of both hands like a Metro-North conductor working through a crowded commuter train. She scanned the length of the square, expressionless, except for a faint vertical crease in the otherwise smooth, honey-colored skin above her pert nose. David was definitely captivated.

"101, but you gotta throw in something extra, if ya unnerstan' what I'm sayin'," Herbie said, grabbing her bare elbow.

"What you mean?" she spat out with an angry shake of her short blonde locks, brushing away the offending hand.

"So how about you come back to the car with Jerry and me, and give us a little, uhh uhh?" Herbie rotated his hips toward her for emphasis, his large paunch quivering.

"Tell me, Herbie, you kiss wife with that mouth? How you like to talk about sex games with that Polish policeman? And me a good Christian girl!" the young woman parried, pointing with a slim, bare arm toward a uniformed patrolman inspecting a nearby fruit vendor. Her hands were suddenly empty of all currency.

"Hey, whaddaya talking about? Just tryin' to do a little biness here," Herbie blustered, looking away from her angry eyes in embarrassment, but noticing the nearby beat cop for the first time.

"Is true, Herbie? Fat old men with long cameras have SHORT PUTZES?" she asked loudly, smirking in David's direction.

"Come on, Herbie. You can buy me one or five beers," the winner of the bet said as he put a hairy arm around his friend's shoulders, leading him away from the fray like a disappointed child. A very impressed David Garvey smiled, his appetite whetted.

Once David had convinced Agnieszczka Czarnocki, Ani for short, that he had no connection with the police, she was willing, almost eager, to explain how she twisted what passed for the Polish financial system to make it work for her. Ani fidgeted with her coffee spoon while repeatedly glancing at the street through the small restaurant's lead-paned windows as she told David just part of her story.

"I am spending half year at school in England. Two days before coming home, my father killed in accident at Nowa Huta steel mill. When I am coming home, Mother only look out kitchen window. Never talked to me again. When Father died, so did she."

David was momentarily distracted by the fullness of Ani's firm breasts thrust up at him from her tight, black lace brassiere as she reached into her purse for a scrap of cloth to wipe the corner of her eye. Yet David couldn't help noticing his new friend sneak a look at his unfinished chicken cutlet out of the corner of her eye.

"Take what you want," he said, pushing the plate in her direction.

"Not now—maybe later. I had no job, no family, except older uncle living in Moscow. Nothing to eat. I sell some of Mother's jewelry to buy food. But I buried most gold pieces in garden, between carrots and potatoes. Then I use gold to get money."

"What do you mean, get money?"

She looked nervously around the crowded restaurant before continuing.

"Needed food. I have two friends, boys, one my age, one younger." Perhaps referring to the urchin David had already met. "Change foreign money for tourists in main square. You know, where you see me. Where foreigners hear tape from tower of, how you call it, sentry playing horn. Killed in middle of song by Turkish arrow. Make money charging tourists not so good price for Polish money or euros but better than state banks."

"But how'd you get money to do that?"

"I take Mother's gold jewelry to house near railroad station. Old man give me money for gold. I must pay him every two weeks. Interest is 5% when I must pay."

David's look of disbelief caused Ani to pause.

"But, still I make money!" she exclaimed, as if preempting anticipated criticism. "One day, when I pay everything, I get all gold back. Now I'm changing money for many foreign tourists. Older men very much like me, maybe thinking they will get something else—you know, like Jerry." She giggled self-consciously.

For just a moment, Agniesczka Czarnocki looked older, tired, as she turned away to avoid David's penetrating gaze.

The wheels were turning in David's head, even as he filed away for further consideration the look of shame that had just flickered across Ani's otherwise open face. What she had described reminded him of the second and third mortgage lenders at home—lending at ridiculous rates and getting decent security to boot. He wondered what else lingered behind her warm smile and mischievous sense of humor.

"What would you think of paying only 4% interest each month?" he asked, carefully watching her finely chiseled features for any involuntary tell.

Only a minute shift of her jaw might have signaled that she even heard his question. *What a tough operator, this one*, David thought. He suspected he'd hate to have her working against him.

"Please, I am not understanding. You are saying I should pay 40% interest every month?"

"No," David answered, doubting Ani had really misunderstood, "what I meant was would you rather borrow money at 4% interest a month than 10%?"

"No one would loan money for so little!"

"If someone would loan you money, enough to pay off the loan shark you are dealing with, at, say 4% interest each month, would you give your gold and maybe your mother's house as security?"

"What you mean loan shark?"

"The old man near the railroad station. He's charging you at least 120% each year. He may not care if you ever pay off the principal of the loan so long as you keep up the payments for at least a year. By then, he'll have all of his money back and then some."

"This 4% person. Also a shark? Why does he want my mother's house?"

"In America, people borrow money and give bankers the right to take away their homes if they don't pay," David explained. "Bankers lend at lower rates because they think they can get the house if the loan goes bad. Most people will work pretty hard to make sure the loan gets paid, so they'll still have a place to live."

"Why you interested in Polish loan sharks?"

David paused to poke at the remains of his dinner, trying to decide what to tell Agnieszka Czarnocki about himself and his business. On one hand, he wasn't really ready to trust anyone at this point in his life. On the other hand, what chance was there he would ever see Ani again after this brief but wonderful vacation?

"Let's say I know someone looking to get into another line of business. Good connections to other people's money. Creative, willing to take risks."

David looked up from his plate. Ani was listening intently.

"What if this person loans money here in Poland? Hard currency," David continued. "If people need money to start a business or send kids to school in the West, where do they get it? Maybe I could raise a lot of cash and lend it out to hardworking people who give back mortgages on their houses or give me their shares in newly privatized companies and—"

"You want to be most biggest loan shark? You make me very wet," she grinned coyly, slowly tracing the outline of her upper lip with the tip of her exquisite pink tongue. Ani reached for David under the table.

STIRRING THE PLAN

Heading south from Krakow and fresh from his first dalliance with Ani, David watched the children's sanatorium in the mountain village of Rabka-Zdrój rapidly recede into grayness in the rearview mirror of his black BMW convertible. Rabka-Zdrój lies on the northern slopes of the Gorce Mountains in Poland's Nowotarski Voivodeship where the Poniczanka and Sionka Rivers join the River Raba. With his left hand lightly guiding its leather-covered steering wheel and right hand firmly grasping the gearshift, David powered the sleek vehicle around a sharp curve and over the next ridge of these increasingly steep foothills in southeastern Poland without even a touch of its brakes. Its eight-cylinder engine humming deeply as David drove toward Nowy Targ and the Beskid Mountains beyond. At once anxious and pleased, David was still uneasy about recent events.

Lying hip-to-hip in an overgrown field high over the Raba River, oblivious to the world around them, David and Ani jumped when someone started pounding on the hood of his BMW and yelling loudly. Angry shouting. David leaped up and tried to pull on his poplin trousers but lost his balance as one tasseled loafer caught on the way through a narrow cuff and he toppled to the ground with a dull thud. Silently motioning for him to lie there quietly, the back of one index finger to her flaming lips, Ani tiptoed down an almost hidden dirt path leading toward a nearby country road. Just before passing out of the range of David's admiring eyes, she hiked up her skirt slightly, leaving even less to the imagination.

David strained his ears to hear what was going on. At first, there was only a man yelling, but that soon subsided. David couldn't imagine what Ani had done to shut him up. He hadn't heard another car on the rough stones of the road to this apparently secluded meadow. As the breeze changed, David could hear Ani talking rapidly in her native Polish, and before long, the bushes parted, and Ani emerged with a saucy grin spread across her honey-colored face.

"So what happened, you charmer? I didn't hear a car."

"We are making love in farmer's field. Farmer walked by and saw German car with—how you say?—Munich license cards."

"Was he mad we were trampling his hay?"

"No. Farmer is pretty old, live in Warshava during war. Hates Germans. Thinks all Germans must pay for what Nazis did to his family."

"What's that got to do with us?"

"Farmer saw German car. Thought Germans here on his land—his family's land."

"Let me explain it to him!" David growled, springing to his feet.

"No good!" Ani warned her new American lover, holding him fast by one black, stockinged ankle. "If he see your blue eyes and yellow hair—be sure you German. Besides, I am telling farmer you big politician. You stole BMW from German tourists. Farmer went away fast."

"Oh great! So now I'm a Polish car thief in addition to being a Nazi war criminal. Let's get back on the road to Zakopane. We can finish our, ah, lunch later."

The wind whistled in David's ears as the nimble sports car seemed to fly up and over the rugged foothills slipping away under its wide-track tires. He grinned broadly at Ani, asleep in the red leather bucket seat beside him. Now David's black BMW hurtled through the thick darkness, coming down hard in a huge pothole with a crash.

The impact jarred Ani from her fitful slumber. She sat up and looked around to get her bearings.

"You know," she said sleepily, "my uncle bought apartment in Moscow, after Wall came down—30 square meters for cash. Now he can sell apartment. It is his. You think he could get big loan for apartment instead of selling?"

"In the West, that would be no problem. Maybe possible for him and others if my plan works."

"So what you are thinking, Mr. Rekin?"

"Whaaaatttt?"

"That Polish word for shark."

"I'm thinking this whole idea is not for the faint of heart. There's probably no law on who owns these buildings and probably even less law on how to take a really enforceable mortgage. But it looks very profitable, if I can organize it to run smoothly and line up the financing."

"You don't have money yourself?"

David snickered.

"Have to get in line after my ex-wife and her bloodsucking lawyer and behind the creditors of my last law firm. My new firm is doing pretty well, but we're talking serious bucks here. If this is structured properly, it should be bankable. I'll need to come up with a workable plan and probably some seed money to fund the start-up costs."

"I have cousin in Czechoslowakia. She got some papers. Traded them for parts of companies used to be owned by government. Can she get cash for her shares, Mr. Rekin? What about some other papers Father got from Polish government? Papers supposed to be piece of action in many Polish companies used to be owned by Polish government. What you think?"

"I don't know without more information, Ani."

Squealing his tires, David swerved to the left to avoid the glaring yellow eyes of a cat in the road ahead. "This whole project sounds pretty simple in concept," he explained. "But it would require a lot of detail work and some good people running the day-to-day operations here in Central Europe."

"Mr. Rekin not going to be big boss?"

"I still have a day job, as a New York lawyer! My two boys live in Manhattan, and I don't see them often enough as it is. Wouldn't even think of living permanently anywhere else. Besides, with good communications, I could keep track of operations from New York and come here when needed. But, like I said before, making all this work would depend on having someone really reliable to be in charge here. And a good central place to keep the records, collect the loan payments, etc."

David noticed Ani had become very quiet. He glanced away from the road whizzing by to see she was staring blankly toward the convertible top, now latched tightly in place against the chilly night air.

"You know, David Garvey," she said to the black canvas over her head, "nobody helped me stay alive and start business. Just because I love you, don't make mistake. I am very tough! Maybe I be local boss?"

David pondered that one for a long moment, wondering how much his response would be dictated by his johnson. He knew there was a lot to be said for personal loyalty, but could he trust Ani with that sort of responsibility? Not to mention trust her with what might become a very important part of his financial life? The operation would surely need many people, mostly men, to deliver the cash for loans and drive around to pick up payments. Would men in this part of the world work for a woman? And then there's the problem of comforting his rod with the staff.

"You need someone who grew up here, David. Me, I know area. Also know many people in other countries. Russians, Poles, and Czechs all have local money under bed or buried in garden. Not enough televisions or cars, so they buy land, shares. Anything that might be worth more later. Using them to get hard currency would work!"

"Why hard currency?"

"Nobody trust local money. Too easy for government to play with. Look how many times old Yeltsin changed Russian money. Better to have euros or Swiss francs. May change some, but won't disappear."

"So we lend US dollars, euros, Swiss francs to people with jobs in Central Europe and get back mortgages on homes or shares in newly privatized companies, or even some of the new start-ups. Loans would have to be repaid in hard currency too? Any problem there?"

"Maybe, maybe not. Some people get paid part in hard currency. Maybe some customers have accounts in foreign banks. Have to see."

"Borrowing hard currency somewhere in Europe or the United States would be simpler."

"So where you get all this stuff you're talking about?"

"I read a lot. It's an important part of my legal skills to know what is going on in my own country as well as around the world. Clients who want to do business in the US expect me to know what is happening. For example, our new President, Cristina Hernandez-Nakayama, sitting in the newly minted State of Columbia, despite her recognized interest in foreign policy matters, doesn't really support meaningful aid to the myriad republics and satrapies born in the Communist bloc's decaying carcass. No one on Main Street in Dubuque is buying the 'buy time for Boris' argument."

David Garvey paused in midbloviation to see how Ani was taking in all this information. She was sprawled awkwardly against the padded leather door, head back and fast asleep and snoring loudly.

Just as the twinkling lights of Zakopane came into sight, huge drops of rain began to pelt the windshield of David's ebony sports car. Slowing only slightly to let the heavy-duty wipers overtake the sudden deluge, he began to look for their hotel, all the time turning the variables of his new project over in his mind. But twirling around the edges of his mentally organizing and reorganizing the Fund were two intertwined thoughts: could Ani handle the challenge, and can he trust her with something this important to him?

THE SEARCH

"Where's Orion's belt, Dad?" David Garvey's son, Will, asked as he pointed toward replicated constellations high in the dome of Grand Central Station.

"Just to the right, Will, and above where you're looking right now. Over the fifth ticket window from the left," David mechanically counted each window and then pointed up toward the glittering restored dome of Grand Central Terminal.

"Peter, pay attention and watch your bag! One of those bums might steal it!" he barked at his older son. "Our train is supposed to leave from Track 18. Let's walk over there and see if we can board yet. As usual, we're early."

A closed pair of metal gates blocked the entrance to Track 18. David squinted through its wrought iron pattern of ivy vines and delphinium blossoms. He tried in vain to force the two sliding doors apart. Through a smudged plastic plate covering the back of the gate, he could just make out a red, white, and blue Amtrak diesel engine sitting at the near end of Track 18. Behind the long-distance train's power unit, a string of silver passenger coaches stretched into murky shadows of the tunnel extending north, toward 96th Street in Manhattan. A baggage cart loaded with what appeared to be cases of Dos Equis and Heineken beer hummed away down the long platform, darting through a throng of passengers like an Austrian slalom skier. Lounging against the idling engine, four crewmen

*were arguing heatedly about something David and the boys could not
hear. Maybe the Subway Series, David mused.*

"Let's go guys," he called out to his sons.

*"Where we going, Dad? Our gate's locked. We can't get on the train
yet."*

"I'm gonna show you a trick."

*David led his sons toward an adjoining gate where a single blinking
green light over glowing red and white letters announced the imminent
departure of the 7:10 Croton-Harmon local. A school of trench coats
and briefcases was swimming smoothly through Gate 23, leavened with
occasional mink and sable coats, nannies with babies in Italian strollers,
and near-teenage children wearing heavy backpacks. David guided his
reluctant boys toward the open gate.*

"But we aren't going to Croton-Harmon, Dad!"

"Remember, I'm showing you a trick."

*David and his boys scurried into the surging crowd of riders and were
swept through Gate 23. He eased Will and Peter toward the right edge
of a torrent of dark suits and ties and then off to the right side, under an
electronic clock hanging from the ceiling, ominously flashing "7:09."*

*"Look, over there," David said, pointing with satisfaction toward the
tricolored engine on Track 18 behind a long green trash bin.*

*"Our gate may be locked, but there are other ways to get where we
want to go. Lots of people are already on our train, veterans who know
how to get around the system. They probably* won't *get around to opening
Gate 18 until the train is about ready to leave the station, maybe even
after it's left."*

*David swung Will's blue nylon bag over his left shoulder. Will skipped
happily down the broad concrete ramp, sliding sidewise along the shiny
chrome railing to inspect the waiting engine more closely.*

*"Dad, I'm famished. Why couldn't we have dinner before we
came down here? I could sure use some pizza or a cheeseburger and a
milkshake," Peter said, rubbing his stomach in mock anguish.*

A nearby door of the engine's power unit stood ajar, starkly framing the nearly liquid grime blanketing two roughly idling Fairbanks-Morse diesels. Ample buttocks testing the capacity of a pair of worn dungarees nearly filled the lower half of the doorway, almost concealing her greasy, brown leather work boots. David saw a meaty arm swinging a tungsten wrench that careened out of her hand, clanking off the access cover for the lower crank throws of the nearest engine. She leaned around the doorframe to cough hoarsely and spit into the track bed, wiping her tobacco-stained lips with the back of her wrench hand. A large indigo tattoo on her bare forearm blared at David and his two young boys: "Get your rosaries off my ovaries."

"What's that mean, Dad?" Peter asked.

"We can talk about it later on the train, but let's get moving. We'll never get a decent seat if we don't hurry! Remember what I told you to say if the car is crowded, and we have trouble finding seats together. Toss me your bag so we can move faster!"

David struggled along the sloping concrete platform leading toward the distant end of the long train, luggage banging against both legs, his head down. He used the bright yellow safety track at the edge of the platform as a guide. Weaving in and out of other irritated travelers trying to push past a porter helping an elderly passenger with her bags and a loudly mewing calico cat in a small plastic cage, David nearly tripped over the outstretched sneaker of a homeless derelict fast asleep with his head and shoulders inside an overturned newspaper recycling cart, an empty Popov vodka bottle clasped affectionately to his chest. First looking into a darkened commuter train on the next track and then circling Peter who plodded glumly along behind his father, Will skipped back and forth across the crowded ramp.

"Come on, Peter, pay attention and get your brother away from that trash bin. The two of you run into that car and get those two seats facing each other we just passed, where that guy is playing a harmonica. And don't forget what you're supposed to say."

Peter led Will by the hand through the next open door into a dark passenger car overflowing with people standing on dilapidated seats, pushing heavy suitcases into cramped overhead bins. Their father followed just a few steps behind with all their baggage. As instructed, both boys climbed into the two remaining seats. Struggling under the weight of all their luggage, David tried to squeeze the larger bags into the overhead rack and push Will's blue nylon bag behind the seat next to Peter. Next to the boys, a lean black man with gold-rimmed glasses was still playing a large silver harmonica to the vocal accompaniment of a very slim young woman sporting dyed platinum hair and two golden safety pins through her right ear lobe.

"Will, get up, you'll have to sit on my lap. The train is crowded and you don't pay full fare yet."

"Dad, did you give Will his Dramamine?" Peter asked.

"Oh no, Peter, I forgot to give him his pills. Let's see. Are there any in my pockets? No. Maybe I better see if there are any in one of the bags."

"That was really dumb, Dad! You know how he THROWS UP! Like, remember that little old lady he puked all over last week? Filled up her whole lap!"

Without so much as a word, the musical couple quickly vanished into the next car. David selected one of the empty seats, stretched out, and put his feet up in the other empty seat. The two boys settled back into their recliners. So smoothly done it could have been rehearsed.

"Now I'm really hungry, Dad, and I just heard that conductor say the bar car won't open until we get outside the City. Can't we get something to eat, somewhere? Puleeeeze?"

"Will, do you mind waiting here a minute while I find Peter something to eat? We'll bring you something too."

David Garvey looked over at his younger son. Will had just turned five.

"Just don't take too long, Dad. I'm afraid the train will leave," Will answered, biting his lip. "Can Mom come down and wait with me in case the train leaves before you get back?"

"*Your mother won't even talk to me on the phone,*" *David snarled.* "*I'll just be a minute. Don't worry, Will, the train won't leave for at least another twenty minutes. We'll be right back. You want us to get you something, Will? Come on, Peter!*"

Together, David and Peter struggled through the incoming tide of passengers and hurried down the platform toward Gate 18 and the cavernous terminal beyond. Suddenly, the gate in front of them began to slide slowly shut, and the speed of the diesel engines behind David and Peter accelerated sharply. The rumble grew louder and its pitch increased noticeably. David spun around and ran back down the platform toward the train as it began to inch down the track.

The train was pulling out of the station. The red, white, and blue engine was backing down the track with ever increasing speed, trailing a thick pall of greasy diesel fumes. David ran, puffing down the emptying ramp, but the train rolled away from him, slowly at first, then faster and faster. Finally, he just couldn't keep up.

David sank to the concrete, breathing heavily, his spirit broken. Peter edged timidly up behind him and reached out to put a small hand on his father's shoulder.

"*Sorry, Dad, I should have waited for the bar car to open.*"

"*Come on, Peter. We've got to find the station master's office,*" *he answered quietly, looking away to conceal the worry that was plain on his face. "Maybe we can have someone from Amtrak meet the train at Croton-Harmon and take Will off. Then we could pick him up in the morning or something. Let's go. How could I be this stupid?*"

Sprinting into the main terminal, the pair hurried frantically toward an ornate brass information booth standing alone in the center of the gigantic open hall. Its golden antique clock with renowned pearl-like face, framed by a Merrill Lynch stock ticker capping the immense polished marble arches in the background, read 8:56. A lone attendant in the booth slowly directed a pasty-faced woman wearing an expensive mink coat toward the next Trenton train downstairs. In his haste to reach the metal-shuttered speaking hole into the booth, David stumbled over the toe of one of her expensive red leather pumps.

"Can you help me? My little boy was left on the Chicago train. I mean, the Chicago train left with my kid on it. I, we, missed it trying to get something to eat. Can you tell me where to find someone who can contact the station in Croton-Harmon?"

A green telephone buzzed inside the booth. As the clerk pressed the instrument to his left ear, he broke into a smile and slowly turned his back to David and Peter. His smile grew into a grin as he adjusted a natty, yellow, polka-dot bow tie and smoothed the few remaining strands of his thinning brown hair. Increasingly irritated, David tapped impatiently with his finger on the bulletproof Plexiglass shield. The attendant scowled angrily over his right shoulder at David and Peter and continued his conversation. David rapped loudly on the barrier with two quarters. Just then, the hovering mink coat observed, "you must be a terrible father to abandon one of your children in this station. You should be locked up!"

Glaring at her for a split second, David began to beat on the information booth window with both fists. At last David got at least part of the amorous clerk's attention. The clerk clamped his hand over the phone and screamed at his tormentor.

"Get outta my face! Take the goddam lift between the grand stairs on the Vanderbilt Avenue side, two levels down. That office closes at nine!"

David Garvey grabbed Peter's hand and dragged him across the marble floor toward the nearby elevator. He punched at the down button with his fist. After what seemed like a lifetime, the double doors dinged slowly apart. Inside the open carriage, David cast anxiously about for some controls to find only two choices: Main and B. In desperation, he pushed the B button hard with heel of his right hand. Nothing happened. David hit the button again, then the 'Close Door' button. Still nothing! Finally, a loud buzz announced closing of the doors. The car ratcheted slowly downward. Click, click, click, clunk, click . . .

Over dusty, exposed steel beams and open skeletal partitions they were passing through, David and Peter could see tracks stretching out toward dark tunnels in different directions, gates and trains of different sizes and colors, all with surging crowds of people passing to and fro on their way to other stations. Finally, the elevator spilled David and Peter into a dark, narrow hall. Dingy plywood doors with no numbers or signs lined both sides of the corridor. Many of the doors were closed; others blocked with fluorescent ocher warning strips made of flimsy plastic tape. The cracked linoleum tile floor was littered with scattered remains of old newspapers, cigarette butts, and dirty Styrofoam coffee cups.

David burst into the first open room. An obese black woman wearing a worn navy blue uniform jacket sat at the only desk, puffing a thin, dark cigar. Pungent gray smoke swirled through the green shaded light above her head.

"Can you please help me? My little boy is on the train to Chicago. It just left without us. Can you please help us find someone to call ahead?"

"Not my yob, mon. And, 'sides, I'm on ma break!" the woman replied.

David lurched out into the hall. He frantically tried the next door. Locked! He tried the next and the next. All locked! David could barely see someone moving at the far end of the shadowy corridor. He ran in that direction. It was the mink coat again. She angrily waved one of her red pumps at him:

"You are such a poor excuse for a father!" she yelled. "First you leave our youngest son on a train. That's bad enough. Now, you've lost our other boy. What have you got to say for yourself? I knew you couldn't measure up!"

David's heart leaped into his throat. He looked up and down the corridor. Peter was nowhere to be seen! Where had he gone? Terrified, David lunged toward the slowly closing elevator doors. He stuck his right foot between the doors to keep them open, but they kept trying to close. Clunk, clunk, clunk . . .

Through the cycling elevator doors, David could see a striking blonde woman in the half darkness. As she came closer to him, he could make out her sparkling blue eyes.

"Marja! You've come back! I've missed you so!"

"Help me, David! They're coming back to finish the job! Don't let them kill me again! David! David!"

He looked frantically up and down the dingy corridor for something to pry open the elevator doors—nothing.

"I'll save you, Marja! I won't let them get you this time!"

"Hurry, David, they're almost here!"

"Leave her alone," David screamed in terror. "Take me! Take me! Don't hurt her . . . please, I beg you—"

Above the banging doors, a crimson light began to flash brightly. A deep chime started to sound.

"Bong, bonnng, closing, CLOsing, BONG, BONNNNNG, BONNNNG . . ."

David lost his balance. He put out both hands to break his fall and tumbled onto the plush crimson Astrakhan carpet beside his carved oaken double bed, dripping with sweat. His right foot was tangled in a web of twisted sheets, blankets and the marigold bedspread. David's antique wooden-geared Waterbury clock had just finished chiming six.

The salmon glow of a new day was waning over the Triborough Bridge, looking across the East River. David was alone. Hopefully Peter and Will were safe at home with their mother.

David shivered. Suddenly, he felt very cold and tired. *I can't give up, as much as I'd like to*, David promised himself as he pulled on his running clothes.

Let's see how fast I can get around the Central Park Reservoir!

MY BANKER, MY PAWN

David had little choice but to seek outside financing for the initial operations of his new business. Realistically, there were only two options open to him: find some joint venture partners to share the cost and burden of starting a complicated new financial institution or seek out a traditional financing vehicle. David quickly discarded the idea of assembling a group of partners to organize and develop the business of the Fund, because that would ultimately require, among other things, having some sort of committee manage the Fund. It all sounded too much like the law firms he had been a reluctant part of, with their "consensus" management. Joint ownership of the Fund would have meant David's suffering on a daily basis with multiple, most likely competing, internal agendas, not to mention the problem of energizing others to make decisions when prompt or effective action had to be taken.

The trade-off for avoiding cumbersome management and ownership issues in his new business would almost certainly require his unlimited personal guarantee of any bank borrowings—something David could hopefully limit to a guarantee of collection rather than payment, if not something more useless to bankers.

David's long experience representing both domestic and foreign lenders inclined him toward traditional bank money to obtain at least the first $150 million dollars he needed. While bank financing might seem like taking in partners, in fact banks could be more effectively controlled. If carefully selected and properly manipulated, banks, particularly in a large and internally competitive group, could be kept from directly interfering in any significant way in the Fund's operations.

Weak loan demand made his search easier, at first. Traditional customers of American banks were continuing to slip away to other sources of funding, notwithstanding substantial increases in the permitted activities of American banks during the late eighties, lavishly portrayed by politicians as helpful deregulation while it gutted the great post-Depression separation of banking and investment banking powers instituted by the Glass-Steagall Act. After much initial spade work, David Garvey was ultimately invited to make detailed presentations to three groups of lenders: a syndicate of North Americans, including American, Canadian, and Mexican banks; a group of Japanese banks and insurance companies; and a consortium of Austrian, German, and Arab banks led by Neu Ost Bank. NeuBank was loosely patterned on the Landesbanks existing throughout the German Federal Republic before reunification, quasi-governmental and slow but solid. After the prolonged beauty contest, the North American group couldn't even decide whether or not to act on David's proposal. The documentary and legal requirements of the German and Japanese syndicates would be essentially the same—no surprise there. Both the Germans and the Japanese were represented by the same New York law firm, a fervent adherent of the "better to say it twelve than nine times" school of legal drafting.

The premium over the European Monetary Fund currency interest rates suggested by NeuBank's group for its loans to the Fund was a full 1/8% lower than the bid of the Japanese bank consortium. NeuBank also offered a lower commitment fee on undrawn amounts under its proposed credit agreement. And David was intrigued that NeuBank was willing, even eager, to accept a cap on legal fees for the entire transaction, in effect to squeeze its own lawyers. Certainly any limitation on legal fees, which the commitment letter specifically stated would include all legal fees for the entire deal, would be imposed in turn by NeuBank on its outside counsel. NeuBank was represented by a large Lexington Avenue law firm, Smythe & Mahoney, P.C., that liked to refer to itself as a "Wall Street" law firm, even though most firms of any significance had long ago moved uptown. Known affectionately in the trade as S&M, in part for its arduous working conditions and long required billable hours, Smythe & Mahoney seemed like almost the perfect adversary for David Garvey. Some of the perks at S&M included mandatory beepers and portafaxes plus billing minimums for beginning lawyers of 3,200 hours per year, considerably higher for more senior employees. There were no real partners at S&M, only employees. All of S&M's voting stock was tied up in protracted litigation surrounding the untimely demise of its founder, Julian Smythe.

During the rush to arrange financing for the Fund and attend to myriad operational details, it wasn't apparent why NeuBank would be willing to make the same loans based upon an essentially identical security package for markedly less. He assumed the lower interest rates offered grew out of the lower cost of funds that NeuBank's syndicate members enjoyed from a considerable retail deposit base in thrift-minded Western Europe. David also credited NeuBank's greater familiarity with Eastern and Central Europe, its proximity to Poland and Belarus as well as its understanding of the value of real estate mortgages and Central European company shares serving as collateral for loans by the Fund, as the real basis for the Fund's ability to repay its loans to the Euro syndicate. David also figured NeuBank might be extending favorable financing to build its Euro portfolio substantially in one highly visible transaction. And perhaps some public relations points for a relatively new and growing institution. He was dead wrong on several counts.

Late one afternoon in August, first drafts of the loan documents arrived from S&M at the offices of David's law firm in the Swiss United Bank/Saks tower. His firm's reception area looked out over the skating rink at Rockefeller Center. Where ice dancers pirouetted before the famous Christmas tree during the December holidays, tourists dawdled under gaily colored umbrellas this steamy Saturday. The helmeted bicycle messenger held out a fuchsia pen for David to sign a receipt for the bulky package. The plastic instrument was so slippery from the messenger's sweat that it escaped David's left hand, but he snatched it out of the air before it reached the polished marble floor of the entrance hall. David watched to make sure the messenger got back into the elevator.

He ripped open the paper pouch and ducked into the office next to his own to hand his junior partner, Cecily Chow, one of four two-pound copies. David halted just inside her doorway, caught off guard by the sight confronting him. The wiry young Chinese woman bowed slowly in front of what appeared to be a gray brick perched on the edge of a sturdy wooden table, supported on each end by another brick of similar size and color. As David watched quietly, she slowly raised her stiffened right hand, fingers fully extended and tightly together, high above her head. The long, straight strands of her ebony hair swung slightly back, exposing a diminutive ear, pierced by a simple gold orb. David held his breath.

"EEEyahhhhh!"

Cecily's right hand sliced through the air. Chunk! The brick fell into two neat pieces as she exhaled sharply. She inhaled deeply and bowed again toward the sturdy table before turning quietly toward David.

"Sorry, Boss. Just warming up for the struggle ahead," she beamed sarcastically.

David must have hoped she would apply the same vigor to the contents of the package under his arm. If there was any type of loan document Cecily hadn't worked on, he couldn't think of it. She had also learned passable German growing up in Salzburg—something arrogant German bankers would never suspect. Cecily had spent the bulk of her career representing banks in loan transactions. She had learned the trade well. Her specialty demanded a particular perspective: a practical and biased predisposition toward the needs of creditors, honed to great precision in secured lending transactions like the one David had in mind for the Fund.

The trick in helping this younger lawyer to represent the Fund aggressively would be to induce a not-too-subtle shift in her perspective, a change in the shading of this chameleon's colors. Now she must appear very sensitive, almost obsequious, to the needs of the banking syndicate and its counsel while doing her very best to negate the practical effect of every important provision of the draft lending instruments S&M could be expected to dump on her. While Cecily's normal role in representing a bank revolved around obtaining all possible protection for the lender and limiting the institution's risk and potential expenses, her only goal now would be to get the money as soon as possible with the fewest possible restraints, both initially and over the longer term. Her changing sides would be made easier by the fact all lawyers at S&M working on the deal knew her only as a banking lawyer. After all, she was a member of the elite Banking Law Committee of the Association of the Bar of the City of New York. Fortunately, Cecily was comfortable with those inherent contradictions. She could argue both sides of the same issue, at the same time, persuasively.

After leaving Cecily's office, David stopped by his own office to check messages and warm a pot of tea. Then he buzzed Cecily.

"Can you come down and talk to me about how you plan to handle Gunther Takimoto and his underlings at S&M?"

David squeezed a slice of fresh lemon into his mug of tea. He was still looking out over the darkening city when Cecily tapped lightly at his oak-paneled door.

"Come in! Sit down," David answered, gesturing alternatively toward a salmon wingback chair and a comfortable overstuffed sofa.

"Thanks, David, I'll stand. It helps me think and process the various alternatives. This will be difficult for me, at first, but I'm a better lawyer than any of those guys at S&M."

The nimble Asian lawyer launched into a tirade. "I'm almost sure Gunther can be sidetracked on some of those academic and theoretical issues he thrives on, the kind that have nothing to do with the real world we're living in or the credit arrangements we're trying to create."

"Can you play that back, on slow speed?" David asked. "What little I know about Gunther Takimoto is that he has a pretty large stable of foreign banking clients. How are you going to keep him away from the meat and potatoes?"

"For starters, Gunther's licensed as a *Rechtsanswalt* in Germany and a *bengoshi* in Japan. Born in Germany of Japanese and German parents—a schizo from the cradle. The Germans and the Japanese love him because he speaks their languages. In this deal, though, his tendency to dwell on irrelevant minutiae can be exploited, particularly if we have limited time and you can get the business people at NeuBank to push Gunther a little bit."

"How about a few specifics?"

David was warming to Cecily's approach to the problem. She was looking at the problem as a potential opportunity, digging for the best way to get what the Fund needed. While the normal response would be to send over some suggested changes to Gunther by fax, David much preferred how Chow's strategy seemed to be unfolding.

"First, I'd call up Gunther when he's already in the office tomorrow morning—Sunday," she said. "I'd go over the legal opinion he wants to get from our firm, a topic of almost no interest to us, but of great interest to a pedant like Takimoto. There are at least twenty really interesting issues in the form of our firm's opinion he sent over this afternoon."

"Interesting, but what's your point?"

"After I get him fixated on the large number of complicated issues in the written opinion his clients will need from us to show the bank examiners, I'll suggest he and I get together with our partner, Archibald Magruder, the head of our legal opinion committee."

"I see what's coming," David grinned.

"No! This is my scheme, and I'm just getting to the fun part," Chow growled possessively, waving at David with both of her hands as if shooing away a swarm of angry bees. "I've had this in mind since the time I had to explain to one of our bank clients what some of Archibald's obtuse drafting meant. Two pages of printed text—a noun (notice I've avoided using the word *subject*) and a stream of words with no predicate and no punctuation other than commas and semicolons. I had absolutely no idea what it meant, except to obfuscate. So we have Archibald do a detailed and lengthy draft of our opinion, complete with footnotes about the law of transporting negotiable instruments across the boundaries of countries not officially recognized by the United States, how to perfect a security interest in a Moldovan deed of trust, etc. Do you get the picture?"

"Sure, that's easy, but how does that get the things we need in the Fund's loan agreement with NeuBank?"

"We both know how thin S&M is on real banking talent, even when Gunther is on the case. But submerge him in extraneous issues, in effect remove him from the board, and I get to deal with some young kid who may not know euro interest rate provisions from the Guangzhou phone book. Even when the lawyer I'm dealing with doesn't know what she is doing, she'll be afraid to ask Gunther. I bet enough of the provisions important to the Fund can be either removed or emasculated by a combination of 'reasonable' requests and my being just my normal helpful self.

"It wouldn't occur to Gunther or his toadies that I could really switch to the borrower's side and abandon my banker's mentality. And, by the time Archibald wears them down, my job will be much easier! Besides, Gunther just got back yesterday from five days in the

Fatherland, after six days in Osaka. His body clock will be all fucked up!"

David looked up from notes he had been scribbling on a yellow pad. Chow was energetically ripping lines through her outline of how to proceed with a dull lead pencil, chomping at the bit to be turned loose on her opponents at Smythe & Mahoney.

"Could you run me through how it might work when we go over to meet with the head of NeuBank's New York operation, Diether Kreuz, and his lawyers at S&M on Tuesday?"

"Sure, we'll walk in to find Diether Kreuz and at least two of his subordinates sitting with Takimoto's draft documents in front of them, mostly unread. Takimoto will be speaking German with his clients. He'll make a point of continuing the conversation after we arrive and probably attempt a joke near the end to show how well he gets along with them."

David nodded.

"You know, Cecily," he interjected, "I'm proud of how well you're focusing on the big picture. That's a scarce but valuable skill."

Chow blushed deeply and looked away but didn't appear to hear David's compliment. She continued.

"Gunther won't have any associates there because his ego won't allow it. You and Archibald will engage in extensive pleasantries with Takimoto and Kreuz, pointedly leaving me out of the conversation. At that point, Archibald will take Takimoto aside to resolve all the IMPORTANT legal opinion issues they've been discussing for the entire weekend, and you and Kreuz will go off by yourselves to finish up the business points. Takimoto won't mind leaving me and his youngster with the credit agreement because, in his warped little world, typing is woman's work."

Before packing it in for the day, David called Diether Kreuz at home to arrange the first negotiating session for Tuesday at ten o'clock in the morning. Then he looked up the Southampton number of Archibald P. Magruder, IV, in the firm's directory.

"Magruder residence, Snively speaking. How might I be of assistance?" a proper English accent intoned through what must have been a starched collar.

"Mr. Magruder, please."

"Who might I say is calling Mr. Magruder, sir?" the collar continued.

"David Garvey."

"Would Mr. Magruder be aware of the reason for your call, sir?"

"Could you tell Mr. Magruder I'm the night clerk at the Ramada Inn, the one just down the street from LaGuardia Airport? The vacuum of one of my cleaners robots just sucked up his American Express Platinum card in one of our, eh, high traffic rooms. I wanted to know what to do with it."

"Certainly, sir! Right away, sir!"

David winced as the plastic handset bounced once on a hollow wooden surface and then twice on the ceramic tile floor a split second later. Footsteps scurried off toward the squeaking of silverware against bone china in the distance. It must be the dinner hour chez Magruder. David smirked at the thought of the old curmudgeon's expression as Snively whispered the message in his ear. Slow, limping steps approached from afar. David heard a wheeze as someone bent over to pick up the phone. A watch fob chain rattled against the receiver on the way up.

"Archibald Magruder, here. May I help you?"

"Archibald, this is David. Sorry to bother you on the weekend, but we have urgent need of your special expertise."

"Why, David, why didn't you say so? And what is this about a, er, ah, credit card?"

"Sorry about that, Archibald. It's been a very long day, and I didn't feel like finishing the game of twenty questions with that dork who answers your phone. But let me fill you in on what we need. Please remind me of your fax number so I can send you the papers."

A molten orange globe was sinking into grey clouds above the Palisades across the Hudson River in New Jersey when David finished giving Archibald his instructions. He neglected to explain the underlying purpose of Archibald Magruder's participation in this transaction. Archibald would do his job with great thoroughness. If Archibald were successful, Takimoto would come to feel like he was trying to swim across the River Spree in a three-piece woolen suit and shoes with a full briefcase in tow.

David assembled his team at precisely 9:15 on Tuesday morning. His personal conference room was set with a light breakfast—freshly squeezed orange juice, raspberries nestled in a cantaloupe basket, fresh cranberry scones still warm from the oven, cappuccino, coffee, and a variety of imported and herbal teas.

"Let's review where we are, before going over to S&M," David opened the skull session. "Archibald, how are you doing with Takimoto and the opinion?"

"Well, David, of course this is very difficult, but we are making some progress. Takimoto-san and I spent all day Sunday reviewing the various issues in detail and acquainting the juniors with the research to be done. He has three associates working on it, and we have four. We've divided it up by country and then subdivided the issues by creation of the security interests—perfection of those interests-"

"Excuse me, Archibald," David interrupted. "Thank you, that sounds very complete, but perhaps we could move on. It's nearly time to go see Gunther and his crew. What do you have, Cecily?"

"I've got extensive proposed written changes as well as the entire document the way we want it on disc. But I'd rather work directly off a Holo right in the meeting. I'll help whichever donkey Takimoto's put in charge of the loan agreement make revisions directly into their system. If my memory serves me correctly, Takimoto thinks lawyers shouldn't be reduced to running Holos, so it'll probably be just me and an operator. If there's an appropriate opening, I'll try to get my chip onto their system, to work off our version."

"Pardon me, David, but I see it's nearly 10:05. Shouldn't we be going? Ought not be late, you know," Archibald Magruder broke in.

"Actually, Archibald, I plan to be late, at least late enough for Herr Kreuz to have worked up a good head of steam. I'll have my secretary call in fifteen minutes to say we're on the way over. We'll leave in about a half hour. Take a few minutes to check your calls and messages so you won't be nervous over there. And, everyone stop by the sandbox on the way out. We don't want to have to leave the meeting before they do. Please meet me at the elevators at 10:40."

When the elevators opened onto S&M's spartan reception area on the 18th floor of 399 Park Avenue, David spotted Diether Kreuz pacing in the adjacent oak-paneled conference room. Herr Doktor Kreuz had undoubtedly been instructed to report promptly to the world headquarters of NeuBank about the results of the meeting. With the time difference between New York and Germany, NeuBank's offices in Schwerin were already beginning to close for the day. Poor Herr Kreuz would not be able to make his report on time. All would not be in order.

A CLIFF OVER THE VOLGA

Drumming hail the size of marbles reached a crescendo on the tinny roof of the four-passenger Polish Fiat where the two waited for one of their Russian managers. A sudden torrent of chilling rain momentarily obscured several irregular blotches of grease on its cracked windshield. David looked out across the windswept parking lot of the Volgograd airport, in what was Stalingrad before the Soviet Union evaporated. He glanced down again at his watch.

"Yevgyeniy's always late," David grumbled to Ani. "I suppose the good news is at least he remembered to leave the car for us."

David Garvey was beyond tired. These sales trips often made him question the wisdom of planting the Fund's European headquarters in Königsberg. All the physical aspects of the Königsberg installation worked well. There had never been a problem with security or electrical power and the neighbors weren't nosy. On the other hand, David's life would have been measurably simpler if his administrative center for Eastern European lending activities could have been closer to reliable public transportation.

The simplest route for today's trip required getting someone to drive them to Kaunas, Lithuania, just over 100 miles from Königsberg over barely passable roads. In Kaunas, they climbed aboard a fourteen-passenger, Brazilian-made Embraer Bandeirante III turboprop bound for Vilnius, Lithuania's capital. After a twenty-minute layover, the same aircraft continued on to Minsk, the governmental seat of Belarus. In the former capital of the Byelo-Russian Soviet Socialist Republic, they changed planes, taking a Lot fan-jet to Volgograd with stops along the way in Kiev and Kharkov. Even with an early start, that made for a very long day. David dreaded the obligatory long liquid meeting and dinner with his Volga River Basin salesmen after the sales calls.

Filling the silence, David observed, "you know, we really have to make significant inroads into the shareholder base of the Togliatti Auto Works, known as Vaz. Before privatization, it was the largest Soviet automaker. The city's called Togliatti—formerly Togliattigrad, and before that Stavropol. They're talking about going back to the old name, just like in the Baltic states. It was renamed in the late sixties for Palmiro Togliatti, a leading Italian Communist."

Ani looked annoyed.

"What's this have to do with anything? I want a coffee!"

"Great idea, but you told me not more than fifteen minutes ago that the airport snack bar is closed because of a strike. Besides, being able to impress the people we're here to meet might help sales. So pay attention! I'll try to be brief."

The young Polish woman snorted, "you are kidding, yes? Brief not part of your dictionary!"

It was David Garvey's turn to look annoyed, but he continued anyway.

"Production at Vaz consists of three main lines: Zhyigulyi station wagons for domestic consumption—"

"Please, David, get to something important!"

"OK. Ownership of the new company is weighted in favor of existing management by a system of voting and nonvoting shares. 103,000 Vaz workers own approximately 51% of the company's initial capital but management has working control of the voting shares. Right now, Ani, the only real players are the workers, who are represented by two labor unions, and the company's management, with the potential 'strategic investor' waiting in the wings. That's why we're here today—to get as many workers as possible signed up so we can get our hands on their shares."

Disappointed Ani had apparently absorbed none of the details of last week's video conference with the Fund's Volga basin salesmen, David watched a pair of rusty beer cans being tumbled by driving rain across nearly deserted parking lot. She had seemed to be actively participating in that discussion and even appeared to enjoy his clowning for the audience during that private telecast.

"*Dobryi vyechyer, tovarjischi*, good evening, comrades," David had joked during the telecast, using the outmoded Communist form of address. "You're probably all wondering why the Fund is so interested in a badly sagging Russian car maker. I'll download to your receivers our sales incentive structure for our new project, the Togliatti Auto Works—otherwise known as Vaz."

"Pleazzzzz," groaned Pyotr Boryisovyitch Myiskavyitch, "Vaz—that old dinosaur! How we are making money? For myself, I am very much more preferring to work instead from Party membership lists to find customers with new apartments or some other company shares from under table."

"Wait until you've seen our compensation proposals, Pyotr Boryisovyitch," David responded. "Then you decide whether to work on those outdated Party lists or not. For myself, I would prefer to eat from a fully laden cherry tree than peck about in the gravel for a few loose grains of barley."

Yet another example, David thought to himself, *of how long real capitalism will be in coming to this land where personal initiative has rarely been rewarded. To be sure, the people he had recruited were among the more adventuresome Russians he could find. While most others preferred the security of a regular wage, even for much lower income, these men were at least willing to work on a commission basis, something quite foreign to the Slavic outlook. Still, his beaters would almost always choose an alternative that appeared to offer the greatest guaranteed results, even where some creativity might yield a much greater return.*

So David was trying to educate his charges and his new deputy, Agniesczka Czarnocki, in the ways of financial incentives. Fortunately, Ani's personal experience in Krakow's black markets before more liberal capitalism arrived in Poland attuned her to some of the potential rewards, as well as some of the pitfalls to be avoided. Unfortunately, her interest in detail was sadly lacking.

David went on. "First, for our purposes, each share of Vaz will be valued at nine US dollars, six euros or 12.50 Swiss francs, for customers signed up during the five-week promotional period beginning next Saturday only. You are allowed to loan new customers up to 65% of the value of the Vaz shares you take in pledge."

David paused to let that sink in. He passed a finger over the holographic privacy button on his speakerphone and remarked to Ani, "This should make them push to get some loans on the books within the next month, because no one knows where the rates will go then. I may reduce the value we assign to the Vaz shares as well as the percentage that can be borrowed against them after the promotional period expires, but my idea won't make them work any harder unless they know about it."

"How much commissions we are going to get?" Anatolyi Pavyelovich Vlasov demanded.

"Every customer who signs up during first five weeks gets a German-made electric skillet on closing plus a discount on commitment fee from 1-1/2% down to only 1-1/8," Ani carefully explained, reading slowly from the term sheet David had given her.

"No, little lady, I meant our commissions—what people doing work get," Vlasov sniffed.

"I was getting to that, if you don't mind! Originating representative will have account in Brussels credited with 1/2 of 1% of principal amount of each loan, four business days after closing. On Vaz only, you will get an additional 1/2 of 1% eighteen months later, IF LOAN IS COMPLETELY UP TO DATE ON PAYMENTS."

"Why we can't get whole fee at beginning? By then we will have done all our work." Yevgyeniy Schevchenko whined.

"Because, if you do a careful check of each customer's credit with the local merchants and make sure our loan gets repaid, payments will more likely be current throughout the life of the loan," David had explained during the telecast.

"I want to pick up the cream of the union and management hierarchy at Vaz as customers. Impress them with your flexibility and efficiency. But don't bring me anyone you wouldn't personally loan hard currency by yourself! You must concentrate on big loans for the large and medium-sized fish in the Vaz pond. If you do that, you'll earn larger commissions faster. We can pick up the smaller fry once some of the more important people at Vaz, like the Secretary of the Auto Workers Union, Sergey Maxyimovich Yershov, and Nyikolai Glyushkov, the General Director of Finance, are our satisfied customers."

"Why don't you review the procedures for the new guys?" Schevchenko suggested.

"Good idea," David agreed before continuing. "You send me each customer's credit file you've worked up and the number of Vaz shares they plan to pledge with our own couriers to arrive in Königsberg at least one full week before closing. NO EXCUSES! Each of you will have his closings in a different place to allow each of you to build your own customer base. We'll arrange for delivery of cash for the closing the same day by our courier. You'll arrange for all of your closings to be on the same day, so we can avoid the expense of multiple cash deliveries. The same courier will deliver you all the necessary loan forms, already filled out. The customer gets the original amount of the loan, less the commitment fee, closing costs, and legal expenses. The courier will wait to pick up the completed loan documents, the shares and the cash fees. Anyone, ANYONE, who asks a customer for any money for himself will be immediately terminated and his foreign currency account in Brussels forfeited. Any questions? Oh, and payments are due monthly, in the same currency as the loan. Make sure every customer understands that."

"Is there a prize on this one?" Myiskavyitch asked.

"Izzzz therrrr a prizzzzza?" David mugged with the speaker phone. "Ani, spin the wheel and tell the lucky contestants about this month's prize for closing the most Vaz loans!"

Ani announced, "Lucky winner of month—one to sell most biggest total loans to shareholders of Togliatti Auto Works during promotional period—gets Kawasaki motorcycle fresh from new factory in Rostov with rationing coupons for 40 liters premium gasoline."

"What model Kawasaki?" one of the salesmen asked in the split second before David's index finger passed through the holographic image of the disconnect button on the communications console.

The Fund employed two Russian lawyers full-time in Königsberg. They were expected to regularly analyze the tea leaves of various Russian, Belarusan, and Ukrainian publications, decrees, laws, and regulations churned out by the many, many layers of those Eastern European governments. These attorneys, with only criminal law experience under their belts before the collapse of the Soviet Union, were responsible for advising David about any necessary changes to the Fund's loan documents and procedures to keep up with the flurry of events swirling around them.

David had given up trying to find any effective private commercial lawyers in Russia, or in any of the other countries the Fund had any interest in, for that matter. Change in the various governmental systems was almost a daily occurrence in nearly every country where the Fund did business. The private lawyers in those countries simply did not have the experience to add very much to the mix. And the American firms that pretended to know what was going on were not only as uninformed but several times more expensive. There were certainly enough risks to go around in tilling this new soil, mostly ambiguous and almost impossible to assess.

David was forced to fall back on common sense in a difficult situation without any understandable rules. Together with his outpost legal staff, he had successfully negotiated with the governments of Poland, Russia, Belarus, Ukraine, Estonia, and Lithuania to allow his couriers border-crossing privileges without subjecting their cash pouches to detailed search. Regular border searches would have allowed border guards to help themselves to the Fund's cash supplies. David's minions were still working on Latvia.

David's couriers had an essential role in the lending process. Without any workable banking system at the consumer level, Russian citizens were in much the same position as ghetto residents in America: "cash talks, paper walks." Making a loan in Volgograd or Rostov-on-Don had to be closed in cash, not a check or other piece of paper because there was simply nowhere to easily cash checks or make deposits. Owing to the continued softness of the Russian ruble, despite Russia's membership in the International Monetary Fund, the Fund's customers wanted small denomination US dollars, Swiss francs, or euros. For each set of closings, bundles of cash had to be moved efficiently from the outpost's vaults to wherever the loans were going to be made. Once each loan closing had been completed, the loan documents had to smoothly find their way back to the Fund's European headquarters in Königsberg.

But David's couriers had an even more important role once a loan had been made. For the same reason making a loan by check would not work in Belarus or any other part of David's territory outside Moscow or St. Petersburg, a borrower in the provinces couldn't easily make loan payments. No debit cards existed there yet, and there wasn't even a moderately convenient way to drop a draft or check in the mail.

To keep its own wheels of commerce greased, the Fund provided its customers the "service" of stopping around at home or work to pick up monthly payments of principal and interest. This service became essential to the Fund should a customer fall behind in payments. In that situation, the direct and personal attention of one of the Fund's couriers was more likely to achieve the desired result than one of those impersonal dunning letters common in the West. Once a loan was more than 60 days past due, the couriers worked on a commission basis to collect overdue amounts. They could be very persuasive.

David Garvey had tried to outline for Ani how the Fund worked in language she would hopefully understand.

"The Fund's three-year loans bear interest at an average rate of 46% per year. These rates are very high by Western standards, almost certainly usurious, but they give the Fund a large margin over its actual cost of borrowing the dollars, Swiss francs, or euros' being lent. You see, Ani, few complain about our exorbitant interest rates, because rates of inflation in Central Europe are very high, sometimes near 150% a year. So long as the customer has a job where pay is adjusted to deal with inflation, we've had pretty impressive repayment rates. And don't forget, we don't really have any competition!"

"But still, why workers want to risk losing shares in company where they work?"

"Anything liquid they can get for new shares seems almost like a gift. So here comes the Fund, willing to give them real cash just for signing some papers and turning over some other paper that might not really be worth anything anyway. Having a little plot behind the outhouse to grow tomatoes is one thing, but to own even a small piece of a huge factory complex that produces real automobiles? That's beyond imagination for the people we're trying to attract as customers. Hopefully loans on the Vaz shares and on the shares of other companies being privatized throughout the region will lead the Fund to more stable loans on apartments and homes and mortgages on hard real estate."

David jumped, spilling credit files on the cluttered floor of the Fiat as a wet face pressed against the car window only a few centimeters from his left ear. Brown eyes, tousled dark hair, and a long, slender nose peered out from under a long coat held high to fend off the waning cloudburst. David wiped away the cloud of condensation on the glass with his shirt sleeve and cracked the window open.

"Yevgyeniy Djenjisovjich, where have you been? We had almost given you up for lost. Don't you have anything to keep dry? Here, take my umbrella," David said, slipping a nondescript grey model through the partly opened window.

"Thanks," Yevgyeniy replied, opening the umbrella and passing his sodden overcoat to Ani in the front seat. "I am now getting wipers out of boot, and we can then be going on."

David could see light through a crack between the rear seat cushions. Myiskavyitch rummaged through the contents of the jumbled trunk until he found two worn windshield wiper blades. He slammed the trunk lid and hurried to install them on two nubs at the base of the Fiat's windshield, trying to balance the umbrella over his head with the crook of his left arm. Myiskavyitch finished his task and gave Ani a thumbs-up sign followed by the motions of turning a key in its lock.

Ani reached over to turn on the ignition and then turned on the wipers. Both wipers completed two passes at the dirty windshield before one clattered onto the hood and bounced off into a mud puddle. Yevgyeniy applied some chewing gum to the socket of the fallen blade and jammed it into place. He squeaked open the driver's side door, squeezed behind David Garvey in the driver's seat, and settled into the cramped back seat while the American lawyer ground the Fiat's gearshift while revving the tiny engine.

"We will be arriving at great economical prosperity when leaving car on street is possible without losing wipers and other parts," Yevgyeniy sputtered good-naturedly. "We are meeting Sergey Maxyimovich Yershov to talk about his loan, yes? He is expecting to meet us outside of town, in parking lot for Mamaiyev. Do you want me to be now giving directions?"

"Of course. Let's get started. We're probably late now. I haven't been to Mamaiyev since the early seventies. I wonder if it's changed," David replied, settling back into his seat as the small Fiat chugged jerkily out onto the highway. "While we're driving, tell me how the sales campaign is going."

"Whole group has 146 completed applications at end of yesterday. Myself, I am leading to win Kawasaki motorcycle with 19 customers ready to take loan, not counting Sergey Maxyimovich. Your idea to sell to bosses and union chiefs was good. Others are hearing about good deal and trying to sign up. We need more help to handle all too much business," Myiskavyitch beamed, slapping at a fly buzzing around his head.

"Good work," David said, congratulating him. "We'll consider your recommendation for additional sales representatives. Keep your eyes and ears open for good candidates. Have you encountered any problems?"

"I am noticing strange thing. We are hearing from one shop in Vaz some Arab janitors objecting to loans because taking interest violates teachings of Allah. Old Communist union bosses complain about program. Don't know why. But they complain about everything since they no longer line pockets from Party membership," Yevgyeniy explained. "Also, you know these people from America come here to bring Western religion to Russian people? They come to factory with Bibles. They are telling workers, your own people from America, these loans no good because money spent for buying things, not the will of God. Besides that, no real problems."

The four-lane highway ahead wound up and over a small hill. Above the top of that knoll, the travelers could see the tip of what appeared to be a large sword extended into the sky, pointing toward the West. As the Fiat wheezed over the crest, the entire statue came into view: a sturdy Slavic matron cast in alabaster with flowing skirts and muscular, bare arms stood at least 50 feet above the crest of a rounded hillock below them. She seemed to be leading a charge, although her army was nowhere to be seen.

"You seen Mamaiyev Hill before, Ani?" David asked.

"No, what it for? Has same kind of monuments built by Russians in my country."

"The turning point of World War II was here, the Battle of Stalingrad," David explained for her benefit. "Russian armies forced the unconditional surrender of the German armies under General von Paulus, against Hitler's direct orders to fight to the death. The rest of the war was all downhill for the Nazis. Once the war was over, the Soviets built this mound out of debris and rubble from the battle—tanks, trucks, shell casings, helmets—and erected that statue on top. It's supposed to be Mother Russia leading the crusade against Fascism. There's an underground monument with an eternal flame in honor of the fallen."

David's visit many years before flickered through the recesses of his mind.

When I was here in the seventies, newlyweds came to visit this shrine after their civil marriage ceremonies—seemed to be genuine interest in the sacrifices made, as if the war was just yesterday. He thought to himself. *Very impressive. Some cynics used to say the Soviets promoted this sort of monument to distract their subjects from the dismal surroundings and lack of economic progress.*

"Here we are now arriving," Myiskavyitch announced, as David Garvey wrenched the little car off the highway into the parking lot at the base of Mamaiyev Hill.

The heavy rain had stopped. The sun was trying to peek through low-lying clouds. A light breeze from the East fluttered the forms on David's clipboard as he stepped from the car. Looking up the path toward the towering woman with her punishing sword, he could only make out part of the inscription on the first monument through a tangle of tall weeds: "*Vyechnaya Slava.*" Eternal glory! What David remembered as an airy, neatly trimmed park had become a dump of

Pepsi bottles, McDonald's wrappers, and even graffiti on some lower parts of the monuments.

Yevgyeniy offered, extending a hand toward the object of this meeting. "David, may I have honor to present Sergey Maxyimovich Yershov? Sergey Maxyimovich, may I present David Garvey, Managing Director of Königsberg Fund. He came all way from New York to meet with you this afternoon."

"I am pleased to make your acquaintance, Sergey Maxyimovich," David responded. "Please excuse my lack of fluent Russian. I'm sorry to say I do not speak your language very well."

"It is pleasure to know you, Mr. Garvey, and to have opportunity to discuss with you and Yevgyeniy Ilyich lending proposals for my workers."

Yevgyeniy and Yershov launched into a rapid exchange about the General Secretary's role in promoting the Fund's loan program with the Vaz shareholders. As David expected, Yershov was looking for a piece of the action, demanding a fee for every loan taken out by one of his members as well as for every other extension of credit made by the Fund in the area. David thought about how little things have changed from the Communist regime. Everyone was still trying to line his own pockets.

Fortunately, David and Yevgyeniy had already discussed this problem and decided how to deal with it.

"Sergey Maxyimovich, because you are first one in union to apply for loan from Fund, you are entitled to greater percentage of value of your shares, more money for you. Perhaps one of your relatives might consider join our growing staff of representatives," Yevgyeniy proposed. "We will provide excellent service to your colleagues in union. But we are prohibited from paying fees to important public officials such as yourself."

Something behind the two men caught David's attention. One stiff leg of a mannequin in threadbare trousers balanced precariously on the rough edge of an overflowing trash barrel, its decrepit cracked boot bobbing slightly while the contents of the barrel rattled as if possessed. As David watched, the military boot teetered haltingly toward the pavement to join its mate hiding behind the refuse bin. At the same time, an overcoat-clad torso emerged from the mound of trash.

Straightening up, the old man slipped something into the outer pocket of his coat, brushed several real or imagined bits of trash from his left shoulder and sleeve, pausing to reposition an oaken cane in his left fist. Clear gray eyes met David's curious gaze. A self-conscious smile cracked his weather-beaten face to reveal two shiny steel teeth. He absently touched a gold-encrusted red star pinned above his outer pocket. Then the old soldier swung his artificial leg slowly along an overgrown path up the grade in the direction of the Soviet goddess. David wondered whether he had been part of the human flood that engulfed the German armies and closed its pincers around Stalingrad, dashing Hitler's dreams of domination and sending Hungarian, Italian, and Rumanian troops fleeing toward the West.

A STRANGLEHOLD

The malignant ebony bull of Neu Ost Bank's coat of arms lumbering across the translucent tray of David's home fax machine exuded as much menace as the letter that followed.

> 700-244-3425
> David Garvey,
> President and Treasurer
> Königsberg Fund
>
> My Dear Dr. Garvey:
>
> Neu Ost Bank, New York Federal Branch, as agent (the "Agent") for the banking institutions (the "Banks") parties to the Secured Revolving ECU Credit Agreement dated as of April 20, 1991 (the "Credit Agreement"), hereby in writing notifies . . .

The letter's clumsy wordiness somehow reminded David just how much the general public disliked lawyers—only slightly less than dentists specializing in root canals or perhaps glad-handing politicians. No wonder Lenin had temporarily abolished the Russian legal profession after the 1917 Revolution, although Lenin's reasons were more likely ideological than aesthetic.

NeuBank's letter used several turgid and convoluted paragraphs just to announce that David's company was not complying with an important part of the Credit Agreement and, if that continued, the banks might do something about it.

One important advantage of AT&T's system of personal nationwide phone numbers to David was that he could receive facsimile transmissions wherever he happened to be. NeuBank had sent this demand letter to David's personal facsimile number. The German bankers had probably sent the same message to David's law firm as well as to the number for the Fund's offices. Still, no one at NeuBank had the slightest idea where David actually might be at any particular time.

At least the letter gave David and the Fund a concrete warning, a signal to prepare for the potentially bloody conflict just over the horizon. Fortunately for David, the NeuBank syndicate of banks lending euros, the currency of a reinvigorated European Community, was managed by a new and somewhat inexperienced German bank, one recycled since the reunification. NeuBank's conservatism made every procedure under the Credit Agreement ever so orderly and slow. Lengthy delays were frequently caused by the German banking management philosophy of *fier augen*—four eyes, meaning two executives were responsible for making every decision, however administrative or ministerial, at every level. And the credit officers in NeuBank's New York branch trudged to the dirge of several layers of required approvals and signatures back at the bank's head offices in Schwerin.

It was terribly infuriating to get the money in the first place, but infinitely more useful when the banks in the syndicate might need to take some definitive action that might harm the Fund. Getting the loan facility in place and closing the first series of loans had been like Chinese water torture. Now, David took a certain amount of comfort from the Byzantine nature of the existing structure and the cumbersome financing mechanism it was supposed to administer—shades of the Azerbaijani Post Office.

In theory, the terms and conditions of the Fund's loans were quite simple. The Fund could borrow from 37 banks in the syndicate. Money borrowed flowed from each of those banks through NeuBank's New York branch office to one of the Fund's bank accounts in New Jersey. To get a loan, the Fund was supposed to give NeuBank documents representing a pool of the Fund's loans to its customers in Russia and other Central European countries. Each pool of the Fund's loan documents delivered to NeuBank was supposed to have a face value of not less than 115% of the amount of money the Fund was trying to borrow. If more than 5% of the loans the Fund pledged to NeuBank fell more than 90 days behind in their payments, the Fund was expected to fix that problem by either repaying part of the outstanding loans, buying back the deficient collateral, or furnishing additional collateral to NeuBank to hold on behalf of the syndicate of banks.

Each batch of loans made by the Euro syndicate was supposed to be secured by delivery to NeuBank's New York office of a pool of promissory notes and real estate mortgages the Fund had received as security for loans to its own customers. Where the Fund had made loans on the security of shares of recently privatized Eastern European state companies, the Credit Agreement required the Fund to turn around and pledge those same shares to the banks, all endorsed to NeuBank and delivered to NeuBank's New York office. Payments of interest and principal were supposed to be transmitted from one of the Fund's bank accounts in some other country to NeuBank's New York office, where a proportionate share of that money was retransmitted to each of 37 individual banks. In theory, at least, that was how NeuBank and its banks were supposed to be protected. But the reality might be something else.

It was almost time to spring the trap David and his law partner, Frank Gillespie, had been setting for some time. David put a handset to his ear and pushed the speed dial for Frank's private number.

On the third ring, a young female voice answered.

"Wendy's Massage Parlor, we get you up when you're down. How can I help you?"

David could make out the sound of tires hissing on wet payment in the background, wind flowing over the top of an open convertible, and a little girl giggling.

"Hi, Mona, it's David. Could you please ask your father to pick up on the scrambler?"

The line went dead. David sighed and passed a finger through the redial holographic image floating above his communications console.

Frank Gillespie picked up before the end of the first ring.

"Sorry, David, we had a little, eh, technical problem with the phone. Mona, if you even think about touching those buttons again, I won't have time to see your piano recital Thursday afternoon. Now get back in that seat and buckle up your belt! What's up, David?"

"I just got the demand letter from NeuBank we've been expecting. We're beginning to run out of time. Can you meet me for sushi at Hinomaru about seven thirty?"

"No problem. We're just coming up on the Midtown Tunnel, right out onto 38th and Second Avenue. I'll drop Mona off at home and park the car. I can grab a cab and meet you in the restaurant. The usual tatami room?"

"Sure, I'll call Motoshige-san to make sure he'll be open. Could you bring your Holo with the federal court papers you and I worked out?," David asked. "And how about giving Cecily Chow a buzz? Ask her to join us, with the credit papers on a chip."

"Can do! See you then. Mona, put down that squirt—"

David flicked off the speakerphone, put his bare feet up on the railing of the balcony overlooking Central Park, and took a cool swallow of seltzer and fresh lime. The park was shadowy and peaceful in this late summer afternoon, an oasis of leafy green in the Big Apple's desert of hot pavement and overcrowded streets. So serene, with so much action and confusion only a few steps away.

Once David had figured out how NeuBank and its syndicate could offer its severely discounted rates in the first place—lots of cheap cash from NeuBank's silent partners—he knew to expect something very unpleasant soon. His up-close and personal discussion at the outpost with NeuBank's field officer for Belarus revealed overwhelming evidence of at least the head of the syndicate's treachery.

David suspected NeuBank was about to be pushed into making its power play. Even though there was little chance anyone at NeuBank or the people pulling NeuBank's strings knew anything about its field officer's indiscretion in telling David what NeuBank was really doing with the Fund's loan customers. For such an attractive young woman, NeuBank's representative had a very bad habit: drying her hair in the bathtub. The morning after David and his colleagues questioned the young banker, the humming electric dryer slipped through her soapy fingers into the full tub where she was lying—shocking carelessness.

David used the apartment's house phone to call down to the doorman for a cab.

"Edward, could you please call me a cab—one of those adapted for wheelchairs? They're roomy just like limos."

David peered over the edge of his balcony to see a red light over the building's kelly green awning begin to blink. David slipped leather loafers onto his bare feet. Despite the warm breeze, he stopped to pull on a heavy-duty sport coat before opening the double-bolted door to his private elevator lobby.

"It's no good, Mr. Garvey, y'all goin' out wif you briefcase and all on de weekennnd. You woik too hahhd. Why ain't you out chasing de honeys today?" the graying elevator operator grinned.

David Garvey returned the smile.

"Just trying to make a buck, Edward," he replied. "How's your family? That daughter of yours home for the summer?"

"Why no, Mr. Garvey. She graduated Wellesley last month," the building's oldest employee beamed. "She woikin' in Boston, makin' money for medical school nex fall."

"That's hard for me to believe, Edward. Seems like just yesterday you were showing me pictures of her senior prom."

"Here's the lobby. Y'all take care now, Mr. Garvey," the operator gestured toward the open door. "Have a naas day!"

Edward Bennington watched David saunter down the long polished marble hall toward the street. Then he plucked a cellular phone from his jacket pocket and punched in a local number. He heard a sharp click on the line and whispered, "right now, he waitin' fo a cab at the front door on Fif'."

The elevator operator pushed the disconnect button, dropped the heavy phone in his jacket pocket and swung the lever to close the elevator doors on the way to pick up a passenger on the ninth floor.

A luminous, yellow boxlike cab screeched to a halt in front of the building's awning and automatically lifted its wide curbside door for David, and lowered its ramp.

"Can I help you with your bags, sir?" the new doorman inquired.

"No thanks. I've got it," David said, climbing nimbly from the curb through the cab's open rear door.

The lawyer slid a black, calfskin briefcase across the wide seat cushions toward the cab's far door. Then he scrambled into the taxi's only seat, sat down, and placed his utility case on the beige carpet between his knees. David reached for his seat belts. Two lovely belts, no buckles. *Great—new technology, less pollution, and still some of the same problems hack riders have faced since the car replaced horse-drawn carriages on the streets of New York,* he raged silently. *At least some of the rude human drivers had been sent to harass customers somewhere outside the Metropolitan area!*

"Where to, Mac?" the cartoon face smiled from the silver screen in front of him.

"49th and Fifth, northwest corner. I'm not a tourist. Please do not take me through Central Park. Just go straight down Fifth Avenue. I know you're supposed to follow under-street electronics to our destination, unless your owner has hacked the system."

"No need to be impolite; I am entirely at your disposal. Please insert your card into the terminal under my screen," the robot countered.

"If you're really entirely at my service, surely you know payment comes at the end of the trip, so you can deduct only what is on the meter and not during the entire trip so your system can play with my balances. And please turn on your meter so we won't have to argue about the fare later."

"Just sit back and relax. You'll be well taken care of; you can count on that," the cartoon face grinned again.

I must be getting old, David thought, *to let these little things bother me so much.*

David poked in his numeric code and flipped open his briefcase to consult his short what-next list about the Fund that he'd scribbled on a yellow pad. Even with all the marvelous advances in computer technology, David still kept written notes on a pad from the beginning of a deal until it was finally finished, adding new things to be done and deleting entries when they became irrelevant or had been completed along the way. He'd been outlining what to do with NeuBank since very late one Thursday night last month when that young woman from NeuBank would not stop screaming in the outpost's basement interrogation chamber.

First, our lawyer deflects their thrust, then very methodically goes for the throat, David thought.

Further downtown, Wesley "Spats" Ungarn ran a leather-gloved hand nervously through tousled blond curls. His deceptively rotund figure and loose jacket concealed two M67 HE-Frag grenades, a 9MM Glock handgun and a Kalashnikov machine pistol, both fully loaded, plus a spare clip for each. He looked across Fifth Avenue toward the Hotel Pierre—no horse-drawn carriage.

"Come in, Jerome," Ungarn whispered into the tiny mouthpiece poised at the left corner of his mouth, "come in, damn it!"

"Relax, Spats, I'm only about 30 feet east of the intersection. Remember, the plan is for me to pull out against the light and block the left two lanes in front of the Pierre just as your customer passes by. For that to work, I have to be stalled in the intersection when the light starts to change and make it look like my horse is giving me trouble."

Spats waited for the green light and looked both ways before stepping across 59th Street. He particularly wanted to avoid getting run over by some tourist from New Jersey or a bicycle messenger. Spats touched the buttons on his wristwatch to display his financial projections for the ninth time this afternoon. Once his bank account in Liechtenstein was credited with the final $20,000 for this job, he would be $7,000 over the price of the down-payment for his dream: the small, ramshackle dairy farm on a back road outside Cortland, New York. It was past time for Spats to start a new life—something with more regular hours, a dependable income, and fewer risks.

Spats leaned over a nearby Good Humor cart as if to look into one of the open freezer boxes. One of the vendor's dreads slipped from under her paper cap as she reached into Spats's coat to retrieve the Kalashnikov and poked it out of sight among the bars of frozen desserts beside a sturdy canvas bag. Then Spats strolled farther down the sidewalk in front of the lavish bubbling fountain. Looking into a dark blue perambulator, Spats whispered into the nanny's left ear, "Car 2359!" He turned and walked briskly back to the southwest corner of 59th Street and Fifth Avenue, clasping the first hand grenade deep in his right coat pocket, its pin now resting on a mound of Creamsicle sticks and candy wrappers under a nearby sewer grate.

Just a few yards north on Fifth Avenue, David's cab swerved sharply to the right to avoid a shiny black horse-drawn coach decked with highly polished brass lamps. The hansom's driver, perched high atop the bench in front, was waving his stovepipe hat to a group of uniformed school children milling under the Pierre's front awning. David's taxi careened on down Fifth Avenue but screamed to a halt beside the fountain in front of the Plaza Hotel. David slammed hard against the front wall. Over his shoulder, he saw the wheels of an overturned baby carriage and a distraught woman almost under the cab's right front bumper frantically trying to gather the contents of her pram. At the same instant, he saw a diminutive woman click something large and hard onto the cab's trunk lid, her dreads flying in the air as she whirled away, behind her cart.

From inside the cab's silver screen and its amiable cartoon face, an unseen observer saw David Garvey tense noticeably. David dropped to his knees on the carpet. He tried to open the right door and then the left—both locked. While taking two rapid deep breaths and looking carefully about the cab's interior, David flipped back the lid of his utility case and reached inside. He snatched up a dense, layered, six-inch square steel plate with two squat handles in the center and held it over the hinge side of the cab's left door.

In less than the blink of an eye, David turned the right handle protruding from the steel plate slowly clockwise, screwing the plate to the cab's door frame and then snapped the other handle smartly to the left. The audio unit linked to the cab's central station began to pick up a faint ticking sound. David quickly slipped the green Glock 19 automatic pistol from the utility case into his right shoulder holster and squeezed both palms tightly against his ears. David tugged the Kevlar-lined jacket over his head and shoulders. One muted explosion shattered the cab's rear engine compartment, flinging bits of shrapnel and pieces of metal through its back window and into the nearby crowd of pedestrians. A second blast hurled the cab's left-rear door outward.

A high-speed, precision video taken from outside the cab at that instant would have shown pressure bursts all along the rear edge of the door as its latch and surrounding door parts vaporized. The door latch held for the briefest of moments, in part because all doors had been remotely locked shut to keep David from escaping and make the cab his coffin. The door latch held just long enough to let the cab door rotate slowly in this blink between milliseconds from its original vertical position into the horizontal plane. It was just long enough to give this metallic bird a good spin as it flew free of the latch's failing grasp.

The whirling door caught Wesley "Spats" Ungarn in midstride between a blue-and-white city bus and the dying cab. Its fierce impact jerked Spats out of his motorcycle boots and smashed his lifeless body against the idling bus. His 9MM semiautomatic pistol clattered to the pavement. Spats Ungarn's final message to the living was borne by his second hand grenade. With its pin gone, the malignant metal pineapple that was designed to finish off David Garvey tumbled between the scuffed brown shoes of an elderly Chinese official of Transport Workers Union Local 100, who had been checking payment of driver dues and the steps leading up into the open front door of the kneeling bus.

In the confusion of shrapnel and the screams that followed, David ducked through an acrid cloud of smoke, Glock in his left hand and bags in the right. He squeezed between two double-parked limos and swung up onto the far side of a muscular green garbage truck gaining momentum down Fifth Avenue. At the same time, the Good Humor vendor began firing her Kalashnikov into the charred skeleton of David's cab. David tried desperately to make himself one with the side of the garbage truck until it stopped beside a pile of oozing black plastic bags on the east side of Fifth Avenue at 45th Street. There, he dropped to the curb and lost his balance for an instant, sliding through the remains of a potato knish and quickly regaining his equilibrium. Then he walked very slowly and deliberately back a half block north then east across 46th Street.

David stepped sidewise into the doorway of a shuttered deli on the north side of 46th Street and drew himself up to his full height of five eleven. He crossed both arms in front of his chest, placed his palms together and stretched them as high as possible overhead, and then relaxed. Next, rotating both shoulders high and back, David quickly dropped them, letting his arms dangle loosely at his sides. All the while, he forced a single thought to cycle through his mind: *I'm OK, I'm OK, I'm OK*

David looked carefully both ways before ambling across 46th Street and up Madison Avenue to 49th. Turning left at the corner of Madison and 49th, David sauntered along the south side of 49th Street, across from the Japanese restaurant, until he was well past it, hoping with every fibre of his being that he looked like an executive on his way to a Sunday afternoon meeting. David stopped to look in both directions, first east across 49th, then west toward the setting sun over the Hudson River, making a point of looking carefully at each of the tall and shorter buildings nearby. Keenly aware of the absence of traffic on this quiet Sunday afternoon, David crossed 49th Street at midblock, then ducked under Hinomaru's awning.

The owner of Hinomaru peered at David through two branches of Devil's backbone framing the deserted sushi bar beyond.

"Mista Galvey, ahh, you rook rike you seen a ghost! Come in, ahh, yaw guests aw waiting in yaw speciarr loom upstairs, ahhh." The proprietor unlocked the outer door and opened it.

"Arrigato, Mr. Motoshige, I can find the way myself. Thank you for staying open for us," a shaken David Garvey struggled with the expected formalities.

"Ahways a preasure, Mista Galvey, ah." Mr. Motoshige bowed slightly.

David slipped quietly past the silent hat check booth and up a flight of narrow stairs to the left. The landing above lay masked in shadows. David found himself reaching for the Glock machine pistol in its concealed holster. Just past the top of the stairs, he slid back the only lit rice paper panel.

Frank Gillespie and Cecily Chow were perched at opposite sides of a low, highly polished birch table, stockinged feet dangling in a well in the floor beneath the table. Frank was writhing in apparent pain, his right arm pinned against the wooden table by an exuberant Cecily Chow. As David stumbled into the tatami room, both lawyers scrambled to meet him at the door.

"What happened? You look like you almost became a hood ornament!" Cecily gasped.

"How'd you tear your coat sleeve?" Frank asked.

"Give me a minute or two to calm down and I'll fill you in on the details," David responded.

He hesitated just inside the paper screen to remove his own shoes.

In front of him was a symmetrical arrangement of yellowtail, surrounded by thinly sliced strips of fatty tuna and smoked eel, both sushi and sashimi, and several handrolls, artistically arranged on a large, round powder blue ceramic serving plate. The feast waited in front of the empty place against the far wall between Frank Gillespie and Cecily Chow.

"This whole project has gotten even nastier since I spoke with you on the scrambler, Frank. I would offer you both another chance to get out, even if it's probably already too late for that now. But I really need all the help you can give me to pull this one off," David began.

He cringed as the waitress slid the door panel aside and bowed deeply before entering the room. Her ivory chopsticks presented each of the lawyers with a scalding towel. David took his carefully by the corners.

"Much too hot for this time of year," Cecily muttered, "but then the Japanese have always overemphasized ceremony."

David found himself chuckling at Cecily's predictable ethnic remark and buried his face in the towel's steamy warmth. As soon as the waitress had poured tea, tucked the damp towels into the obi at the center of her back, and quietly departed, David replayed his latest encounter with the opposition's assassins for his law partners. They both listened raptly as David recounted his most recent brush with death.

"Are you sure who was behind the attempt?" Chow asked.

"I can't imagine anyone but NeuBank's hidden partners having any interest in taking me off the board."

David patted each of his pockets twice before finding two rumpled sheets of paper inside his jacket pocket that he then handed to Cecily.

"Here's the default notice from NeuBank. What do you make of it? What can we do about it? While she's looking at the demand, what do you think about our litigation alternatives, Frank? Along the way, let's not let the sushi get warm!"

David leaned forward to select a pungent lump of green wasabi paste with the large end of his ivory chopsticks. He mixed the lime-colored horseradish paste carefully into a small, shallow dish of soy sauce the waitress had poured from the spout of a gilded ceramic pot to his left. Then David dipped the open end of a salmon skin handroll into the mixture and took a large bite of its chorus of crispy roast salmon skin, cucumber, avocado, rice, and seaweed paper enlivened with sprouts and more wasabi. The wasabi made his eyes water!

David swallowed the pleasing mixture and gulped a mouthful of hot green tea followed by a swig of ice water.

"So, Frank, what can we do besides waiting for NeuBank to shut down the Fund?" David inquired.

"Depending on your nerve, we have at least two options. Our ace in the hole is that video you took at the outpost. That ought to give us pretty good grounds for a temporary restraining order and then hopefully a permanent injunction. The cases are pretty clear we have a cause of action for tortious interference with the Fund's contracts, namely the loan agreements between the Fund and its borrowers."

"This is starting to remind me of my first year contracts course at Penn Law School," David said.

"Can't ever lose sight of the basics," Frank continued. "The basic elements of a tortious interference claim in our case are: a contract, NeuBank's knowledge of that contract, and their deliberate interference with it. We have the last one on that delicious tape. It shouldn't be very hard to show that NeuBank learned about the Fund's insides from whatever due diligence they should have conducted while putting together the Credit Agreement in order to protect the other banks in the syndicate."

"Where would you try for an injunction?" David wondered out loud. "We don't have much time."

"I wouldn't recommend Germany because NeuBank would have the home-court advantage, if you'll pardon the pun. Also, the German courts probably grant this sort of preliminary remedy very sparingly, and German lawyers have a fee schedule, including large amounts for just showing up. NeuBank's clearly subject to the jurisdiction of New York courts because it has a branch in Manhattan and because the Credit Agreement was negotiated and closed here. So we have the choice of the Federal courts in the Southern District or New York County Supreme Court. You no doubt remember that Supreme Court in the State of New York is somewhat of a misnomer, being the court of first instance that has general jurisdiction."

"When you got that temporary restraining order last month in the bank fraud case, who was the judge?" David asked.

Frank nibbled a piece of fatty tuna before continuing. A lump of wasabi-stained rice dropped from under the slice of dark red fish into the shallow ceramic dish of dark brown soy sauce, splashing over the front of Frank's white shirt and an already spotted, rumpled brown necktie. He didn't seem to notice.

"We were really in a hurry that time. I picked state court because temporary restraining orders are usually easier to get in state court, if you're lucky enough to get a judge who will either act quickly without trying to understand a complex case or a judge willing to take the time to understand something difficult. In that case, we got lucky. I sent Aaron Muckler down to file the papers and do the request for judicial intervention."

"Muckler? I haven't seen much of him."

"Been with us over four years, David," Frank said, rubbing his unkept mustache with the back of a knuckle, as if he were about to sneeze. "Aaron cajoled the clerks into walking the paperwork through the bureaucratic maze, got the case entered into the computer system and tried to get us a good judge, even though that's not supposed to be possible. We got Justice Winston Hong. He's a very bright and practical judge, rumored to be under consideration for a federal judgeship in the Southern District. His cases move! We got our temporary restraining order the same day."

"Then what?" David hurried on.

"The other side got more agreeable and we were able to work out an arrangement to freeze things until the merits could be sorted out. What impressed me with Justice Hong was that he allowed me to style the document as both a stipulation and order. Whether or not the other side understood, it couldn't be appealed."

"Could NeuBank make us put up a bond in response to our request for an injunction? Any substantial bond could present a real problem. I suspect the local bonding companies would probably require substantial collateral from an off-shore company like the Fund, maybe 100 percent cash. You know cash is a problem, caused by our tormentors at NeuBank."

"The rules in state and federal court both say you must post a bond to get a temporary restraining order. Fortunately, the judges in state court often exercise some discretion on that question. I've been known to convince judges in New York Supreme to at least postpone putting up the bond for a while, so that might not be an immediate problem. Hard to know if NeuBank will push for a bond of any significant amount. Assuming NeuBank taps S&M, as I fully expect,

Maggie Wilbur will most likely get the case. She has more of this type of litigation under her belt than anyone else there. No way to tell how much of her attention this one would get, particularly if the Huns are trying to cheap on the fees, as usual."

"State or federal court? You got great results in state court last time," David noted.

"A real crap shoot! In state court, we might get one of the judges who has been waiting to retire for the last fifteen years or some former Legal Aid lawyer who would be completely baffled by anything more complex than a simple promissory note. Sure, to some degree there is a similar problem in federal court, but, in NeuBank's case, we have firsthand evidence of venality. Even with a good judge in state court, we could be hamstrung with preliminary issues and stonewalled on discovery. That is less likely to happen in federal court. In the end, David, you're the client. You have to make the choice. Whichever you choose, I'll strap on my buckler, pick up my lance and gallop into the lists to do battle. There's an awful lot to be done, and time is running out!"

Frank settled back from the now nearly empty table.

David paused for a swallow of hot green tea. He absentmindedly chewed the remaining salmon skin handroll before turning to Cecily, whose finely chiseled features were a picture of angry concentration.

"What can we do about the default notice?" David demanded.

"This is just garden-variety dreck from someone's Holo over at S&M. They missed the provision in the Credit Agreement I added requiring arbitration of any dispute about the existence of an event of default, like this one."

"So what do we do?"

"While you were talking with Frank, I put together a letter you should send tomorrow. Basically it says the Fund will do its utmost to comply with the requirements of the Credit Agreement. No sense in appearing to be troublesome. They'll figure that out as soon as the injunction papers are filed and served," she sneered.

LUCK OF THE WHEEL

Federal Rule of Civil Procedure 65:

(b) <u>Temporary Restraining Order; Notice; Hearing; Duration</u>. A temporary restraining order may be granted without written or oral notice to the adverse party or that party's attorney if (1) it clearly appears from specific facts shown by affidavit or by the verified complaint that immediate and irreparable injury, loss, or damage will result to the applicant before the adverse party or that party's attorney can be heard in opposition, and (2) the applicant's attorney certifies to the court in writing the efforts, if any, which have been made to give the notice and the reasons supporting the claim that notice should not be required.

(c) <u>Security</u>. No restraining order or preliminary injunction shall issue except upon the giving of security by the applicant, in such sum as the court deems proper, for the payment of such costs and damages as may be incurred or suffered by any party who is found to have been wrongfully enjoined or restrained.

The first blush of morning crept down the broad alleyway leading to the rink at Rockefeller Center. From his spacious office high above the waking city, Frank Gillespie could see a lone brown-uniformed woman scraping tiny patches of different colored chewing gum from the sidewalk beside the huge bronze statue of Atlas. Someone had told him the Freemasons had been instrumental in locating that statue directly in front of the altar of St. Patrick's Cathedral as a challenge to the Catholic hierarchy.

Frank looked up as Aaron Muckler stuck his head in the open office door.

"You want me to take a look at the affidavit?" Aaron asked. "I JUST found a an e-mail message from the client demanding that we go for a temporary restraining order as soon as the Federal courts in lower Manhattan open this morning."

"Please look over this draft. I worked on it through last night and again this morning," Frank responded between double gulps of steaming black coffee from what appeared to be an ivory ceramic pail. "What do you propose to do about notifying S&M?" He rubbed his scruffy mustache with the knuckle of his left index finger as he waited for the young associate's response.

"Well, how do we know for sure NeuBank will hire S&M for this litigation?"

"You know, Aaron, getting this done right and as soon as possible will be tough enough. I'd rather not piss off the judge at the very first opportunity. One of us has to sign the affidavit saying we notified NeuBank's lawyers, we tried to, or why we didn't. I'd rather be straightforward and not play games. Let's just call Maggie Wilbur and be able to put that in the affidavit. If they show up, fine. If they don't, it won't be our fault."

"Anticipating your point of view, I just left a message on Maggie Wilbur's voice mail, since she isn't in her office at six thirty in the morning. Do you want to hear the message I left?"

"Will it make my day?" Frank worried his gray-speckled mustache once more.

Aaron opened his ham-sized hand to reveal a tiny disc. He popped it into Frank's communications console, passed a finger through a blinking holographic image floating above it and reached over to adjust the volume of the speaker.

"This is Margaret Wilbur's office. We're not able to answer your call at this moment. If you would care to leave a message, please do so after the electronic tone and we will return your call as soon as possible. BEEEEEEEEP . . ."

"Margaret, this is Aaron Muckler calling from Garvey, Stahl. The time is Tuesmab ast thirty mglflmmks un bosfglmoss dirxcalowiznstk vor wiltter Southermndistrum temporinity morining caleder urgerintly musttifflum—"

"Cute, very fucking cute!" Frank exploded, cutting off the recording. "What can you tell the judge with a straight face about that hodgepodge of drivel?"

"The rule says the affidavit has to describe notice given or why it wasn't. I don't see why they deserve anything more than that. She knows I called. And besides, we don't really know whether they will handle the case. Ethically, we can't call NeuBank directly to find out who will be appearing for them. And we have to win this one or David is out of business, washed up."

Frank didn't respond immediately. Retrieving his favorite glass paperweight from a stack of pleadings in another case, he stared down toward Fifth Avenue far below, where the narrow sidewalks were beginning to fill with pedestrians rushing headlong into their days. But Frank didn't notice any people in the street below.

"You all right, Frank? We gotta finish this affidavit, make arrangements for a bond, and polish our canned memorandum of law for TROs if you think one would be useful. We don't have a lot of time."

"I was just thinking maybe we're putting too much pressure on you to win. When you were trying to justify ignoring the substance of Rule 65, I—"

"Wait a minute, Frank. I'm trying to do my very best for the client, who, incidentally, is your law partner and my employer."

"No, you wait a minute, Aaron!" the older lawyer snarled. "No one wants to win this case for David more than I do, but we're both going to be practicing law in this city for a long time. You and I can't expect others to play fair if we cut corners when the going gets a little tough. Make a genuine effort to contact Maggie Wilbur or whoever is taking her calls."

Frank paused to inhale two gulps of coffee, followed by a lemon-flavored Maalox.

"Errp! Excuse me. This affidavit needs to be shorter, but beef up the description of immediate and irreparable injury and damage to the Fund if we don't get the temporary restraining order. Make the telex from Königsberg you helped David draft an exhibit to the affidavit. It has all the gory details and came from the client. If that part doesn't bring tears to the eyes of both of the judge's clerks, we're in serious trouble. Got that?"

"OK, Frank. I'll be on my way in an hour, tops." Aaron assured him.

"Call me as soon as you have an index number and a judge. I'll join you for the hearing. In the meantime, I'm going to try to find Maggie Wilbur. And I have to call David at home to let him know where we stand. He may want to go down to court with us."

GOING TO COURT

The beggar stepped back quickly to avoid a rush of commuters boarding the downtown Second Avenue express under Bloomingdale's at 59th Street. He waited for the coach's double doors to swish shut before beginning his pitch:

"Lays an gennemen, I bin put outta ma house and cain't feed ma fambly. I'm tryin' to feed ma kids but I shoah do need your help. Any change you could spare would be mos 'preciated. God bless you. Have a nice day."

The young black man turned and began tapping through the crowd with his candy-striped cane. Every other step he rattled some loose change in a battered tin cup for effect, emphasized by a sagging limp in his left hip.

Suddenly, the beggar's path was blocked by one very large man in a smartly tailored blue suit, clutching a dark leather briefcase to his bosom as if to protect its contents from the teeming rabble around him. Aaron Muckler's carefully pressed suit and freshly starched shirt suggested a commuter on the way to work downtown, but the brown eyes behind his wire-rim glasses were bloodshot and the circles under them were deeper than usual. Even through his heavy dark lenses, the beggar, a bank data processor who had just finished the night shift at a downtown brokerage firm, could tell Aaron was exhausted. In fact, Aaron had not been home to his apartment on East 62nd Street since Friday night, except to shower and change clothes before catching the electric sewer downtown to the Brooklyn Bridge station under City Hall.

Aaron's worn satchel contained the Fund's application for a temporary restraining order, the first step toward obtaining a preliminary injunction designed to freeze the Fund's dispute with NeuBank in place until it could be resolved. David's lawyers needed an injunction to keep the Fund's enemies at bay long enough to give him some breathing room to strike back. Some of the lawyers in the office understood David Garvey's business hung by this slender thread, but most of them were not even dimly aware he was fighting for his very life. Just to be safe, Aaron had stuffed a duplicate set of the papers in his belt behind his back, concealed by his ample suit coat.

Aaron and Frank had spent the end of Saturday and all day Sunday getting ready for this short and noisy ride to the Federal Court for the Southern District of New York. Humming rubber tires under Aaron's subway car, a novelty inspired by equipment in the Paris Metro, whispered into his weary brain "*go to sleep . . . go to sleep . . . go to sleep.*"

"Hey, man, can ya spare a dollah fo' a cuppa coffee?" the beggar demanded, stretching forth a bony hand. He had long ago learned not to hold out the cup. Some people would help themselves.

"Sorry. Gave at the office."

"Man, you surely could afford DOLLAR."

"Can you change a $100?"

"How 'bout you stop playin' wif me and gimme some green? I bet you wouldn't miss a couple of bucks."

"How do you possibly know that, my man, unless perhaps you really can SEE?" Muckler countered, punctuated with a quick right cross that stopped only centimeters from the beggar's nearly opaque glasses.

The bum jumped back then quietly pivoted on his heel and began tapping his way slowly in the opposite direction. As Muckler stepped out into the polished marble of the Brooklyn Bridge station, the refrain began once more:

"Lays an gennemen . . ."

Aaron headed down the slot between the uptown and downtown express tracks of the Second Avenue subway toward dark stairs at the north end of the platform, and through a dimly lighted tunnel under a rabbit warren of walkways in the floors above., He quickly dodged a bag lady squatting just around the next corner and then up more steps, two at a time, and out through the electronic turnstiles. The token booth attendant was snoozing soundly in her armored redoubt. Aaron was in a terrible hurry. Dashing up another flight of concrete steps, he remembered one of his late father's pearls of wisdom: "Always keep your jaw closed when running up or down stairs. You'll be less likely to break teeth if you fall."

Dad, Aaron thought to himself, *I hope you would be proud of me today. We never got to talk about that before you died.*

Finally, Aaron stepped out into the urine-free air. He crossed a small park in front of the old Federal courthouse, 40 Centre Street, scattering a flock of pigeons in his wake. Next, he scurried down a side street to the Park Row entrance of the new Federal Building, built over an early slaves' graveyard. After a long dispute, the powers that be had decided that these involuntary residents of old New York should be honored by preserving the graveyard as a museum located in the bowels of the courthouse. The graves remained in their original locations, accessible to the public, while the halls of justice ascended into the sky over them.

Aaron Muckler, Esquire, stepped from the street into the first of two secure entranceways. One of the uniformed guards motioned for him to put all contents of his pockets, including papers, watch, keys, and pocket change, on a conveyor belt, where it all promptly disappeared from sight. At the guard's direction, the lawyer added his bulging briefcase to the moving belt. As requested, Aaron punched his Federal Bar identification card into an adjacent computer terminal.

A loudspeaker instructed Aaron to put both hands, palms down, through a hole in the Plexiglass partition in front of him. He spread his fingers to facilitate a check of his identity. With a perceptible snap, his hands were clamped gently to the dirty glass plate; at the same time, a portion of the wall where Aaron was standing rotated while a body scan hummed around him, depositing the bulky advocate inside the security system's first set of barriers. Inside the second secure chamber, his hands were released to allow Aaron to step away from the machine. While another guard was carefully searching Aaron, a voice to his left inquired about his destination.

"Second Floor, Clerk's Office," Aaron replied. "I need an index number."

"Mr. Muckler, please go directly to the Second Floor. The waiting elevator is programmed to go only to that floor," the armed security guard directed without looking up at the young lawyer through her bulletproof faceplate. "Kindly exit the elevator as soon as it reaches its destination. If you do not, the elevator will immediately return to this floor."

"No problem, ma'am. I'm in a hurry," the young lawyer muttered.

Aaron hurried toward the elevator doors. Once the elevator doors swished shut, he was momentarily alone in a gleaming chrome cage. Almost instantly, the glistening panels opened again. Counselor Muckler adjusted his blue silk cravat and lumbered across the gleaming marble hallway. He inserted the same identification card into a terminal between two opaque, unmarked doors. One of the heavy portals slid quietly into the wall, permitting him to step through. He found himself standing before a ponderous aluminum wall, devoid of all ornamentation except the Great Seal of the United States. From atop that barrier, at Muckler's chin level, a slight, uniformed woman peered down from her wheelchair through thick creme-rimmed spectacles. White letters on her navy plastic name tag read "*CONSTANCE BROWARD*."

"May I be of assistance?" the woman asked.

Aaron suppressed the sudden impulse to snicker. He wholeheartedly endorsed all aspects of courtesy, but this woman's only job was to assign index numbers to new cases in the United States District Court for the Southern District of New York. Like he really might be coming in through this elaborate screen of security to order a pizza or something? And how can she stand sitting in that wheelchair all day?

He kept all that to himself and mumbled politely:

"I have a complaint to file plus a request for a temporary restraining order. Rule 65. Here's my Federal Bar card to debit the fees. Could I have a receipt please?"

"Could you please hand the papers up with your card? I can't reach that far," she asked, stretching out a spindly arm in his general direction.

Aaron stood on tiptoe to pass her his filing package. She received the weighty stack with both hands and let it drop to her work surface with a dull thump.

Ms. Broward tightly gripped the right wheel rim of her chariot. She took a deep breath, pushed, and then strained to reach a recessed shelf below Aaron's line of sight. Her fingers found the knob of the Wheel, a polished oaken wooden box measuring twelve inches across at the widest point of its octagonal sides resting on a rough iron spindle. The gadget's sides were made up of seven 8" by 5" panels of similar material and an eighth of comparable size and shape attached to the frame with a pair of hinges. Each time a new case arrived in the United States District Court for the Southern District of New York, the plaintiff or the plaintiff's attorney had to come to Constance Broward's office to be assigned a number for the case, its index number. To equally spread the torrent of pending litigation among the Southern District's 43 active judges and to keep parties from picking the judge they want, Ms. Broward employed this antique device, rather like a small, thick wooden Ferris wheel, to assign a judge to each new case. That judge would then attend to the matter until it was either finally settled, dismissed, transferred, or went to trial and usually if the case was returned after any subsequent appeals. Her choice determined which federal judge would be responsible for the case until its journey through the trial part of the judicial system was finished. She spun the Wheel and opened its door panel.

Deputy Clerk Broward plucked a rectangular wooden marker from the Wheel and read aloud:

"Nathaniel D. Fischbein! Congratulations, Counselor, you or should I say your client, has been commended to the care of the Court's oldest judge and one of its most colorful, I might add."

She stamped all three sets of Garvey, Stahl's papers with Judge Fischbein's name and an index number indicating the matter's sequence within civil cases for that year and handed one set of the papers over the counter to Muckler.

Not a good sign, Aaron Muckler thought to himself darkly. Judge Fischbein had tried to hold him in contempt in another case for making a motion without asking the judge's permission to submit his motion papers. What a terrible way to start such an important case!

"One of those is a courtesy copy of the papers for the judge. Should I deliver it to his chambers myself on the way out?" Aaron asked.

"Not allowed! Very tight security, you know," the clerk clucked. "Since this case involves a temporary restraining order, I'll see to it myself that the papers are delivered to Judge Fischbein's chambers promptly."

The young lawyer thanked the clerk for her help, retrieved his Federal Bar card, and turned to hurry on his way.

"Wait a minute," the clerk called after him. "You forgot to take your copy of Judge Fischbein's individual rules."

"Thanks, I had another case before Judge Fischbein last summer. I don't need his rules unless they have changed since then."

"He hasn't changed his rules since we moved to the new courthouse. I guess you know what you're up against. Good luck."

The paraplegic functionary returned her attention to the mountain of files on her desk.

"On second thought, ma'am, I'll take a copy of Judge Fischbein's rules. I can review 'em while we're waiting to see the Judge."

Moments later, Aaron was reporting to Frank Gillespie on his bulky cell phone from the street outside the Federal courthouse.

"We got Judge Fischbein. He prides himself on being a big-picture judge. I could tell you some stories. But I checked with his clerk. The judge is hearing a capital drug case this morning, but he'll consider our application during the lunch break. That would be in about forty minutes. Are you coming down? I could handle it, but I'm really tired."

"As soon as we hang up, I'll get on the electric sewer," Frank said. "Will he hear us in his courtroom or chambers?"

"Chambers. Did you get Maggie Wilbur?"

Gillespie paused, remembering Aaron was only an associate, an employee, however competent a young litigator he might be. There was no reason to share with Aaron Muckler how he was able to contact Maggie Wilbur, no need to tell him about calling David at home to report on status of the TRO and mentioning the trouble they were having locating S&M's senior bank litigator. Frank was also pretty tired and now a little confused. Just a few moments after Frank had hung up the phone from talking with David, Maggie Wilbur called back on his direct line. Frank had not had a case with Maggie Wilbur in a couple of years, but then she was reputed to have an almost photographic memory.

Time to charge onto the field of battle, Frank thought to himself. He opened an ebony calfskin briefcase on his coffee table and tossed in two copies of the NeuBank papers and a set of the opposing party's papers in a summary judgment motion he was defending in another case in New York Supreme. Frank Gillespie's Rule No. 27-1/2: always bring other work to a conference or hearing. That's the best way to have your case called before you have time to start the other work. If you don't bring other work, it will take forever to be heard.

To the collection of documents in his slim briefcase, he added a cab voucher and two candy bars. Frank Gillespie removed his suit jacket from its hangar on a mahogany hat rack and slipped into it. On his way toward the elevator, Frank stopped in front of Olivia Ojeda, the group paralegal and communications specialist, to let her know where he would be and to retrieve his pager from the recharging bank. The office sentry unlocked one of the firm's double doors to let Frank out into the elevator lobby. As the senior litigator waited for his elevator, he rubbed and rubbed the stubby bristle of hair under his nose with the knuckle of his left index finger.

The same set of guards who had ministered to Aaron earlier attended to Frank Gillespie as he stepped into the alabaster lobby of the Federal Building. This team was overdue for a lunch break and a little cranky from two attempts by security supervisors to sneak dummy explosives through their sector a few minutes earlier.

"Mr. Gillespie, please go directly to the waiting elevator, which is programmed to go only to Judge Fischbein's floor," the slender young guard pointed toward the nearest elevator bank, stroking his auburn ponytail in the process. "Kindly exit the elevator as soon as it reaches its destination. If you do not—"

Frank rode the iridescent chamber to its preprogrammed destination. His adrenalin was already pumping! He fervently wished there had been time to go to the bathroom before leaving his office. Frank needed no notes for this presentation—the bare bones of a temporary restraining order argument were burned into his soul: irreparable injury to the Fund, absolutely no damage or even inconvenience to NeuBank in complying with the TRO, minimal bond.

Frank stepped out of the elevator into a long corridor with windowless doors along both sides, each with a terminal in place of a doorknob.

It was a sharp contrast with the old facilities at 40 Centre Street. Those old chambers were rambling, somewhat chaotic, and reasonably comfortable. In the old building, bathrooms were easily accessible, and every judge had a chamber and courtroom known to all practicing litigators as well as any interested members of the general public. Here in the new building, judges were randomly reassigned both chambers and courtrooms. Each judge's calendar of cases was still published in the Law Journal, but neither judges' chambers nor their courtrooms were revealed to the general public. Access to judges was tightly controlled. You couldn't even find out where you're going until after the end of the thorough security check downstairs. Even then, no one would tell you what floor you're going to. You just stepped into the assigned elevator and hoped it delivered you to the right place.

All correspondence and legal papers must be delivered to a central facility in the basement where everything was meticulously screened for explosives and other dangerous devices. Outsiders were allowed in the courthouse only on court business; after passing the initial security checks, they too were directed to the appropriate room on the floors above. On the destination floor, only one door terminal was remotely reprogrammed to receive the coded access card provided to a visitor at the completion of lobby security checks. Access to the computer terminal controlling access to the judge you wanted to see expired ten minutes after leaving the security lobby to keep people from wandering around inside the building.

Frank looked down at his access card. Having been informed Judge Fischbein's chambers were located today in the third room on the left after leaving the elevator, he walked quickly down the hall and inserted his small white plastic card into a black metallic slot in the door. The heavy metal slab clicked and rolled smoothly into its casement. Frank stepped inside.

"Hi, Frank! We can get started unless we have to wait for opposing counsel," Aaron greeted him sarcastically.

"I spoke to Maggie Wilbur after you left to come down here. She wasn't sure whether her firm would be retained on this one. Then I called Maggie back to let her know about this hearing, the time, judge assigned, and everything else. By then she had talked to Diether Kreuz at NeuBank. Maggie's been hired. She's been directed to vigorously oppose our application. I expect she'll be here shortly."

As if on cue, the steel door behind them slid sideways, and a haughty Margaret Wilbur strode through the portal trailing a very sunburned and heavily perspiring young blonde woman dragging two bulging litigation bags.

"You're Frank Gillespie, aren't you? I'm Margaret Wilbur," she said, extending her unadorned right hand. "Didn't we work together on the Donner case?"

"That's right. You really ate us up on that one! Maggie, this is my associate, Aaron Muckler. You can talk to him whenever I'm out of pocket."

"Aaron, nice to meet you. Margaret Wilbur. This is Gesine Walter, one of our foreign lawyer trainees from the legal department of Neu Ost Bank in Schwerin. She will be helping on this one, but please direct all correspondence and other communications to me personally. Do you have some papers for me to look at while we're waiting for the judge? I don't have any papers for you, but I'll reserve the right to put some in later."

Aaron Muckler snapped open his briefcase to remove S&M's copy of the application for temporary restraining order, the affidavits, and accompanying memorandum of law. Frank watched carefully to see how Aaron behaved when dealing with opposing counsel, particularly someone as pushy as Margaret Wilbur. From what Frank could remember from their prior encounters, Margaret had changed little over the years, except to look a tad more severe—no colored nail polish, makeup, or lipstick, and what looked like simple, almost orthopedic sandals.

"Would you mind receipting for these papers, Ms. Wilbur? It sure would save me some trouble," Aaron asked.

"Actually, I would prefer you serve and file them the usual way," she answered in a deep voice, shrugging absently. Then turning away abruptly, she began to leaf through the hefty stack of motion papers.

"Aaron, could you ring the judge's bailiff?" Frank said. "I think we're ready to see him."

"No need for that," a deep voice rumbled from the monitor screen on the freshly painted wall. "Judge Fischbein will see you now."

With that, the compound's inner door clicked open to reveal a highly polished mahogany conference table surrounded by eight cordovan leather chairs. At the far end of the long table, an elderly man sporting polka-dot suspenders and a Kelly green bow tie was wolfing down an overstuffed sandwich—turkey and cheese with Russian dressing judging from the debris on the floral placemat in front of him. He held out a Limoges cup to his rotund black bailiff, who disappeared into the next room to add another tea bag and some steaming water.

Judge Fischbein carefully wiped the tips of his fingers with a crumpled paper napkin and motioned the new arrivals to join him. Frank squeezed into the seat on Judge Fischbein's immediate left and motioned Aaron to take the seat beside him. Margaret Wilbur slid into an empty chair at the end of the elongated table, her acolyte struggling into the seat beside her after tripping over her baggage.

"Tell me what this is all about," the judge demanded. "The jury in my capital drug case is coming back in less than ten minutes. Make it snappy! I see from this electronic contraption we have papers from Plaintiff but none from Defendant. Security says Gillespie and Muckler are here for Plaintiff from Garvey, Stahl. Who's up, Gillespie or Muckler? Muckler . . . that sounds familiar."

"Frank Gillespie, Garvey, Stahl, Your Honor, for Plaintiff, Königsberg Fund. This is pretty simp—"

"Where the hell is Königsberg, Counselor?"

"I believe it's in a small part of Russia between Poland and Lithuania. Was Kaliningrad under the Soviets. As I was saying, Your Honor, this case is pretty simple. Our client makes loans in what used to be the Soviet Union. The Fund borrows money from Defendant German bank from its Federal Branch here in Manhattan. Our client pledged Eastern European loans the Fund made and mortgages as collateral for loans the Fund got from the German bank, all delivered here in New York. The German bank has been telling our customers to not make their payments and interfering with our contractual relationships with our customers. We're out of business if this continues. We want the German bank and all of their subsidiaries, agents, and affiliates restrained from interfering with our collections until the Court can hear our request for a preliminary injunction on the basis of more complete papers. That's it in a nutshell, Your Honor, although more information is contained in our application, including correspondence from the client setting out more of the details."

Frank took a deep breath, furiously rubbed his mustache with the knuckle of his left index finger, and looked around expectantly, first at Judge Fischbein and then at his opponent.

"Nasty place, that Eastern Europe," the judge observed. "I was a very young lad in the OSS in Czechoslovakia during World War II. Lied about my age to get in. Who is appearing for the Defendant?"

"Margaret Wilbur, Smythe & Mahoney, for Neu Ost Bank, Your Honor. We just learned about this case a couple of hours ago. We don't think the Court has jurisdiction over business transactions in Belarus, Poland and Russia. It would be entirely proper for the Court to refuse to hear—"

"Young lady, this Court is entirely capable of determining the extent of its own jurisdiction. Do you have any substantive arguments? Tell me how your client would be harmed by a temporary restraining order of limited duration, say, five days?"

"Your Honor, I'm hardly a young lady," Margaret Wilbur growled, her anxiety betrayed only by a slight catch in the movement of her jaw as she gathered steam. "I've been an active member of the bar of this Court for nearly twenty years. The Bank's activities in Europe should not be regulated by this Court. If the Court chooses to restrain the Bank, a substantial bond should be posted to insulate the Bank from any damages from wrongful restraint; I would suggest at least $3 million."

"Your Honor," Frank jumped in, "we're only asking that this German bank stop interfering with our customers. Any reputable financial institution should be willing to agree to that without the necessity of having to come down here for a temporary restraining order. There's no damage to anyone in being required not to interfere with our client's customer base and cash flow. A minimal bond ought to be sufficient, particularly in view of the short delay before the Court's proposed hearing on the preliminary injunction. If the Court believes a bond is necessary, $2,500 ought to be sufficient. Here is another copy of our proposed restraining order."

Frank handed the additional copy of the order to Judge Fischbein.

"Restraining order granted," the judge said, marking on the copy as he spoke. "Bond is $5,000, to be posted not later than 4:00 P.M. today. The restraining order expires at 4:00 P.M. Friday. Hearing on the preliminary injunction is . . . can I see our calendar for Friday morning, William? You're on for 10:00 A.M. this Friday. Mr. Gillespie, have your papers to me and Miss Wilbur by 4:00 P.M. Wednesday, by hand delivery. Miss Wilbur, your papers are due by 4:00 P.M. Thursday. We're done for today. I have to get back to my jury."

Judge Fischbein stepped quickly into the small adjacent robing room, where Frank watched the towering bailiff help the jurist, first into his bulletproof vest and then flowing black judicial robes. The judge whispered something inaudible into the attendant's ear and disappeared through a side door beyond Frank Gillespie's line of sight. The judge's bailiff, William Pilkington, laid a large open hand with a heavy gold ring on each finger on the table in front of the four lawyers.

"If y'all give me your access cards, I'll aks our system to reprogram 'em and call you an elevator to the street."

A few moments later, the four litigants stood in the nondescript lobby awaiting transportation to the building's exit lobby. The tension was palpable.

"Maggie, how could we settle this without prolonged litigation?" Frank ventured, cringing inwardly in anticipation of Maggie Wilbur's stinging response.

"That's easy. Withdraw your complaint and have the Fund agree to discharge its obligations under the Credit Agreement. Schwerin sees this as simply the Fund's attempt to avoid paying its bills. That's the only basis I'm even willing to discuss settling this with you. See you Friday morning, and don't be late with your papers."

Margaret Wilbur pointedly turned away from the two Garvey, Stahl lawyers toward Fräulein Walter and began explaining to her in German what had transpired during their whirlwind conference with Judge Fischbein as the elevator doors opened.

Frank looked Aaron straight in the eye and shrugged. In what seemed like a split second, the elevator doors swished open, spilling the lawyers into the first floor lobby. David Garvey's two spear carriers hurried into the street.

Frank was already in motion, right hand raised to hail a cab just coming into sight from around the next corner, the knuckles of his left hand busily worrying his graying mustache. On to the next crisis.

THE SKIM

"Mr. Garvey, what should I do?" she asked, hovering behind the corner of David Garvey's desk.

He looked away from his bird's-eye view of the alleyway in the front of Rockefeller Center that would lead to the Christmas tree later in the year and realized he'd been absently tapping the point of his lead pencil on the surface of his desk, faster and faster as the minutiae of the bookkeeper's explanation unfolded.

"Can you run the details by me once more? I've got too many things going on," he said to the bookkeeper as she looked from him to his computer screen, her thick lenses hanging in a beaded chain around the wrinkles of her neck. She was only slightly more appealing than a Pondicherry turkey vulture but fortunately a whiz with financial records and uncovering hidden variables.

"In summary, you may remember we had to do an audit of our financials for the Konigsberg Fund banks. In the course of that audit, we were required to confirm our law firm's receivables. You know, of course, confirming receivables requires us to send a letter to businesses that owe the firm money, asking them to confirm outstanding balances. You've always hated doing that because it suggests to clients that they have an opportunity to quibble about bills. While this audit unfolded in a more or less normal fashion, several clients of one of the law firm's partners claimed their bills had already been paid. Upon further investigation, it was discovered that each of those businesses had paid one of your partners directly, instead of paying the firm. What do you want me to do about that?"

"Who's the partner and how much is involved?"

"Frank Gillespie. We figure the amount of receivables paid to him instead of the firm is at least $580,000, but our accounting analysis is still in process."

"Did you talk to any of the clients involved?" David asked.

"Knowing your point of view, just two. Both said the bills were paid as Mr. Gillespie instructed, to him personally. They volunteered to show me cancelled checks, an offer I accepted. Disappointing. Their point of view is it's not their problem; what he did with the money is not their problem," the bookkeeper reported.

Yarding her medicinal marijuana gum, the obese accountant went on, "a complication here is that we regularly ask partners to confirm status of receivables at year's end in preparation for putting together tax returns. Last time around, Mr. Gillespie confirmed the receivables in question were still owing but collectible even though they had already been paid to him."

Christ on a crutch, David Garvey thought to himself. *Bad enough Peter and Will's mother reported to the IRS that my firm was making up expenses just to be troublesome. I already had to hire still more accountants to deal with IRS bureaucrats while fending off NeuBank and its not-so-silent partners.*

"Tell you what," he said to the elderly accountant. "How about you complete your compilation and report the results with complete details only to me?"

As the bookkeeper gathered up her files and waddled out of his office, David Garvey continued tapping his lead pencil on the desk, faster and faster. Then he snapped the yellow pencil into three jagged pieces and hurled them at the view out over Rockefeller Center.

Damn, damn, damn! One more traitor!

THE HUDDLE

The last rays of Monday's early evening sun burnished an antique, gold-framed indenture hanging on the east wall of Frank's spacious office. His rush of excitement from the conference with Judge Fischbein had faded earlier in the day. The afternoon had fluttered by like a stack of so many disposable pages on his desk calendar. He had many little things to attend to—work to assign, briefs to read, and an avalanche of calls to return.

Aaron had gone home to get some rest with the promise of a very early start in the morning to assemble materials needed for Garvey, Stahl's memorandum of law to reach both Judge Fischbein and Maggie Wilbur by late afternoon Wednesday. Here in the quiet dregs of a busy afternoon, Frank surveyed his domain from the soft cushions of his plush sofa.

"Got a minute to bring me up-to-date on how the hearing went today and where we go next?" David asked through the office's open door, rattling a nearly empty glass of seltzer with lime. "Do you want something to drink, Frank? I can duck into the kitchen before I come in."

"No thanks. Just finished a couple a coffees. Sure, come on in, put your feet up. That's what I'm about to do. This day has been longer than some others recently."

David cautiously eased himself into an upholstered wingback chair and dangled his right leg over one arm. He thought: *Frank's one of the firm's most able litigators, but he's been looking worn out and unkept for quite a while and seems even more distracted than usual. Not to even mention our accountant's revelations.*

David was still trying to assess whether Gillespie could handle this crucial case. Particularly in light of what David had recently learned from his bookkeeper, he continued to watch his partner closely, carefully considering his every reaction. He wondered if Frank's divorce, which had been even nastier than David's own, had introduced unmanageable financial pressures.

"So, tell me more about the hearing," David said. "Besides granting our request for a temporary restraining order, how'd the judge react to our claim? Whadda we need to do next? And how'd Muckler do?"

Frank retreated into the comparative safety of the depths of his couch before answering.

"Fischbein heard us on very short notice. I couldn't tell if he had even looked at our papers. Set bond at $5,000 even though Maggie Wilbur asked for $3 million. I sent Aaron home for some sleep after he took care of making arrangements with the bonding company to get the bond delivered to the clerk before the deadline."

"Any problem getting the bond?"

"Shouldn't be if the papers are filled out correctly. One of our paras will chase that. Aaron's done a fine job. Probably could have handled the TRO hearing himself. Apparently Aaron had some difficulty with Judge Fischbein on another case, so I didn't see any point is risking a problem on this one."

"Is that going to cause a problem?"

"Probably not. I did all the talking myself," Frank said. "The preliminary injunction hearing is on Friday, 10:00 A.M. By then, we must have served our papers and laid out our claim in as much detail as humanly possible. Judge Fischbein strikes me, in this case and others, as someone who makes up his mind early on. We got past the first hurdle—getting the TRO. Now, we have to build on that and convince Judge Fischbein our case is meritorious and likely to succeed at trial, even if we never ever intend to get to trial."

David and Frank dissected the case that might determine whether the Fund, David's lifeblood, would survive, as if it were so much used furniture. So far, Frank was doing pretty well, but fleshing out the details about what he planned to do next would give David a better idea of whether or not Frank was up to the challenge.

"Do we need witnesses for Friday? What about discovery? Should I be trying to talk to NeuBank?" David continued excitedly.

"Slow down, Mr. Corporate Maven!" Frank barked, repeatedly worrying his mustache with the knuckle of his right index finger. "Let's not overdo this now I'm the client, now I'm the lawyer bit. Anyway, I was just making some notes that address your questions, as well as some of the other more relevant issues. Let's start with whether you should give Diether Kreuz a call. How do you suppose that would go?"

"Good morning, Herr Doktor Kreuz—"

"And, what's the punch line?" the litigator interrupted testily.

"What do you mean, what's the punch line? I'm calling to see if we can make a deal," David Garvey said hopefully.

"Well, the concept is pretty damn stupid. I just wanted to see if the execution was any more helpful. I guess not," Frank mumbled, appearing to brush something from his sleeve with the backs of his fingers, as if shooing away a beggar in the street. "It's almost like you've been taking correspondence courses from Client School. You rushed in here a couple of days ago with this wild story about how the German bankers for your outside business, secretly backed by Iraqi money, are trying to take over the Fund—running around all over Eastern Europe telling your customers to default on their loans so the Germans can grab all the local mortgages and other business collateral. You helped us do up an affidavit demonstrating you caught one of their operatives red-handed. Aaron and I spent the entire weekend preparing for today's hearing. We got a temporary restraining order with only a small bond. There's still a ton of work to be done in only a couple of days, and YOU WANT TO JUST FUCKING CALL DIETHER KREUZ?"

Frank repeatedly banged a clenched fist on the arm of the sofa in his frustration.

"Calm down, Frank. I know you're tired. I just thought there might be a way—"

"Before you share that terrific idea with me, tell me what the hell is going on here," Frank demanded. "I may be beyond tired, but there's something going on I can't quite figure out. I can't get this job done right unless I'm working with a full deck of cards!"

"I haven't the faintest idea what you're talking about, Frank!"

"For starters, how did Maggie Wilbur know where to call me this morning?"

"Jesus, Frank! Relax! We're probably in every phone book printed in the Big Apple, not to mention Martindale and the City Bar directory! How to reach us is not exactly a closely guarded secret."

"Don't act like I'm a moron, David, just because I don't have a lot to do with how this place runs on a day-to-day basis. Even I know the partners' private lines aren't listed anywhere. Now, what gives?"

"Oh, she called you on your private line? How do you know which line she called on?" David parried.

"I just happened to be looking right at my console when it started ringing, Frank explained. "At that hour of the morning, I didn't expect anyone to be calling me. I looked directly at the blinking red light. It was right on my private line! Besides, the switchboard wasn't open yet. I checked!"

David slowly crossed his right leg over the other knee, stared silently at his partner, and took a deep swallow of icy seltzer. He paused, hoping Frank would continue. He waited and tried to outlast him. But his law partner would not be intimidated!

"It's probably pretty simple. I suppose she had your direct number."

"And now, Mr. Garvey, having in mind you have sworn to tell the whole truth and nothing but the truth, could you explain to the Court and the jury why one Margaret Wilbur needed your assistance in locating your law partner, Frank Gillespie, early on the aforementioned morning?" Frank continued his mock interrogation as he got up to quietly push his office door shut.

David cleared his throat nervously. He didn't like where this line of questioning was heading, but at least his colleague's vigorous assault suggested maybe Frank still had the balls to manage this crucial litigation.

"Frank, you yourself told me when we spoke this morning you had been trying to reach Margaret but had been unable to. You called me at home, about 6:45, as I recall. I was still in bed. You asked if I wanted to go see whatever you and Muckler had put together and whether I wanted to go down to court with you."

"But tell me something about Maggie Wilbur, David. I suppose you're going to tell me she just happened to remotely check her voice mail at 6:30 on a summer Monday morning, and found a message to call yours truly."

Frank plowed on, following the time-honored litigator's rule of never asking a question you don't know the answer to.

"Sounds good to me. Yeah, that's possible."

"And what would you say, Mr. Garvey, if I told you the only message on her machine from anyone in this office was almost entirely unintelligible and offered to play it for you?"

Frank reached into his coat pocket and produced a tiny disc.

"I'd probably say let's stop playing games and get on with what needs to be done before Friday morning and, along the way, I'll tell you whatever you need to know about the case and any related circumstances that bear on how you manage it. Now, what is SOOOO STYOOOOPID about trying to reach some accommodation with NeuBank?"

David could see Frank was caught off balance by the inner turmoil of his own conflicted feelings, maybe even thinking about the receivables he'd diverted for his own use. David had always suspected it made Frank really mad that David used the firm to do legal work for his outside ventures. Maybe it didn't matter to him that David's companies paid regular rates and promptly.

Perhaps Frank resented the fact he had little else in his life except the office and its seemingly endless supply of litigation. Frank probably envied the fact that David got to travel to exciting places on short notice and often seemed to have interesting people in tow around the office. Frank, on the other hand, usually went to court in New York or took long and often boring depositions. His most interesting trip during the past calendar year had been to Birmingham, Alabama—hardly anyone's favorite travel destination.

Or maybe Frank was jealous of the increasing volume of business David attracted and his clout around the office. On the other hand, maybe Frank was reluctant to goad David on an issue their partners might think was silly—Margaret Wilbur, for one. David could tell Frank thought there was probably something going on between David and Maggie. But Maggie was so different from the sort of women Frank occasionally pursued that he probably couldn't imagine David wanting anything to do with a high-powered woman like Maggie Wilbur. David hoped those competing considerations would introduce gridlock into Frank's thought processes on the subject.

Frank looked over at David, who appeared to be adjusting Frank's pink balloon curtains.

"It doesn't advance the ball one bit to sue NeuBank first thing on Monday morning, alleging all sorts of evil and vicious deeds, and then call over the next day and ask permission to kiss and make up," Frank observed. "Most people, particularly non-Americans, take getting dragged into court very personally. They react to being described in nasty terms in a very negative fashion. I raised the question of settlement at the conference by pointing out NeuBank should be willing to leave your customers alone without putting you to the trouble and expense of getting an injunction. That bitch Maggie Wilbur dismissed that concept out of hand. She made some catty comment about how her client thinks the Fund is trying to welch on its obligations. Maggie gave every indication of wanting to play hard ball on this one—said she could only make a deal if that involved the Fund complying with all of its duties under the Credit Agreement. How very German!"

"Well, it seemed like a good idea to me," David replied. "I would really rather get on with the Fund's business. That's difficult enough without all this added pressure."

"You really sound like a regular client. First you come in here all full of piss and vinegar and want us to go out and rip off the bad guy's head. Then, when it starts to look even a little bit difficult, you want to back off and pretend it never happened. Really, David, you've been practicing law long enough to know better. Besides, calling over to NeuBank smells like weakness. If you're right about the Iraqis having a stranglehold on NeuBank, that's another reason to avoid the impression of being too willing to be reasonable. You know more about the international stuff than me, but everything I read suggests the Iraqis only respect someone who can beat their brains out."

"Probably right. What about witnesses for the hearing on Friday?"

Before Frank could answer, there was a light tap at the door just before it opened a crack. Olivia Ojeda stuck her head in.

"I thought you might be in here, Mr. Garvey," she said. "You have a bunch of messages, and I'm going home. Perry's on the night desk this evening. I'll tell him you're in here, 'case something urgent comes up. See ya."

David stuffed the sheaf of flimsy telephone messages into his starched shirt pocket.

Frank continued his analysis of the case. "Whatever attention we get from Judge Fischbein's Friday morning is the most we're likely to get for the rest of the litigation. If we don't convince him of the merits of our case on Friday, we may never have a better opportunity. We have to play Friday as if it's the whole ball of wax!"

"What's that mean as a practical matter?" David asked. "Can we get some discovery?"

"What do you really need to find out at this point that you don't already know? We've gotta have a credible witness to tell our story convincingly and some carefully crafted arguments that anticipate and neutralize each of NeuBank's defenses and objections. In a nutshell, we have to present our case in a way that Fischbein will be convinced. Plus, we have to anticipate Maggie's arguments in our papers before we've seen her briefs. No pun intended."

"Well, let's get started," David suggested. "I can testify about the structure of the deal with NeuBank as well as the problem we are having with them right now."

David could see Frank was feeling better.

"Have you thought about our firm's being disqualified from representing the Fund in this case?" Frank asked.

"No. Why would I want to do that? What does that have to do with whether or not I testify at the hearing?"

"You might not wonnnt to do that, but the law in this Circuit is, if an attorney becomes a fact witness at trial, his firm cannot represent one of the parties. Calling you as a witness could put us out of action. That could delay the process because the Fund might have to hire replacement counsel. Besides, it seems like generally a lousy idea for you to testify."

"Why's that?" David asked. "I can probably tell the story better, and I know enough of the law to avoid some of the traps."

"Do you really want to get too deeply embroiled in the daily routine of the hearings, not to mention the discovery process that is sure to follow unless this is settled quickly?"

"Well, I suppose we could—"

"And, if you get on the witness stand, Maggie can ask you all sorts of questions about other parts of the transaction, background, whatever. At least for the Friday hearing, we must keep the discussion focused on the narrow issue of whether NeuBank is telling your Russian customers to renege on their payments. Why not have someone with pretty limited knowledge, say the specifics of the Credit Agreement and what's is going on in Eastern Europe? Is there anyone like that we could get here well before Friday so there would be plenty of time for preparation?"

What had started as a minor irritation in David's right eye now felt like a piece of steel wool under his contact lens. Add to that the tension of having the opposition trying to rub him out, worrying about how this might affect his boys, and the prospect of Margaret's cross-examining him on the witness stand and what do you get? A migraine. David knew his attention span, not to mention his patience, was growing exceedingly short.

"Could we use Agnieszczka Czarnocki?" David suggested.

"Which one is she?"

"Ani's about 5'5", almost platinum blonde hair, blue eyes, and a complexion the color of an eternal tan. She was here last month for our round of meetings of the Fund's management. I seem to remember you drooling a time or two."

"That's funny. I surely noticed her—very attractive. But I thought she must be Swedish or Finnish. You sure she's Polish?"

"I'm certain, Frank. Don't forget, the Swedes occupied part of Poland when they were in their expansive and warlike mode. Many Poles look Nordic, but with just a touch of slightly darker skin. Some people find that captivating."

"How's her English, and does she own a brown suit?"

"Look, Frank, I'm bushed and have a splitting headache, I don't need the jokes. Let's just get done so we can all go home," David complained.

"No jokes, Counselor. Someone that delicious must be properly packaged to be persuasive with a judge, particularly an old letch like Fischbein, and with a jury later—God forbid we get that far in the process. If we don't do that, Judge Fischbein will have one thought: bed. And after that he won't really hear anything she has to say. A nice warm brown suit, conservative white silk blouse buttoned at the neck and some horn-rimmed glasses, even if the lenses have no prescription. That should do it. But how good is her English?"

"Pretty good, but then I understand some Polish and speak Russian, so I'm used to listening hard to what people say, particularly when they're speaking another tongue. You'll probably tell me Judge Fischbein and a New York jury cannot be counted on to listen carefully to someone who doesn't speak English easily."

"Not sure, probably luck of the draw," Frank noted. "Most people do tune out when it's difficult to understand the speaker or at least take them less seriously than someone who speaks fluent English. Judge Fischbein mentioned at the conference he spent some time doing undercover work with the OSS in Czechoslovakia, so maybe he's interested in foreign languages or maybe has some languages under his belt. But that was a long time ago! I'll have someone try to check that part of his background in the morning. On the other hand, if we get a courtroom where the witness stand is on his right, that could be trouble. That's his deaf ear. He's too vain to use a hearing aid, so he pretends nothing is wrong."

David leaned forward out of the wing chair and stood up to leave, rubbing his left temple slowly with the first three fingers of his left hand.

"Unless you need something else from me right now, I'll stop by my office to try to call Ani at home on the way out. Maybe she can grab a morning flight to Kennedy. If she needs different clothes, we can take care of that Wednesday morning or Thursday. Presumably you'll need a fair amount of time to prep her for Friday morning. She'll also need some time to get over jet lag to be fresh in court. See you in the morning."

With that, David Garvey stumbled across Frank's cobalt blue Persian carpet and out into the hall, looking as if all of the world's cares were perched on his shoulders.

Frank Gillespie didn't get up from the sofa. He pondered the swirl of issues the two old friends had tussled over, trying as best he could to isolate what they had resolved and what had been skipped over.

Frank wondered if he had accomplished anything. He'd gotten the witness business taken care of and probably kept David from causing more problems by calling Diether Kreuz. He and Aaron Muckler could get the papers out, so there was no need for David to be involved in that part of the process but he still wasn't sure what was going on with Maggie Wilbur. For the time being, though, he'd better leave that one alone.

It was probably just as well Frank couldn't read the thoughts tumbling through his senior partner's mind as David moved slowly down the darkened, book-lined corridors and up a circular staircase to his corner office on the next floor. David was now somewhat more comfortable about Frank's ability to handle the Friday hearing. While he now understood why it would be a bad idea to regularly intrude into the day-to-day machinations of the case, he couldn't afford to just let Frank run alone with this one. There were simply too many important business risks to the Fund outside the scope of Frank's technical expertise. Yet David couldn't escape the feeling Frank might not be sufficiently aggressive whenever crunch time appeared around the corner, when least expected. Like most people, Frank probably wanted to be treated as the boss, king of the mountain, but he could be distracted by side issues—witness the Wilbur quiz. While that whole set of questions might remain quietly submerged beneath the waves, David hoped against hope that they wouldn't porpoise at the wrong time.

David was well aware it would be counterproductive to discourage Frank's independence and critical analysis, much less challenge his partner's fragile self-confidence. On the other hand, he couldn't let the reins escape competent hands entirely and flop in the dust and gravel under this careening buckboard. There was simply too much at stake for David to abdicate even a small part of the most basic decisions in the fight for his financial life.

The beleaguered lawyer slowly limped into his own office, casting a dirty look out of the corner of his eye at the blind sensor in the light switch nearest the polished mahogany door. This device had been installed by the landlord in every office to turn on the overhead lights whenever a warm body entered the room and extinguish them when the room was empty, supposedly to save electricity. In an occasional more cynical moment, David wondered whether the lights came on when the cleaning crews made their rounds.

As soon as his firm moved in, he had disabled this particular annoyance himself, because he despised glaring overhead lights and the overhead lights often went out anyway if he sat quietly at his desk. A bright glow from Rockefeller Center's outside lighting across Fifth Avenue filled David's office. He swept a finger through the floating holographic speaker button on his communications console and touched the holographic image glowing "Czarnocki-Home." After a series of thirteen melodic electronic beeps, David found himself listening to the emptiness of the phone system's international circuitry, not unlike a passive sonar sweep from a submarine into the deepest part of the ocean.

Seven hours toward the new day, a ringing telephone roused Agnieszczka Czarnocki from the fitful torpor that usually followed too much wodka. She tensed noticeably. The irritating ringing continued, but Agnieszka did not move from her bed. She just cracked open one bloodshot eye to sneak a look at the clock.

"Even chickens are still sleeping," she muttered to herself.

Finally a click of her answering machine silenced the noisy phone. ". . . message after beep. BEEEEEEEP!"

"Krasavyitsa, this is David. Please pick up if you're there. We have an emergency! I need you to come to New York this—"

"You know I don't mind when you wake me up in person, David," Ani grinned sleepily into the phone as she reached over the slumbering body beside her. "Not fully light here yet. What's happening in Big Apple?"

Ani listened as the lawyer gave her a brief and sanitized version of recent events in New York. Then David asked her to get someone to fly her to Warsaw and to grab the next LOT or American flight to Kennedy or Newark.

"Please call my office before you get on the plane to let us know the flight arrangements. We can have someone pick you up at the airport and take you to your hotel. We're using a different hotel as the result of some recent difficulties. I'd rather not talk about that over the phone. I need some time with you this evening so we can talk with Frank Gillespie about what you need to do on Friday, but we can set that up after you arrive. Watch out for him, Ani, he has a worldwide reputation for fondling beautiful women under the table."

"Why you don't sit between us? Then I can handle you under table! Call you from airport in Warshava!"

Ani returned her turquoise telephone to its resting place on the nightstand next to a pair of empty tumblers and an empty bottle of Vyborowka wodka and peered absently through lace curtains and across the rainy street.

"This is important, Waldemar," she said, reaching under the sheet to focus his attention. "It shows David Garvey has at last begun to trust me and I will be in middle of whatever is going on in New York."

"You will miss me while I'm gone?" she giggled as the tips of her manicured fingers lightly traveled the inside of both his thighs until she found the source of his warmth.

A hairy arm connected to the lump under the nearby mound of satin sheets roughly grabbed her hand and dumped it on the chenille bedspread.

"I'm still drunk, and we just did that. Even if you don't want more sleep, I do. Good night!"

Ani withdrew with a resigned sigh. She was too excited to sleep any longer and began thumbing through her little black book to find the number of the helicopter service in Kaunas that might get her to Warsaw quickly.

With the clank of her phone, David found himself again listening to the ocean's hollowness. He selected another outgoing line and touched speed dial number three on the Holo.

"Hello?"

"Can we get together tonight? Maybe my place for a simple dinner?" David asked.

"Kimberly is with her father for the night, but I have this huge stack of court papers to plow through before morning. This is going to be a lot more difficult than I had imagined. Is it a good idea for us to be together any time soon?"

"This could go on for a very long time. I don't like the idea of not seeing you just because of big projects at work," David answered. "Besides, the pressure is squeezing me twelve different ways. I really want to see you. I promise to be good, at least for a while."

"You always promise to be good, but we always seem to end up in the same place."

"But isn't it a pretty nice place?"

"I'll be over in about two hours. Just remember, I'm more than a little cranky. We really must talk about how to handle this one. But first, let me get some of this work out of the way."

David passed a finger through the "Off" holographic image floating above his communications console, disconnecting the call. He opened the nearby closet door, took out a polished maple hangar, and began to remove his dark blue pinstriped suit, dress shirt, club tie, and shiny black wingtips. From a vinyl shoulder bag emblazoned with the vibrant green and yellow of "Nathan's Famous," David retrieved a pair of dark gray Gore-Tex pants, a hooded pullover, and dilapidated Reebok running shoes. His carefully selected and tailored office uniform quickly migrated into the closet, replaced by decidedly nondescript jogger's garb, plus a belt with cash, keys and identification in a compact fanny pack.

Just in case this turned out to be a bad idea, David slipped his Glock 19 into the lightweight holster positioned between his shoulder blades within easy reach of his left hand. As he began stretching on the carpet beside his antique, mahogany Portuguese partners' desk, David telephoned his home computer from the Holo and instructed the electronic household manager to ready the lava rocks in his electric sauna. Before slipping out into the internal stairs to the street, David popped open a panel in the back of a double drawer of his desk. Without looking inside, his fingers quickly found a pair of night-vision lenses. David plucked the black rubber goggles from their hiding place, doubled their strap, and lodged them high on his right arm, just below the shoulder.

He stole silently out of his office but then stopped for a moment to gaze out over the city that never sleeps through a clear panel of floor-to-ceiling bulletproof glass.

David Garvey was very much in need of someone with whom to share his desperation—someone with no axe to grind. Everyone around him seemed to have his or her own agenda, although perhaps that was simply the reality of life. But that invariably got in the way of really hearing what David needed to talk about. Not unlike meeting people at a cocktail party for the first time, asking about them, listening to a lengthy exposition on that subject and then having the new acquaintance excuse himself to get another drink without the slightest inquiry about David Garvey.

What would you say to me right now, Marja? You were always so good at listening and putting aside your own needs when we talked. I miss you all the time, David thought to himself. *We were so close and now I'm so completely alone, just when my world is coming apart at the seams. There's no one to trust in the same way I trusted you! Ani made a decent effort at picking up where you left off but she doesn't really connect with me anymore or with what I'm trying to do. It's just too complicated for her.*

Remember you said you didn't mind if I slept with her as long as I didn't love her? Well, not to worry! Ani and I don't speak the same language on several different levels. What Margaret and I have is growing slowly. She's so bright and articulate. Sometimes it frightens me! What should I do, Marja? Somehow I've got to deal with this unbearable pressure. If only I could be with you again, just for a while.

The lights of the city that had become his home were blurring for David Garvey. He looked down the dim corridor, hoping no one on the night staff would happen by and see him like this. Like all of the people in his life, the firm's employees looked to him for strength and leadership. They wouldn't understand any sign of weakness.

He turned away from the city's glowing nighttime face and disappeared through a green door crowned with glowing crimson letters: FIRE EXIT.

SWORDS GENTLY CROSSED

Twinkling lights of the Triborough Bridge taunted David Garvey. Despite a challenging run through Upper Manhattan's darkened streets, including nearly becoming a hood ornament on a runaway gypsy cab and a slow roast in the moderate temperature sauna followed by an icy shower, he couldn't really relax. Even after a light dinner of General Tso's chicken and savory broccoli, stir-fried in his well-worn wok, and a pair of Tsingtao beers in frozen glass mugs, sleep continued to elude him.

Every tick of David's metal-geared Waterbury clock emphasized the fleeting nature of these quiet hours and seemed to roil the goblins squabbling inside his head. A lump of covers on his right rose and fell with regular breathing. Two pinned curls of chestnut hair facing him indicated she was turned toward the wall. Having tried the usual mind tricks for falling asleep with no success, David leaned over on his right elbow and whispered loudly into her naked ear, "Call your next witness, young lady! The court will not tolerate your continued inattention and delay!"

"Not funny, for two reasons. First, you promised to be good, so let me try to get some rest. Second, I get enough of that sort of grief in court. And that brings us back to how to handle this litigation." Margaret Wilbur turned toward him, her anxious ginger eyes almost charcoal in the faint light.

All of David Garvey's anxieties bubbled to the surface.

"That's three reasons," he said. "But I'm very worried about this case too, for some reasons you can't possibly understand. I suspect you're mainly concerned about the ethical problems and what your partners and your client might think if they found out about our relationship—quite common, you know. These issues come up whenever two people with close personal ties work on opposite sides of the same case, any time married litigators are involved in the same matter. Basically there are two concerns: conflict of interest and client confidences. Our situation is probably more common but less obvious, so it ordinarily attracts less attention. Also, I'm not directly involved in the details of the case while, at the same time, I'm the client. Quite a jumble, but I must tell you, these are theoretical and trivial—"

Margaret Coolidge Wilbur lunged to staunch the almost incoherent flow of David's rhetoric with the open palm of her right hand. Her aim was spoiled by near blindness from putting her contact lenses to bed for the night. David easily deflected her thrust over his head. Margaret's momentum carried her on top of him, nearly suffocating David with her ample breasts. She shrieked in frustration, trying, with only limited success, to pound on David's chest with her clenched fists.

"I just practice law," she screamed. "That's all I do. I can't just fly off to run some other business if things don't go well! You act like this is some child's game, like the normal ethical rules don't apply to us. You don't care about my responsibilities or how I feel!"

"Come here," he whispered softly, sitting up and putting an arm around her shoulder. "Tell me everything about how you feel."

Margaret started to sob, not daintily but with huge, wrenching wails. Tears began to roll down her cheeks as she lost control of her seething emotions.

"I'm being torn apart," she cried. "NeuBank deserves my undivided loyalty, but you're on the other side. How can I do a professional job without hurting you? I don't know what to do, and

I can't talk to anyone at my firm about it. Parts of it I can't even talk about with you."

"Would it help you to know I understand how you feel? I didn't know you very well when we were negotiating the Credit Agreement with Gunther Takimoto. What a sanctimonious asshole! Ever since the Fund started having problems with the esteemed Neu Ost Bank, I began to worry about the problem we're talking about right now. By then, I cared very much about you. I couldn't do anything about it by the time it slapped me in the face!"

He put his arm around her shoulder and drew her close. Her tears of frustration warmed his bare chest.

"But what are we supposed to dooooooo?"

"Unless we stop seeing each other for good, I'm not sure there's a clean or simple way to fix these problems right now," David conceded. "I couldn't bear to stop seeing you, not now or ever! Besides, there are some other entanglements I've deliberately concealed from you. Please forgive me."

"What do you mean?" A startled Margaret Wilbur looked at him through red-rimmed eyes, clearly taken aback, and loudly blew her nose into a paper tissue plucked from a flowery box at the base of a brass lamp on the nearby night table. She dabbed at her brimming eyes with another tissue that was rapidly becoming sodden.

"For starters, have you been keeping up with the local news since the end of last week?" David asked.

"Not really," she sniffed. "What's that have to do with the subject we're discussing?"

"I'm not sure it does. But let me fill you in anyway. You have to know. We're probably in this together! Last Saturday afternoon, a cab was blown up on Fifth Avenue, right in front of the Plaza. At the same time, a hand grenade killed several people in a city bus trying to get through the snarl of traffic that mess created. I was on my way to see Frank Gillespie about NeuBank's default notice and—"

"I still don't see what that has to do with us or the case," Margaret interrupted.

"Margaret, I was the only person in that cab," David revealed. "I barely got out alive!"

Margaret buried her face in his neck, sobbing more loudly than ever.

"Why didn't you tell me?"

David quietly caressed her curls, letting her warm tears run freely down his chest. He felt a lump in his own throat. Except for Frank and Cecily Chow, David hadn't told anyone yet about this latest attempt on his life. He'd even concealed the two prior attacks in Finland from all of his friends and business colleagues in New York. In part, David felt personally responsible for this leapfrogging violence, for getting involved with Eastern Europe and for attracting the now malevolent interest of the Iraqis. It was almost as if his creative plans to start the Fund had indirectly killed all those innocent people on the bus. Now, as the terror accelerated, David felt very much alone. He had nowhere to turn. Iraqi hit squads in the lake country of Finland were one thing, but now this wave of selective brutality was spreading, lapping on the home shores and threatening his loved ones. Everyone around David might be at risk.

"Your heart is beating very fast, and you're shaking, David. Can't you tell me more and let me inside?" Margaret asked.

"I'll tell you just enough to give you the flavor of the mess I'm in and what's probably spilling over onto those around me. Too many details would only add to the problem we were discussing and might be dangerous for you. There's no reason to discuss the specifics of our dealings with NeuBank that led to our application for a preliminary injunction. That would really compromise us both."

He looked around the bedroom, as if half expecting someone to be watching them.

"Just tell me whatever you can." Margaret tried to coax some vital information from him, softly tracing the line of his clenched jaw.

David took a deep breath and let it out slowly. This was so very difficult for him, but he had to do it. Margaret was in mortal danger, either from the unreasoning hand of an unknown killer or because she might be too close to David at the wrong time and get caught in the cross fire. He shuddered to think of what these people might do to her or his two boys. Choosing his words carefully, David tried to describe all the frightening things that had happened to him since construction of the outpost at Königsberg had been completed, in a way that hopefully this woman he cared so much about could accept and understand.

"It was early September," he said almost inaudibly, with a faraway look in his eyes. "The late summer frosts were already painting the rustling birches of the lake country around Savonlinna with yellow, then crimson. The Fund's offices in Königsberg were up and ready to run. Marja and I were—"

"Who is Marja? You've never mentioned her before." Margaret was no longer looking directly at David, her gaze seemingly trapped by the pattern of quilt over their legs. The proud woman choked back a sob.

"Is Savonlinna in Finland?" she then asked.

Margaret's unmanicured index finger worried the seam of a plaid panel of the colorful quilt.

David nodded, his own eyes filling with tears.

"Marja and I built the Fund's offices together. The intensity of that project made us very close. You have some idea of the difficult times I've been through. Her story was even worse. I couldn't imagine it would ever possible for me to really care about anyone again after my divorce, but I did. I cared for her in a way that didn't seem possible and then—"

David's words trailed off, as he found himself unable to continue. His anguish was burning brightly. Margaret's attention was riveted on the same seam between plaid and deep purple panels of the quilt next to her naked thigh. David gently raised Margaret's chin with the tip of his left index finger so he could look directly into her eyes.

"If you really care for me, you probably don't want to hear this, but it will always be a part of me. The lake country of Finland is an indispensable ingredient of what is happening to us right now. That was another time and place. It doesn't diminish how I feel about you in the slightest."

She looked back down at the quilt.

"Keep going. Right now, everything you say makes me feel like just another part of your collection, but I'll try to put aside my personal feelings for a while—"

"Early one morning at least two heavily armed visitors came calling," David jumped in as he continued Marja's epitaph. "There may have been more. Maybe a helicopter let them off in a small clearing up the hill from our cabin in the forest. I'm certain they were after me. Instead, they killed Marja, probably by mistake. They came through the skylight. She didn't have a chance! I was dozing by the fireplace downstairs. One of the gunmen died jumping into the bedroom. I got the other one; killed her myself. Both Iraqis. Their fingerprints had been surgically removed, and they had no identifiable dental work. Marja died in my arms. Part of me died there too. I must have been responsible for her death."

Every vivid second of the last moments of Marja's life had flashed across the screen of David's mind thousands of times, but until now he had never before shared this private hell with anyone. Suddenly spent, David slumped onto the mound of down pillows.

"How can you bear the weight of feeling responsible for someone's life?" David asked.

Margaret gently pulled a silky sheet over David's naked torso.

"Do you think the bombing on Fifth Avenue and the attack in Finland were part of the same plot?" she asked.

"I can't be sure," David said. "Another piece of puzzle is probably the fellow who tried to kill me at Vantaa airport right after Marja was murdered. I can't imagine these three separate incidents are all just coincidences. They must be somehow related to the Fund! But I'm certain Marja wouldn't have died absent her relationship with me."

"Aren't you being too hard on yourself?"

"Please, please." David begged. "Explain to me how she could possibly have bled to death from multiple bullet wounds in our bed if I hadn't come into her life. I killed her! I can't change that. I'd give anything to make my peace with it and say good-bye to her, but I relive her death in my arms every day. It haunts my sleep!"

"Maybe her time had come."

Margaret was already off balance. She had accepted David's dinner invitation to vent her frustration at being caught between her ethical responsibilities as advocate for NeuBank and her growing affection for him. Even though she professed to being horrified at the prospect of her partners' discovering her relationship with David, in fact no one at her law firm would have even the faintest interest in this esoteric point so long as she got all the work done and kept her billable hours unreasonably high. Most of her law partners couldn't imagine her having any life outside the office, much less a torrid and clandestine love affair with someone as handsome as David Garvey. Margaret was simply uneasy because her own rigid ethical code, nurtured by membership on Law Review and a clerkship on the Eleventh Circuit Court of Appeals, couldn't cope with these multiple ambiguities. Margaret desperately needed someone to tell her she was doing the right thing. She was appalled to learn that her worries paled beside the very real physical danger facing David, his family, and perhaps even her and her daughter. At least no one had tried to kill her yet, but that was scant comfort when David was in such grave jeopardy.

David plumped another goose down pillow behind his head and gently drew her close to him.

"You know, that's just exactly what Marja said as she was slipping away from me. I would give anything to truly believe it was her time and that I wasn't responsible for her slaughter."

Margaret lightly traced a figure eight on the back of David's right hand, over and over again.

"I'm not sure how I'm the one to grant you solace. Everything you've told me is so completely foreign to me. Many other places and times. I know it's entirely unreasonable of me, but I wish you had always been just for me, that there had never been anyone for you but me. It makes me very sad to feel your pain but I wonder whether you could ever care for me the same way you must have cared for her. Silly, but I can't even bring myself to say her name."

"Our cabin in the forest seems at once only a brief moment ago and several lifetimes away. My rational side knows she's gone but my heart can't accept it. If I could only let go of the way she looked into my eyes at the end, that would be an important step in the right direction. What worries me most right now is the Iraqi nets seem to be casting in ever-widening circles. Until the attack on Fifth Avenue last weekend, somehow I felt safe in New York. Of course, there are always the ordinary random violence problems that go with living in Manhattan but not trained assassins from the Middle East!"

"How can I help? Just tell me, and I'll do the best I can, even if I hate even the idea of sharing you," Margaret offered.

"For starters, please let me arrange for an unobtrusive bodyguard for Kimberly."

"Why's that necessary? What does this have to do with my daughter?" The normally staid Margaret Wilbur looked around the cozy room frantically, caught up in the threatening web of violence David Garvey had only briefly described.

"The people you and I work with may not have made the connection between us, but lawyers are famous for missing such important subtleties. Did someone in the lobby downstairs open the outer door to let you in from the street? Who was running the elevator that brought you up here? Do you think either of them might remember you if questioned with large denomination bills to refresh his memory? What about the other times you have been here? Or my visits to your place?"

Something tore at their bed's dust ruffle. Margaret glanced nervously over her shoulder toward the carpet under David's bed. It was only his obnoxious Siamese cat! She was already caught up in the turmoil clinging to David.

"Hold me, David, I'm so very weary. I can't deal with so many things at once. Help me fall sleep in your arms," she sighed, burrowing into the hollow of his neck.

To avoid disturbing her, David pulled the covers up with his left foot until he could grasp a hem and then spread a sheet, thick blanket, and the quilt over both of their naked bodies, some measure of warmth against the heavy air conditioning. He gently massaged a knot in the muscles between her taut shoulders until the rate of her breathing slowed and its rhythm became more relaxed. While Margaret Coolidge Wilbur sought relief from her demons by escaping from the waking world, David watched the twinkling lights of the Triborough Bridge until they faded into dawn, examining each piece of his dilemma like an interesting pebble found on the beach—carefully inspecting one surface and considering its features then turning it over and imagining the possibilities suggested by the other side, to see what potential alternatives might come to mind.

ROUND ONE AND ONE-HALF

David Garvey never appeared in Federal court in Manhattan without feeling at least a little bit intimidated by the trappings of justice. The low-ceilinged but windowless courtroom was dominated by a shining Great Seal embedded in the wall directly above the judge's bench, set off by a large, freestanding American flag directly to its right. In front of David's seat, the high bench towered over the courtroom's rows of highly polished oaken seats. On the right side of the bench, a somewhat lower enclosure connected to the bench contained desks and computer terminals for the judge's three law clerks. The left side of the courtroom was occupied by a jury box filled with twelve upholstered swivel chairs and several computer terminals. The jury box was surrounded by a hip-height wooden composite wall that everyone knew contained transmitters intended to blank out all signals from cell phones and other personal electronic gadgets. Directly in front of the bench, two rows of tables for the lawyers, also with computer terminals, stood empty.

A bolt clanked loudly somewhere in the wall behind the high bench. A section of the back wall swung outward and William Pilkington in his uniform stepped in, closely followed by Judge Nathaniel Fischbein in his flowing black judicial robes. The hulking bailiff banged on the nearest side of the bench with a meaty palm.

"All rise! Hear, Ye! Hear, Ye! The United States District Court for the Southern District of New York is now in session. All persons having business before this Court draw near and ye shall be heard. God save this great nation and this Honorable Court, the Honorable Nathaniel Fischbein presiding."

David silently said a small prayer and peered slowly to his left, down the file of his assembled cohorts, to see how they were reacting to this unfolding drama. Seated at David's left elbow, Frank Gillespie's lips moved slightly as he appeared to watch Judge Fischbein settling in his swivel chair and beckoning his clerks to hand him papers.

On his law partner's immediate left, Agniesczka Czarnocki looking almost scholarly in her brown tweed suit, dark-rimmed glasses, and blonde hair pulled back in a pert bun, winked slyly at David. Her darting pink tongue peeked wickedly through slightly parted ruby lips. David hoped she would take this process seriously.

Farther down the long, polished oak pew, Aaron Muckler's massive frame nearly hid Ambrose P. Jett, one of Garvey, Stahl's first-year associates. Jett nervously leafed through a stack of cases behind his neatly folded wheelchair, apparently oblivious to the arrival of the hearing's central character.

"What's the first case, William?" Judge Fischbein demanded testily.

"Konashta against The Sumo Federation of—"

"My name Konashita! You must pronounce my name properly!" an enormous Oriental man wearing a tent-like gray suit bellowed at no one in particular, shaking his topknot in frustration.

"Restrain yourself, Sir. This is not a circus! Sit down or I will have you removed from my court!" Judge Fischbein thundered. "William, what's the full caption of the case?"

"Konasky, AKA Jerry Matsuda, against The Sumo Federation of Japan. On the calendar is Defendant's motion to dismiss Complaint for failure to state a claim. Konasky just fire his lawyer so he appearing *pro se*."

Nathaniel Fischbein peered deeply into his cup of steaming English Breakfast tea, as if trying to perceive some wisdom in its murky depths. *Pro se* cases always troubled Judge Fischbein. People representing themselves in this kind of complicated litigation invariably created problems for the court as well as everyone else involved—a lose-lose situation! *Pro se*s didn't know most of the procedures—couldn't be expected to. Even with some experience, handling your own case mixes up advocate and client, so the lawyer side is hobbled by whatever personal animosity is really at stake. And a *pro se* plaintiff almost always becomes frustrated that victory is not easier. Not that Judge Fischbein was more of a stickler on procedure than other judges in the Southern District, but trying to make sure this fellow was not disadvantaged would make the case go much slower. Hopefully, the pending motion would do the trick.

Judge Fischbein motioned for Pilkington to come closer. He flipped through his electronic stack of court papers on the case before him. There was a copy of the Complaint, Defendant's Motion to Dismiss, and supporting Memorandum of Law and little else. Apparently nothing from Mr. Konashita in opposition to the Motion to Dismiss. The judge noted that Defendants were represented by Yamato & Goldberg, but he didn't remember seeing that firm before. He wondered if Yamato was related to that Japanese admiral, later the name of a battleship.

He leaned over to whisper in Pilkington's ear.

"Did we get any papers from the Plaintiff? Anything else you know about the case that might help me move it along?"

"No, Your Honor." Officer Pilkington shook his head slowly. "I mean, like, we didn't get nothing on the modem from this wrestler. I aks him why he here *pro se* when he aks me where he supposed to stand. He say he fire his attorney before the brief got finished. Maybe there be some argument about what the papers would say. Maybe Mr. Green absent. Who know? This dude seem more annoyed than most. He gave security downstairs a big bunch of trouble. Claimed asking those questions and looking in his things dissed him, so they searched him extra thorough. One of the other court officers follow Japanese wrestling; he say our Plaintiff very good and extremely strong. I can take care of myself on the block, but I sure wouldn't want to mix it up with this specimen!"

"Got any ideas?" the judge asked.

"Just follow what you was telling that new judge yesterday." Pilkington cupped his pudgy fist to direct his comments straight into the judge's good left ear.

"What's that? I have an abundance of advice for everyone, particularly recent arrivals. Probably talk too much."

"You told her you got one most important piece of advice from an old judge when you first put on the robes. He tell you never rule from the bench. Always send your decision in the mail."

"Good advice then; not always possible, but good advice now. Thank you!" The judge clapped him on the shoulder affectionately.

Judge Fischbein deliberately furrowed his brow and turned to the litigants before him. On his left, standing behind the table meant for the attorneys, the enormous Plaintiff, weighing in at no less than 380 pounds, glared directly into the Judge's eyes. Even from the height of Judge Fischbein's seat behind the bench, Konashita's head seemed almost level with his own. On the Court's right, cowering safely behind the far end of the same table, stood a slight Oriental man, most likely Japanese, wearing a dark linen suit, colorful four-in-hand tie and horn-rimmed spectacles.

The judge reached under the top surface of the work surface in front of him, retrieved a pair of gold-rimmed half lenses, and perched them precariously near the end of his nose.

"Defendant's motion to dismiss the case. Who's up for Defendant?"

"May it please the Court, I am Iwao Yamato, Yamato & Goldberg, counsel for Defendant The Sumo Federat—"

"No! No! This is my case, not more chance to keep me out!"

Yamato cringed under the verbal assault.

"Mr. Konashita, you must be quiet!" Judge Fischbein banged in cadence with a large oaken gavel on a circular wooden block poised on the bench in front of him.

"You will have your turn to speak. Just like your profession, we have procedures here. We are here to listen to Mr. Yamato's reasons for moving to dismiss your Complaint. He believes your claim is not allowed by the law and will hopefully explain that to us. When he has finished his SHORT presentation, you will have the opportunity to address the Court. Do you have any questions about this specific part of why we are here this morning?"

Fortunately the Garvey, Stahl group was sitting in the second row outside the well of the courtroom, where the judge, for the most part, could be understood without using the courtroom's installed headsets. Since David and his colleagues would be waiting in this particular courtroom until their case against NeuBank came up on Judge Fischbein's calendar, David couldn't help becoming just a little bit interested in the drama unfolding before him. This was not the usual duel of lawyers in conservative suits with briefcases crammed full of documents, arguing arcane points of law of little interest even to the business people involved. Here someone was fighting for something he believed in. But what's this little bit of Japan doing in court in New York City anyway? But even with this amusing little sideshow, the mounting peril to the Fund and his personal survival continued to gnaw away at David Garvey.

"I am very best sumo wrestler!" Jerry Matsuda, known as Konashita in his chosen profession, thumped his broad chest for emphasis. "I have followed Japanese custom and ceremony for many years, but they do not allow me a chance for the right contests. I do not fight the top sumo wrestlers. Because I am not native Japanese, I am second-class citi—"

"Mr. Konashita! You are not listening! Since this is Mr. Yamato's motion, he is permitted to present his arguments before you have a turn," Nathaniel Fischbein interrupted patiently.

Suddenly sensing an inspiration, the judge continued. "Have you been formally introduced to your adversary, Mr. Konashita?"

"No," the titan mumbled, fidgeting with his enormous pudgy fingers.

"Good! Mr. Konashita, may I present Dr. Iwao Yamato. Dr. Yamato is a distinguished member of the New York Bar. He is a member of a profession which is very much respected here in the United States." Judge Fischbein only slightly rolled his eyes. "Dr. Yamato, may I present Konashita, a most distinguished sumo wrestler."

The adversaries turned to face each other and bowed deeply, feet together and hands rigidly at the sides. Konashita bent somewhat lower in keeping with the hierarchies of his training and adopted country. Both turned to again to face the Court.

"Thank you, gentlemen," the judge beamed. "Could we please continue, Mr. Yamato?"

"Thank you, Your Honor, as I was about to say, it is Defendant's position that, first, Defendant was not properly served in this action. Second, Defendant is not subject to the jurisdiction of this court. And, third, even accepting as true everything Konashita alleges in his Complaint, the way my client deals with its wrestlers in Japan violates no American law and—"

"Counselor, are you telling the Court that an American's rights can be abused in Japan, perhaps through activities which might, if conducted in the United States, violate US civil rights statutes, without giving this Court jurisdiction to provide a remedy?" the judge asked.

"Well, Your Honor, as I was saying—"

"Just answer the question, Mr. Yamato," Judge Fischbein demanded. "I've read your papers!"

"What I meant, Your Honor, is that American civil rights laws are not supposed to protect people in Japan, even if they are American citizens."

"Does the Sumo Federation have an office in New York?" the judge inquired.

Attorney Yamato smartly returned the judge's easy lob.

"Your Honor, my client not only doesn't have an office in New York but it doesn't have an office anywhere in the fifty-two states of the Union."

Judge Fischbein cleared his throat.

"Tell me, then, how was your client served with the Complaint?"

"Mr. Kikuchi, the President of the Federation, was traveling from Tokyo to Geneva, Switzerland, on vacation. He landed at Kennedy Airport to change planes. He was served with the Complaint while having dinner with his family in the airport transit lounge. Maybe good service, but still no jurisdiction."

Mr. Yamato looked around the crowded courtroom and sat down.

Judge Fischbein looked down at the blank yellow pad beside his now cold cup of herbal tea—no help there. He balanced a new pencil on its eraser, slowly running his right thumb and index finger from the lead tip to where its top touched his bench. So far, the applicable law seemed pretty clear, but perhaps Konashita had something to add. This really might be easier if the wrestler were represented by counsel.

Nathaniel Fischbein's private thoughts were interrupted by loud shouting at the counsels' table. Konashita was towering over Mr. Yamato, waving a clenched fist like a small ham and yelling down at him.

"Why you didn't mention how badly they have treated me for many years? You forgot that?"

Konashita screamed, his jowly chins quivering with rage. "I am treated like dirt every day by the Federation, and you don't even mention that!"

Yamato scrambled to stuff all of the briefs, affidavits and other documents on the table in front of him into a worn satchel with tarnished metal buckles, all the while backing quickly away from

Konashita toward the courtroom's exit, ignoring sheets of paper trailing behind him on the floor.

Rap, rap, rap!

"Order, order in the court!" Judge Fischbein shouted, banging the gavel smartly on its pestle, his temper rising. "If you do not control yourself, Mr. Konashita, I will hold you in contempt for disobeying the instructions of the Court. Please approach the bench, Mr. Konashita!"

The gigantic pugilist brushed aside a chair blocking his path, lumbered around the end of the counsels' table and padded toward a scarlet-faced Judge Fischbein. Konashita stood before the bench, fists clenched defiantly at his ample waist.

"What you mean contempt?"

"If you do not behave properly, the Court will impose fines on you and, if you still do not act in accordance with the rules of this Court, you might be sent to jail!"

"Who's this Court?"

Judge Fischbein answered slowly and deliberately. "I am the United States District Judge hearing this case. In this case, I am the Court! I will not permit my courtroom to be disrupted in this fashion!"

"You gonna give me money and make them treat me same as Japanese people, Judge?"

Nathaniel Fischbein raised himself to his full 5' 6-1/4" and leaned over the bench to speak directly into the wrestler's nearly purple face.

"The Court will not be intimidated by your outrageous behavior. While the Court has yet to hear your arguments, the Court will not grant anyone, not even you, relief on the spot. It is incumbent on the Court—"

David was momentarily distracted as Ani leaned across Frank to ask if their case would be next. He looked further down the row to see Margaret tensely waiting for their motion to be called.

A dull, hollow thump drew David's attention toward the front of the courtroom. A pair of bent gold-rimmed glasses sailed through the suddenly silent courtroom into the empty jury box. Konashita's meaty hands held Judge Fischbein's bloody head firmly by both ears. He continued pounding the bench with the judge's head. Chunk, chunk, chunk!

William Pilkington leaped over the low railing to the judge's defense and was promptly thrown aside by a sharp backhand. Konashita continued pounding Nathaniel Fischbein's motionless torso. The judge's right arm hung limply over the front edge of the high bench. The polished oaken gavel slipped from Nathaniel Fischbein's failing grasp to the floor with a faint ping. Pilkington crawled slowly behind the bench. A loud klaxon erupted in the hall outside Judge Fischbein's court.

After what seemed like an eternity, three heavily armed guards in riot gear burst through the courtroom's closed doors. The only law clerk still standing ducked down behind her steel-lined desk. The squad's leader pushed through the swinging gate and stopped several paces in front of Konashita.

"Freeze! Hands on your head! Kneel on the floor!" the black-garbed lieutenant screamed, pointing her .45-automatic at Konashita's left knee. "If you so much as breathe, I'll make you a cripple! Get down on the floor!"

Over her shoulder, she barked at her second, a spindly Hispanic woman.

"Get emergency medical! The Judge is in bad shape!"

Konashita showed no sign of comprehension. He stared quietly into the growing pool of blood lapping at his sandaled feet.

"Spider 'em, Harvey!" she ordered, stepping out of the line of fire.

The third member of the team, a chunky officer with shaved head gleaming from under his ebony helmet, lifted a large blue plastic tube to his shoulder and pointed it at Konashita's nearest side. With a whoosh, the sergeant's weapon belched a mound of wriggling, finger-sized white cords. Once free of their confinement, the wriggling cords spun into a circular web, encasing Konashita in its glistening grasp. The wrestler struggled to free himself, lurched to turn toward his attackers and then crumpled to the floor with a deep thud that shook the entire courtroom.

As if on cue, two young orderlies and an older woman in green scrubs with a battered stethoscope swinging from her neck burst into the courtroom, pushing through the same gate as the security team had used to reach Judge Fischbein's side. William Pilkington steadied himself on a corner of the bench, tears streaming down his furrowed cheeks.

"Y'all don't move from your seats. We aks you not to move until we gets a stretcher for the judge. If you try to get out now, you'll only block the way."

David looked down the row of his colleagues, again at the drama unfolding in the well of the courtroom, and then back again at his team. Jett was retching quietly on the tires of his wheelchair. Aaron looked especially glum. Ani looked from side to side as if trying to figure out what was happening and whether she might be in any danger. Frank was simply ashen.

David stepped over Frank's legs to squeeze in between Ani and Aaron Muckler. "This is awful! I'm no medical expert, but it looks like the sumo wrestler just finished off Judge Fischbein," David exclaimed. "Please don't think me hard-hearted, but, while we are trapped here, be thinking about what we have to do to preserve our preliminary relief. Frank, you go ask Margaret if she'll let us keep the temporary restraining order in place until we can sort this out."

David watched as Frank picked his way carefully to the third row and made his way toward his adversary, climbing over the legs of other spectators where necessary, eyes averted from the medical team working feverishly on Judge Fischbein under the lip of the empty bench. Finally, he reached Margaret and bent to whisper in her ear. David Garvey watched his law partner ponder her curt response then straighten up. Frank looked back at David and shook his head.

JUSTICE DELAYED

"How do you suppose they'll invalidate the sumo wrestler's access card?" Aaron Muckler asked.

David Garvey scowled at the young attorney beside him.

"What the hell are you burbling about, Aaron?"

"Well, you know how the security access cards are scrambled automatically by the exit gates if you forget to turn them in? Their memory is also scrubbed by guards when you surrender them on the way out. Konashita probably isn't leaving the building either of those ways, and I just thought—"

Aaron's normally commanding voice trailed off into silence. He looked about the courtroom nervously, probably wondering what to do.

Just then, two heavily armed guards and the three medics rushed the shiny steel gurney bearing Judge Fischbein through the courtroom's double-hung doors like a battering ram, its chrome railings rattling noisily against the heavy oak panels on the way out. During the momentary hush that followed, the sound of hard rubber wheels squealing down the long marble corridor outside was punctuated only by the tock, tock, tock of the swinging double doors.

Suddenly the dam burst! 37 lawyers, five secretaries, nine paralegals, 14 clients and three spectators surged toward the courtroom's only door with all of their briefcases, documents, books and other paraphernalia. David raised his hands to stem the tide of his own colleagues' escape from the horrible scene.

"Wait a goddamn minute. What's the point of going anywhere? Time's running out. Getting out of here just to be somewhere else won't help. What's the quickest way to get the TRO extended, Frank?"

Looking around the tight circle of anxious, expectant faces, Frank blanched.

"I've never had this problem before," he mumbled. "Rule 63 says if the trial or hearing has started when the assigned judge is unable to continue, we get another judge. Has a trial or hearing has started for our purposes? Maybe we have to start again. Research is probably useless. There's no question Judge Fischbein is disabled, but I'm not sure whether what we're doing right now is a hearing, since our hearing never got started. On the other hand, we surely can't be expected to wait patiently while the TRO runs out. Aaron, why don't you ask one of Judge Fischbein's law clerks if they know the answer. If they don't, ask if you can use the phone to speak to the Clerk's office."

"Help me out, Frank!" David shouted in exasperation. He was scared to death his preliminary injunction would simply expire at four o'clock, the time originally set by Judge Fischbein. That would leave NeuBank free to keep right on interfering with the Fund's customer base, cutting his financial throat.

Frank Gillespie was hyperventilating. His face had turned almost scarlet. He shuffled frantically through all the papers in his open briefcase, looking for an answer—any help at all in this crisis. Then his gaze chanced upon Aaron Muckler. The young litigator was engaged in animated conversation with Judge Fischbein's only remaining law clerk, a short and very pregnant young woman in a brilliant red print smock. Aaron beckoned to his boss. As Frank rushed forward, Aaron stepped back from the clerk's armored desk and whispered in his ear.

"This woman's understandably distraught. She only wants to be somewhere else. Her horseback guess is that we should go talk to the Clerk but she figures we probably couldn't get to the second floor now anyway because the attack on her boss has probably disrupted the building's security system and locked the security doors between here and there. And her phones are dead."

Frank gestured in David Garvey's direction.

"What the hell do you suggest? Our senior partner is about to have a cow, and WE'VE got to come up with a solution!"

Aaron ventured, "the good news is I went to law school with her and her husband. Her name's Eloise Ramirez. She volunteered to use her pass key to let us out into the stairwell and back in at the second floor. Eloise has to go by the Clerk's office on the way home anyway to report that Judge Fischbein's calendar for today didn't get taken care of—sort of related to our problem."

"Now that's creative," Frank agreed. "What do we do with our entourage?"

Aaron suggested, "if we're lucky, someone in the Clerk's office will assign us a new judge. If we're not that fortunate, we get to go back to the office. Assuming the gods are smiling on us today, and I sure hope we have better luck than Judge Fischbein, we get another judge. If the gods are positively beaming, the replacement judge will be available sometime today. Should that happen, we ought to jump at the opportunity to present our case. The question would then be: would the new judge conduct the hearing we came here for or would she or he make us start again?"

"What does he mean by that?" David puzzled, looking at Frank.

"Aren't there two possibilities with a new judge?" Frank offered. He continued, "Case one: new judge looks at the Complaint and Application for Preliminary Relief, a copy of which I just happen to have in my briefcase, and decides, just to be on the safe side, to treat it as an Application for Temporary Restraining Order—back where we were on Monday with Judge Fischbein. Even there, the Court might expect notice to our worthy opponents, and that sullen bitch Maggie Wilbur would have hung us up by disappearing. Can you believe what she said when I asked if she would stipulate to continuing the TRO until this, eh, scheduling problem could be sorted out? She looked me straight in the eye, then put her nose in the air and said, and I quote: 'That is NOT my problem, I'm leaving as soon as they will let us out of here!'"

Frank added, "not necessarily, because we may be able to convince the new judge, in effect, to continue Judge Fischbein's temporary restraining order until another hearing on the preliminary injunction can be scheduled. In that event, the witness we brought along will be unnecessary."

"But what's case two?" David asked.

Aaron looked over his shoulder at Eloise Ramirez, who was crying and becoming increasingly agitated.

Frank tried to answer David's question, "the other alternative—unlikely in my worthy opinion—is the new judge would agree to have the preliminary injunction hearing today. That would only work if at least Maggie could be found and made to show up, something she and her client presumably have no interest at all in doing. I can't imagine any Federal judge would grant an injunction without a proper hearing, which is why case one is most likely. We only need the witness and perhaps Mr. Garvey if there is some kind of hearing. But let's get going, because we may lose our pass key! You decide who we should take along."

With that, Aaron Muckler stepped close to his friend's side and put a massive arm around her shoulders. He helped her slowly toward the rear door of the courtroom. Frank started to follow them, then remembered his senior partner and client was waiting for guidance, and obviously fuming. Frank turned on his heel and walked back toward the other Garvey, Stahl lawyers.

Frank announced, "she's going to let us into the Clerk's office on the second floor. I think we have some chance of getting a live judge this afternoon. God, I hate myself for saying that. If we can get another judge, we may be able to put Agnieszka on the stand. I know you want to be there too, David, just in case. We'll have to walk down the fire stairs. If you want to come, we need to go now. I'll talk to Jett. He'll have to hang on here until the elevators are back in service."

David pushed past Frank and hurried to follow Aaron and his friend. On the way out the courtroom's rear door, he looked back over his shoulder to see Jett setting up a portable Holo on the polished oaken pew beside his folded wheelchair. Frank was feverishly reassembling the sheaf of papers he had spilled on the floor in his haste to follow David toward the Clerk's office.

REARRANGING THE CHESS PIECES

"Smythe & Mahoney, good afternoon, may I help you?"

"Margaret Wilbur, please."

"Mizzz Wilbur's office, may I help you?"

"Margaret Wilbur, please."

"And who may I say is calling?" the cluster receptionist repeated concisely, eyeing nine other blinking lines nervously.

"This is Judge Garcia's chambers. Could I please speak to Margaret Wilbur?" The enthusiastic young law clerk reveled in his newfound importance.

Without looking up from her work, Maggie Wilbur passed a finger through the speaker button's floating holographic image. She listened to the playback of the caller's greeting. Puzzled, Margaret Wilbur retrieved the list of all her pending cases—no Garcia. Next, she retrieved the list of all New York and Federal judges sitting in New York—one Garcia, in Housing Court in the Bronx.

"This is Margaret Wilbur. May I help you?"

"Ms. Wilbur, this is Ernest Brothers. I'm one of Judge Milagros Garcia's law clerks. Judge Garcia has been assigned the case of _Königsberg Fund, Inc. v. Neu Ost Bank_, from Judge Fischbein's calendar, under Rule 63. Judge Garcia has set 3:00 P.M. today for hearing the preliminary injunction motion Judge Fischbein was to have heard this morning at 10:00. Judge Garcia regrets the short notice, but she asks that you be present at that time if your client wishes to present any evidence or witnesses in opposition to the motion."

Margaret Wilbur paused long enough to finish writing down what the clerk had just said.

"I'm sorry, but is Judge Garcia a new judge?"

"Judge Garcia was sworn in as a UNITED STATES DISTRICT JUDGE last Friday afternoon. Will you attend the hearing this afternoon?"

"My witnesses have already dispersed. Could we adjourn the hearing until Tuesday?"

Maggie chewed her lower lip during the brief silence that followed.

"Are your necessary witnesses still in the city?"

"Well, I'm not sure . . . . they may be . . . but the hearing is less than two hours away."

Ernest Brothers looked at his watch, glad he had discussed this possibility with the judge. "I'm sorry, but Judge Garcia wishes to complete the hearing this afternoon. As you may recall, the temporary restraining order in this case expires at 4:00 P.M. today. May I tell Judge Garcia your intentions?"

"You may tell Judge Garcia that I will be present at the hearing although I cannot speak for my witnesses!"

Passing a finger through the speaker disconnect button's holographic image floating above her console, Maggie passed the same finger over the floating image of the number of Gesine Walter's pager.

"Here is Fräulein Walter," the foreign trainee dialed the phone in Maggie's office almost instantly.

"Gesine, this is Margaret Wilbur. Looks like we have another judge in the NeuBank case. Hearing at 3:00 P.M. Bring your things down to my office so we can talk. On your way, get the librarian to give us anything he can find, immediately, about a brand new Federal judge in the Southern District, Milagros Garcia. We need background, comments, and whatever is available. In the meantime, I'll break the bad news to Herr Doktor Kreuz."

While Maggie Wilbur assembled her ammunition and sought instructions from her client, David Garvey and his troops caucused on the sidewalk outside the courthouse, having miraculously obtained a new judge who seemed prepared to act decisively.

"I'm so hungry I could eat the north end of a southbound skunk," the always tasteful Aaron Muckler groaned. "Can we go over the Chinatown to get something to eat?"

"What is skunk?" Ani asked.

"Sure, let's head in that direction. We don't have time to go anywhere else," David Garvey said, ignoring her question. "What do you know about this judge?"

David looked annoyed at the blank stares Aaron and Frank returned.

"While we've been standing around talking, I used my Holo to look up Judge Garcia," Ambrose Jett chimed in brightly. "I'll fill you in. We have no printer and the screen is almost impossible to read in this bright sunlight. Let's see. Stuyvesant High School right here in Manhattan. Yale College, chemistry degree, *summa cum laude*. Columbia Law School, Order of the Coif. US Attorney's Office. Racketeering prosecutions. Looks like a fair number of high visibility cases. Private practice doing criminal defense work in the litigation department of Dwayne & Fuelner. Recently nominated to the bench by President Cecilia Hernandez-Nakayama, on the suggestion of New York's senior Republican Senator, Beatrice Rendleman. No prior judicial posts. Found 'Qualified' by both the American Bar Association and the Association of the Bar of the City of New York. Nothing on Judge Garcia's judicial temperament or decisions. She was just sworn in."

"Thanks, Ambrose."

Looking around the group, David interrogated his team. "How does any of this change what we're after in the hearing this afternoon or how we go about getting it? Think it over and we'll talk about it during lunch."

The Garvey, Stahl lawyers straggled around the corner of the new courthouse toward Chatham Square. They were looking for a quick lunch between acts of the life and death struggle over the Fund's very existence.

The gaggle of lawyers presented a strange tableau. Aaron Muckler boldly trudged toward his favorite dim sum parlor on East Broadway, closely followed by the young black lawyer, Ambrose Jett, furiously cranking his wheelchair to keep up with his more senior litigation associate. Ani positioned herself on David's right. Frank tried to stay close to her, which worked well while the sidewalk was wide enough to accommodate three people walking abreast. As the group entered Chinatown itself, however, the cracked sidewalks became narrower and more cluttered, causing Frank to fall behind David and his statuesque young business colleague. After crossing the first intersection, Frank tried to remedy the situation by walking on David's left but soon lost ground once again when David stopped abruptly to let Ani step in front of him over several crates of snow peas blocking the sidewalk.

Aaron herded the flock of attorneys down a dark alley and into a dimly lit restaurant. As soon as everyone in the group had found seats around a single table in the back of "Exotic Taste of Wuhan," David Garvey impatiently interrupted the din of lunchtime conversation.

"Before you get caught up in what you want to eat for lunch, please give me a minute. We're really under the gun now. Our TRO expires at 4:00, but we don't see Judge Garcia until 3:00. Let's talk about how to get the new judge to see it our way in the short time we have. There may not be another chance!"

Frank mildly added, "as you probably know, David, Judge Garcia shouldn't let the TRO expire while we're making our arguments. If that looks like a risk, I'll remind her of that."

"I probably knew that. What I would really like here, Frank, is for you to make your argument while we're eating. Aaron, Ambrose, and I will pretend to be Margaret Wilbur and try to shoot you down. OK?"

The lawyers grew silent as the waiter approached their table.

SECOND DOWN

At precisely 2:50, David Garvey and his colleagues were standing rigidly behind identical sets of polished birch tables in front of the elevated bench of the Honorable Milagros Garcia. The judge leaned forward to confer with her bailiff about what may have been matters unrelated to their case.

Frank Gillespie considered the scene skeptically. Even Judge Garcia's tent-like black robes couldn't conceal her girth or the fact she was quite short. Her stringy auburn hair looked particularly unkept. Was there was any truth to the rumors Judge Garcia had been nominated for this important post because of her ethnicity, her difficult childhood, her being a diabetic, or the fact she allegedly played for the other team?

"I hope we didn't get another political correctness appointee to deal with this important case," Frank muttered.

Frank clicked into supplicant mode as Judge Garcia motioned to the two groups of attorneys standing behind counsel's table.

"Please be seated," Judge Garcia directed. "I'll take a brief opening statement from each party before hearing any evidence either side wishes to present. Would counsel for the Königsberg Fund take the first turn?"

Frank Gillespie stood up, glanced down at his fidgeting law partner seated on his immediate left and sneaked a look at his notes—the same outline he had prepared for the morning's aborted hearing. He took a deep breath, cleared his throat and launched the attack.

"Good afternoon, Your Honor, I'm Frank Gillespie of Garvey, Stahl, counsel to Königsberg Fund, Inc., the Plaintiff in this action. In very brief summary, our client is in the business of making loans in Eastern Europe. The Fund has a credit agreement with a group of banks. Defendant Neu Ost Bank is one of the lending banks under that credit agreement and also acts as agent for the entire group of banks. We previously obtained a temporary restraining order from Judge Fischbein to prevent NeuBank from telling the Fund's customers to stop making payments on their loans from the Fund."

Frank paused, looking up at Judge Garcia, and then continued. "We're here today to get a preliminary injunction for the same reasons. As illustrated by the cases in our brief, the test for granting a preliminary injunction is whether irreparable harm to the Fund would likely result without the granting of the injunction. We must also show a *prima facie* case. In this tortious interference with a contract case, our affidavits show, and our witness will verify, that NeuBank gained intimate knowledge of the Fund's lending arrangements with its customers during the structuring and negotiation of the credit agreement between NeuBank and the Fund. Our witness will testify that customers of the Fund in both Russia and Belarus informed her that representatives of NeuBank told them to stop making payments on their loans. It is beyond argument that a lender will suffer irreparable injury if its customers stop making loan payments—far beyond the obvious monetary injury. Thank you, Your Honor."

Milagros Garcia looked up from her video display of Garvey, Stahl's papers to consider the parties appearing in only her third hearing as a United States District Judge. Already the new judge had noticed an indicator of her separation from lawyers on the other side of the bar: she no longer had a first name.

Frank hadn't even finished his final sentence when a tense, plainly dressed woman leaped to her feet. Before she could begin speaking, a graying bespectacled man in a wrinkled dark brown suit seated beside her tugged at her sleeve and began whispering loudly in her ear. A flustered young woman on the German bank executive's right listened intently to his staccato instructions.

"Ve VILL haf an end to zis foolishness!" Herr Doktor Diether Kreuz demanded in a voice easily audible to others nearby. "Ve pay you much good money. Make zis nonsense stop! Der Peoples, er, State government vill not be meddled vith by zis Amerikan judge!" The angry branch manager's tirade at Margaret Wilbur continued unabated.

"I will do my best, Herr Kreuz."

Margaret Wilbur scowled deeply. *It's bad enough my illustrious partner, Gunther Takimoto, in his infinite wisdom, had negotiated an arrangement with David's company where NeuBank wouldn't get reimbursed for any of this,* she thought to herself. *More likely than not, that likely means my colleagues and I are probably working for free.*

Margaret had already advised this arrogant little functionary there was no meritorious defense to this particular part of the Fund's claim. But Herr Doktor Kreuz insisted on fighting to the last drop of blood—her blood—even though he would most likely refuse to pay anything outside of whatever David reimburses the Bank. Knowing David, Margaret realized that would be zero! The crowning touch was that Margaret had to pretend this worthless paralegal from the Bank's head office was really working on the case, when she could use some real help. She snapped a pencil in frustration.

"Please proceed, Counselor."

"Thank you, Your Honor," Maggie stammered, hoping the occasional slight catch in her jaw would not betray the almost overwhelming pressure she was feeling. "I am Margaret Wilbur. My firm, Smythe & Mahoney, represents Neu Ost Bank in this action. Quite simply, Your Honor, this is a blatant attempt by the Fund to avoid paying what it owes NeuBank and a number of other banks—substantial amounts of money. For the reasons set forth in our brief, this court should not interfere in NeuBank's operations in Eastern Europe. Even if the Fund's allegations were true, which they are not, this court has no jurisdiction over the activities of a government bank like NeuBank, in general, or this dispute over events supposedly taking place in Eastern Europe, in particular. The Fund should be required to bring any claim it has against NeuBank in the German courts. Thank you, Your Honor."

Judge Garcia finished reading Judge Fischbein's summary of the competing sovereign immunity arguments advanced by both litigants. She was not convinced NeuBank could isolate ordinary business activities such as commercial lending from the jurisdiction of American courts, particularly since the credit documents were negotiated in Manhattan and the loan activities were managed from New York.

Milagros Garcia's experience at the US Attorney's Office had not prepared her for this type of complicated commercial litigation.

"The Government may call its first witness!"

"Excuse me?"

Frank Gillespie looked confused, and worried his scraggly mustache vigorously.

"The Government may call its first witness," Judge Garcia repeated, enunciating each word carefully. Suddenly, her jaw dropped.

"I mean, Plaintiff may present its first witness."

"Thank you, Your Honor. Plaintiff calls Agniesczka Czarnocki."

Ani fingered the collar of her brown tweed suit and adjusted the unfamiliar horn-rimmed glasses. She stood up and meekly followed Gillespie's direction toward the enclosed witness stand on Judge Garcia's immediate right. The Fund's star witness settled herself in the witness chair and looked expectantly at the judge.

"Ms. Czarnocki, I'm going to ask you to take an oath to tell the truth. Do you know what that means?"

"Yes."

Ani tried her very best to concentrate her attention on the one rule Frank had told her to always follow, many, many times: "Just answer the question. No more, no less."

Judge Garcia raised her right hand and motioned for the witness to do the same.

"Do you swear to tell the whole truth and nothing but the truth, so help you God?"

"Yes."

"Your witness, Mr. Gillespie," Judge Garcia directed.

"Thank you, Your Honor," Frank responded. "Please tell us your full name and the address where you live."

"My name is Agniesczka Maria Czarnocki. I am now living at Borisova, 8, Königsberg, Russia."

"If you are employed, could you please tell us the name of your employer and your duties at that company?"

David Garvey sat alone at the table assigned to plaintiff's counsel. Aaron Muckler and Ambrose Jett were parked in the first row of spectators' seats, on Frank's theory counsel's table shouldn't be overloaded when plaintiff is trying to look helpless. So far, Frank had handled the hearing in an aggressive yet professional manner, making the essential points without trying to argue untenable positions. At the same time, Frank kept worrying his mustache, which made him appear extremely nervous. However, even recognizing a lawyer's willingness to believe his own bloviation, it seemed to David that Margaret didn't have much to work with. From where he was sitting, it looked like Herr Doktor Kreuz was about to jump out of his skin. David Garvey hoped the NeuBank executive would do something really stupid to jeopardize his case.

". . . and, Miss Czarnocki, when you were speaking with Misha Schteinberg that afternoon, what did he say the NeuBank field director had told him?"

"OBJECTION!"

Maggie Wilbur jumped to her feet, right arm flailing almost spastically.

"Hearsay, Your Honor, the witness cannot testify about what someone else has said. That other person is not here to be cross-examined."

Frank weighed in: "Your Honor, the witness is not being asked to testify as to the truth of what Mr. Schteinberg said, but only what he said. The witness will testify that Mr. Schteinberg was told by the NeuBank representative that he, Mr. Schteinberg, did not have to pay back his loan from the Fund. This sort of testimony is allowed under an exception to the hearsay evidence rule. I have a short memorandum of law on the subject, for the Court's consideration."

Frank handed a single page up to Judge Garcia and leaned over to pass a copy to Margaret Wilbur at the same time.

"Objection overruled," Judge Garcia opined. "You may continue, Mr. Gillespie."

Nicely done, David silently congratulated his partner. He wondered how Ani would fare under Margaret's cross-examination. David really didn't know what to expect from Margaret in the courtroom. He'd never see her at work before.

"Although I have no further questions for Miss Czarnocki at this time, Your Honor, I reserve the right to recall her to the stand," Frank said.

Gillespie turned toward his seat at the counsel's table, with a faint smirk on his face.

"Ms. Czarnocki, you will have to wait in case opposing counsel has questions for you," Judge Garcia cautioned Ani as the slim, young blonde bent down to retrieve her purse and stood up to leave the witness stand.

"Your witness, Ms. Wilbur."

"Thank you, Your Honor."

NeuBank's counsel crossed the courtroom toward the elevated chair where Ani was again sitting.

"Ms. Czarnocki, you have testified that you are in charge of loan marketing and administration for the Fund at the headquarters in Königsberg, is that correct?"

"Yes."

"Does your job require you to know the details of each loan made in your area by the Fund?"

"I do not understand question," Ani responded. Her shoulders relaxed slightly, perhaps proud of herself for remembering Frank's admonition about not guessing the meaning of questions.

Maggie paused momentarily, apparently to reconsider her approach to this crucial witness.

"Let me rephrase the question," she said. "You previously testified that three different customers of the Fund told you my client's representative encouraged them to withhold loan payments from the Fund. Is that correct?"

"I am sorry. What withhold mean?"

The Fund's local manager looked like she was beginning to enjoy this game ever so slightly.

"Did you testify in this courtroom that three of the Fund's customers told you that NeuBank's representative told them not to make their loan payments to the Fund?"

"That's correct."

"Can you tell me whether one of those customers, Mr. Schteinberg, has made all required loan payments?"

"Yes."

"Yes he has made all required loan payments?" Maggie asked.

"No, I was only answering question you asked. Yes, I can tell you whether Misha Schteinberg is making all required loan payments."

"Did he make all his loan payments? Did the other two customers you previously mentioned make all of their required loan payments?"

"Yes to both questions," Ani confirmed.

Maggie leaped at the chance to roll over Frank's witness.

"Can you tell the Court of one customer of the Fund that you are certain did not make a loan payment because of something a representative of NeuBank told him?"

"No."

Margaret Wilbur lunged at the scent of blood.

"Then how can you be certain NeuBank's field representative told the Fund's customers not to make payments?"

Ani tripped the trapdoor under Maggie Wilbur, using the lines she and Frank Gillespie had carefully rehearsed. "Because I am having right here a wideo of her admitting in front of witnesses she did that!"

Ani reached into the leather purse at her feet and picked out a small disc.

Judge Garcia reached over the edge of the bench, hand open and outstretched.

"May I see that? It looks like it fits our equipment. Surprise. It fits quite nicely."

Margaret Wilbur strode angrily toward Judge Garcia, clenched left fist jammed tightly against her waist, and shaking a sheaf of notes dribbling from her right hand. She suspected, with good reason, that she had been set up.

"Your Honor, I strenuously object to the introduction of that video."

"On what basis, Counselor?"

"Er, ah, the video is not competent evidence of anything," Maggie tried tentatively, her stress betrayed by a slight catch in the movement of her jaw.

"Have you seen it?" Judge Garcia asked. Hearing no response from NeuBank's counsel, the judge continued, "No? Well, I'll decide whether or not it is competent evidence."

The judge popped the video disc into the courtroom's display console.

Despite his considerable affection for Margaret Wilbur, David respected the way Frank had lured her into this ambush. He settled back in his straight chair beside Frank, as if the bailiff might actually come over and offer them some buttered popcorn just before the movie started.

A shadowy flicker and garbled voices drew David's attention to the computer screen bolted to the polished wooden table in front of him. His quick glance around the courtroom confirmed that everyone's eyes were glued to the fluttering video of a disheveled and visibly distraught Ulla Cerpinski. She was speaking into the video recorder in response to questions put to her by a harsh male voice outside the camera's range.

"What were your instructions about the Fund's customers?" the voice asked.

"I was first given a list of the Fund's customers and told to find as many as possible. And then tell them to stop paying their loans from the Fund," NeuBank's representative responded.

"Who gave you the list?"

"My supervisor at the Bank's head office in Schwerin . . . Herr Reichnagel, and—"

"Did you actually contact any of the Fund's customers in order to carry out your instructions?"

"Yes, but please, could I have something to drink?"

A hairy arm reached around from behind the camera to offer a cup of clear liquid to Ulla Cerpinski, who remained seated at a worn linoleum-covered table, alone in the camera's unblinking eye.

"How many did you tell to stop paying their loans?" the voice continued. "Just a few more questions. It won't be long now."

"More than fifty, probably less than one hundred . . ."

"Just one more question, if you please, Fräulein. Who ordered you to contact customers of the Fund and tell them not to pay their loans?"

Ulla Cerpinski tried in vain to shade her eyes, to look behind the operator of the video equipment, squinting into the glaring lights. She looked frantically from side to side, as if searching for help.

"Please, Fräulein Cerpinski! Answer this one final question," the disembodied voice directed.

"It was—"

"Speak up, Fräulein, I can't hear you!"

"It was Herr Doktor Diether Kreuz, the manager of our Bank's office in New York."

David dared a glance at Margaret Wilbur. Her face was ashen. A blank stare occupied her normally attentive features.

"Why isn't Ms. Cerpinski here to testify in person today?" Judge Garcia inquired, ejecting the disc from its slot in the console. "Mr. Gillespie, can you explain that?"

"Well, Your Honor, she's well beyond the 100 mile limit of this Court's subpoena power. We thought it futile to even try to get her here. Given she is under Defendant's control, we didn't think there was much chance of locating her, much less convincing her to come here voluntarily to testify. The Fund cannot be expected to go into court in Germany just for the purpose of getting live testimony from this witness."

"I'm going to grant the Fund's application for a preliminary injunction. Bond will be continued at the amount originally set by the late Judge Fischbein. Would counsel join me in the robing room to flesh out a discovery and trial schedule? Since I am only recently appointed to the bench, my calendar is still manageable, which would permit an accelerated schedule and perhaps . . ."

The Honorable Milagros Garcia disappeared into the adjoining conference room outside followed closely by Frank Gillespie, Aaron Muckler, Ambrose Jett, Gesine Walter and Margaret Wilbur.

From his chair, David reached over to pick up a few papers from the table and place them carefully in his open briefcase. Without looking up, David could sense someone standing very close beside him.

"You may consider zat you haf won a wictory here, but you MUST withdraw zis case!" Diether Kreuz spluttered, his face black with anger.

"Why would I want to do that?" David asked. "You didn't even put up much of a fight today!"

Herr Doktor Kreuz drew himself up to his full height, towering over David ominously.

"You do not understand ze danger of your situation. You vill surrender zis case because ze personal danger to you and your family vill become unbearable. DO YOU HEAR ME? You vill do anysing to give up zis case! You vill bek zem to stop!"

THE FUN HOUSE

Peter and Will Garvey, David's two sons, now twelve and nine, having both successfully navigated a year at The Buckley School, watched from seats near the back of the bus.

Cleary Wentworth yelled above the bedlam, "sit down, Miguel! Listen campahs! This is the first year we're takin' all you boys to the Bangor State Fair. Ya might think of it as a test. Anyone misbehavin' gets a week of kitchen dooty. Buddy system! Don't leave the caahnival grounds. Back heeah at the bus at nine thuhtee. Any questions?"

Wentworth's tongue worried the cud of smokeless tobacco tucked behind his lower lip as he looked warily up and down the rows of school bus seats, all overflowing with boys of different sizes, shapes and colors. Each young camper wore a forest green pullover sporting the camp's crest and a matching baseball cap, mostly turned backward.

The Camp Longbow bus rattled and rumbled slowly through dusty summer evening streets and lanes of Bangor, Maine, toward the Bangor State Fair on Dutton Street at the edge of this city on the banks of the Penobscot River. Leaving Camp Longbow in late afternoon for its 28-mile trip through St. Albans, Stetson and Levant, the green 1985 Chevrolet P30 School Bus, with traces of its original orange paint peeking through Wentworth's dark green paint job, rolled along back roads toward Bangor, its windows wide open to make up for its lack of air conditioning.

The lumbering vehicle's youthful occupants jumped and rolled over its tattered faux leather seat backs like so many kits of young foxes. Despite the rumpus, Wentworth instructed the bus's driver to wait for a few minutes in the parking lot of the St. Albans Walmart so he could chat with his sometime love interest, Temperance Miller, a stocky but surprisingly amorous cashier at that bargain emporium.

The Garvey boys sat quietly by themselves in the seventh row of the Camp Longbow bus, engaged in serious conversation, as if somehow immune from the general ruckus going on around them. Peter, a strapping blond, appeared to have his younger brother Will's full attention as he spoke directly into his downcast and worried face.

"You heard Dad say he was sending someone to pick us up, that we were leaving camp early!"

"But did he tell Mr. Wentworth?" Will wondered.

"Why would he tell that dork? We'd probably get in some kind of trouble for having 'speshul 'rangemints,'" Peter noted.

Will blurted out, "we can't just leave camp without telling anyone. What about our stuff? Are we supposed to just leave our clothes and sleeping bags? Who's gonna tell Mom? She'll be really worried if she calls to talk to us and Mrs. Wentworth can't find us."

"Dad didn't cover all of those details. He just made it very clear to me we have to leave camp quickly! Dad said he'd call tomorrow to make arrangements. He was just emphasizing the importance of our passwords when he had to take another call. Dad sounded pretty worried. I'd sure like to know what's going on!"

"Why do we have to leave camp right now?" Will wondered aloud. "I'm just about to get my waterskiing badge."

Peter turned to look across the crowded aisle, out the grimy window of the wheezing bus. The busload of campers was passing through a tree-lined residential neighborhood of well-kept older homes, one with a gas lantern mounted on a wrought iron pole near the sidewalk, its yellow glow casting a warm light over two children playing nearby. In one spacious, green backyard surrounded by a white picket fence, Peter could see a baby girl in a pink bathing suit splashing vigorously in an inflatable blue wading pool. A young woman in loose blouse, linen skirt and leather sandals—probably the baby girl's mother—was squirting fresh water into the pool with a green plastic hose. Off to one side, the little girl's father dozed in a hammock slung between two towering maple trees. The scene was so idyllic. Part of Peter longed for that kind of simple existence—a mother, a father and a backyard with grass and trees.

Living in New York City had never been anything like Harmony, Maine, or even Bangor, but so much had changed since his parents' nasty divorce. Oh, they were outwardly friendly enough, but now there were two homes. Only one really belonged to Peter and Will. With all of their father's business trips and the many demands of his new law firm, Peter and Will didn't spend as much time with him as they wanted.

I wonder, Peter thought to himself, *would Dad have to work so hard if he didn't have to pay Mom so much money from the divorce?*

Camp wasn't bad, but it was still a long way from New York City and even farther from the sort of traditional home and family Peter craved.

Will, a wiry kid, looked to be fretting over their situation. Will defined anxious. Nearly everything worried him, from his father's constant business travel in various parts of Europe and Asia on airplanes to his mother's new boyfriends. Now he was beside himself, trying to figure out what calamity would make his father need to take them out of camp before its regular season ended. Will didn't like camp very much anyway because it wasn't home. But now he was concerned about the problems involved in getting ready to go home, not to mention how they would get back to New York since their tickets were for nearly two weeks later.

Through the trees, Will caught a first glimpse of the twinkling white lights of a slowly whirling Ferris wheel. His worries were swept aside as he was caught up in the excitement of the other boys around him.

The dark green Camp Longbow bus leaned into the Bangor State Fair's swarming parking lot, punctuating its arrival with a loud and squeaky jounce caused by climbing a high concrete curb during the sharp right turn. That made the young campers inside yell even louder. The first rows of cheering boys tried to push by Cleary Wentworth as he stood with his back to the bus's front door like the last line of defense against chaos.

"Remembah what I told ya. Don't leave the caahnival grounds. Back heeah at the bus at nine thuhtee. You each get ten dollaahs for spendin' money—charged to your camp account, a'corse." He fished a wad of worn bills from the front pocket of his baggy khaki trousers, licked his index finger and began to slowly hand one to each outstretched hand leaving the dilapidated bus. He was happy to at last be able to relieve himself of the considerable quantity of tobacco juice generated since he had last leaned out a window, without spitting on the floor.

"OK to Beck's Lite, Mr. Wentworth?" Miguel Quinoñes asked with a snicker.

"Anybody caught drinkin' anythin' strongah than tonic gets a week of kitchen dooty and . . ." Cleary Wentworth's admonition was drowned out by the rising squeal of excited youngsters. "Rude, insolent, rich city kids," he observed to the bus driver, rubbing his now empty right hand through thinning gray hair as he wandered away from the bus.

As Cleary Wentworth stood back to escape the wave of excited children, the dam broke and a flood of screeching boys burst upon the Bangor State fairgrounds.

"Come on, Will. Let's get something to eat," Peter suggested. "I smell hamburgers!"

"Let's take our time," Will admonished. "We haven't had much grease for several weeks. Eat slowly. Sometimes cheeseburgers make you sick, you know! It's probably the same thing that gave you those horrible headaches from eating pizza."

Together, the two Garvey boys picked their way along the midway, past the freak show and a grizzled barker extolling the virtues of several bored "exotic" dancers toward a motley collection of mobile food stands and tents dispensing fried dough, cotton candy, pizza and other offerings of carnival food. Picking his way along the midway, Peter stopped at a counter run by the local American Legion Post and instead ordered two cheeseburgers with french fries—his father once told him their food was likely to be cleaner than from the stands lurching from town to town around the countryside with the carnival caravans. Will stepped over a pair of thick, black power cables to the beverage stand next door and came back with two cherry snow cones in blue plastic cups. Together, the two boys settled down to eat their dinner and figure out what games and rides to try first on the midway.

"Excuse me, you are Cleary Wentworth, executive manager of Camp Longbow?" a delicious young voice crooned into his ear.

"Why, why, yes, ma'am. I don't believe I've had the pleashah," Wentworth mumbled through his pizza as he struggled to extricate himself from the rickety wooden picnic bench. "And who might ya be?"

The statuesque young woman arranged an errant blonde lock behind her right ear with a scarlet manicured index finger and extended a tanned bare arm between Wentworth and his dripping slice of ham, onion, and pineapple pizza. The musk of this young lady's scent obliterated any passing thought of Temperance Miller's abundant thighs. Wentworth was hungry but for more than pizza.

"I am mother of Peter and Will Garvey. I will be taking them back to New York as arranged. My driver is waiting to take us to airport."

He stopped in midchew.

"Nice to meet ya, Mrs. Gaahvey but I'm not awaya of any 'rangements. Who did ya speak ta?"

"Oh, your mother, Louise, I am not long time ago speaking with her," she beamed, wickedly teasing her crimson upper lip with the tip of her sharp tongue.

"Gee, I'm not shuah, Mrs. Gaahvey. I wouldn't want ta do anything I wasn't supposed ta." Wentworth parried ineffectively, suddenly confused. "Maybe I bettah call my motha."

Agniesczka Czarnocki pointed over Wentworth's shoulder, nearly touching his bloodshot nose with her pleasantly scented arm.

"Isn't that a paying telephone there behind trucks? I have some money if you need it," she said, digging into the large bag slung over the delicious bare shoulder that was increasingly occupying the older man's attention.

Cleary Wentworth leered; he gulped down the rest of his lukewarm Budweiser and stuffed what was left of his pizza into his pants pocket. Then he ambled around a humming generator truck in the direction of two pay phones next to a dimly lit pair of restrooms barely visible behind an adjacent bingo tent. Wentworth turned back to get another look at Ani's bare, slender legs as he scooted sideways to slip between two heavy metal tent poles.

A muscular mahogany arm reaching through a tent flap covered Wentworth's mouth as another grabbed him firmly about the shoulders and jerked him inside the darkened tent. Ani looked up and down the midway to see if anyone had noticed her conversation with Cleary Wentworth.

Farther down the midway, Peter Garvey handed two gray tickets to a pale and dirty little man wearing a torn T-shirt and tattered Nike athletic shoes crouched near the gate to the Wellington's Spectacular fun house. The attendant reeked of cheap domestic vodka.

"You'll love this one, Will. It looks just like the one I went in last summer in the country while you were visiting Gramma in Memphis. Watch out for the shaking pipes in the floor! Stay close to me."

Will Garvey cast a jaundiced eye toward the noisy contraption. The two brothers tiptoed across a moving ramp, through a pulsing bank of strobe lights, and into the darkness beyond. Ani watched all of this from her vantage point behind the attendant's booth and quickly ducked under the barrier.

Will worried, "I don't like this, Peter. I'm scared! What if we fall? Who'll help us?"

"Not a problem," Peter said, trying to reassure his brother. "These things are really pretty tame. Just watch for the pipes like I told you. Right here, the wall turns into a pretty dark space. Hold my hand. Oops, I just tripped over something or someone. Who's there?"

The boys heard an anguished female voice in the dark: "Can you please help? I fell down and I can't get up. Please help me!"

"Will, give me a hand! Sounds like a woman needs help. Smells like a woman too!"

Trying to get his bearings, Peter dropped to his knees on the creaky plywood flooring. Will fumbled in the pocket of his jeans and brightly announced, "I've got a penlight!"

Peter and Will saw a very pretty blonde woman lying in a heap against a badly scraped green plywood panel, one ankle turned sharply behind her.

"I am hurting foot. You please can help me with getting outside? I think there is door ahead."

Peter peered back toward the entrance and then ahead into the darkness.

"How'd you know there's a door nearby?"

Ani silently gnashed her teeth, probably already wondering why she had gotten into this dangerous scheme, this deep. She could deal with passive children she was used to back in Poland. The Garvey boys seemed like tough city kids!

"You want to check and see if I am correct?"

"Come on, Will. Let's see if we can find that door!"

Peter took his younger brother by the hand. The two boys disappeared around the next corner, Will charging ahead with his penlight.

"You are just going to leave me here?" the woman called after them.

"Back in a minute . . . Look, Will, there really is a door. Push it open."

The panel's rusty hinges creaked shrilly as Will peeked outside.

"It leads down some rickety little steps into a patch of weeds and bottles behind the ride. Looks gross!"

"Come on," Peter said. "Let's go back and help her out."

Will left the small door ajar as they both returned to where Ani lay propped against the dirty wall. Peter motioned for Will to get under the young woman's left arm while he draped her right arm over his own sizeable shoulders. Together, they raised her to a standing position and guided their limping charge toward the stream of night air pouring through the open door. Soon all three were standing in semidarkness between two rows of trailers and parked flatbed trucks.

"Can I have your light?" she asked Will sweetly.

"Not to keep!"

She grabbed the light and shone the beam in Peter's face.

"You are Peter Garvey?"

Peter drew a shocked breath.

"Who are you? How do you know who I—" Peter clammed up as quickly as he had begun.

"I am Villa Martin. I am working for your father. He sent me to take you home."

"You have a strange accent. What's the password?" Will demanded.

"What you mean pass—"

"Run! Run, Peter!" Will screamed at the top of his lungs. "She's going to kidnap us!"

Peter vaulted easily over a low fence and ran toward the brightly lit rows of rides and stands, crawling with hordes of people. Ani frantically grabbed Will by the throat then tried to add a choke hold with her left arm. Will bit deeply into her tanned forearm, growling like an angry pit bull. Trying not to lose her grip, she swore loudly in

Polish and fumbled in the shoulder bag with her free hand, looking for something, anything, to bring this hellion under control. The angry young woman pulled an evil-looking pistol with a silencer from the satchel and roughly forced its sinister barrel into the near corner of Will's mouth. She yelled to Peter above the pulsating hum of a nearby generator truck.

"Stop! You don't come back, your brother is dying!"

"Run! Run! Get help! Call Dad!" Will cried, pushing the gun away from his face.

She whipped Will sharply across the forehead with the barrel of her pistol.

"SHUT UP! Your brother is out of range of fire but you are not! I am not here playing with games!"

As if to emphasize her determination, she jerked a pair of open handcuffs from her bag and clipped one tightly around Will's right wrist. Then Ani wrenched Will's right arm behind him and attached the other cuff to a belt loop at the left hip of his jeans. She relaxed her hold on Will's throat slightly and spread her legs in case he should try to kick her where it might hurt most. Ani was still breathing hard from the scuffle as she peered into the gathering darkness toward where Peter had disappeared from sight.

From his vantage point behind the rear wheels of a lighting truck, Peter could see she was still standing with her back to the fun house, long-barreled pistol poked into Will's cheek. At first, Peter tried to ignore the pungent odor of whatever he was lying in. Once he traced the flow of brown liquids back to a dun colored plastic booth nearby, Peter was sure his new jeans were ruined for good. But as much as Peter wanted very much to be somewhere else, he couldn't bring himself to abandon his brother. Will worried about almost everything! Peter knew Will must be very frightened right now.

Suddenly, Peter had a flash of brilliance! He crawled away from his hiding place under the truck and ran around to the corner of the next ride. Right in front of him was a pay phone! Fortunately, no one was using it. Peter plucked the handset from its cradle and feverishly punched the 11 numbers needed to call his father's private line at work using a credit card. After the tone, he carefully tapped in all 14 digits of David Garvey's AT&T calling card, reading them in order from the databank of his wrist watch.

"STRUUuum. STRUUuum."

"Come on, Dad, answer the phone!"

"STRUUuum. STRUUuum. CLICK! The person you have dialed is not available to take your call. If you would like to leave a message with that person's voice mail, please do so after the tone. If you are calling during business hours in New York and wish to speak with an operator, please dial O and stay on the line. BEEEEEEP!"

Peter look nervously in both directions. He could see several Longbow campers waiting in line to ride the Ferris whirling wheel with one of his least favorite junior counselors. Obese Adam Heine, known behind his back as the Fat Knish, hailed from Flatbush Avenue in Brooklyn. Heine had tried very hard all summer to strike up a friendship with Peter. If the Fat Knish spotted Peter talking on the telephone, he would probably come over and try to make conversation. Peter would never be able to get back to Will!

"Dad, this is Peter!" he blurted out. "We're at the Bangor State Fair, a day trip from camp. A thin blonde lady with a foreign accent tried to grab us. She caught Will and is holding him with a gun. First she told us you sent her to take us home. Now she's gonna kill him if I don't go back there! Help us, Dad!"

Peter quietly slipped the handset back into its place, ducked under the empty phone book rack and ran toward the fun house feeling very helpless. In the distance, he could hear crickets faintly chirping in the tall grass and the occasional churump of a bullfrog in a nearby pond. He spied the young woman leaning against a lattice of black steel framing as he rounded the corner, her left arm still tight around Will's throat. The dusk-colored weapon now rested against Will's neck.

Just a few moments ago, his brother had seemed distraught. Now Will just looked really mad. Peter was surprised this woman had not moved. How did she know he would come back? Peter stopped just outside the circle of light cast by the humming generator truck. He was still trying to formulate a plan. Peter hollered at the truck right in front of him, hoping to disguise the direction of his voice.

"Who are you? What do you want?"

By now, Ani knew there was little point to pretending she was someone else; the boys had seen her face.

"I work with your father," she said. "He sent me to get you. He couldn't come."

"Why do you need a gun, then? And why don't you know the password? Dad wouldn't send anyone we don't know to pick us up without the password. What's going on?"

"Come here, NOW!" Ani said firmly. "I am very tired of children's games!"

It had never occurred to her this would be so complicated. Knowing David Garvey and his strong personality should have given her some clues, but she hadn't paid attention to them. Besides, Czarnocki was accustomed to relatively docile European children.

"I will come over, but you have to let my brother go first."

"No talk, no negotiations! Come here right now! I am losing patience. If you do not come here right now, I am quickly shooting your brother in head! I have nothing here to lose!"

Peter was in no danger right now. If Peter gave up, he would be in great jeopardy. Maybe this lady was not serious. What if he was wrong? Even though his younger brother was often a pain in the neck, Peter was at least partly responsible for his safety. Perhaps together he and Will could figure something out. And they could count on Dad to help. Peter swallowed hard and stepped out of the shadows.

"I'll come over there if you promise not to hurt us."

"I am never wanting to hurt you. Just come over here! We must get to car. Put out your hand."

Peter extended his left hand as instructed.

Ani grabbed a second pair of handcuffs from her shoulder bag, clipped one over Peter's left wrist, and snapped the other through the locked cuff dangling from Will's left waist. She removed two curly blonde wigs from her satchel and pulled one roughly over each boy's head. Next Ani draped a large dark green plastic raincoat around the shoulders of both Garvey boys.

"I am taking you to far edge of parking lot. We will walk behind lorries and trailers. I am putting gun in bag. My hand will be staying on trigger. If you try to escape or talk to anyone, I will shoot little one first."

The trio shuffled clumsily off into the Maine darkness, a wobbly green bundle in front followed by a chic blonde with a stunning tan.

Peter's mind whirled in confusion as he tried to figure out a way to escape from this horrible predicament, and save his brother from the even worse things that probably waited for them, wherever this woman might be taking them.

GEARING UP

"Garvey, Stahl, good morning."

"Mistaah Gaahvey, please."

"And who might I say is calling?"

"Louise Wentwuth from Camp Longbow."

"One moment, please, I'll see if Mr. Garvey is in."

"Hello, Mrs. Wentworth, I've been expecting your call," David answered as he picked up the phone. "What took you so long?"

"We didn't find out there was a problem until almost midnight last evenin'. That's when one of the old boys called the camp to say my son didn't show up when it was time ta come back on the bus. Police found him layta. Someone hit him on the head. By the time we got ovah theya and tried to figah out which boys was on the trip, it was neahly three in the monin'. Both of your boys seem to be missing. I called your home numbah as soon as we figahed that out. Ya wan't home, which ain't unusual for you city folk. I'm callin ya as soon as I thought the office would be open."

"I sure am sorry to hear about your son, Mrs. Wentworth. I can't imagine what that might have to do with my sons. When I called the camp—what was it, nearly two days ago now—I told the boys we would be sending someone to pick them up. I believe you answered the phone. Family emergency. Didn't have a chance to speak directly with you about it. Planned to do that later but never got around to it. Sorry if my sloppiness has caused you to worry. It was just quicker for my person to pick them up in Bangor, near the airport, and save the extra drive out to the camp. She probably looked for your son and couldn't find him because of the other problem. Would you mind shipping all of the boys' things to my home address? I'll see that everything gets to the proper place and take care of letting their mother know what is going on. Does that leave any loose ends? I sure hope you did not add to local police problems by reporting my boys missing."

"Wanted ta speak with you first. We have such an excellent recad heah at Camp Longbow. Always glad when we don't have a problem. I'll send the boys' things off tamarah by Federal Express. If you don't mind, I'll be seein' ta my son—got quite a lump on his head. Doesn't seem to remembah what happind. Keep us in mind for next yeah!"

Since listening to Peter's message, David was certain the last thing he needed was some of the local Barney Fifes or even Maine State Troopers stumbling around trying to find his boys and perhaps kicking up so much dust it be difficult, if not impossible, to find Peter and Will. There was no good reason for Mrs. Wentworth or anyone else at Camp Longbow to have the slightest appreciation of the seriousness of his sons' predicament. And, if David was right about how this calamity would unfold, he could get the Feds into the picture later, if he couldn't solve the problem privately.

As soon as Peter's frightened call from the Bangor State fairgrounds had finished blaring from David's console, he had his former brother-in-law on the speaker phone.

"Good morning, Harry Cochrane. What can I do for you?"

"Harry, it's David, I've got a serious problem! Is this a secure line?"

"Maybe not. Let me call you back. I see from my caller ID that you're in your office. Light off that scrambler I gave you. Punch in my sister's blood type."

Despite the nasty divorce, David Garvey and Harry Cochrane not only remained close friends, but David regularly used the services of Harry's security firm. At first, he'd hired Harry and his detective colleagues to satisfy Garvey, Stahl's appetite for investigative services. Later, after the

Fund was born, David came to appreciate Harry's cunning and expertise even more. Fresh from government service, Harry was both discreet and creative but didn't shy away from messy assignments. In a split second, David's unlisted private line winked at him.

"Thanks, Harry. One of my European people grabbed Peter and Will—probably bought by the opposition. I can give you whatever details you need, but, while we're talking, line up some top level electronic intelligence talent in the Boston area. Someone who can be available as soon as we can get to Logan this morning. We'll need them for a minimum of a couple days, if we're lucky. Among other things, we'll need tracking on two frequencies I'm going to give you."

Harry interrupted what seemed like a casual description of some routine chore.

"Jesus, David, are they all right? I know it's still early, but what do these frequencies have to do with finding my only nephews?"

"Please make a list while we're talking of every piece of information you'll need from me. Once this Fund business started getting bloody, I took the precaution of installing some extra, eh, equipment on both boys. It's a tiny transmitter implanted where their upper-right wisdom teeth will hopefully grow in someday. Peter and Will don't even know it was done. I had Dr. Zuckerman knock them out during routine cleaning."

"How's it work?" Harry asked.

"Let's talk about that on the plane. I'll fill you in on the specifics on the way up to Boston. Can you be down in front of your office in ten minutes? I'll be in a black BMW 728i with tinted windows. Get in the back. One of my people will be driving so we can work on the way to the Marine Air Terminal at LaGuardia Airport."

"Sure thing! I'd do anything for those kids. You call my sister yet?" Harry inquired.

"Let's both call her from my plane. I'm on the way down to the garage. And, Harry, this one will likely be wet, so bring your whole bag of tricks!"

NEEDLE IN THE OCEAN

The leased Lear jet leaped into its takeoff roll down the short runway in front of LaGuardia's main terminal building. The sleek little plane quickly accelerated toward what David imagined were the steps in the air that would whisk him and Harry through a quick turn over the Riker's Island prison compound before climbing into the traffic pattern that became an upward spiral toward cruising altitude and the greater Boston area. No Goshawk available for this trip.

David had gone over and over with Harry every conceivable detail about the boys and their trip. Looking across the aisle at his friend with his feet up on the next seat, David could almost hear Harry's wheels turning. David was spent—sick with fear about what might and might not happen next. He tightened his seat belt, leaned back and tried to think of anything else.

RRRReeep! RRRReeep!

"Conning tower, Chief Fahnestock. Wait one, sir. Mr. Garvey, it's the Captain."

Garvey, David A., LT, USN, looked up from his perch over the lower conning tower hatch, his worn sea boots propped on the coaming where he could hear everything going on in Picuda's rigged-for-red control room below. The young, red-haired diving officer directly under David swung listlessly from the ladder leading to the conning tower, deep in obvious boredom. David stood up, abandoned his stale cup of blond-and-sweet coffee in a nearby aluminum coffee holder, and groped for the handset of

213

the helm's sound-powered telephone fixed to the pressure hull, immediately to the left of the conning tower's helm station. He watched Torpedoman Third Class Jawicki, a two-week summer reserve, fresh from Boston University's doctoral program in applied mathematics, slowly adjust the helm from right five degrees rudder to amidships, check his compass heading dead on ordered course of 083° and look over his shoulder at Lt. Garvey, the Officer of the Deck (Submerged), smirking expectantly.

"Morning, Captain, this is the Officer of the Deck."

Lieutenant Garvey could hear the tinny rendition of the Captain's voice through the World War II-version sound-powered communications system.

"Mr. Garvey, let's go up to 100 feet and check out the neighborhood. We're assigned to intercept a Russian squadron coming through the gap. Put on some turns. After you check out 100 feet, take her to periscope depth and snorkel on two engines. Fill up the can. The XO will be up with a new course once we're up and running. What kind of seas?"

"Sounds pretty quiet on Gertrude, Captain, but I'll check with Sonar when we're coming up to clear the baffles to make sure nothing's sitting above us on the way up."

Lieutenant Garvey snapped the ancient instrument into its aluminum cradle and squinted at his watch in the red night lighting—0147. Only two hours of the midwatch left. David couldn't wait for a warm slice of the fresh bread, with real butter, he could smell baking back aft in the galley even through the pervasive aroma of stale diesel fumes that permeated every nook and cranny of Picuda.

"ALL AHEAD TWO-THIRDS!" he ordered.

"All ahead two-thirds, aye," Jawicki confirmed his instructions by repeating them. The helmsman then released the helm for just a split second to deftly click one engine order telegraph one either side of the conning tower helm simultaneously two stops clockwise, one annunciator for each of Picuda's slowly rotating propeller shafts.

A "ding" from each engine order telegraph in front of Jawicki and another at the same time from a second helm, the emergency helm in the control room below positioned to the left of the hatch leading toward the boat's bow into the forward battery compartment. This emergency helm was presently unmanned but remained available in case the regular helm station in the conning tower was disabled, either through collision or hydraulic failure.

Instantly, David's instructions and Jawicki's response were acknowledged by the engineering watch atop the boat's slowly turning propeller shafts back aft—a second set of arrows in each annunciator matched the change in speed signaled by Jawicki. A faint jingling of the annunciators underlined the change in speed, a sound repeated in the control room directly beneath Lieutenant Garvey and his crew in the conning tower of this decrepit diesel-electric submarine.

"Answers all ahead two-thirds, sir!" Jawicki said in a high voice to no one in particular.

In front of the so-called Christmas tree on the port bulkhead of the control room below, with its unbroken row of green lights indicating all major hull openings shut, the Chief of the Watch, the senior enlisted man in the watch section, looked up from his daily fuel and water report as the annunciators at the emergency helm station beside him jingled. Ensign Luther Marsden pulled himself up the ladder, eyes at the level of David's scuffed and oil-stained boot tops.

"What's up?" Luther asked

"Back to work, Luther! MAKE YOUR DEPTH 100 FEET! SMARTLY!"

"100 feet, aye!"

The tall, gangly, and freckled Diving Officer dropped lightly to the diving stand, running his long fingers through a short, red crewcut. David could tell from the tension in the young Ensign's voice that he was keenly aware of the attention he would be getting during this evolution, his first dive by himself.

"Full rise on the bow planes. I want a two up bubble. Don't let your bubble run away from you! Give me five up on the stern planes to get it started. No, Clarks, the other up!"

. . . cycle the head valve, start number one main engine . . .

Lieutenant Garvey was only part way through the beginnings of what had happened long ago when the air around him became very cold and even nearby voices of the crew began to fade into silence. A quick glance at the depth gauge confirmed David's suspicions—63 feet from keel to surface and slowly sinking! Through the hull, David could hear his precious rock crushers back in the engine rooms begin to labor. Suddenly, the vacuum began to subside as Luther Marsden regained control of the dive and the boat rose to 59, then 58 feet. David could feel the pleasing rush of cool air on his face from the conning tower's ventilation ducts.

"DON'T BROACH ME, LUTHER . . ."

"Wake up, David." Harry Cochrane was gently shaking his arm. "You were about to rip the armrest out of its socket. Where were you?"

"Back on the boats, starting out on that Northern run where we lost Luther Marsden and his Chief Torpedoman," David sighed. "They were on deck in a fierce Arctic gale, trying to free a cable from the after messenger buoy that got tangled up in my propellers. Even with old-fashioned safety belts locked into the track along Picuda's flooded main deck, since replaced with the new "cross-your-heart" versions, the waves broke their backs. We couldn't even recover their bodies. I can't let go of that one any more than I can stop feeling personally responsible for Marja's death. Where are we?"

"Just touched down at Logan," Harry confirmed. "I called ahead to the spook we normally use in the Boston area and gave him all the information I thought might be relevant to finding the boys. He's meeting us at the airport with a vehicle and his full complement of high-tech electronics. You want a Coke? I'm having one."

David took a deep swallow of the bubbly liquid.

"Did your electronics specialist have any ideas, Harry? What'd he say?"

"He liked the concealed transmitters your Dr. Zuckerman hid in the wisdom teeth of each of your sons. Says he's never worked with them before, but has read the specs," Harry burped. "The type of structure the boys are being kept in apparently has a lot to do with how easy it is to locate or track the signal. That's a matter of luck unless the kidnappers know about the transmitters and deliberately try to mask their effect or remove them from the kids' mouths and leave the transmitters somewhere along the way to throw us off the track. See that Verizon truck over there? That's our spook, Johnny Tsai. He's more than a little odd, but very competent."

The small jet squeaked to a halt on the hot tarmac of a deserted arm of the airport's runways, far away from the main passenger terminal. David stuck his head through the open cockpit door and addressed the pilots: "Thanks for the ride, gentlemen. Please stand by until 9:30 P.M. When I need you, I'll call through the head office. If you don't hear from me by then, you can call it a day and return to New York."

With a curt wave over his shoulder, David turned and bounded down the tiny folding steps of the slightly humming Lear jet to where Harry was busily loading cases of equipment through the back door of a white rear-entry truck with familiar phone company markings. A gaunt Asian man wearing a black cotton turtleneck, black, polyester-blend slacks with no cuffs and black athletic shoes with no noticeable labels stood beside the vehicle's rear fender, quietly smoking a thin cigar. David's attention was drawn first to the skintight white cotton gloves the technician was wearing and second to his cold and detached manner.

"Johnny Tsai, meet my brother . . . ex-brother-in-law, David Garvey. They're his two sons we're trying to find."

The electronics specialist bent forward ever so slightly and extended a gloved hand toward the worried lawyer.

"How do you do, sir?"

"Pleased to meet you, Mr. Tsai," David said as he received the limp handshake. "Can we go? There's no time to lose!"

Once the trio had settled in the overstuffed brown calf's leather seats of their mobile command post, Tsai slid open the window to the driver's compartment and whispered instructions into the right ear of Sue Yin, a diminutive Oriental woman poised behind the truck's black plastic steering wheel. Without another word, he slid the shaded glass partition shut and turned politely toward David.

"Wait a minute," David objected. "How do you know where we're going? I thought we would be going to your office to work on the frequencies."

"Mr. Garvey, as soon as Mr. Cochrane called my office from your aircraft to provide us with the base frequencies of the transmitters you were so wise as to install on your sons, we immediately began our work. Only one of the transmitters appears to be operative. Its location seems to be roughly on the longitude of the border between Maine and New Hampshire."

Tsai paused to adjust a lighted dial on one of the large banks of electronic gadgetry occupying one entire wall of the remodeled truck, holding a headset to one ear. The equipment reminded David faintly of Picuda's sonar room. Although the truck's walls blocked David's view of their route, he could vaguely see occasional road signs through the front windshield, indicating they were headed toward the entrance to I-95, north toward Portsmouth, New Hampshire. Johnny Tsai laid his pair of headphones on the seat beside him and continued his explanation.

"As you may know, the border between New Hampshire and Maine extends almost directly north from the port city of Portsmouth, New Hampshire, to the wilderness of the Canadian Province of Québec. Even assuming your children are still in the United States and have not been taken out to sea, that border covers many long and difficult miles. I took the liberty of speaking with two of my cousins. One lives in Portland, Maine, and the other happened to be passing through Manchester, New Hampshire, on business. Without receiving your permission, I asked them both to take a bearing on the signal from your portable transmitter. I hope that does not disturb you.

At that time, about one hour ago, the bearings taken with my own equipment and those supplied by my family members intersected roughly at a point somewhat to the west of where the Salmon Falls River separates Berwick, Maine, and Somersworth, New Hampshire. That point is some twenty-five miles north of Portsmouth, New Hampshire, on the New Hampshire side of the border. My two cousins have kindly agreed to provide me with another reading at . . ."

Without taking her eyes from the road, the driver tapped twice on the glass partition with a leather-gloved knuckle. She made the shape of a telephone with her fingers next to her right ear. Tsai picked up a receiver at the truck's elaborate instrument panel and pushed the single blinking button. After a brief conversation in what David thought was probably a Chinese dialect, most likely Hakka, Johnny Tsai returned the instrument to its cradle.

"Good news! Our signal has not moved appreciably since the last check," Tsai announced.

Peter and Will's father looked at Harry Cochrane with a mixture of relief and concern. At least they were making rapid progress, but why was only one of the transmitters showing up? Perhaps a malfunction. Maybe one of the boys is somewhere else or worse. Mr. Tsai appeared to be absorbed in his maze of cables, connectors and gadgets, otherwise oblivious to his surroundings.

"I hope you have a plan, old friend," David said.

"First, they've apparently crossed state lines," Harry indicated. "That means we can get help from the FBI if this doesn't go as smoothly as we'd like. I suggest we follow the signal until we can't get any closer without alerting whoever is holding your sons. If we chase the signal on Tsai's direction-finding equipment, that ought to work. As we get closer, we may overshoot the exact location. At that point, we'll set out a couple of portable receivers tuned to the magic frequency to help with the final triangulation and in case your, eh, colleague makes a break for it. Once we've identified the location, maybe we'll try to figure out the phone number using the reverse phone book and, one way or another, put a tap on the landline. It will be even easier if anyone in the house is using a cell or cordless phone."

"Do we just drive up to the door and knock?" David asked, a faint glimmer of his humor returning.

Frank patted his brother-in-law's arm.

"Look, this telephone truck shouldn't even interest any of the locals, but tell me more about our opposition. They're foreign, aren't they?"

David warmed to the task, eager to do whatever he could get save his children.

"Peter left a message saying a pretty blonde woman grabbed Will. That may have been Agnieszka Czarnocki. She was born and brought up in Wrocław, Poland. That used to be Breslau, Germany, before the end of World War II; it was actually the last place the Nazis surrendered. She's very tough from growing up in the disintegrating Polish economy," David said. "If she's the kidnapper, I don't really know why she has done this, but she may have been bought off either by the German bankers trying to take over my businesses in Eastern Europe or by the Iraqis who are pulling the bankers' strings. Or maybe she is just jealous! No way to tell how tough she'll be when the chips are down. As far as I know, Ani's not married, but she once mentioned a daughter still living somewhere in Poland."

"If you had to guess, who would be with her?"

"That's a tough one! She always impressed me as a loner. But you need to know Ani and I have been romantically involved on and off since the project in Königsberg got off the ground. I couldn't name any of her friends, but it wouldn't surprise me if she has some Iraqi muscle with her. Maybe her participation in this mess was coerced."

The Verizon telephone truck wound tentatively around a treelined curve to the left, as if looking for an address amid the brilliant foliage of this autumn afternoon. Johnny Tsai's dark eyes were riveted to the display of his direction-finding console as the road straightened out.

"It's on our right side, moving rapidly from front to rear. The transmitter must be very close!" Tsai blurted out.

David was beside himself. All he could see through the front partition was a narrow country lane in poor repair. Their vehicle pulled up beside the next driveway, off the soft right shoulder of the crumbling asphalt. The female driver, who Harry now noticed was wearing the uniform of a telephone repairman, jumped to the street and sauntered over to the mailbox. She looked carefully in both directions, paying particular attention to the telephone lines and the house hidden far behind a bank of scraggly evergreen trees. Seeing nothing moving except a groundhog in the neighboring field, the technician rummaged around in the right leg pouch of her jumpsuit, retrieved a small, dark object mounted on a silver spike and jammed it sharply into the wooden underside of a rectangular metal mailbox bearing the inscription "Living Free and Dead in New Hampshire—Somersworth RFD 2 Box 136." She climbed back onto her elevated seat, backed into the same driveway, then slowly turned the white truck back toward town. Just past the treelined curve, an overgrown hunting road led into a stand of birches. Tsai tapped on the partition and motioned the driver to enter the darkening byway.

Once off the highway, David felt the truck lumber ponderously along a soft woods road for what seemed to him like forever. Then, Johnny Tsai tapped again on the partition with a gloved knuckle and made a fist, which he then twisted sharply in the air to signal the driver to stop. The vehicle squeaked to a halt in the middle of the wooded trail. The driver stood up on her seat to reach out through the open cab window to release rolled canvas covers—they dropped rapidly from the truck's roof to cover the truck's windshield and, from what David could hear, its side panels as well. He turned his attention to their electronics consultant, who removed his earphones and smiled faintly.

"Combining our bearing from this location and the tiny receiver Sue Yin attached to the mailbox confirms the transmitter is in the house we just now passed on the left. It is a fairly modern, one-story ranch set back about fifty yards from the road with woods on both sides and a narrow field running down to the road. The edge of the woods near us is marked with an old stone wall."

"How did you know all that? I couldn't see anything back here!"

The Chinese tech blushed.

"I'm so sorry, ah, I was so involved in what I was doing I forgot to mention we have a tiny video camera on the roof of this truck. The picture is right here on this screen."

He pointed to a small computer screen out of David and Harry's line of sight.

"Wonderful! Let's get out so we can see what it looks like up close. Do you need help with any of the equipment, Harry?" David asked as he started picking up equipment and girding for the task ahead.

Shortly, David and Harry crawled through wet leaves on the ground toward a break in the crumbling stone wall in front of the last line of birches. Each wore a full-sleeved Kevlar jacket, buttoned under the crotch and zipped up tight around the neck. Harry dragged a bulky utility bag behind him. In front of the two heavily armed New Yorkers, a doe and her two fawns grazing quietly in the overgrown meadow looked at the two men dismissively. On the far side of the road, Sue Yin climbed nimbly up a solitary telephone pole and began working on the wires, a charcoal silhouette against the remaining sliver of papaya sunset.

David could see patches of green moss on the gray shingles of the ranch's roof and the rusted gutters that hung under the roof's eaves, which were overflowing with dead maple and oak leaves and pine needles. The part of the house's foundation David and Harry could see behind irregular, overgrown azalea bushes was cracked in two places. Near the center of what might have once been a front lawn, a septic tank had fallen in on itself and was now a sunken brown patch in the center of patches of sandy soil and leggy crabgrass.

At that moment, a light came on in the back of the house they had been chasing since early morning.

TOUGH BAGELS

Peter Garvey surveyed the spartan laundry room that had become his prison, deliberately ignoring his ruined jeans although he couldn't escape their pungent odor. He decided for the fourth time today that his accommodations at Camp Longbow had been just fine. Peter's right wrist ached from the constant chafing of a single handcuff that bound him to the brass supply pipe of a baseboard hot water heating unit recessed under the cracked pine windowsill above him.

Peter could just see out one of the rear windows of the aging ranch-style home if he strained to pull himself up. To his left, against the far wall, beside another pair of double-paned windows that faced a stand of dense pine trees in the yard outside, a top-loading Sears washing machine and an electric dryer were jammed against the wall between a wallboard partition and a deep mop sink. The whole room reeked of liquid bleach, which had splattered on the worn linoleum tile floor during Peter's gallant but futile attempt to overpower Ani's heavy-handed accomplice. In front of Peter, his only brother was calmly playing chess with a frail elderly woman perched in a worn rocker, knobby knees covered by a torn, knitted afghan.

Will danced around the wobbly little table holding the chessboard.

"I'm gonna beat you this time, Mrs. Kronfeld. Check again," he squealed.

"Don't be too cocky, young man. You're only ahead for the moment because I'm worried about having these criminals in my home."

Surveying the black-and-white squares, Sadie Kronfeld moved her king one space to the right, out of the reach of Will's white knight.

"Tell me again why that woman brought you here," the older woman said. "I didn't understand what you told me the first time."

"My dad has this business making loans in Eastern Europe. She worked for my father. I think she's trying to blackmail him or something."

"What, WHAAAT?"

Mrs. Kronfeld thumped the pocket of her smock. The room promptly rang with an ear-piercing whine.

"That's better. Now tell me again. Your move, Will," she said, reaching into the baggy pocket of her smock to turn down the volume on her hearing aid.

"I said my dad has a loan business in Poland, Russia, and other parts of Eastern Europe. I think this blonde woman works for him in Russia," Will explained again. "She kidnapped us from our summer camp in Maine while we were at the Bangor State Fair so she can make him do something he doesn't want to. I haven't figured out what that is yet."

"Poland. I was born in Germany near Poland, a city called Breslau. My family lived there for generations until the Nazis sent every one of us they could round up to the camps. I alone survived."

Mrs. Kronfeld paused to tuck a wisp of carrot-colored hair behind her ear with a long pin.

"Have you always lived here?" Will asked. "You don't sound like you're from New England."

"Check," she exclaimed, withdrawing a gnarled hand from the mitre of her remaining black bishop.

"I grew up in New York City. My late husband Sidney and I, we ran a small bakery in the 160s just off Broadway until the neighborhood went to hell in the late sixties. The best bagels in Washington Heights we made! That part of Manhattan was heavily German at one time, but many of the Germans died out or moved away. That area's mostly Puerto Rican now, or at least it was when we left."

"How'd you get up to Maine?" Will asked

Grasping its wooden arms with both hands, the widow heaved herself out of the rocker and clumped toward the deep sink.

"New Hampshire," she said, correcting him. "We're just a few blocks from the Maine border, but you probably missed that coming over the Salmon River Bridge from Berwick in the dark. My genius husband, Sidney, figured we'd be better off in a place like New Hampshire, with no estate tax. Turns out that doesn't matter if you have no estate. And it's hard to get the help we need around here—too many people on unemployment or welfare, and no one wants to work."

She selected a maroon ceramic mug from the wooden shelf over the open top of her washing machine, let the cold water run noisily from the chrome spigot and drank deeply.

"You want some water, Peter? How about you, Will?"

"No, thanks," Peter said. "I'm pretty thirsty, but that guy may not let me out of these handcuffs to go to the bathroom."

"Don't worry about that! I've got a plastic pail in the closet over there.

"Sidney convinced me to buy this house on foreclosure from the Resolution Trust Corporation. We got a good price, and it didn't need that much work at the time. It seemed like a mansion after our two-bedroom walkup in northern Manhattan. I still can't imagine why Miss Fancypants decided to get me involved in this mess! Or why she picked me to bother."

Will leaned over toward Peter with a smirk on his young face.

"You want me to bring over the PAIL yet?"

"Not yet," Peter replied grimly. "But see if you can find some tools in that gray metal toolbox I see through the crack in the closet door. I'd ask you to drag it over here, but I don't want our jailer to see what I'm doing if he bursts in unannounced. Maybe I can break the joint on this pipe I'm chained to. And push that pile of dirty laundry toward the door, so maybe we'll get some warning next time that towel head comes in. Have you noticed? We haven't seen that woman since we got here. Think she's ashamed to see us?"

Will squeezed around the corner of an aquamarine folding ironing board where Mrs. Kronfeld was now meticulously pressing freshly laundered embroidered sheets with a hot electric iron plugged into a dual wall outlet above the washing machine. He didn't remember ever seeing anyone actually iron clothes before. A clear plastic bag of what looked like wet laundry lay on the floor not far from the door to a tiny bathroom. She removed a sheet from the bag, squirted part of it with an aerosol can of spray starch and then smoothed its wrinkles with the heavy, old-fashioned electric iron.

Will opened the nearby closet door and pawed as quietly as he could through the contents of the gunmetal gray box until he found an adjustable wrench. He held it up for Peter's inspection, looking furtively over his shoulder toward the door to the hall.

"That's fine," Peter said. "Bring it over here. I can't stand just sitting here doing nothing. We really don't have any idea what they intend to do with us. Will, see if you can twist together the wires of that telephone the towel head ripped out of the wall. It's hard work—you have to reattach each individual wire. Match the colors. Use some more of that dirty laundry to cover up where you're working. Maybe we can call Dad to let him know where we are."

Sadie Kronfeld looked up from her ironing.

"What's a towel head?"

"An Arab," Peter said. "He's obviously an Arab! He's been jerking us around since they grabbed us from behind the funhouse at the fair. Big and very strong but not very smart."

Mrs. Kronfeld reached under the shoulder of her floral smock to rearrange a bra strap. She sniffed, "he certainly ruined my side door. I was just putting on some coffee for breakfast. All of a sudden, this van pulls into my carport and out climbs this muscular towel head. I like that word! Rings my door buzzer. Says he has car trouble. Can he use the phone? Well, even here in the country, I'm real careful who I let in. When I refused, he pushed in the door and knocked me down on the kitchen floor. Hit my head on the corner of the table. That's how I got this egg on my forehead. Next thing I knew, I was on the floor in here with you two boys!"

"I was awake before we got here," Will said. "Peter was still asleep on the floor of the van. They were looking for a house with a telephone and not too close to the road, where no one was home. When they didn't see a car in your driveway, they thought nobody was here."

"My old Dodge is having its brakes relined—won't be ready until the day after tomorrow," Mrs. Kronfeld explained. "Until then, I don't have a car. But don't normally need one anyway. Where would I go?"

"Do you have any tape, Mrs. Kronfeld?" Peter asked.

"What kind of tape? What do you need it for?"

"If Will can splice the phone wires, it may be important to cover the receiver so we can listen in when they are making calls. No offense, Mrs. Kronfeld, but that looks like a really cheap phone. We may be able to hear them dialing a call from in here. That might let us listen in without disrupting the dial tone. We need a plan to get out of here. They each have at least one gun. We have to assume the worst. If I could get free, can you get around well enough to climb through that window and go out into the woods with us?"

Sadie Kronfeld drew herself up to a full five feet, two inches, planted a gnarled fist on her left hip and brandished the other liver-spotted hand in the air.

"This is my home! They ain't gonna push me around! But the short answer is just barely. I'm eighty-four; I've got high blood pressure, arthritis, a pacemaker, and a hip replacement and am very hard of hearing, but I still get around by myself, at least when there's no snow on the ground. I could probably get out the window and down onto the lawn, but what good would that do us if they followed us?"

"I hadn't thought of that," Peter responded dejectedly.

Suddenly, the cheap knob of the door into the hall rattled as if someone were trying to take it apart. All three captives looked around to see what was happening. Finally, the door swung inward, trailing several feet of white clothesline that had apparently been holding it firmly shut from the outside. Ani swore as she pushed aside a heavy pile of dirty laundry.

"Here is orange juice and cakes. I couldn't find other things. Refrigerator is empty. Something is wrong with phone, old woman! Every time I am making call, operator says she must make call for me because tree has fallen on wires."

"You makin' toll calls?" Mrs. Kronfeld demanded.

"What you mean toll calls? You be quiet, old woman, and we will not hurt you. As soon as we are getting instructions about what to do with these two, we are going away. You be good, and Abdul won't hurt you or your house."

"Where's the cake? You said there was cake." Will chirped hungrily.

"Right here." The bedraggled young woman pointed disdainfully to several round rolls of cooked dough with holes in the middle.

"You never before seen bagels? Where you from? The Moon?" Sadie Kronfeld demanded incredulously.

"I am being from big city in southwestern Poland," David Garvey's former lover yawned. "I am now remembering, an old Jew baker in my neighborhood used to sell those things—very tough. Eat! When I get instructions, we will soon be going away."

Mrs. Kronfeld appeared interested in this woman for the first time.

"What city in Poland?"

"I am first living in Wrocław before moving to Varshava, but why you are wanting to know?"

Ani inspected the tiny old woman, from her pair of scuffed black-laced shoes with stumpy heels to the unkept knot of badly dyed red hair.

Mrs. Kronfeld looked intently into her young captor's dark eyes.

"You remember the German name?"

"I am not understanding. Varshava has no German name."

"I mean where you were born. What was the German name?"

"Oh, you are meaning Wrocław. Let me think . . . . that is Breslau. But why you are wanting to know?"

"Just a foolish old woman," the widow observed sadly as she turned her back on Ani and resumed her ironing.

"I am again locking door tight. No tricks," Ani warned, as she turned to leave the room.

She clicked on the ivory wall switch, and two rows of overhead fluorescent lights came on with a slight buzz.

"It is getting dark. You need light to see what you're doing, old woman."

The door slammed behind her. Peter and Will could hear Ani fumbling with the rope around the outer doorknob. Peter motioned for Will to look under the door. Will crawled quietly across the linoleum floor on his bare knees to peer under the wide gap between the hollow-paneled door and tufts of grey-green shag carpet on the floor of the hall outside. Will tiptoed back to stand beside Mrs. Kronfeld, who was now ironing a child's red skirt, as if having kidnappers and perhaps murderers in her home was not at all unusual.

"Why are you doing this?" Will asked. "Don't you have a cleaning lady?"

"Not everyone has a cleaning lady, Will. I do all my own chores here, but this really isn't work!"

"Why're you doing kids' clothes? Do you have grandchildren?"

Will traced the warm outline of the skirt pocket on the ironing board with his left index finger.

"Hadassah's collecting used clothing for Jewish refugees from Russia, especially children. We take donations of old or dirty clothes, wash them, and put them in boxes to ship to the resettlement camps and their new homes in Israel. Funny how some things don't change. When I was a little girl in Poland, people treated the Jews badly. This woman who brought you here seems to have the same attitude. My people in Russia were leaving to go to Israel long before the Soviet Union was failing. Now they're leaving even faster because the Russians are mistreating them again. Just like before World War II in Poland."

"You don't seem very worried, Mrs. Kronfeld," Peter said softly, watching her expression. "Don't you know how these kidnappings usually end? The ones you read about in the papers?"

"I'm a very old woman," she sighed. "My husband's gone. We had no children. When my time has come, that's it."

Mrs. Kronfeld squinted as she skillfully maneuvered the hot iron through the maze of the skirt's lace hem. Then she clomped over to a small card table against the wall facing Peter, where she added the finished skirt to a growing pile of folded laundry. Then she turned slowly into the tiny bathroom and shut the door. She fumbled with the door lock and then the boys could hear the sounds of water running in the bathroom sink. As if on command, a shadowy figure appeared in the lower window pane over Peter's head, a single finger pressed tightly to his lips. Will saw him first and shrank back in fear. The man outside made a lifting sign near the bottom of the window, still with one finger to his closed lips.

"What're you looking at, Will?" Peter demanded, looking about wildly.

Will scurried across the floor to his brother's side and whispered in Peter's ear.

"Someone's outside in the backyard. It looks like Uncle Harry, but what would he be doing here? He wants us to open the window."

Peter winced as he strained to peek above the sill, the annoying handcuff cutting even further into his wrist.

"That is Uncle Harry! Open the window! Can you reach the latch?"

"I can reach it, but it's too tight," Will said. "I can't open it!"

"Don't get excited," Peter said, trying to calm Will down. "Get Mrs. Kronfeld to help. Be sure she knows it's our uncle, so she'll help. Remember, she's pretty deaf."

Will sneaked toward the bathroom door. He tapped lightly against its empty plywood panel.

"I'll be out in just a minute," a muffled voice from inside answered his inquiry.

"Please, please, Mrs. Kronfeld, let me in right now. I'm going to throw up!"

Sadie Kronfeld pushed open the bathroom door. Will squeezed in past her, immediately pulling the door shut behind him. In a moment, the bathroom door opened again, and Mrs. Kronfeld peeked hesitantly around the door post toward the window over Peter's head. This time, Harry Cochrane gestured urgently toward the window sash. Will and Mrs. Kronfeld hurried to the jammed window, crawling over Peter in their haste. She struggled to boost Will onto the windowsill, where he tried again to best the obstinate latch. Then the elderly woman clapped a leathery hand over Will's straining fingers and grunted. Finally, the brass latch clicked.

Mrs. Kronfeld easily slid the window up slightly on its tubular plastic sash. She bent to inspect the catches on both sides of the closed storm window before pulling them both toward the middle of its frame, allowing the window to be moved upward. Sadie lifted the storm window two notches before its stops clicked into place, allowing coolness to pour over the windowsill. Smells of wet leaves and grass were in the air.

"Uncle Harry! What're you doing here?" Will whispered through the small mesh plastic screen.

"Your dad and I've come to take you home. Help me with this window and screen so we can get you all out. How many are there in the house?"

Harry activated a tiny microphone at the corner of his mouth, putting him in direct communication with the boys' father as well as Johnny Tsai in the van.

"Just me and Peter and Mrs. Kronfeld here. It's her house," Will blurted out. "And Czarnocki and this big Arab guy that brought us here from camp."

"Peter, that you down there? What's wrong with you?"

"Not much. I'm handcuffed to this radiator. You got anything to cut off this handcuff?"

"Sorry," Harry replied. "I don't have any tools for that right now. I'm afraid they might hear us if we try to come in this way. We're going to try and lure one of them outside to break up the pair. Your father really wants to take the woman alive. He needs her in the litigation that started all of this. What I want you to do is—"

The quartet froze as someone tried to open the door to the hall outside. Harry Cochrane dropped out of sight below the windowsill. Mrs. Kronfeld stood up, picked up a pile of dirty clothes and began stuffing them into the open lid of the electric washer. She pulled out a silver control knob with a snap, sending a powerful stream of scalding water coursing over a pile of towels, underwear, and summer curtains in the machine's perforated metal basket. Then Mrs. Kronfeld calmly heaped three full scoops of blue laundry powder on top of the sinking clothes, maintaining her balance by leaning on the teetering ironing board. David's boys looked at each other in amazement as Mrs. Kronfeld appeared to be quietly going about her business as the door burst open. The washing machine's agitator began to rotate back and forth as its operating cycle began in earnest.

"Old woman!" Ani yelled. "Show me where you are more food keeping right now! Abdul is demanding food, real food. He is now watching television, but you come cook!"

"Sure, but can you help me find my glasses? I think they fell into the washing machine," Sadie warbled, reaching down into the hot, soapy water with her left hand.

Ani bent over to peer into the swirling mound of soaking linen just as Mrs. Kronfeld quickly scooped up a dripping fistful of soggy laundry detergent and clapped it to the young woman's eyes. Her shrieks of surprise and pain were muffled by several sodden bath towels Sadie jammed against Ani's face. Ani coughed hoarsely, sneezed once, and slipped in the growing puddle of soapy water on the scratched linoleum tile floor. She tried without success to catch her balance, grasping frantically at the white enamel edge of the washer. The dilapidated washer continued to churn its load of laundry, soap, and hot water, adding to the slippery mess as it splashed on the floor under the young blonde's feet.

"Jew baker!" Mrs. Kronfeld growled angrily in a guttural voice, grabbing the handle of her iron firmly. "Probably one of my relatives who just went home die."

Mrs. Kronfeld swung the heavy iron with a force that amazed and delighted Will and Peter. The broad base of the iron's triangular metal face caught Ani near the left ear, just behind her tiny gold earring, and then escaped Mrs. Kronfeld's grasp and careened against the nearby wall. Ani's head bounced heavily against the washer's tinny front panel and a second time more softly in the puddle of dirty soap suds on the floor.

Peter and Will's lips moved in unison.

"Yes!"

Wiping her chin with a gnarled hand, Sadie Kronfeld leaned over to push in the control button of the humming machine. The laundry room suddenly became deathly still, except for the occasional dripping of water from the front edge of the washer. The muffled sounds of crowd noise could be heard from the living room. Harry Cochrane popped back in view through the window.

"Good arm, Mrs. Kronfeld!" Harry Cochrane observed. "That certainly breaks up the pair nicely! I hope you didn't kill her. Will, get that piece of rope off the door so you can tie her up, just in case. Then push everything in this room against the door to the hall and get down in the corner right next to Peter. The big guy in the living room is just about to reach the end of his sports program."

Peeking over the sill of a living room window, David watched a barrel-chested Iraqi forward dribble the soccer ball skillfully through the pack of Saudi defenders on the large screen of Mrs. Kronfeld's entertainment center. The dark green-shirted player sidestepped the remaining Saudi defenseman between him and the wide posts framing the net and bore down on the exposed goaltender. The Iraqi looped the ball well above his shoulders and caromed it off his forehead toward the goal mouth with an adroit snap of his thick neck. The crowd was on its feet! The goalie leaped frantically into the air!

"HHIIIISSSSSSSSSS!"

With a slight click, the cable box went dark. The television picture dissolved into a cloud of black snow. Abdul sprang angrily toward the wide screen and began pounding mercilessly on the channel selector box. Behind the enraged Iraqi, the New York lawyer had silently slipped into the hallway outside the living room through the door to Sadie Kronfeld's basement. In addition to a double-barreled shotgun slung over his shoulder, David held a lightweight rifle in his left hand and a green-and-gray orb the size of an apple in his right.

Cradling the rifle in the crook of his right elbow, he twisted the top half of the green-and-gray sphere one-quarter turn and rolled it slowly between two woven rugs centered on the living room's polished maple floor boards toward the irate giant. The ball began to emit a deafening squeal. The noise made Abdul snatch the cable controller from its resting place and beat it even more vigorously against the particleboard shelves of Mrs. Kronfeld's fake birch bookcase.

David calmly raised the smaller weapon to his left shoulder and pointed its muzzle between Abdul's massive, heaving shoulder blades. Its sharp "POP" was drowned out by the high-pitched whine coming from the metallic globe now resting under a plastic-covered chair to Abdul's immediate left. The bulky Arab winced and tried to reach between his shoulders as the hypodermic dart plunged deep into its target. Abdul turned to lunge at David, stretching to reach for a menacing Kalashnikov machine pistol lying on the coffee table next to a dilapidated fuchsia easy chair covered in cracked but clear plastic. The Iraqi's legs began to wobble. He slumped slowly to the floor in disbelief.

David leaned the spent rifle against the nearby chair and laid his pump-action shotgun on the glass-topped coffee table, pointing straight at Abdul's flickering eyelids, beside the Arab's own useless weapon. Only then did David remove both of his soft rubber earplugs. He pulled a packet of elastic thongs from the pocket of his vest and carefully bound the twitching Abdul, hand and foot. Then David buzzed twice on the intercom, suspecting Harry and Johnny had turned off their receivers as soon as he started the noisemaker.

"All quiet back there?" David called out.

"You didn't need to buzz," Harry chimed in. "I wouldn't have missed the show. Good work! The boys are both fine, but Peter is handcuffed to a radiator in the laundry room. Hopefully your blonde squeeze has the key. I could break through the back window, but Mrs. Kronfeld has already suffered enough today. I'll get them to move things away from the door, and you can walk right in."

The proud electronics expert almost beamed through David's return feed: "Mr. Garvey, Sue Yin was able to tap into their phone line by convincing the young Polish woman we were repairing damage from a fallen tree. She sounded a little confused or not very smart. I have very clear tapes of every outgoing call, as soon as you are ready, sir!"

David heaved a sigh of relief.

He hurried down Sadie Kronfeld's back hall. Behind the closed door, he could hear the squeak of a heavy appliance being dragged across a linoleum tile floor. Suddenly, the door banged open and a curly-headed young boy in a dirty Camp Longbow T-shirt bolted out and fiercely hugged both of David's legs. The weary father picked up his second-born son and held him so tightly it seemed he might break. David buried his face in Will's strawberry blond curls and sprinkled them with his hot tears, starkly aware this episode might not have ended so pleasantly.

"I wasn't afraid, Dad. I was waiting for the chance to kick butt!" Will exclaimed.

"It's all right to be afraid," David said softly. "It's even OK to cry. It makes me cry just to think of the danger you were in. And now this adventure is over for you and Peter, and you're both safe. Is Peter OK?"

"He's fine 'cept he's cuffed to a radiator and hasn't had anything to drink today because he didn't want to piss in a pail," the youngster grinned mischievously.

Suddenly serious, he looked thoughtfully into David's deep blue eyes.

"Does Mom know what happened?"

"Uncle Harry and I talked to her on the flight up here, but she doesn't know the whole story yet. She's pretty mad—blames me for exposing the two of you to this danger. You can call her as soon as we get Peter unhooked from the radiator.

David gently lowered Will to the floor. The two turned the corner into the laundry room to see Peter, still attached to the radiator, with his left hand raised toward David. His father knelt down to embrace his nearly grown son as best he could without knocking over Mrs. Kronfeld. Sadie stepped aside, interrupting her direction of Harry's efforts to free Peter.

"Careful with that rusty saw blade. Please don't break my heater," Mrs. Kronfeld implored.

"Harry, why don't you stop cutting for a minute and see if either of these scumbags has a key? Besides, we'll need the cuffs for Miss Polish Trustworthiness," David suggested.

"Sorry, David. I forgot. Got carried away in the heat of battle. God, it's good to see you guys!"

"Harry, you make sure I don't do anything I might be sorry for later," David said with a hard voice as he stood over his once-trusted colleague and former lover.

Ani lay in a pool of cooling soapy water and no small amount of blood, her dirty blonde hair only partly covering a darkening bruise as she tried without much success to keep her nose out of the pool of blood, soap, and water beneath her. Some value of Camp Longbow's exorbitant tuition was evident. The young woman was trapped in a cocoon of knots that would have made Will's woodsmanship instructor proud—three pair of timber hitches around her ankles, a bowline around each wrist, two sheepshanks connecting arms and ankles, and a taut line around her throat thrown in for good measure.

He prodded her with a worn boot. She glared at him with a mixture of rage and shame.

"I've got only one question. Why?"

"You not understand," she mumbled through puffed lips.

"Try me!" David challenged her. "Maybe I could understand stealing from me in the loan operation, although that possibility probably needs some attention. But kidnapping my children? What have I ever done to deserve that?"

"I thought we were having something together. When I am arriving here in New York this time, I am for first time truly understanding you and me from very different worlds," Ani explained sullenly, looking away from David. "They also offered me much money."

"Who is they, Krasavitsa?"

"I am not telling you. They kill me!"

"How do you know I won't kill you? I've every reason to toss you out in the middle of I-95 on the way back to Boston. Let the highway crews pick up the street pizza that's left after a couple of semis do a dance on your lovely body," David growled. "Besides, we have every detail of your calls from this house. Your talks with Herr Doktor Kreuz were most enlightening. While we're packing up to leave, try to think about why we should allow your treacherous existence to continue!"

David permitted himself a sharp kick to her rib cage.

"Mrs. Kronfeld, would you mind searching this one to see if she has a key to the handcuffs and anything else of interest?"

Sadie Kronfeld warmed to the task as she roughly turned the Wrocław native first to one side, then the other. First she laid a snub-nosed pistol on the laundry table, then a folded sheet of paper covered with pencil notes, and finally a small key. The widow passed the key to Harry Cochrane, who quickly clicked open Peter's handcuff.

"'Cuse me," Peter exclaimed as he ducked into the nearby bathroom, "I've been waiting for this all day!"

A visibly incensed David Garvey jammed the heel of his left boot into Ani's slender neck and growled: "Your note says 'NeuBank 2258.' What does that mean?"

"I don't remember." Agniesczka cried out in agony as David shifted more of his weight to the heavy heel behind her left ear, recent recipient of Mrs. Kronfeld's swinging iron.

"Harry, would you mind taking Mrs. Kronfeld and the boys outside on the lawn," David suggested. "I don't want them to hear what it sounds like when I crush her larynx and she chokes to death from lack of oxygen!"

David motioned them toward the door, his further shift in weight bringing a low moan from the supine body.

"Code to alarm system in New York office of NeuBank," she coughed through the puddle of dirty wash water. "Please don't kill me. Diether Kreuz gave me code in case I needed to enter his offices outside normal business hours."

David touched Mrs. Kronfeld's shoulder before she could leave the room.

"Do you have a full-length dress we could borrow? If you wish, I'll send someone here tomorrow to repair the damage to your home. I apologize for the damage and distress these thugs have caused you. I'd appreciate it if you could help me get this one ready to travel. That would involve stripping her and letting her use the bathroom. I will be standing here with my shotgun. It shoots multiple slugs and makes big holes in whatever it hits! Then, if you don't mind, clean her up, put the cuffs on her and put that long dress over the handcuffs. What I mean is leave her cuffed inside the dress. Then, I'll finish getting her ready to travel. We'll keep her alive as long as she cooperates with us."

The old woman looked David squarely in the eye.

"You've got two fine boys. Polite and only a little spoiled. I'm happy to do whatever I can. This *shiksa* is absolutely no good!"

David helped Sadie Kronfeld untie the young Polish woman. As soon as the last rope dropped to the floor, the old lady roughly jerked Ani toward the bathroom with surprising strength. His mind already on to the next problem, David buzzed Johnny Tsai.

"Would you mind calling up our transportation at Logan and asking them to wait for us? I guess we'll be there in just under two hours. Could you also bring your van over here and back it into the upper driveway? We need to load up and get going."

He called through the partly closed door to Mrs. Kronfeld.

"Could you please put those handcuffs on behind her back? I want to hear them click before I leave you alone with her. Would you mind if I use your telephone to make a credit card call?"

"Help yourself! And, you, you miserable bitch, make one move, and I'll do you with the iron again! If you so much as—"

David chuckled as he picked up the chartreuse kitchen wall phone and dialed Frank Gillespie's private number in the office.

239

Before the system asked for his calling card number, he shouted to his brother-in-law: "Harry! Get Abdul ready to travel. Make sure everything is removed from his person—everything. All he gets to keep is pants and that pullover. Don't even let him keep his shoes. We're going to dump him in one of the worst parts of Boston on the way to Logan."

"Hello, Frank?" David turned his attention to the phone. "We got the boys back, no casualties. Do whatever you must to get us on Judge Garcia's calendar absolutely as soon as possible. We may have a live witness to confess to kidnapping Peter and Will on behalf of NeuBank to get us to withdraw the action. And now's the time for the showstoppers."

"And get together a racketeering brief to cover wire fraud, mail fraud, extortion and kidnapping," he continued. "Remember the other line of attack you and I've been talking about for so long? Dust off that brief so we'll have something to hand the judge next time we get to see her. See if you can serve that subpoena we have on the shelf. I'll put Harry in touch with you once we're rolling to work out the details. If everything goes according to schedule, we may even have documentary evidence of all basic parts of this treachery by tomorrow morning."

Hanging the plastic handset on its smudged chrome cradle, David motioned to Peter and Will. "Time to call your mother, he said. "I'll dial and try to explain some of what's happened. Then you can fill her in with any details you want. Just make sure you emphasize you're OK. Hello, it's me again. I apologize for the long delay—"

David held the phone away from his ear and shook his head sadly. When the noise stopped pouring from the receiver, he said quickly, "they're both just fine. Here's Will."

David watched his boys talking excitedly with their mother, his former wife and sweetheart.

Mrs. Kronfeld hobbled into the living room pushing Ani in front of her, the young woman now draped with a long, faded grey woolen gown.

David grabbed a soft leather helmet from an olive duffel bag lying in front of the wide-screen television and pulled it over Ani's sodden curls. He explained to Mrs. Kronfeld: "Properly adjusted, she'll be as deaf as you claim to be without your hearing aid. And with these goggles, she'll be as good as blind. Both lenses have very strong prescriptions she doesn't need; the left eye is adjusted for an almost disabling astigmatism. That should keep her quiet until we get back to New York. Thanks again for your help. Have you thought about my offer to send someone to fix your back door and probably your television?"

"Don't know why you haven't already killed her, messing with your kids," Mrs. Kronfeld said. "Guess you have your reasons. The neighbor boy will help me with the repairs. All I ask is that you let me know what finally happens with this court case and your business in Eastern Europe. I probably won't understand some of the details, but I was born in Poland and those people need help, even if some of them are no damn good."

She gestured dismissively in the prone young woman's direction.

David watched Harry Cochrane and Sue Yin drag the comatose Abdul toward the waiting electronics van on a canvas sheet. Abdul's head clunked softly on the door sill and again on the top flagstone step outside as his bare feet disappeared into the darkness. Shortly, Harry came back to drag Ani toward the nearby truck. David looked around him for any missing pieces of equipment and called to his sons: "Tell your mother I'll drop you by her place in about three and a half hours. We've got leave now."

Peter and Will emerged from the kitchen. Each boy gave Mrs. Kronfeld a long hug, then turned toward the carport expectantly.

The New Yorkers disappeared through Sadie Kronfeld's front door, leaving her in much the same condition she had enjoyed before the assault on the Fund burst into her quiet life, except for a severe headache, a smashed back door, and one very wet laundry room.

PLANNING THE ASSAULT

The heavily laden Verizon truck swayed ever so slightly to the left as it rolled smoothly up the southbound ramp of the Spaulding Turnpike, toward Portsmouth. David surveyed the vehicle's crowded rear compartment.

Both palms together as if in prayer under his left cheek and a Camp Longbow sweatshirt over his head, Peter was fast asleep on his left side on the van's plush beige carpeting, the curtain rung down on his cameo appearance in this dangerous drama. Will looked over Johnny Tsai's shoulder as the electronics consultant quietly explained the workings of his console. Harry was methodically cleaning and wrapping the tools of his trade, suspending the weapons in oilcloth and rolling the Kevlar vests tightly into their heavy-duty plastic bags in readiness for his next operation. Abdul, clad in wrinkled blue summer-weight trousers, lay bound and gagged, his muscular but inert body facing into the lower seam of the van's barred rear door.

David Garvey was reclining in one of the van's padded armchairs, which was bolted to the floor against the vehicle's left wall. Both of his legs rested on the truck's carpeted floor beside his former friend and sometime lover. He was silently plotting how best to make use of her unexpected treachery.

He reached down to unfasten the chin strap of her headgear and flipped up the leather flap covering over Ani's left ear.

"Let's talk about your future," David whispered sharply into her ear, intent on feeding her mixed messages. "Can we do that without hysterics?"

The subdued young woman wearily nodded twice.

"I am paying better attention if you remove glasses. They are making me sick."

"I really wish I could, but that's not possible 'til we get to where you can't do any more damage. You testified in court once already in this case. Your testimony was credible and very useful to our cause—one might even argue indispensable to our getting the temporary restraining order and then the injunction. I think you'll need to give testimony in court one more time."

"What you are talking about," Ani gasped.

"Who told you to kidnap my boys?"

"How am I knowing you will not just kill me along highway to New York? Why should I help you?" The slender woman attempted to bargain, squirming on the vibrating floor of the van, trying to ease the pressure of her handcuffs. She tried to look up at David out of the corner of her left eye but couldn't see around the cloud of distortion caused by the heavy lenses he was forcing her to wear.

David continued, "try to remember that walk in the forest, Krasavitsa, and looking up at the stars from our bed of pine needles. You must know that I've loved you. I gave you important responsibilities and trusted you with the management of a vital sector of my business. Why should I want to hurt you? Just because you kidnapped my children?"

David understood he was deliberately bombarding his captive with a mix of conflicting messages in hopes of manipulating her to suit his needs, both now and as they presented themselves later.

"Maybe I'll just throw you out on this busy highway right now," he suggested. "Can you hear the wet tires on the road and the large trailer truck passing us right now? Or perhaps I could let you swim in the East River from the 59th Street Bridge. In case you don't know about that bridge, it's very high over the East River, from 59ᵗʰ Street in Manhattan to Queens. Maybe we'll have to stop on the bridge to fix a flat tire. No one would probably even notice if you happened to fall over the side, maybe with your hands still in cuffs. I was hoping you might think of some good reason why those terrible things won't come to pass, some reason to let you go home to Poland unharmed after this is all over. Wouldn't you like to see your daughter again?"

"How are you knowing I have daughter?"

David smirked. "You often talk in your sleep, mostly in Polish. Once you mentioned your daughter and how much you missed seeing her grow up. I thought you might enjoy spending some time with her once this unpleasantness with NeuBank has finally been put to rest. There are ways to make that happen, Krasavitsa. When this is all over, maybe we can both think of it as only a very bad dream. And remember the good times!"

"What you are wanting?" she asked.

David paused for a moment to savor the tranquility surrounding him, a lull on the way to dealing with the many threats to him, his family and his business. The hiss of the Verizon truck's tires slowly subsided as the weary band of travelers approached a toll booth on this stretch of New Hampshire highway meandering south toward Dover Point, then skirting Portsmouth to the west onto Interstate 95 with its five lanes and 75 miles per hour speed limit in the direction of Greater Boston.

The thump, thump, thump of the truck's heavy-duty windshield wipers provided a calming contrast to the chaotic search for the boys and the burning anxiety David had felt. Tears blurred his view of Will sitting in Johnny Tsai's chair and entering instructions into the van's console for some task the electronics consultant had given him. It would have been so easy for some mishap to take the boys from him forever.

"All I want, all I require, is for you to tell Judge Garcia the truth about everything that happened before you took Peter and Will. Why you did it, who paid you to do that and any other details we ask you in court."

"Is that all you are wanting, Mr. Shark?"

"That's pretty much it. You know me pretty well. I never ask for Rockefeller Center when I'm willing to settle for a newsstand in Hoboken. Can you do that, convincingly and well?"

"They will kill me if I am doing that," Ani observed wryly. "But I suppose you will hurt me if I do not. Right now, you most able to do bad things to me. How you find us so easily in old woman's house?"

"Not an interesting topic. You're not on my side anymore," David Garvey said bitterly.

"We'll need to review a lot of questions this evening and each of your answers," he explained. "In preparation for this, I've already asked Frank Gillespie to arrange hearing in front of Judge Garcia tomorrow morning. You won't mind if we discuss each of them right now so you will have a chance to think about your answers and whether or not I like them. Later we'll want to put your answers on videotape, just to make sure the answers don't change at the wrong time."

Ani shuddered. Perhaps she was thinking about the final interrogation of poor Ulla Cerpinski. At the beginning, Cerpinski had been tough and defiant. As the hard questioning the young banker could never have imagined wore on, she became weaker and less certain. Without food or water, the young German was exhausted and confused, unable to resist her captors or see any way out of her downward spiral. Near the end, Cerpinski would have confessed to being Hitler's love child, willing to say whatever the people behind the bright lights wanted, even though creating a compelling record of her treachery was only a matter of form, because she'd been caught red-handed. While Ulla Cerpinski had done exactly what David wanted, she'd quickly become expendable as soon as he was finished with her. Ani was undoubtedly wondering how she could avoid ending up like that unfortunate young German banker.

Ani kept both eyes tightly shut to lessen her nausea and shifted her weight again, trying to reduce the chafing from her manacles and find a more comfortable position. More than anything else, David knew she wanted to let the humming of the tires lull her to sleep on the plush beige carpet.

"I am ready to answer questions," she finally admitted.

"Who told you asked to help snatch my kids?" David began, motioning for Johnny Tsai to hand him a microphone. Tsai turned on the console's video recorder and adjusted its volume control, even though the lawyer had no intention of using any resulting images, which would show Ani's restraints and perhaps question the admissibility or veracity of her statements. He tapped the microphone's wire mesh and noticed the electronic tech's indication that a clear signal was being captured by the van's equipment.

"Go ahead," David directed.

"When I am returning to hotel from courtroom in New York where woman judge rule in your favor, foreigner called me about 'business opportunity.' He wanted to come to my room, but I am not that stupid. I met him in hotel bar. He ask me if I want to earn $400,000, easy way. He said only picking up your boys at camp was required and delivering them as instructed. Then, he—"

"Can you describe him? Do you know his name?"

"He never told me real name. He's smaller than me, about my age but more thin, black hair and dark eyes. He had heavy gold ring on third finger of left hand. Kind with writing on it."

Ani struggled to describe the Arab without using of her hands.

"I think he from somewhere in Middle East. He said to call him Mr. Weatherly. Clothes European, very expensive."

So far, nothing clashed with what David already knew from the information Johnny Tsai had obtained from the recorded telephone conversations. He winked at Harry, who was listening carefully to every word. David reached over to softly rub the back of the distraught young woman's neck.

"That is very helpful. Tell me more. How were you to be paid? When, where, and by whom?"

"Please do not touch me. You make me think of our time together. That makes me very sad . . ."

The young woman's voice trailed off into silence. After a moment, she continued, "at first, I refuse to be part of plan, but he said they would kill me if I did not do what they want. Mr. Weatherly said my bank account in Luxembourg would be credited with $200,000 next day, balance to be paid same way once your sons delivered."

"Where was the money from?"

David watched her formless gray body turn blindly toward his voice.

"I DO NOT KNOW! You can do whatever you want with me, but I do not know! Money can come from anywhere. All I know is my account was credited as promised. I telephoned during night to bank in Luxembourg and instructed account officer to transfer entire balance to another bank. Then I called you to ask for few days of holiday."

"What happened next?"

"Can someone scratch my nose?" Ani implored her unseen captors. She sighed as Harry complied with her request. "They send car to take me from hotel to airport. Driver gave me a ticket on plane to Bangor, Maine. Abdul met me at Bangor airport; airfield looks like old military base. We drove to Bangor Fair where I met your children. Now, tell me. How did you find us so quickly?"

David looked through the front windshield as the telephone truck rounded a curve, now on local roads leading eventually to Boston's Logan Airport. The Verizon vehicle's headlights played over a rundown diner, an automotive parts supply store, and two abandoned cars before the two-lane road straightened out once again. The lawyer waved a hand to get Tsai's attention and then pointed toward the right side of the three-lane highway. At the same time he leaned down to pull down the left flap of Czarnocki's headgear and buckle it tightly under her chin.

"Time to shed a few ugly pounds," David grinned at the gaunt Chinese.

"I'm sorry, sir. I do not understand," he replied.

"About a half mile down this stretch of highway, there's a burned-out Exxon filling station on the right. I'd like to pull in there, next to what used to be a pay phone. We'll turn off all the lights just before we leave the highway. Then I'll help Harry chain this giant to a couple of pipes behind the station."

He pointed to the motionless Abdul against the rear door of the van.

"Of course, I'll give Sue Yin instructions," Tsai agreed.

A few moments later the Verizon truck lumbered away from the decaying skeleton of the abandoned gas station, toward their rendezvous with what was probably by now the humming leased Lear jet. The road toward Logan Airport stretched around a curve and into a crowded rotary before them. David reached over to unbuckle Czarnocki's leather helmet. He carefully removed her headgear and glasses and stuffed them unceremoniously into the nearby olive duffel bag.

"I'll take this off for now. But if you cause even the slightest bit of trouble, it goes right back on—glasses, earplugs, and everything."

She looked around, savoring unhindered sight.

"Where's Abdul?"

David tried to look very solemn.

"I have some familiarity with the teachings of Islam. Every serious Moslem's goal is to be with Allah. We were able to help Abdul on his journey to join Allah and perhaps enjoy his virgins. Now, where were we?"

Ani swallowed hard.

"I thought you had been learning everything about what you were wanting to know from me."

"Oh yes, what you told us was very helpful. Mostly consistent with what we already knew. But, gosh, I must have forgotten to mention something. I guess this has been so tiring, some things have escaped my attention. Did I tell you about going to NeuBank's offices tonight?"

Ani looked startled.

"What you mean? I thought you were only wanting some information, then talking to judge tomorrow. What about NeuBank's offices?"

"Your testimony will undoubtedly be very helpful, but we need documentary evidence of the connection between NeuBank and the Iraqis. I'll just bet there are some paper tracks in NeuBank's offices on Park Avenue, and you can probably help us find them most quickly!"

"You are not expecting me to help you break into NeuBank's offices. If they find out—"

David was distracted by bright lights of the airport's parking lots and terminals, whetting his appetite to gear up his counteroffensive.

"Sorry, Krasavitsa, looks we are coming to our magic carpet. As uncomfortable as it may be, I have to put your helmet and glasses back on. You're not allowed to see or hear what's next. If you're quiet and behave, I'll take off the glasses later so you can sleep on the plane. Don't worry. No one will see you in NeuBank's offices, if we're lucky. Here we go."

David cinched up Ani's leather headgear tightly even as she whined.

"Get your things together, boys," he directed his sons. "Time for a short plane ride. Maybe the pilots will let you fly the plane!"

David turned to bespectacled electronics technician.

"Your services have been truly exceptional. We would not have found my boys without your very quick and imaginative assistance. I'll be eternally in your debt."

Tsai bowed slightly, pressing his thinly gloved fingers together.

"It has been my pleasure, ah, to stretch our humble capabilities for you and your family. Please do not hesitate to call upon me if you need further assistance."

"I have one small further request. We must be certain Abdul is not available to interfere with the remainder of our efforts. I read in the *Boston Globe* there have been at least two murders in this neighborhood recently, perhaps with Arab gang connections. Maybe Abdul's heavy hand was involved. After our plane is in the air, would you mind calling the Boston homicide detectives to explain where Abdul can be found? That should keep him out of circulation long enough for our purposes."

"You may consider it done." Tsai smiled for the very first time since David had first seen him on the runway at Logan. "But that is a very tough neighborhood, Mr. Garvey. Your Iraqi friend may have, in fact, already joined Allah by that time. I suspect he might be impolite to anyone who happens by."

A MEAL GROWN COLD

Tariq al-Tikriti surveyed the north dining room of the Four Seasons from his usual table, looking uptown from the center of the room. An intricate curtain of tiny metal links shimmered gently in front of banquette-to-ceiling windows overlooking 53rd Street—a silver cascade. And all the right people were there. Two ornate Belgian crystal wine glasses filled with the finest Dom Pérignon champagne graced the expanse of freshly pressed white linen table cloth in front of the young Iraqi, adorned with a single violet orchid poised in a cut-glass vase of Swarovski crystal. Tariq must have felt like licking his lips, as he fondled the angular redhead on his right with his eyes, eager for the chase.

He raised one goblet in her direction.

"To your health and happiness, most beautiful one, and to an exciting evening ahead."

Her green eyes sparkled brightly as he explored her taut thigh and higher under the table with the nimble, searching fingers of his right hand. He smiled smugly to himself—she might be a professional, but surely one of the best.

He beamed benevolently as the tuxedo-clad *maître d'hôtel* glided sedately nearer, with a grim but well-dressed wine steward in tow. Tariq leaned forward to examine an amber bottle wrapped in a crisp white serviette graciously presented for his consideration by the wine steward. He reached into the cloth to examine the bottle's label.

251

Apparently distracted, the maître d' turned to look across the crowded room, away from the elegantly dressed couple's contemplating the wine offering of Chateau Margaux '67.

Tariq yelped as a finely honed blade tacked the fold of tan skin between the thumb and index finger of his left hand to the plain plywood table concealed beneath its sumptuous linen table cloth.

"Mr. Weatherly, I presume," the maître d' whispered menacingly in the young Arab's ear. "If you make so much as a peep, I'll slice off a couple of your finely manicured fingers. Right here. Just keep your other hand in the young lady's crotch, and we won't have any problems. Maybe we can even leave here quietly without any further bloodshed."

"And you, Miss, please reach slowly into his left inside jacket pocket to remove his bulging billfold. I am—how did my father used to say it—packing heat. That means I'll blow your brains out if you move too quickly or not fast enough. Take out his wallet, open it in your luscious lap, look it over carefully, and count out what he owes you for the evening plus a generous allowance for the fact you'll not be dining at the Four Seasons tonight. Oh well, on second thought, take whatever you want but be sure to leave me all identification."

Tariq looked furtively around the crowded dining room, reminded of the weakness of his position by the sinking feeling at the pit of his stomach and the warm and growing moisture in the crotch of his silken trousers.

"Could we perhaps make some arrangement?" Tariq squeaked. "I don't know what this is about."

"This is about kidnapping innocent children to further some unpleasant business transaction, scumbag," the maître d' continued. "I'd derive extreme pleasure from gutting you like the piece of trash fish you are, right here in front of all these beautiful people. For reasons that need not concern you, my own days are denominated in rather small numbers. I wouldn't be deterred from terminating your loathsome existence by whatever punishment our creaky system of justice might someday mete out to me, even if anyone nearby would even look up from their meals while you bled out," the pale young man snarled into Tariq's quivering ear. "How ya doing, Miss? Find anything interesting?"

"Just fine," the hooker grinned. "This camel jockey carries lots of large denomination bills, euros and dollars, but I can't seem to find my coat check. You know, you're really doing me a real favor, Mister. No telling what kind of perverted tricks this little twerp would have demanded later. Isn't there something I could do for you? I give great head."

The maître d' grinned wickedly. "Under the present circumstances, that might be a little awkward. How about a rain check? Perhaps you could slip your card into my coat pocket. Where's the ticket for the coat room, asshole?" he demanded, twisting the blade sticking through Tariq's hand. "You wouldn't want this young lady to be uncomfortable outside in the night air without her wrap."

Exalted Leader's esteemed nephew grimaced with pain.

"It's in my right front pants pocket."

"Miss, please extract your coat check from his pocket, quickly and quietly," the maître d' said. "We really must be going. And you, Mr. Weatherly, enjoy the feel, it's the closest thing to sex you'll be having for a very long time."

The redhead observed brightly, "this one reminds of a line from that old Bette Midler movie—needle dick the bug fucker. Oh, here it is!" Then she recoiled. "Ewwww, it's wet! If you'll excuse me, I really must powder my nose and, after this turkey, wash my hands."

She winked at the tuxedoed domestic, slid away from her customer, stood up gracefully, stretching her delicious legs, and paused for a moment to slip a red lock of short hair behind her right ear.

Tariq sadly watched his evening's entertainment, most of his cash, and probably all of his credit cards sashay smoothly across the crowded room to the obvious relish of several male diners and the consternation of their wives, girlfriends, or mistresses. Just then, a tall and angular waiter scurried up to Tariq's table.

"Mr. Weatherly, you have a telephone call. The jack beside your table is not working. I do apologize. Would you mind terribly taking the call at the center island?"

"How convenient! What took you so fucking long, dipshit?" Harry Cochrane's man muttered under his breath.

"Here's the script, Mr. Weatherly or whatever your real name is," the maître d' hissed. "I'll withdraw this razor-sharp blade just enough so you can move your hand into that swell linen napkin in your lap while you hope it doesn't damage your special trousers any more than you did while pissing your pants. Then you slide slowly toward me and stand up, ever so carefully. One move in the wrong direction or anything clever, and I'll slit your scrawny throat. And don't even think about trying to do me with the table! It's firmly bolted to the floor. I checked that before you strolled in with your hooker. Together, we'll walk calmly toward the front door, like we're the very best of friends or something. If you're a really good boy, I may not kill you right here, as much as that would make my entire week. Any questions?"

Tariq shook his head glumly.

"Cheer up, Mr. Weatherly, you could be dead already. Worse still, you could be in one of your esteemed uncle's famous prisons for failing so miserably," Harry Cochrane's operative snickered. "Now move, ass wipe! We've got places to go, people to meet, and all that other good shit."

Tariq tentatively slid toward this dangerous man as he had been instructed, his eyes averted. He covered his bleeding left hand with the ample dinner napkin that also draped over the growing dark patch on his trousers where he had wet himself. The young Iraqi picked his way carefully across the rich expanse of claret carpet and up the steps toward the maître d's console where a heavyset man in a three-piece black linen suit and a Burberry trench coat was arguing with the head waiter.

Tariq stood obediently beside the glowing tank of tropical fish, feigning interest in the exotic clownfish, blennies, and electric blue damsels lazily swimming among clouds of flowing green vegetation. Sneaking a look over his shoulder, the Leader's most highly educated relative discovered the nasty wine steward and his helpers had disappeared. He was just quietly turning toward the stairs leading down to the street exit when the man in the Burberry trench coat whispered loudly in his ear.

"Why, Mr. Weatherly, how nice to see you here. Do you suppose we might just step outside for a chat?" Martin Gluck urged Tariq in the smoothest of voices while jamming the barrel of a .45-automatic into his ribs from under the trench coat for emphasis.

"Do you have a coat? Oh, I'll bet you misplaced your ticket. Well, not to worry. You won't be needing that fine camel's hair overcoat anyway. Why don't we just amble casually down these stairs? Please do smile occasionally. And, just so I'll be welcome next time the wife and I come in for dinner, why don't you hand the doorman a fifty on the way out, from the sterling silver money clip in your left trouser pocket?" the detective sniggered. "Smoothly now, let's go!"

At the bottom of the restaurant's circular staircase, Martin Gluck and Tariq stepped down onto the shiny marble floor in front of gold-framed double doors opening onto East 52nd Street, between Park and Lexington Avenues. Tariq looked beneath his feet to see reflections of the ceiling lights. A red-faced doorman in mufti waited patiently beside the expansive pair of doors facing 52nd Street, his white-gloved hand poised at the door's brass handle.

"Taxi, sir?" the doorman asked.

"What do you think, Mr. Weatherly? Ah, as always, you're so right, Mr. Weatherly. A stroll in the crisp evening air would the best thing after such a fine dining experience."

Gluck nudged Tariq with the hidden pistol barrel.

Without a word, Tariq reached into his left trouser pocket and retrieved a shiny money clip. As he numbly counted the bills, al-Tikriti saw three twenties and a five. He looked at Gluck for instructions. The detective nodded his head in the direction of the waiting doorman. Weighing the matter carefully, the Iraqi handed the three large bills to the attendant as he held open the door to the street. Tariq stepped out onto the sidewalk, oblivious to the doorman's effusive response.

Two oversized white limousines idled beside the curb. Pedestrians crowded the side street as traffic whizzed by, east on 52nd.

"We have an urgent appointment presently in the Pan Am building," Martin Gluck explained in a low voice as he directed the Leader's hope for economic survival toward Park Avenue. "Please don't even think of running. You'd be dead before the third step. I'm a crack shot. Oh goodness, I've forgotten an important administrative matter. You are Tariq al-Tikriti, aren't you?"

The young man stared at his captor blankly.

"What difference does it make?"

"Here's a subpoena directing you to appear to testify tomorrow morning at the United District Court for the Southern District of New York in the matter of *Königsberg Fund, Inc. v. Neu Ost Bank*, but I'll save you the trouble of finding the courthouse. In fact, I'll personally see that you have both the time and the opportunity to be present for the hearing before the Honorable Milagros Garcia at 9:30 A.M. I'll just put this subpoena in your pocket. You know, it doesn't work like the old George Raft movies. You don't have to accept the subpoena or even read it. The fact I have served you and submit an affidavit to that effect to the Court is enough. It would be naughty of you to ignore this legal process, but I'm going to make sure you honor your obligations to our legal system, Mr. Weatherly."

As the two men reached the east side of Park Avenue, Martin Gluck gestured expansively from north to south along the elegant stretch of roadway where Christmas lights were already sparkling from evergreen trees planted in the avenue's center island well in advance of the early holiday season. At 46th Street, a stream of southbound taillights disappeared into the old New York Central building, now the Helmsley Building, ornately decorated in gold leaf. High over the Helmsley Building towered the Pan Am Building, glittering atop Grand Central Station.

"See that tasteful Pan Am logo," Gluck commented to his silent companion. "We're meeting some people there in a few minutes. How's your German?"

"Not ba . . . wait a minute," Tariq exclaimed. "What's that have to do with anything?"

"Good question. The answer is we're going to stop by NeuBank's offices to see if they have any documents that might be useful in the case I mentioned. You seem like a clever chap. I'll bet you're wondering why a bank would be open at this time of night. You might say there've been some special arrangements made for us. Let's hurry along—wouldn't want to be late."

Gluck prodded Ani's controller along the east side of Park Avenue toward the dingy pedestrian tunnel under the Helmsley Building, passing the stairway down into walkways into the bowels of Grand Central Station in the process.

"Your job, when we get there, is to pretend that you can't talk. Probably difficult, but I know you'll do your very best. Whatever anyone outside our party says to you, you don't understand. *Capisce?*" Martin Gluck continued.

Gluck and Tariq emerged from Helmsley Walk East onto a nearly deserted 45th Street. Two cabs idled quietly on the south side of the narrow road—one driver apparently asleep, the other bobbing to a distinctly different drummer somewhere behind white plastic buds that filled both of his ears. Across 45th Street, the young Iraqi noticed two men in the shadows to the right of the Pan Am Building's brightly lit entrances, near Cafe Centro II, an attractive blonde wedged tightly between them. Gluck looked up and down 45th Street before poking respected Leader's nephew in the ribs with his heavy-duty pistol. "Let's go! It's showtime. Remember what I told you before: don't talk to anyone unless I tell you to once we get inside the building. If you can be some help to us, that might prolong your miserable existence. Personally, I don't care if you have a fatal accident right here. If, for example, you should happen to fall down a long set of fire stairs in the Pan Am Building, I would get home to my football game all the more quickly."

When they approached the trio, Tariq must have been shocked to discover these people had captured Agnieszczka Czarnocki. She really looked worked over. Nasty bruises on her forehead and the left side of her normally pretty face were obvious, even in the pool of shadows near the building's doorway. Tariq cast about for some, any, means of escape. *Where is Abdul?* he wondered. *Maybe he could help me out of this mess.*

An angry blond man, who the well-dressed Arab suspected might be David Garvey, watched Czarnocki like a hawk as the two men drew closer. She flinched as Tariq stumbled into the glow of the bright entranceway, urged on by Gluck. The American lawyer looked at them both contemptuously. "Ms. Czarnocki, may I introduce Mr. Weatherly? Oh, I see that's not necessary. Let's be on our way."

David scrutinized each of the other four, mentally cataloguing the different pieces of the puzzle now falling into place. He wondered what parts of the jigsaw puzzle were unaccounted for or beyond his reach.

"Harry, you're in charge of the honey blonde from the south of Poland. If she tries anything, blow off her left knee first. Other friendly, you keep Mr. Weatherly on a very short tether. At the slightest provocation, you're authorized to do whatever seems most effective. We'll be passing through a guard station on the way up to NeuBank's offices. Do not mistake my good manners for lack of resolve. You are both responsible for endangering the lives of my only children. I haven't decided what to do with either of you, yet."

With that, David snatched up his black leather briefcase, pushed through the revolving doors, and trudged up the motionless escalator to the mezzanine level. The others followed close behind, Tariq dragging an overflowing canvas bag of litigation documents cuffed to his wrist, a burden Harry Cochrane had suggested in order to make the young Iraqi's movements more cumbersome. David crossed the highly polished tile floor toward a raised desk. Behind the wide, black Formica counter, a young security guard in a gray-and-red piped uniform was lost in the roar of a flashing television set.

"'Scuse me," David yelled above the din.

The guard only half looked at David and his freshly pressed suit and suspenders.

"Say what?" she barked from the corner of her mouth without taking her eyes off the colorful screen and its rapidly moving images.

Martin Gluck leaned over the lip of the wooden counter, his pistol jamming into his captive's bruised rib cage. "Who's winning?"

"Chuggers! Man, 'nem Skins really suck this yeah," the security guard answered without turning her brace of tightly wound corn rows.

"Where y'all goin'?" she asked absently.

"Duplantier, Merman and Schultz on twenty-three. We have a meeting there," David said, slowly enunciating the name of a law firm with offices in the building.

Rolling a large, pink tongue around the full circumference of her lips, the guard yawned.

"Y'all gots a building card or do I gots to call up?"

"No problem. Here's my card." David passed Harry's pilfered Pan Am Building access card across the flat surface, hoping nothing very elaborate was in store from the distracted security guard.

"No problem."

She waved the plastic card back at David without even looking at it.

"Run you mothah! Go right up, second bank on ya right. 'Dose othahs wif you?"

"Sure are," David answered. "Thanks for your help."

With a sharp poke to the base of Ani's spine, David Garvey directed his entourage toward the one working elevator in the middle bank of eight, a light glowing over its pair of open doors.

Looking suspiciously around the nearly deserted mezzanine just before the elevator doors slid shut, Harry Cochrane satisfied himself that no one was following them.

"You know," the detective observed, "there's a chance someone will be working in NeuBank's offices. It's a week night."

"Not very fucking likely." David muttered. "It's nearly midnight, and NeuBank's offices are staffed mostly with former servants of the East German workers and peasants. I'll bet someone could get trampled standing outside NeuBank's front door at quitting time. The chance of anyone's burning the midnight oil is probably somewhere between piss-poor and dog shit. Even if you're right, we don't have many other options. And besides, Little Miss Hot Pants here has permission to enter NeuBank's offices. She even has the code to the Bank's alarm system. Here we are at twenty-three. Around the corner to the right, swing open the fire door, into fire stairs, and down one flight to twenty-two. Harry, I hope you have the tools we need to get in at twenty-two."

"Does the Pope wear little white shoes?"

"I thought he wore little red shoes," David ventured.

"That was the last Pontiff. Nothing but the best for St. Peter's direct successor," Harry explained.

Shortly, the two sleuths, David Garvey, and their two unwilling companions were poised expectantly in the darkened corridor in front of the nondescript entrance to the New York Federal Branch of Neu Ost Bank on the twenty-second floor of the Pan Am Building. David, Martin Gluck and the two captives stood waiting quietly around a far corner near a set of fire stairs while Harry Cochrane busied himself with the door locks. David heard a sharp click and peered around the corner to see that Harry had disappeared inside. The sound of "tap, tap, tap" reached David's ears as Harry entered the alarm's pass code.

"All clear," the gumshoe whispered from the open doorway, a faint glow from lights of surrounding skyscrapers spilling onto the hall's faded gray, standard office-building issue carpet.

"Ani, here's where you have the potential to add some value," David said sharply. He grabbed Ani's head with both hands over her ears and forced her to look directly into his eyes.

"Now's your chance to prove I didn't make a mistake by bringing you back alive from New Hampshire. Don't disappoint me again—there won't be a third chance."

David jerked the slender woman toward the opening created by the open door. Over his shoulder, he snarled at Tariq: "stay close behind. Your job is to provide instant analysis of the Iraqi connection."

Harry Cochrane met them inside the Bank's main entrance.

"I've located Diether Kreuz's office. Is that the best place to look, Ani?" he asked.

"Yes, that is where he keeps papers," the young woman answered with a sigh as she watched David pull on a pair of milk-colored plastic surgical gloves, just like Harry Cochrane and the other American were wearing.

David disappeared down the long, dark hallway, dragging the stumbling Polish woman close behind, the industrial grade gray carpet in front of him marked by a small moving circle of intense light from the piercing LED on headgear he'd taken out of his briefcase.

BARE KNUCKLES

"All rise!"

David Garvey watched Thomas Mullaney, the Honorable Milagros Garcia's temporary bailiff, loudly pound the side of her bench with his callused palm. The civil servant absently pressed his groin slightly below the belt with the heel of a gnarled left hand.

"Please be seated," Judge Garcia muttered as she plopped into her seat under the gigantic polished aluminum Great Seal.

"Now what's so urgent here? As you probably know, I'm new at this judge business, but it strikes me as most unusual to receive motion papers just yesterday, returnable today. That's certainly less than the normal notice."

She peered down indignantly at Frank Gillespie. "This better be good, Counselor! Why are you in such a hurry to amend the Complaint? Why couldn't this wait for the normal amount of notice? May I assume it was a simple oversight that my copy of your motion did not include supporting affidavits or any memorandum of law?"

"No, Your Honor," Garvey, Stahl's senior litigator gulped, scouring his bushy mustache with the knuckle of his right index finger. "We feared for the personal safety of our witnesses. If we'd filed the usual affidavits and supporting materials with the Court, the normal five days before our motion was to be heard, our witnesses might have been killed. But I can expl—"

"Make it short and sweet, Counselor! You're trying my patience!" the jurist barked.

"Of course, Your Honor," Frank blurted. "The short answer, Your Honor, is the Fund is amending its complaint to include racketeering claims based on wire fraud, kidnapping and extortion and to assert a cause of action based on the Bank's knowing violation of the Treasury Department's Iraqi sanctions. We have a live witness who'll testify that NeuBank arranged to have our client's children kidnapped in order to force the Fund to withdraw its complaint in this action."

Continuing to rub his mustache nervously, Frank gestured toward the second row of benches where a subdued Agniesczka Czarnocki sat directly in front of Martin Gluck who, out of the judge's line of sight, was nearly choking Ani with her own ornate gold necklace.

The Fund's counsel continued, "I have the necessary supporting affidavits and memorandum of law right here. With the Court's permission, I'll hand them up and provide Defendant's counsel with copies as well. This is simply too urgent to delay."

The judge leaned over the bench to receive a bundle of papers and a tiny chip from David Garvey's law partner. Judge Garcia looked truly puzzled. "Isn't this the same witness who testified on behalf of the Fund during the initial hearing?"

"Yes, Your Honor," Frank responded quickly, pausing in midsentence to pass a similar stack of documents to Margaret Wilbur, while pressing on the scraggly growth under his nose, as if trying to rub it off his face. Frank was beginning to hit his stride, to fall into the rhythm of the hearing, if the fact he was worrying his mustache less and less was credible evidence.

"Well, then why didn't she testify about these supposedly urgent matters back then? Really, Counselor, this makes no sense at all. You're stretching the Court's tolerance by showing up here at the last minute without allowing either the Court or opposing counsel some time to digest your claims and legal arguments," Judge Garcia continued without missing a beat.

"The fact is, Your Honor, the kidnapping took place almost immediately after the last hearing. We only recently obtained conclusive proof of NeuBank's wire fraud and violation of the Iraqi sanctions. Ms. Czarnocki will testify that she participated in the kidnapping of Mr. Garvey's two sons, under the Bank's instructions and was well paid by NeuBank for doing so.

"And we also have another witness who has firsthand knowledge of the connection between the Bank and the Iraqi government, as well as the business transactions between them. That violates our government's Iraqi sanctions. We ask the Court to bear with us while we put on our case—it won't take long. Our new evidence will conclusively demonstrate NeuBank's liability to the Fund and will sufficiently detail the illegal acts complained of that the Court should consider referring the matter to the US Attorney's office for criminal prosecution."

"Thank you, Mr. Gillespie."

Judge Garcia turned to Margaret Wilbur. She was already standing, her face a deep beet red.

"You have a request, Ms. Wilbur?"

Maggie lunged verbally from her standing position next to S&M's young associate, Michael Peng, her jaw locking slightly in the open position: "Your Honor, this is worse than outrageous!"

Although it would have been against his best interests, David Garvey fervently wished that he could somehow help Maggie.

NeuBank's senior counsel continued. "I would never, ever, have expected such a sleazy ambush from Plaintiff's counsel. I've been trying to get papers from Garvey, Stahl since they served us with this motion very late yesterday, I might add. Although I tried to contact Your Honor, both in writing and by telephone, I was told first by your law clerk that the Court does not entertain telephone conferences and then that our written requests would be heard today. We really had no choice but to show up here as scheduled, trying to guess what Plaintiff had in mind. I need some time to consider these materials and to discuss them with my client. To make matters worse, my client's US representative has been unavoidably detained by other matters and is unlikely to arrive before the Court hears argument. He would be grossly prejudiced if this hearing went ahead without his being able to participate, with full knowledge of the implications to Neu Ost Bank. We demand an adjournment of this hearing for at least two days."

Margaret Wilbur sat down abruptly and yanked the newly admitted attorney beside her down by the sleeve.

Frank Gillespie had already jumped to his feet. "Your Honor, both of our witnesses may evaporate if any delay is allowed. Ms. Czarnocki is appearing as a hostile witness since she has admitted to being on NeuBank's payroll in kidnapping David Garvey's two young sons from their summer camp. Our other witness runs a serious risk of not being able to appear any other time."

"What does that mean, Counselor? What are you trying to tell me?" the visibly irritated judge demanded. "Who's this other mystery witness you keep referring to? I don't see anyone else in the courtroom."

"Your Honor, once the identity of our second witness is known, his very existence will be in jeopardy. Agnieszcka Czarnocki can provide personal and direct testimony concerning the kidnapping of Peter and Will Garvey as a direct result of the Fund's starting this litigation. But we could, if necessary, prove her role in the kidnapping and the related extortion by other evidence, including the testimony of the two children, if the Court considers that necessary or appropriate. Once our other witness enters this courtroom, or if someone from the opposition catches a glimpse of him in the corridors, his days will be numbered in single digits unless we can get him into some kind of protective custody arrangement with the government. In fact, once this hearing is over, we'll ask that he be placed in protective custody pending the Court's reference of this case to the criminal authorities. In the interim, I have taken the liberty of placing him in the Court's witness room."

Frank sat down, probably thinking he seemed to have gotten the judge's attention.

Judge Garcia announced, "you're in luck, Ms. Wilbur! I have a sentencing in the last of the late Judge Fischbein's capital drug cases to complete this afternoon. If that goes according to plan, we can resume this hearing in about forty minutes. And, if you don't mind, in view of what Plaintiff has alleged, please do not leave the courtroom."

The judge gathered her files, stood up to leave and turned toward the door behind her raised bench.

"Your Honor," Margaret Wilbur shrieked, "what are you suggesting? Is the Court inferring that I might somehow endanger the safety of the Fund's mystery witness?"

"Nothing of the sort, Ms. Wilbur. But it seems to me if Mr. Gillespie's accusations are wholly or even partly true, it might be dangerous to allow anyone in this group to reach a telephone or leave this room. If his accusations are false, no damage will have been done, and you'll have a chance to read the papers right here in this comfortable courtroom. I'll reserve decision following argument pending receipt of any papers you wish to submit. And, if Mr. Gillespie's accusations are false, I can have his head later for wasting the Court's time and attention," the judge tossed over her shoulder as she hurried into the adjoining robing room.

From a cramped corner of the hard oaken bench in Judge Garcia's witness room, behind the rear wall of the courtroom, Tariq al-Tikriti looked skeptically at Harry Cochrane. Harry sat in a gray folding metal chair with his back to the smudged pale green wall, where he could easily reach Tariq, while still keeping a watchful eye on the single door between the witness room and the courtroom. He had locked the exit to the corridor passageway from the inside.

In the silent courtroom, David Garvey was struck by how much Ani seemed to have aged since the last hearing only a week ago, as if the recent turbulent events had sucked away the remainder of her youth, leaving behind only a dry shell to mask her physical pain.

Tariq, from what David had observed in the limo on the way down to court, although appearing genuinely concerned, gave no indication of having figured out what was really happening. If the Iraqi understood what was in store for him personally, he was doing an excellent job of covering it up. David could only imagine the Leader's reaction to his nephew's appearing in an American court to spill the beans. Two otherwise productive individuals had suddenly made themselves very disposable!

A harried, overweight blonde woman wearing a faded navy blazer with a metal badge and rumpled grey woolen trousers peered furtively through the swinging doors of Judge Garcia's courtroom. Seeing the bench momentarily empty, the young marshal reached back into the passageway to reel in her reluctant charge.

She hauled a muscular black man dressed in the loose fitting blue smock and matching pants of the prison world into the quiet courtroom, stumbling over one of her shoelaces in the process. The manacled convict was hobbled by a pair of leg irons. His clean-shaven pate gleamed in the harsh lighting of this penultimate stop in the Federal criminal justice system. Both of the prisoner's arms were shackled securely behind his back with a pair of chainless handcuffs, and heavy leg irons clinked on the courtroom floor. His piercing scowl searched the lawyers seated near the bench; they scattered like a flock of sparrows in face of a hawk. David landed next to Ambrose Jett and his mound of case law, Frank in an empty polished wooden bench, and Maggie in the back row with the pile of papers received from the Fund's head litigator, glancing only furtively in David's direction as she passed him.

An independent observer might have thought both litigators were trying to avoid this tangible evidence of society's shortcomings, as if they had both suddenly chanced upon a leper. As a corporate lawyer, David had never witnessed a criminal sentencing of any sort, much less for a capital offense.

The prisoner strained against his restraints to look over his broad right shoulder, perhaps hoping to find a friendly face in the courtroom. Except for the cast of characters in David's case, the rows of benches were empty.

One of the courtroom's swinging wooden doors opened slightly, then was poked aside by the tip of a carved maple cane, followed by a slightly stooped old man in a spot-stained dark brown houndstooth suit. The public defender, Benijah Davis, shuffled slowly into the room, an unruly thatch of graying black hair and goatee seeming to add to his burden, dragging an overflowing canvas satchel of papers. The elderly lawyer moved haltingly toward the convict and sat down heavily beside him, placing his cane carefully on the floor under the highly polished table. He cast a jaundiced eye in the hovering marshal's direction and began to whisper quietly into the ear of his client, the bound black man.

Both men looked up abruptly when the pair of swinging doors parted noisily to admit the stocky form of F. Leonard Smiley, Esq., Assistant US Attorney, the prosecuting attorney in the matter of *United States v. Lemuel Washington*. Smiley carefully placed his alligator-skin briefcase on the adjacent table and paused to consult an antique gold watch attached to a golden chain passing through one of the buttonholes of his silk vest.

"All rise. The United States District Court for the Southern District of New York is now in session. Draw near, give your attention, and you shall be heard. God bless these United States and this Honorable Court, Judge Milagros B. Garcia presiding," Judge Garcia's interim bailiff, Thomas Mullaney, announced loudly in a gravelly voice.

"Please be seated," the jurist directed as she walked hesitantly toward the raised bench at center stage.

"The clerk will call the next case!"

Mullaney cleared his throat noisily, fumbled with a pair of cheap drugstore reading glasses, and read from his copy of the Court's docket sheet:

"*United States v. Lemuel Washington*."

His initial obligation fulfilled, the bailiff looked around nervously, absently felt the lump of metal below his waistband, and tiptoed toward his tiny office at the rear of the courtroom when he expected no one would have the faintest interest in what he might be doing.

Harry Cochrane looked up as Mullaney peeked through the witness room's partly opened door at the back of the civil servant's government office.

"Just need a file from that cabinet you're sitting in front of, sir," the bailiff said.

The clerk bowed respectfully as he tiptoed across the space between them and deliberately crowded the detective against the wall behind his folding chair, pretending to reach a locked file drawer high overhead.

"Sure, but—"

Harry was lifted out of his metal chair by the shock of Mullaney's first rising swing with a short length of lead pipe snatched from its hiding place in the clerk's waistband. A second slashing blow struck Harry behind his left ear, and the third smashed the detective on the chin! The gumshoe gamely raised both hands to protect himself, but Mullaney dropped Harry to the floor, first with a rabbit punch to the solar plexus and then another quick chop across the back of his head with the heavy pipe. Harry Cochrane clutched feebly at the back of his flimsy seat for an instant but then collapsed heavily onto grimy institutional green tiles.

The young Iraqi froze in the far corner.

Mullaney fished a bulging key ring out of his left pants pocket and clicked open the wooden door to an adjacent utility closet. After dumping the unconscious detective into the tiny space's shadowy confines and snapping its lock shut, the court officer turned to Tariq. By now, he had regained some of his composure.

"I'll bet you've come to help me," Tariq offered brightly. "Did my uncle send you to get me out of this awful place?"

"Half right." Mullaney smiled wickedly through a wide gap between two nicotine-stained front teeth. "Just sit right there and don't move or make a sound. I'll be right with you."

Tariq breathed a small sigh of relief as he watched the room's interior door swing shut behind Mullaney. He heard the court officer's rubber-soled shoes squeak across the small adjoining cubicle and another door's opening, perhaps into the courtroom. "Excuse me, ma'am." Mullaney put a hand on Margaret Wilbur's shoulder. "Are you the counsel for Neu Ost Bank?"

"Ah, er, yes," she mumbled, pushing the clerk's grimy fingers against her ivory silk blouse and exhaling against the odor of his rotting teeth.

Maggie was distracted by the rising tide of claims against NeuBank detailed *ad nauseam* in the lengthy affidavit recently provided to her by Frank Gillespie. She felt betrayed because her client had obviously not told her the full story.

"What can I do for you?" she ventured faintly.

"Well, ma'am, there's an urgent telephone call for you. If you wouldn't mind terribly, could you please take the call in my office, so it won't interrupt the sentencing?" Mullaney suggested.

"Oh, sure. Where's the phone?" Maggie answered, reflexively correct and polite.

Mullaney pointed toward his cramped office. Leaving her stack of half-read papers on the polished wooden bench next to Michael Peng, Maggie followed Mullaney. She padded across the patchwork of dingy green tiles toward a solitary telephone perched on the civil servant's dilapidated metal desk. As the S&M litigator reached toward the instrument, Mullaney pulled the door firmly shut behind him.

"Which line?" Margaret Wilbur squinted at the instrument, wishing she'd remembered to pick up her reading glasses from the courtroom bench.

"Whichever one you prefer," the clerk answered, noiselessly drawing a 9-millimeter German Luger with silencer from his left waistband and pointing it between the unsuspecting lawyer's shoulder blades.

"But, none of them are blinking," she said, turning to face her tormentor.

"Right, but that doesn't matter. We've got a busy day ahead. You may live to tell about it if you decide right now to forget about doing anything stupid. This gun's fully loaded, and I've got another clip. I've burned lots of bridges today, so I don't have much to lose, except perhaps the appointment as a Supreme Court Justice Senator Rendleman undoubtedly has in mind for yours truly." Thomas Mullaney laughed at his captive, his raspy voice rising and rising in pitch until it became a demented croak.

Maggie was confused and scared out of her wits. She cast frantically about for some trail of bread crumbs that might lead her out of this madness.

"What could you possibly want from me?" Maggie begged, rumpling her chestnut brown hair. "I'm just a lawyer. Surely not worth kidnapping!"

"My—how shall we say, employer—very badly wants something only David Garvey can produce. Your personal security and safety is near or at the top of Mr. Garvey's list of important things." Thomas Mullaney peered at Maggie, searching for any sign of weakness.

She cowered under the intensity of his piercing scowl and felt the nearly liquid heat of panic and indecision paralyze her arms and legs.

"I, I don't really know what you're trying to say," Maggie stammered. "I mean, er, many things are very important to David—his boys, his job, his business. I don't know," her voice trailed off into a half sob before she allowed herself to utter the forbidden words tumbling inside her head, "what to do."

"Right," the clerk muttered, extracting a worn blue spiral notebook from the pocket of his white polyester shirt and flipping through its smudged pages.

"I suppose that's why, for example, the two of you had a late dinner on Tuesday at that little out-of-the-way Italian place just above Canal Street. You had pizzocheri, a small green salad, and a glass of the house white wine. Then you went back to his place for the night. Only stopped by your own apartment in the morning to change clothes and send your daughter off to Nightingale before going into the office," Thomas Mullaney read from his notes and looked carefully at David's lover to see how his information had affected her resolve.

Licking his lips, the government employee added softly, "such a beautiful little girl, such smooth, young legs."

Margaret Wilbur's eyes widened, but she could only gasp. "Where'd you get that garbage?! You're making it all up!"

"Whatever! We're leaving this building the normal way—out through the front door," Mullaney instructed the quivering lawyer. "There aren't any metal detectors on the exit side. All you have to do is act normal, and don't try anything stupid. We're leaving this room by the rear entrance, so you'll finally get to meet your honey's mystery witness. He'll be going with us as well, so the two of you will walk in front of me, like you're really good friends or even lawyer and client. I'll be close behind, and I won't hesitate to shoot. Don't expect any help from him though. Besides being a wimp, he's a devious little shit. Just give me a reason to ignore the money they're going to give me because I'll bet I can dish out more pain than you can take." Thomas Mullaney rambled on, his voice rising again, ending in a liquid gurgle.

The renegade clerk nudged Margaret Wilbur toward the witness room with the silencer at the end of his pistol. Ordering her to face away from him, Mullaney carefully opened the wire door of a small cage almost hidden at the back of his jumbled desk and reached inside, toward a tiny green-and-yellow parrot.

"Rosabelle, my queen. They're conspiring to drive me away from you. I can't come back. There'll be no one to feed you. Here, give Daddy a good-bye kiss," he crooned as softly as his congested lungs would permit, letting the brightly colored bird hop onto his outstretched palm.

Glancing at Maggie's slightly trembling back over his shoulder, Thomas Mullaney gently caressed his pet with an index finger. Then he averted his eyes and squeezed Rosabelle with every ounce of his strength until Maggie could hear a series of tiny snaps. Mullaney quickly tossed the inert, feathery corpse back into its cramped wire coffin and rammed his gun into Maggie's lower back, urging her toward the witness room and the bustling corridor beyond.

". . . taking into account the mitigating factors advanced by your counsel, the Court sentences you to transportation and forty years' confinement without the possibility of parole at the Federal detention facility on Herschel Island, Yukon Territory, in lieu of the death penalty. This Court stands adjourned!" the Honorable Milagros Garcia intoned.

Then Judge Garcia energetically rapped a small maple disk on the bench in front of her with a polished antique gavel as if washing her hands of that tawdry affair.

"Where's my bailiff?" she barked.

The judge leaned over the left corner of the bench to question one of her nearby law clerks while impatiently punching the bailiff's buzzer several times.

"You find him!" Milagros Garcia directed her only male law clerk, a recent graduate of the University of Virginia Law School, with uncommon harshness.

The convict, Lemuel Washington, heaved a sigh of relief. His public defender had repeatedly warned Washington about the possibility of being sentenced to death by lethal injection. This multiple drug offender had been willing to go to trial before Judge Fischbein, without a jury, knowing that judge had a long record of opposing mandatory Federal sentencing guidelines. But Judge Fischbein's untimely demise shortly after the completion of his trial had thrown all of Washington's careful planning into disarray. A new judge, and worse, a former prosecutor. From what Davis told him, Judge Garcia had sent a number of mobsters to the needle in her time as a prosecutor. Lemuel Washington could endure the frigid climate of the government's Alcatraz of the north in far northwestern Canada, leased from the region's indigenous peoples, better than he could deal with the official needle.

The prisoner rose slowly in response to the marshal's jerk at his manacles, kicked away the government-issue chair, and moved toward the courtroom's double doors at the fastest pace his leg irons would permit. Behind prisoner 637956641, Washington's public defender dropped his ragged file folder into the waiting sack, deliberately avoiding his client's backward glance as he disappeared into the maw of the Federal prison system.

"Ya Onah, I can't faaahnd Mista Mullhaneh," the lanky West Virginian reported, teasing the tip of his curly red beard thoughtfully. "I looked in his office an the witness room. Both empty exceptin' for some scufflin' and hollrin' comin' from one a them cabinets in the witness room. That door's locked. I'm fixin' to call someone to come up from maintenance with the master keys."

David's ears instantly perked up. He bounded out of his seat beside Ambrose Jett and into the bailiff's vacant cubicle, quietly pulling the door shut behind him.

"Harry! Harry!" David yelled frantically, circling the cluttered desk and file cabinets.

Forcing his way into the adjacent room, he pushed aside two sagging cardboard boxes of files and pounded on one of the larger closet doors. From inside, David could hear the thumps of someone's leather soles kicking sheet metal and loud but muffled swearing.

"That you, Harry?" he yelled at the vibrating door handle, putting his ear to the scratched gray metal panel.

David could barely hear an angry male voice beneath the flurry of loud thumps booming from inside.

"Fuckin' right it's me! That mother fucking court officer's working with the opposition. Get me the fuck out of here. Right now! He's been gone about five minutes with Weatherly and your girlfriend—both involuntarily! Sounds like a real pervert!"

The enraged detective continued to batter the locker's insides.

"Suppose you could stop kicking the door long enough for me to jimmy the lock? I'll have you out in just a minute," David said.

David Garvey deftly inserted a thin metal tool into the latch to probe for its catch.

"There—just like I promised."

The door finally slammed open and an embarrassed Harry Cochrane tumbled out sideways, breaking his fall with both hands.

"He got the drop on me, David, and then worked me over with a lead pipe. What the fuck do we do next?"

Harry reached into his pocket for a crumpled linen handkerchief to blot a patch of congealing red-brown blood oozing from his cracked and swollen chin.

"My jaw and head ache like you wouldn't believe, but we've got to get moving. This guy is serious and well prepared. From what little I could hear, this guy Mullaney or his controller will be in touch with you very soon. What do you want me to do?"

"Take a few minutes at Mullaney's desk and see if you can find something to write down every address and telephone number that might lead us somewhere. Get your people together with Olivia Ojeda to put a high-quality bug on my portable number, including caller tracing so we can nail whoever calls me. Have Olivia alert the office to have all calls sent through to my pager. Have my office tell all callers that's the only way I can be reached. I'm going back into court to make sure Frank has got the rabbit's neck firmly between his teeth and give him some ideas about how to most effectively shake the rabbit!"

David disappeared through the door into the corrupt bailiff's office. *How, in God's name,* he wondered, *could NeuBank be finished off and Margaret saved, all at the same time, when no one friendly had even the slightest idea where Mullaney might be taking her?* Even worse, David's overburdened brain kept exploding with thoughts of all the awful things that pervert might do to his soul mate.

Back into the courtroom, David confirmed Maggie was gone, her purse and documents abandoned on the rear bench of the spectators' section. He scooped up the purse and carried it toward the well of the court, where Michael Peng and Judge Garcia were engaged in a heated discussion, to Frank's obvious amusement. Noticing Attorney Peng was seriously distracted, David slipped Margaret Wilbur's purse under her chair at the defense table and moved to his own place, motioning Frank to join him. Just then, Diether Kreuz blustered into the courtroom, sat down in Maggie's unoccupied chair, and turned to glare at David and his law partner.

"We have a couple of additional problems," David announced tersely through a hand cupped to Frank's ear, as the senior litigator sat at the counsels' table. "The bailiff that was hovering around here apparently grabbed Margaret and Tariq. Without Tariq, proving our case will depend entirely on the documents we stole from NeuBank's offices in the Pan Am Building. From what little I know about the Federal Rules, those documents must somehow be authenticated. Diether Kreuz is probably the best one to do that."

David continued: "I want you to call him to the stand, as our first witness, and see if you can get him to blow up. At worst, it doesn't work and you put on Ani to prove the kidnapping and extortion, backed up with Johnny Tsai's recordings of Herr Doktor Kreuz giving her instructions about how to handle the kids and whatever. Don't let NeuBank have one, not one, centimeter of slack! Harry and I will try to find Margaret, Mr. Weatherly, and the bailiff, in that order."

"Oh, and the first chance you get," David plunged ahead, "give the judge some bullshit about our witness's having left by the back door when our man had his head turned, and how we can't understand what her law clerk was talking about, the noise in the closet and all. Gotta keep security from getting interested in this one for right now. But, before I go, let me give you some ideas about how you could get NeuBank's star witness to spit up on himself. First, I'd—"

"Mr. Peng, your relative inexperience really isn't an excuse for delaying this proceeding any further. Why, I tried cases myself soon after I was first admitted to the Bar. If we're supposed to wait for Ms. Wilbur, where is she?"

The visibly flustered young lawyer stumbled: "Your Honor, I have no idea where Ms. Wilbur went. She didn't tell me. I've only been helping her for a few days on this case and probably couldn't—"

Michael Peng looked over at an expectant Diether Kreuz and thought better of making a point of his ignorance in front of the client.

"Your Honor," Peng continued, "we request a continuance until Ms. Wilbur can be located."

"Mr. Gillespie, would that be agreeable to your client?" Judge Garcia looked toward Frank Gillespie as David disappeared through the door at the back of the courtroom.

Frank feigned interest in his sheaf of handwritten notes for what seemed like an eternity and then cleared his throat loudly, worrying his bushy mustache for good measure. "Regrettably, Your Honor, I've been instructed by my client to do everything in my power to resolve this matter as quickly as possible. Of course, I always do my best to accommodate opposing counsel, but here it's really out of my hands. We want to move ahead as soon as the Court will permit. The Fund is ready to proceed."

He looked expectantly at Judge Garcia.

"Unless you have further objections, Mr. Peng, I'm going to allow Plaintiff to present evidence in support of its motion."

Michael Peng looked anxiously about the courtroom for some source of support or comfort. His frantic search stumbled accidentally upon Diether Kreuz's piercing glare.

"Yes, I mean, no, Your Honor. No further objections at this time, except to object generally to proceeding in the absence of NeuBank's senior litigator."

"Good! Please present your first witness, Mr. Gillespie."

"Plaintiff calls as its first witness Diether Kreuz!"

Thoughtfully rubbing his mustache with the knuckle of his right index finger, the Fund's senior counsel savored the moment.

The General Manager of the New York Federal Branch of Neu Ost Bank appeared to not hear Frank Gillespie's announcement. His young lawyer looked toward the courtroom doors in vain and then leaned over to whisper in his client's right ear.

"You are perhaps crazy?" the German banker exploded. "Vy vould I vant to give testimony in ziss matter, you idiot? Ver iss Margaret Vilbur?"

"I wish I knew where Ms. Wilbur is, Herr Doktor. You are required to testify upon the request of the other party, since you are present in the courtroom. There's no basis for refusing to testify. If you refuse to give testimony, the judge can hold you in contempt."

"You better get me out of ziss mess!" Kreuz demanded.

"If you weren't here, you couldn't be called to testify without being served in advance with a subpoena. I'd like to accommodate your wishes, Herr Kreuz, but I'm powerless to keep the Court from ordering you to give testimony now that you're present in this courtroom. I'd strongly suggest you go to the witness stand. Let Judge Garcia administer the oath, and then you should answer Mr. Gillespie's questions. I'll do my very best to make sure he doesn't ask you any improper questions."

Herr Doktor Diether Kreuz drew himself up to full height and sneered angrily down at Margaret's acolyte. "If ze Bank is damached in any way by ziss circus, I vill haf your head!" He turned abruptly and trudged toward the witness box.

Frank had deliberately positioned himself to block the banker's path toward the witness stand. Gillespie danced from side to side as if trying to get out of the witness's way, only to confuse him. Under his breath, the Fund's lawyer whispered in the German's ear.

"Stasi informant! Kisser of Walter Ulbricht's Stalinist ass! You only got your job because of your subservience to the DDR state functionaries. You should be in prison like those border guards. I will see that you do real time in an American prison. Your father was probably a guard in the death camps!"

An enraged Diether Kreuz lunged for Frank Gillespie's throat. "You svine! You vill not blacken my name in zis court!"

Frank easily evaded Herr Kreuz's grasping fingers. "I really didn't mean to get in your way, SIR. Please proceed to the witness stand so we can get on with questioning."

Diether Kreuz glowered at Michael Peng. The young lawyer pointed hesitantly toward the oaken chair on a raised platform located on Judge Garcia's right side. The banker thought better of grabbing for the Fund's lawyer again and climbed reluctantly into the witness box.

"Herr Kreuz, do you require the services of a translator?" the jurist asked.

"No, my English is wery excellent, sank you," the banker growled.

"Great! Please raise your right hand."

Milagros Garcia barely suppressed a snicker as the German functionary lifted his right arm straight and high without bending the elbow.

"Do you swear to tell the whole truth and nothing but the truth, so help you God?" the judge repeated from memory.

"Ja," the witness responded solemnly.

"Your witness, Mr. Gillespie."

Agniesczka Czarnocki tensed noticeably in her seat on the hard wooden bench facing this impending interrogation. She reached up to push Martin Gluck's pudgy fingers away from the front of her blouse, where they had strayed from their resting place on her right shoulder. For Ani, the jaws of this trap were grinding shut. Diether Kreuz could clearly see her from his elevated seat in the witness chair. What little bargaining power she had left might evaporate if the German banker revealed the Iraqi connection himself.

"Please state your full name for the record, SIR," Garvey, Stahl's senior litigator directed the banker.

The witness looked at Michael Peng for instructions before answering. Receiving an affirmative nod from the young associate, he replied, "My name is Diether Kreuz, and I am ze General Manager of—"

"Could you spell that please?" the court reporter asked. He pushed thick-lensed glasses up on the bridge of his nose with the tip of his left index finger. "I got the first name, Dither, but I missed the last one entirely."

"My name iss Diether, not Dither, Kreuz. Ze first name iss spelled Day, ee, er, tay, ha, er, air," the witness distinctly repeated each letter of his given name phonetically, in German.

The stenographer looked perplexed and wiped his brow with a monogrammed handkerchief. "Maybe it would be easier if you could write your full name for me on this sheet of paper, please, sir. Would you mind spelling your family name for me, in English?"

Herr Doktor Kreuz already looked very annoyed.

"K-R-E-U-Zed, pronounced Kroitz," the NeuBank civil servant enunciated very clearly.

"Lead? What does lead have to do with your name?"

"ZED, you idiot, ze last one of ze English letters," the witness said emphatically, clearly exasperated.

"Perhaps you would be so kind as to write that one down as well, SIR? Come to think of it, please keep that sheet of paper. I heard the name of your bank. I'll need you to write that down as well," the court reporter continued, looking unhappily at the witness. He imagined how arduous and unpleasant this was going to be until his replacement arrived in one hour and thirty-two minutes.

"Patience, Simon," Judge Garcia admonished the nattily attired stenographer. "We cannot expect all of our witnesses to speak Queen's English. ¿Comprende Herr Kreuz. If you speak more slowly and keep in mind it will be necessary to stop each time you get ahead of our very professional court reporter, who is trying very hard to transcribe each and every word you say, it will be much easier for everyone. You may continue, Mr. Gillespie."

"Your Honor, I would like to treat Mr. Cruise as a hostile witness, in the event I need to ask him leading questions."

"Go ahead," the judge answered.

"Mr. Cruise, what is your occupation?"

"I am a banker. Zat is a recognized profession in Germany. I am ze General Manager of ze New York Federal Branch of Neu Ost Bank."

"Are you in charge of the banking activities of NeuBank here in New York?" Frank plunged ahead with his outline of questions for this witness, sneaking another look at his first exhibit.

"Subject in all respects to ze directives of ze Bank's Senior Management in Schverin, ze answer is ja," Kreuz conceded.

Herr Doktor Kreuz was already beginning to feel increasingly confident in giving his answers.

Frank leaned over to consult with Ambrose Jett before posing the next question. Deliberately squinting at the collection of documents in his left hand, he continued while giving his mustache a suitable rub with the index finger of his right hand.

"Do your responsibilities include accountability for transfers of funds by the New York Branch of your Bank, Mr. Cruise?"

"My name iss KROITZ! You vell know how to pronounce my name!" the witness spit back.

"Your Honor, could you please instruct the witness to answer the question? I don't know German, but I sure would like to get a straight answer to this simple question," Frank tightened his grip another notch.

"Herr Kreuz, I must ask you to be tolerant with those of us who are unfamiliar with your language. Please be patient. I'm sure the Fund's counsel is only trying to do his job," Judge Garcia observed.

"Yes, my position is including responsibility for transfers of funds," the senior NeuBank official admitted.

Frank stepped back to his table. The exhibits he planned to use were arranged in neat little piles in front of Ambrose Jett. The senior litigator once again surveyed the hoard of booty snatched in the evening raid on NeuBank's offices. He selected four very clear copies of the first exhibit.

"I would like to mark this as Plaintiff's Exhibit A for identification," Frank Gillespie said, handing a copy of Exhibit A to the reporter, who marked the document and handed one copy up to the judge, and another to Michael Peng, then turned to confront the witness.

"Mr. Cruise, I'm showing you Plaintiff's Exhibit A. Could you please tell us what this document says?"

Diether Kreuz felt his stomach muscles tighten involuntarily.

"Ver did you get zis?"

"If you don't mind, Mr. Cruise, I'll ask the questions. Please tell the Court what this document says."

Diether Kreuz was beginning to perspire heavily. Already deep stains were showing under the armpits of his summer-weight suit. His arrogance was dripping away. The German banker looked anxiously toward Michael Peng for guidance. The young lawyer shrugged and looked down at Plaintiff's Exhibit A, a copy of an electronic message directing the transfer of funds.

"Zis is an instruction to transfer by wire $566,773.20."

"Mr. Cruise, please tell the Court where the money was being transferred from and where it was being transferred to."

"Ze money vas being transferred from an account at Citibank to an account at Banque Moyen Est de Liban."

"Whose account at Citibank, Mr. Cruise?"

Frank continued to tighten the knot of this series of questions.

"Our Bank's account at Citibank," the banker admitted.

"Please speak more clearly, Mr. Cruise. Your answer was the money belonged to your Bank, isn't that correct? Whose account at Banque Moyen Est de Liban, Mr. Cruise?"

"I don't remember."

"Whose account?" Frank repeated.

"OBJECTION!" Michael Peng had a sudden inspiration and jumped to his feet. "Asked and answered."

"Sustained," Judge Garcia responded crisply.

Frank Gillespie tried a new tact.

"Isn't $566,773.20 a substantial portion of a quarterly interest payment on the Fund's loan from your Bank?"

Michael Peng stood hesitantly, half raising his right hand like a young school boy.

Without a word from the Bank's lawyer, Judge Garcia barked:

"Sustained! Really, Mr. Gillespie, you have to do better than that! Please continue and remember you promised this would not take very long!"

Frank reached over to receive four copies of the next exhibit from Ambrose Jett's outstretched hands.

"Your Honor, I would like to mark this document as Plaintiff's Exhibit B for identification. Mr. Cruise, I'm handing you Plaintiff's Exhibit B, a facsimile transmission of a letter addressed to your Bank. Could you read the second paragraph of the letter for us?"

"Please transfer ze entire amount of interest payable to us for ze interest period ending on 23 July with respect to Königsberg Fund,

$566,773.20, to our account 48556125-006 at Banque Moyen Est de Liban . . . . Ver, ver did you obtain ziss document?"

"Who signed that letter addressed to your Bank?"

"Khalaf Alwan," the disgruntled banker read from the bottom of the letter.

"And, could you please tell the Court, just who is Khalaf Alwan?"

Frank poised for the kill.

"I'm afraid I don't know," Diether Kreuz ventured. Was the old banker enjoying playing this silly game Frank had taught Ani? He seemed to be bouncing Frank's ball right back at him.

Undeterred, Frank Gillespie scooped up the next set of Exhibits from the table facing him on the counsel's table in front of Ambrose Jett.

"With the Court's permission, we'll mark these as Plaintiff's Exhibit C for identification," Frank continued methodically.

Receiving a nod from Judge Garcia, the Fund's counsel continued.

"Mr. Cruise, I am handing you a copy of Plaintiff's Exhibit C. You will see that it's page 653 from Volume II of Comford's Directory of Government Officials, the most recent edition. Could you please read the name and title I've highlighted for you?"

Diether Kreuz felt icy fingers closing around his throat.

"Khalaf Alwan," he croaked, almost inaudibly.

"Please speak up, Mr. Cruise; the court reporter cannot hear you!"

"Khalaf Alwan!" Herr Doktor Kreuz bubbled over angrily, his face darkening.

"And what is Khalaf Alwan's title, Mr. Cruise?"

"Deputy Minister of Foreign Trade."

Herr Doktor Kreuz suddenly rose from his seat, jumped down from the witness box and hurried toward the two double doors leading to the outside corridor, eyes on the floor.

"Excuse me, Mr. Cruise, I still have some more questions for you. Please sit down!"

Frank Gillespie set his teeth firmly in the desperate rabbit's neck and began to vigorously shake the struggling animal.

"Deputy Minister of Foreign Trade of which country, Mr. Cruise?" Frank persisted, trying even harder to break this rabbit's neck. "What country, Mr. Cruise?"

"I vill not receive ziss kind of abuse!" Diether Kreuz shrieked at his tormentor. "I haf business at ze office I must attend to!"

The German banker turned again toward the exit doors and the corridor outside, a possible oasis in this unexpected turmoil.

"Your Honor, let the record show Plaintiff's Exhibit C is a copy of the listings of government officials for Iraq." Frank Gillespie fired at the fleeing Diether Kreuz. "Your Honor, I have more questions for Mr. Cruise. Would the Court please instruct the witness to return to the witness stand?"

"Herr Kreuz, you cannot just turn your back on this Court and leave whenever you want. You must allow the Fund's counsel to complete his questions." Judge Garcia's voice rose as she stood up. "Please return to the witness chair!" she ordered, rapping the gavel twice sharply.

"You cannot tell me vat to do," the enraged banker screamed at Judge Garcia, brushing Michael Peng's hand from his sleeve. "Ve are a German bank! Ve are subject to real German courts, not ziss sort of circus! I vil not take instructions from some fat woman sitting even behind a big desk!"

Rap! Rap! The red-faced judge banged the gavel on the bench until its handle splintered.

"If you do not immediately return to the witness stand, Herr Kreuz, the Court will hold you in contempt! Call the marshals . . . ."

DESPERATELY SEEKING MAGGIE

Softened by large flakes of an early snow shower, the kaleidoscope of lower First Avenue buildings fluttered across David Garvey's field of vision like the frames of an old-fashioned celluloid movie or the threats besieging him. Irregular rows of brownstones, some with shop windows in place of street-level floors, squat apartment buildings, a pizza parlor, a corner bodega, a sidewalk artist sketching on the concrete sidewalk with multicolored chalk, passed ever more quickly by as Harry Cochrane's limo sped north while the pair digested the information found in Thomas Mullaney's office.

David turned his attention to his former brother-in-law. Harry reclined stiffly against the back seat of his company's utility limo, still tense from his earlier confrontation. The detective's neck was supported by a large, clear plastic bag of ice from the first Korean deli they'd been able to find north of the Federal court complex, another smaller version held tightly against his swollen chin. Harry's knees were locked, his black stockinged feet pressed against the divider separating the two front seats from the vehicle's roomier passenger compartment.

"I used to think having my own detective business would get me out of getting banged around regularly—wrong!" Harry exclaimed as he moved the smaller bag of ice to one side of his chin so it would not interfere with conversation. "For someone whose work should be pretty tame, David, you sure give me some interesting assignments.

After this one, I could use a few weeks of boring matrimonial or corporate embezzlement cases!"

The detective continued despite the fact his speech was still affected by the drubbing he'd received at the wrong end of Mullaney's vicious hands. "How do you suppose a Federal court employee gets involved in something like this?"

With everything else going on, David was very glad Harry had not been lost to him and his sons during the nasty divorce from Harry's sister. He answered Harry's question: "I'd guess Mullaney makes a passable living as a court officer, but probably spends more than he takes in. Booze from the looks of his complexion and nose and the gravelly sound of his voice—maybe the ponies too. Mullaney probably has a continuing case of the shorts. With his union seniority, it probably didn't take much skill to get assigned to Garcia, once he became, er, ah, employed by the Iraqis. Hopefully he won't have the time or opportunity to find a burrow that will escape our attention. Wha'd ya find digging around in his desk?"

Harry Cochrane said, "as you might expect—lots of junk. From the age of some of the things in his desk drawer, Mullaney came with Judge Garcia's courtroom. Lots of phone numbers, all being tracked down by my team as we speak. A two-year-old ConEd gas bill from an address on Flatbush Avenue in Brooklyn. We're checking to see if it's still a working account. I tried some of the phone numbers on the desk blotter myself. One of them was a real estate broker specializing in Upper East Side co-ops—not the usual sort of high-end, beautiful people you'd expect to have anything to do with a career civil servant. On a hunch, I sent one of our young yuppie-types over there to see if the broker would show her some of the same apartments the broker showed our friend with the lead pipe."

Harry Cochrane smirked, causing him to wince from reopening the split in his lower lip. "You see any other wild cards here, David?"

"I don't think Diether Kreuz got involved in this mess voluntarily," David declared.

Harry sat bolt upright.

"What the hell gives you that idea? He's a nasty enough bastard!"

"Nasty is one thing—might even have been a requirement for getting by in East Germany. I just don't think Herr Doktor Kreuz has enough imagination to cook up a plot like this. I'm betting someone is leaning on him very hard—most likely something more than money. That's why I asked you to seriously monitor the bug we put on his phone when we were in his office to liberate the documents Frank's hopefully using right now to wire up our case against NeuBank."

David's attention was drawn to the car phone's visual display of connected electronics. A flashing red light signaled an incoming call.

"Here's apparently a call from Will or Peter," David noted. "Are your people still stuck like glue to both of them? While I'm thinking of it, could you put a discreet tail on Diether Kreuz as he leaves the courthouse? That might give us some lead we wouldn't otherwise stumble over."

"One of my best men is assigned to each of your boys, with hourly call-in, so we'd know quickly if anything happened." Harry reassured his former brother-in-law.

"Hi, Will," David said. "What's going on in your life? Your Spanish teacher's a dork? Wasn't the dork of the week last time your history teacher? Anything unusual going on in your life? Say hi to Peter for me. Look, we're right in the middle of something important. I'll have to call you both back. Bye."

"Gotta check with the office," Harry said, passing a finger through the floating holographic image of the first speed dial icon. "So whatcha got for me, Cheryl? Hmm, well, OK, call me if anything urgent comes up."

The detective replaced the handset in its cradle and turned to David. "Nothing from the real estate side yet, but it seems our nefarious bailiff used his good payment record with ConEd to open a new account at an address in the Sutton Place area. 400 East 59th Street. Southeast corner of 59th Street and First Avenue. Couldn't get the apartment number from Con Ed. That apparently takes more than a little while to get into the part of Con Ed's computer system—some privacy issues, you know."

As David and Harry's limo sped north, a seething clot of people spilled onto First Avenue in front of the entrance to Bellevue Hospital, attended by a crowd of photographers. A transmission truck from Channel 4, the local Cosby network affiliate, its mobile transmission tower high above traffic, flashed by on the right-hand side of Harry's vehicle as it carried the two uptown.

He said to Harry, "please check the emergency rooms to see if Maggie ended up there." Continually turning variables over and over in his overheated brain, he said to his former brother-in-law, "Why don't we stop in front of the bronze boar?"

"What in hell are you blathering about?"

"You're the New York detective, and you don't even know about the bronze boar? Have your driver take a right at 57th and First and park in the cul-de-sac at the extreme end of 57th Street, just off Sutton Place. Down a ramp toward the East River, there's a bronze statue of a randy boar in the pocket park, surrounded by ugly bronze frogs and grotesque snakes. It's anatomically correct to the point that some of the neighborhood nannies are embarrassed to even look at it. If your driver pulls in there, we can get our bearings and figure out what to do next. Hopefully, by then, your minions will be reporting in, with something we can grab with our teeth."

Harry Cochrane leaned through a sliding acrylic panel in the partition separating front and back seats to direct his driver toward the tusker's playground. The limo's tires splashed through occasional puddles of melting snow, just enough to sustain the limo's clacking windshield wipers. The detective kept one eye fixed on the car's telephone console, remembering that David had told his office to forward his personal number to the speeding limo in addition to his pager.

"Can we get a high-quality recording of the call I'm expecting with the equipment in this sedan?" David asked nervously.

"You won't believe the fidelity. We'll be able to tell if the caller has heartburn, whether he has shaved recently, and maybe even how long his toenails are," Harry Cochrane said as he adjusted three separate settings on the wide electronics panel in front of him. "Ready whenever you are!"

Before long, a blinking red light captured the detective's attention. Harry waved his hand in front of David's nose and directed his friend's attention toward the console's screen.

"An 838 number—that's for an exchange in this part of town," David exclaimed. "Make the driver to pull into the cul-de-sac I mentioned, quickly! It's right ahead. And have him turn off the engine? It must be completely quiet when I take this call."

Cochrane Strategic Services Inc.'s armored, black BMW limousine rolled quietly onto the 1,250 square feet of asphalt pavement at the extreme eastern end of 57th Street, high over the deep, churning waters of the East River separating Manhattan from Queens.

Harry Cochrane passed a finger through the blinking holographic image as David held the handset tightly to his right ear.

"This is David Garvey . . . . Hello? . . . Hello?"

Suddenly, he was listening to a dial tone as the lights on the limo's communications console blinked twice and went out!

DAMSEL IN PERIL

"Jesus, Harry! What's wrong with this equipment?" David pounded the console.

"Calm down, for Chrissakes, David! It's working fine."

"Then why'd I lose the ca—?"

David held his breath as the first incoming line began to blink once more.

"Hello?"

In the slight pause that followed, David heard traffic noises in the background, buffeted by the wind, a whispering hum and someone changing positions in what sounded like an upholstered chair resting on some sort of polished wooden floor.

"Listen carefully, Mr. Garvey," the male caller announced in artificially clipped tones with a slight British accent. "This will be short because I don't want you to trace the call. Our nonnegotiable demand is full access to your facility in Königsberg, including the storage spaces for all collateral for the NeuBank loans. I'll give you a number to call in one hour. You provide the necessary access codes and you get Miss Wilbur back two hours later. We need the intervening time to make sure the codes you give us work on your facility's security system. No working codes, no sweetie."

David could hear some mumbling not very far from the phone, the gravelly tones of an older man's voice.

The tenor voice continued: "the number is 646.987.5730. Call in exactly one hour. Don't disappoi—"

"I'm not dumb enough to give you the codes without being 100 percent sure Margaret is alive and unharmed," David interrupted. "Put her on the phone or you can stuff the entire proposition!"

David chewed the second joint of his left index finger. He wondered how smart the caller really was. Why was he worried about the calls' being traced when caller ID had long been in effect in Manhattan?

"Here she is. Make it quick!" the caller directed, pushing phone against flesh.

In the background, David and Frank could hear fine steel rubbing against a somewhat rough surface. A whetstone! Someone in the background was sharpening a knife and humming a tuneless ditty in a throaty, gravelly tone.

"David?"

David could almost feel Maggie's trembling, this terror in the woman he adored.

"I'll do my best," David gasped.

Then David's whole body collapsed into the limo's cold, ebony leather seat as a dial tone replaced the sounds of Maggie's fear.

"God, that makes me feel helpless!" David moaned. "Play the tape. I pray it has something to offer us. Now!"

"You sure it was Margaret?" Harry inquired as he started to replay the recording.

David just nodded emphatically, his eyes filling with tears.

They had both listened to the entire conversation twice. Then David turned to Harry. "See if you can filter out everything but that hum, and run the whole recording again, slowly."

The detective adjusted two dials on the electronics console, listened to the headphones for a split second, and then started the conversation from the beginning, over the sedan's built-in speakers. The two voices faded into the background as one sound overshadowed all others: "zummmmmmmmm, whishhh, whishhh, whishhh, zummmmmmmmmm, clunclunk, zummmmmmmmmm, whishhh, whishhh . . ."

A rapidly blinking light on the phone console caught Harry's eye. The detective picked up a handset, listened, put down the phone and turned to interrupt David's concentration.

"We're either very lucky or someone's trying to set us up," Harry announced. "We got a line on some of the apartments Thomas Mullaney looked at very recently. One went to contract with a very large cash down payment just last week. Closing's being held up pending approval of the building's Board of Directors, the usual reasons—what's the purchaser's blood type, what color doorknobs does he have in mind, you know the silly drill. But apparently our boy managed to wangle use of the place until the paperwork's done. Want to guess which building?"

"Goddamn it, Harry! Don't keep me in suspense!"

"Would you believe 400 East 59th Street?" Harry Cochrane ventured.

David fidgeted as Harry started the recording again. Both men listened intently to the strange sounds on the recording, the detective carefully watching numbers on the counter advance while the lawyer gazed blankly north toward the southern end of York Avenue, under the 59th Street Bridge. Suddenly, David's face lit up like the bright morning sun.

"Wow!" he exclaimed so loudly Harry's driver Clyde turned around to see what was happening. "Look, Harry! Look up there!" David pointed excitedly toward the 59th Street Bridge.

Harry Cochrane looked toward the structure but still looked puzzled. "I don't see what you're talking about. There's just the street, the bridge, and the buildings . . . . Oh shit! And there's the cable car coming over from Roosevelt Island!"

"Exactly!" David blurted out. "The clunk, clunking sound is from the tram's going over one of those pylons. The caller must have been talking from an apartment facing the 59th Street Bridge, at or above the level of the upper roadway. And, I'm sure I could hear wind whistling past the open windows of the apartment."

"C'mon, Harry! We're running out of time!" David hollered impatiently. "Tell your driver to go up York and then across 59th Street, westbound. Maybe we can figure out what apartment Mullaney's holed up in. How do we get in and rescue Margaret?"

"That's a plumber's job!" Harry promised as he leaned forward to give his driver instructions, while at the same time the chirping speed dial connected the sleuth with his office.

"Yo, Cheryl! Get Rocco to call me in the limo, pronto!"

The heavily loaded ebony sedan lurched out into growing evening traffic, starting and stopping northbound on York Avenue, formerly Avenue A in less toney times. As Harry Cochrane's mobile office nudged impatiently into the queue of crimson taillights, its horn blaring, David could see an unbroken line of red traffic lights extending north, well past New York-Presbyterian Hospital. Suddenly, the traffic signals rippled from red to green, from the light in front of them at 58th Street until they disappeared into a wisp of snow showers somewhere above 70th Street. David grabbed at a nearby door handle to catch his balance, as the limousine squealed in front of a blue, smoke-belching cab to turn onto 59th Street, horn honking in anger.

Harry's telephone buzzed, and he immediately answered: "Hey, Rocco. You and your boys got a furnace job at 400 East 59th Street," he announced and continued with instructions for his crew. "Bring the heavy stuff. Pull right up in front of the building's service entrance. We'll meet you there. And, Rocco, this has got to be very, very fast. We're almost out of time!"

"Slow down as much as you can, Clyde. Harry told his driver. "We need to get a good look at this building's north face, the gray brick job on the near corner, the east side of First Avenue."

He handed David a pair of binoculars. David grabbed the heavy-duty optics from Harry's outstretched hand and dropped to his knees on the carpeted floor of the limo to get a clear view of the brick facade of the apartment building coming slowly into view on the south side of 59th Street. Standing almost by itself, the older building was set off by a long, dark green awning with "400" in large, white numbers.

The lawyer scanned two vertical rows of larger apartments facing 59th Street from the center of the structure. Those above the third floor had casement windows from waist-level to the ceilings in the living rooms. David scrutinized the western bank of apartments. No casement windows were open except on the fourth floor. He concluded noise from the Roosevelt Island tram would probably have been different than the way the recording sounded if the open windows were below the fifth or sixth floors.

Turning his attention to the eastern bank of similar, larger luxury units, David spotted open casement windows on two floors—the ninth floor, just below an apartment where the owner had replaced all of the casement windows with plate glass, and on the fourteenth floor.

"Whadda ya think, Harry?" David asked.

"From the volume and sound of traffic noises on our recording, I'd bet the ninth floor. That's the only place with more than one window open. My ears tell me there were several windows open from wherever we were called. Let's see how that apartment's laid out," the sleuth suggested.

"How ya gonna do that?" David asked impatiently.

Harry Cochrane momentarily ignored David's question while yelling through the partition: "Clyde, pull around the corner at First and stop almost under the 59th Street Bridge but not so far under the brickwork that we can't see 400 East 59th out the back window."

"David, pass a finger through the floating holographic icon of 'Plans' on my installed Holo and you'll see the digital collection of Manhattan building plans we bought two years ago. Let me help you . . ."

Soon plans of each floor of the multifamily dwelling at 400 East 59th Street fluttered across the screen of Harry's Holo.

In the gathering dusk, a dented gray panel truck bearing the legend "Soldati & Son—Plumbers at Large" and no small amount of graffiti rattled up First Avenue, slowed and chugged through a right turn onto 59th Street. Soldati's battered truck jerked to a halt at the building service entrance for 400 East 59th Street, just a few yards east of the conspicuous kelly-green awning leaning over the edge of the concrete curb on 59th Street.

"Christ, what a weird layout! The whole structure is divided into two halves—east and west," David began reading from the Holo's screen. "Each half of the building has its own elevator bank and service elevator. The apartment where we think Maggie is being held has its main entrance off the eastern bank of elevators, on the ninth floor. But the service entrance is on ten. Looks like there are three ways to get out of this apartment—main door, service entrance, and the windows. At least there aren't any external fire escapes. The apartment's pantry backs up to the service entrance, and the service entrance opens onto interior fire stairs. The large living room and den are on nine; the rest of the place is on the tenth floor."

"Remember, Harry, our only real interest is getting Margaret out safely. Getting Mullaney and maybe Mr. Weatherly is only secondary. Focus, focus on how we get into that particular apartment."

Harry Cochrane looked directly into David's eyes, trying to absorb his scattered instructions.

"Here. Put on these coveralls and follow me," he said, reaching into one of the limo's bins and handing David a dirty brown work uniform sporting a worn Roto-Rooter emblem.

Harry pulled on his own jumpsuit before David Garvey could hide his conservative, dark blue business suit under the nondescript uniform he'd been given.

The lawyer shifted his Glock 19 from its shoulder holster to an internal pocket in the right side of his jumpsuit within easy reach of his left hand. Then he looped his cell phone's lanyard around his neck so the device hung inside what was supposed to look like work clothes.

Harry opened the curbside door of the limousine, and the pair clambered out onto the busy sidewalk, without giving a second thought to how strange it looked for two laborers to be getting out of luxury transportation.

Harry leaned back inside to give his driver detailed last-minute instructions. "Clyde, put on that set of diplomatic plates you keep under the spare tire in the trunk and idle on the north side of 59th Street, just across from the building. Whatever you do, don't leave the phone! Let's go, David!"

Harry turned to hurry David along but saw his friend was already running across 59th Street in midblock, toward the plumbing truck as he dodged a pair of bicyclists.

The detective sprinted to catch up, beating David to the truck by just one stride. Harry rapped the back door of the vehicle twice, paused, and then rapped it twice again with his gloved fist.

"Party time, Rocco," Harry Cochrane announced.

The dented driver's door of the plumbing truck creaked open. Its portly operator hopped down from the torn, high seat.

"David, this is Rocco Soldati."

Harry gestured toward the rotund Italian, who cracked a wide smile, revealing a single shiny gold tooth.

"You ready, Rocco?" the detective blurted out. "It's up to you to get us all inside, into the service elevator for the east wing. If we get stopped, you and your two boys are here to answer an emergency call on the furnace. We've got to get into apartment 9E, but we'll take the service elevator to six and walk up the fire stairs, so they're less likely to hear us. If the service elevator's in use, send the operator out for a break, if ya know what I mean. Bring your firepower and electrical equipment. This is serious, Rocco. David's main squeeze is probably being held in that apartment, by the same people who kidnapped his two boys a couple of weeks ago. There's a lot of money involved, so we can expect serious resistance."

Rocco Soldati took a drag on his wilted green cigar and looked David up and down.

"So, David. You gonna be any help on dis one?" Rocco asked. "Dose look like pretty fancy shoes to be gettin' doity or woise. Ever have someone try to blow ya brains out?"

"I've seen more than my share of real blood in the past couple months," David spit right back. "I'm ready to rip someone's face off for messing with my family! So, Rocco, if you'll move your fat ass in the direction of those stairs into the basement, we can get this show on the road and not waste time standing here pulling each other's putzes. We've got twenty minutes, max, to carry this one off."

"I can do dat!" Rocco chuckled.

He jerked open the back door of the van.

"Vinnie, Jock, grab da tools and folla me."

Vinnie Soldati, a younger and only slightly slimmer version of Rocco, rolled out of the dark recesses of the rear compartment of the plumbing truck closely followed by Jock Jefferson, a lanky black man with his hair tied up tightly in an indigo kerchief. Each carried two bulging canvas satchels of equipment that clinked and rattled as they landed on the pavement. Jock bent over to slide a stiletto into its place in the upper of his work boot. Rocco locked the van and clicked a heavy padlock in place on its rear doors.

David, Harry and the three plumbers disappeared into the dimly lit arch leading down into the bowels of 400 East 59th Street.

Before long, Rocco Soldati eased the service elevator to a jerky stop on the sixth floor of the prewar building. Behind him, the janitor lay sleeping peacefully behind a large plastic trash barrel, his hands securely bound and a gag stuffed in his mouth while the rest of David's team strained to spring into action.

"I'll take out the key ta dis contraption so it don't disappear," Rocco whispered softly.

He swung a long, bronze lever to slowly open the outer door of the service elevator and peered into the brightly lit hallway outside.

"All clear except for dis pile of gahbage outside da back door of de apartment on dis floor like we're trying to get into on nine," Rocco said quietly.

"I'll make the call from in here," David Garvey announced softly.

Harry pointed outside the elevator and said, "Rocco, you listen at the front door on nine. I get the service entrance on ten. See if you can hear a phone ringing inside when I call!"

"How many people in dere?" Rocco asked.

Looking around the expectant faces, Harry Cochrane laid out the assault plan. "There's probably three people in there. Maggie and a thin, well-dressed little Arab, who'll probably try to just slip away. Plus the guy who snatched Maggie from the courtroom—he's red-faced and probably sixty plus. We'd like to hang onto the Arab if possible. But the Irish guy, name's Mullaney, probably isn't worth saving. David'll make the call in exactly two minutes. Oh, and Rocco, have Vinnie and Jock tap into the control circuit and surveillance system for the passenger elevator in this bank. Remember, protect the woman at all costs!"

"No problem. We'll get right on it!" Rocco replied.

David Garvey rocked back on his haunches against the thin aluminum paneling of the rear wall of the cluttered service elevator. He watched absently as the two helpers scampered quietly down freshly painted gray fire stairs and Rocco and Harry hurried to their posts. His heart racing as he tried to fathom what was roaring toward him like a freight train, David quickly reviewed the variables to see if he had forgotten anything that might endanger Margaret.

The cell phone deep inside his jumpsuit chirped loudly. David groped for the instrument in panic, bobbling it in his haste to stop the incessant tone that might alert Maggie's captors. Blinking in time with its electronic chirps, the heavy plastic gadget slipped from his grasping fingers and clunked to the lift's rough wooden floor. Finally, his left index finger found the button connecting him with the cellular network as David held the phone to his ear.

"Hello," he whispered nervously, both eyes fixed on the empty hall outside.

"Mr. Garvey!" an abrupt male voice demanded.

"Yes?"

"Diether Kreuz here. Because of you, I am now in jail sitting. This is your last chance to make ziss go avay! Do as they are now demanding!"

"I . . . I'm pretty busy right now. You'll have to get in li—" David Garvey responded sharply as he deliberately ended the call in the middle of one of his own words.

Watching the numbers of Herr Kreuz's phone fade from his cell's tiny screen, David held it tightly for a split second, hoping against hope to find his way through this terrible mess. Then David poked its stubby antenna of his bulky cellphone outside the elevator door for better transmission and carefully tapped out the number he'd been given.

WHATEVER IT TAKES

"Hello?"

The same refined voice with the clipped British accent answered after the second ring. In the background, David could hear the noise of traffic building on the 59th Street Bridge from the evening rush hour, outbound from Manhattan.

"This is David Garvey. I have all the access codes for you, if you can convince me Margaret is still in good health."

"No more games. Here she is," the voice snapped.

David heard someone jam a receiver phone against Margaret's cheekbone. She exhaled sharply as someone held her much too tightly.

"I'm all right, David. But, this obnoxious . . ." the angry woman wheezed. "Pleeeez, pleeeeez, put that knife away! No! No! Don't cut me! Help me, David, this Mullaney's crazy . . . he's going to . . ." she shrieked.

Her sobbing screams were cut short by clunk of a telephone handset smashing bone. Something hit the parquet floor with a bulky thump. Rough hands grabbed for the fallen instrument.

An enraged gravelly voice riveted David's attention. "Give the little twerp the fucking codes, Counselor, sir. I'm getting sick and tired of these stupid fucking games! Yes, sir, yes, ma'am—all my fucking life I've had to play Stepin Fetchit for you fucking lawyers. Now I'm the boss. If you want to see this fucking frigid bitch ever again, give this slimy little Arab the fucking codes, or I'll start carving her into Mrs. Potato Head!"

"Calm down. I've got what you want." David gulped.

"Here, Mr. Garvey, sir, would you kindly provide the access codes to Mr. al-Tikriti, sir? I'm going to hand him the telephone, sir, and then I have to take a call from Senator Rendelman's Judicial Nominating Committee, the Supreme Court, you know. Thank you in advance for your cooperation, sir."

Once the one he knew as Tariq al-Tikriti took the phone, David Garvey could barely contain his fear and anger. He carefully outlined for the subdued young Iraqi the detailed procedures for bypassing the Konigsberg outpost's several layers of electronic security. In excruciating detail, the chief of the Königsberg Fund explained how each of the codes would enable the intruders to enter first the office area and then the additional special set of ciphers needed to gain access to the heart of David's operation—the vault area where all of the loan collateral documents vital to the Fund's existence were stored.

When David had completed his explanation of the outpost's security barriers, he made Tariq read back the entire outline, word for word.

"I'm not exactly a moron," Fearless Leader's nephew whined.

"No offense intended," David placated him. "My outpost's security system was designed to be complicated. I want to be certain that when I call back, you won't tell me your friends had some problem getting into the vault. Is there anything else you need to know?"

Biting his tongue almost until it bled, David listened to the background noises on the other end of the phone as if Margaret's life depended on it. One thing he heard clearly was a resigned sigh from the young man holding the receiver. Suddenly, David Garvey's waiting ear was assaulted by Thomas Mullaney's rough voice:

"You better hope this works, Sir Counselor. If it doesn't, your girlfriend and this fucking little Arab twit won't ever see the light of day again. Oh, and there's been a change of plans. I'll call you at the number we used the first time, once the Iraqis are in your vault. Ha, ha, Counselor, Sir, most honorable member of the Bar! Don't call us, we'll call you. This phone's out of order, starting right no—"

David found himself staring intently at the silent phone, as if his desperate attention would bring the connection back to life. After a few seconds, his concentration was interrupted: "If you would like to make a call, hang up and try again . . . BEEP, BEEP, BEEP."

David looked up as Rocco and Harry padded softly toward the service elevator door. Rocco's gold tooth was plainly visible through his broad grin.

"Like my gran'daughter says," the older Soldati beamed, "he said da 'F' woid! I could hear 'em with my good ear to da crack under da front door. Sounded like he was also beatin' someone up while you was talking."

David winced.

"He hit Margaret with the phone," he reported calmly, trying his very best to put his fear in a box, on a faraway shelf. "Wha'd you hear, Harry?"

"I was listening under the back door, you know, at the south end of the kitchen. Someone opened the refrigerator while you were talking to Mullaney. I heard some bottles rattle, like the sound bottles make when drinks are stored inside the door, and then the top of a can being popped. It couldn't have been Mullaney. If you're right about Maggie, it probably wasn't her either. Was it the devious Mr. Weatherly? Or perhaps some muscle the Iraqis sent to help out their tool?"

Harry Cochrane looked down at David, who was still sitting on his haunches against the elevator's rear wall, apparently oblivious to what his brother-in-law had just said.

"What do you think, Counselor?" Harry asked again.

David Garvey's face felt hot, and his features were contorted with rage. He tried to speak but couldn't. Fortunately, Harry Cochrane picked up the ball.

"Rocco, I want you to go back and see if you can hear anyone—the little Arab or Mullaney—giving instructions to someone about how to get around a security system. As soon as you think that's happening, duck back into the fire stairs and toss this Jolt Cola can down to the landing, right in front of me. Whatever you do, DON'T let them get away with Maggie."

"They'd have ta walk ovah my dead body! But whose dis Weatherly?"

"That's the little Arab guy we were talking about. Doesn't look strong, but watch out for wild cards. Now get going! We're outta time."

Harry Cochrane pushed the plumber out the narrow opening in the service elevator door.

"Before you go, Rocco, can I borrow a couple of your really terrific cigars and your lighter? I've got an idea, David!"

The older man reluctantly passed a silver cigar lighter and two stogies back through the partly open door to his employer and disappeared up the internal fire stairs.

David and Harry both jumped as Vinnie Soldati poked his dark, curly head of hair through the freight elevator door.

"Whassup, Vinnie?"

"My dad said to give you this. The screen duplicates the passenger elevator's surveillance camera and the buttons override the floor selector," Vinnie explained.

The younger Soldati handed Harry a small black box and disappeared as quickly as he had come.

"What's your idea, Harry?" David pleaded. "We desperately need something creative."

"You noticed those blue garbage bags on the landing outside?"

David Garvey looked annoyed.

"Sure, so what? How's that help?"

"You're looking for a chance to break down some doors and, as soon as possible, some heads. Save Maggie and make up for everything they've put you through in the past couple of months. Right?"

Harry put his hand on David's shoulder. He continued, "Maybe we can get Margaret out alive quicker, with less bloodshed."

"Jesus Christ, Harry. Just get on with it!"

Harry Cochrane flicked the top of Rocco's lighter. Instantly, a bright blue flame shot from a tiny opening atop the silver canister.

"You and I are gonna take some of those blue bags up to the ninth floor in the service elevator. A hot cigar left in one of those plastic recycling bags by some careless slob will quickly generate more than enough black smoke to set off the smoke detectors in the ninth-floor landing, and maybe on the tenth or eleventh floors as well. This building is wired directly to the Fire Department."

The detective looked at David, beaming proudly.

"Great! So we set off the fire alarm. I don't see how that saves Margaret," David observed, sounding very annoyed.

Harry Cochrane looked chagrined but quickly explained, "Those open windows in 9E's living room, toward the bridge, should suck the clouds of black smoke under both doors of the apartment. We maybe ought to cover up the crack under the door to Mullaney's kitchen, so whoever's inside will think that's the safe way out. Even if that doesn't work, we should have a gaggle of axe-happy firemen to help us break down the door to 9E. If the fire brigade arrives as planned, the black smoke should be billowing out of the casement windows over 59th Street to whet their appetites. What do you think now?"

"I love it!" David exclaimed. "Get Rocco's two sidekicks up here to help, right now! We can use some extra muscle, particularly if Mullaney has some backup in there! Let's go!"

David pounded a clenched fist into his palm in anticipation. He looked up as an aluminum can emblazoned with a crimson lightning bolt pinged down the concrete stairs from above.

Harry Cochrane leaped toward the freight elevator's controls.

"Going up! Ninth floor! Time to kick ass!"

Just before the elevator door closed completely, he halted its progress and looked at David.

"Why don't you pull in two or three of those blue garbage bags? We wouldn't want to run out of raw material."

Shortly, the pair peeked out through a partially open service elevator door onto the ninth-floor landing. The detective disappeared around the corner into the main hall to find Rocco Soldati. David tiptoed up the stairs to the landing on ten. Reaching into the inner pocket of his business suit to find a small coil of piano wire, he strung it tightly from a rusty radiator leg in the corner next to apartment 9E's back door across the door frame, just at ankle level. Then, David attached the other end of the wire to the base of a heavy electrical cable conduit running between the door frame and the door to the service elevator. He lightly plucked the taut cable with the tip of his left index finger, the jade ring Margaret had given him catching his worried eye. B flat, he hummed to himself, tripping lightly down the fire stairs to nine.

Just then, Harry Cochrane and Rocco Soldati slipped noiselessly through the door between the landing and the ninth-floor elevator lobby. Harry motioned toward the open service elevator door and the three stepped inside. The elder plumber swung the heavy lever down to shut the elevator's door and flipped open his communicator: "Yo, Vinnie! You take da service elevator when it comes to ya and come up ta nine after removin' da operator. Have Jock come up da fiyah stairs! It's almos' showtime and it's up ta you ta make sure none of da bad guys gits away wit da girl. Lemme describe da . . ."

Now David Garvey had only a few seconds to make a life or death decision. The pressure felt like a tight steel bank around his temples—tighter and tighter.

Should the three of them try to rescue Maggie themselves? Or should they hope Tariq's accomplices had broken into the outpost's defenses and that both Tariq and Mullaney would honor their promises to let her go unharmed? There were terrible risks in both cases and no guarantees.

Whatever alternative David chose would subject everyone involved to certain danger, and perhaps death. Both plans had too many moving parts.

He rubbed both temples with his fingertips to ease the tension and thought to himself: *Just one more time, Marja! Please help me! It seems like you've been gone so very long and I may have disobeyed your instructions. You see? I really do care about Maggie. Forgive me, for everything! If you could only give me some practical inspiration here . . .*

Harry tapped David anxiously on the shoulder.

"Time's running out, David!"

David Garvey stared fiercely at Harry Cochrane and the older plumber, his eyes filling with tears. "We've only got two choices, both dangerous. I vote for not sitting here expecting Mullaney to be smart, rational or honorable. Start the fire!"

Rocco Soldati yanked a length of heavy iron pipe from inside his overalls.

"Fine wit me," he said. "Let's do it."

Harry Cochrane shook his head wearily. "Rocco, take a couple hard puffs on that smelly thing and lemme have it."

Rocco Soldati took three deep drags on his wilting green cigar, as if kissing a dear friend good-bye, and handed the stogie to Harry. The detective pushed its glowing orange tip against the edge of a plastic drink container and blew on it lustily, until a small curl of dingy, then thick black smoke swirled up from the blue garbage bag. Turning his head to take a deep breath of clean air, he fueled the growing conflagration with a powerful breath at the base of the flames before motioning the two others to leave the elevator and setting the empty metal trash barrel on the floor outside. Then he pushed the elevator's control in the direction of the basement and let the heavy door slide shut.

David heard the elevator humming slowly downward, carrying the unconscious porter away from the fray, as his best friend Harry fanned the peach-colored tendrils of fire in the open garbage bag at his feet. David could already feel the radiant heat from the burgeoning blaze nipping at the exposed backs of his hands. He suppressed the need to cough from the growing cloud of acrid black smoke. Harry turned the dented trash barrel on its side and kicked the burning pile of refuse into it, cracked the outer window slightly, and dumped another bag of garbage on the bonfire. Looking away to avoid the growing heat, Harry Cochrane righted the trash barrel in front of the closed elevator door, squarely under the red, blinking eye of the smoke detector.

"Let's make sure this mess gets under the front door of 9E," Harry Cochrane ordered.

The detective pushed Rocco Soldati into the outer hall. Stepping tentatively into the hall, Rocco Soldati jammed the door to the main elevator lobby open by crunching a smashed metal soft drink can into its hinge side. Surging clouds of black ooze disappeared under the front door of apartment 9E.

INTO THE LISTS

Harry and David didn't notice black smoke also flowing under a similar apartment door immediately behind them.

"What the hell's going on out here?"

A tiny old woman with owlish spectacles shook a bony fist at both strangers standing in her hall, threadbare stockings rolled down just below knobby knees under the torn hem of a shabby pink night dress.

"Smells like a goddam fire to me! You guys work for the building or something?"

The woman tried to step out into the hall. "What's going on?" she rasped.

Rocco Soldati turned to glower over his puny interrogator, smacking the length of worn pipe repeatedly against the meaty palm of his left hand.

"Besides we'll take care a da problem . . . , if ya don't git back in yer hole and shaddup, I'll rip off yer arm and beat ya wid it!"

The plumber immediately turned his attention back to Harry Cochrane as Thomas Mullaney's new neighbor scurried back into her cramped studio apartment, slamming the door shut, and double locking it from inside.

Rocco exclaimed, "I hear a couple a sireens out front and da honking fire trucks coming down da block. Lemme take care of da firemen when dey get here. De'll be up in da main elevator wid de odda one outta commission. Ya betta help ya fren. I'm afraid he might not be careful."

"Probably right," Harry replied. "I'll try to keep David out of trouble. Make sure no one in 9E slips away during the confusion. You be careful, Rocco! These Iraqis are plain nasty. No regard at all for human life."

The detective clapped Rocco Soldati on the shoulder.

A white light over the passenger elevator door dinged, prompting Rocco to push Harry into the service elevator lobby and kick the crushed soda can out of the door hinge. Rocco could already hear the clanking of equipment and shoulder radios blaring inside the overcrowded passenger elevator.

Just as the elevator doors parted to spew out a horde of stamping firemen on the red tile floor of the small lobby, Rocco Soldati thought he could hear the vacant honk of a CO_2 fire extinguisher behind the closed service lobby door. In the distance, a heavy metal window frame slammed against the top of its stops.

"Da fire's in dere," the graying plumber yelled, pointing frantically toward the door to apartment 9E. "I was bangin' on da door, but no one's home. Hurry up! It might spread!"

The roiling tide of yellow raincoats and heavy rubber boots grew calm for just a moment. Mahogany eyes glaring through the clear visor of his breathing apparatus, the fire company's first member pushed roughly past the senior Soldati.

"Outta da way," he commanded.

A fire lieutenant stepped into view and pounded vigorously on the door of 9E with a heavy gloved fist.

"Open up! Fire Department!"

Hearing no answer, the officer backed slightly away from the dark green door and pointed a sturdy black flashlight toward its bronze door knocker, urging his troops forward.

"Knock it down," he ordered.

The crowd parted, allowing a pair of young firemen to leap up and gleefully splinter the apartment door with a fusillade of blows from two massive, silver fire axes.

The lieutenant held up his right hand to halt the destruction momentarily and reached inside to undo both double latches. The flood of firemen squeezed through the narrow door and disappeared from sight.

Rocco Soldati tensed as a pair of double locks clicked open loudly behind the door to the fire stairs. He turned to peer through the crack between the frosted glass-paned door and its molding. Without warning, two fists clenched together hit the burly plumber from behind, knocking him to the ground.

The last thing Rocco Soldati saw before slipping away into unconsciousness was a pair of highly polished cordovan loafers disappearing into the open door of the descending passenger elevator.

CLOSE COMBAT

His legs spread wide for better balance, Harry Cochrane braced his fully loaded .45-automatic against the wall and drew a bead on the middle of the center panel of the back door to apartment 9E.

David Garvey squeezed into the small alcove created by the freight elevator's recessed door, Glock 19 drawn and cocked in his left hand, and both eyes trained on the co-op's rear entrance, scant inches from his right shoulder.

They didn't have long to wait.

The steel-sheathed door swung inward, banging against a wooden kitchen table and knocking over a yellow, ceramic sugar bowl, framing the former court employee's sweat-stained back in the narrow portal. Thomas Mullaney's hammerlock on Margaret Wilbur's heaving torso was supposed to help him drag her out of the apartment, but she was struggling ferociously and kept slipping from his grasp, toward the floor.

"Bite me again, you miserable bitch, and I'll blow your fucking brains out, so help me God," he yelled. "I've had more than enough of your shit! You're gonna help me get out of here or you'll Goddamn well die in the process. And get your fucking foot out from under the leg of that chair. Jesus fucking Christ!"

The aging clerk grunted under the strain of a sustained tug on his captive, just as his left foot found David Garvey's trip wire and he lurched sideways. Mullaney tried to get his balance by holding

Margaret tightly but, at just that moment, she released the chair leg and wrapped both arms tightly around his ankles. Teetering precariously, Thomas Mullaney lurched forward, kissing the cold steel edge of the ascending fire stairs with a dry, crunching sound.

Maggie crawled crab-like away from her tormentor, wispy shreds of her shredded panty hose catching momentarily on the door frame.

"Freeze, Mullaney!" Harry Cochrane screamed. "Give me any reason to splatter you all over that wall behind you. Don't move a muscle! Over here, Maggie, we've come to take you home." The angry detective waved her in his direction.

His right hand preoccupied with retrieving a large shard of broken denture from inside his bloody mouth, the battered bureaucrat raised an open left hand weakly over his head. He paused to spit the remains of a shattered front tooth on the gray floor in front of him as he doggedly pulled himself to a crouching position, using the low windowsill as a crutch. Mullaney smiled wickedly at Harry, drooling crimson clots of blood and saliva onto his rumpled green polyester shirt.

"I'm not afraid of you, Mr. Detective, Sir, not one little bit," he cackled shrilly. "The Federal marshals guarding me will make short work of you. When Mr. Chief Justice Thomas Mullaney is finished with you, you'll wish you'd never been born."

Unnoticed by everyone except the sneering court clerk, a large shadow clouded the milky door panel behind the enraged Harry Cochrane.

The door from the hall slammed open violently, throwing Harry Cochrane against David, knocking them both to the floor. Momentarily deafening everyone in the tiny space, Harry's .45-automatic pistol accidentally fired from the unexpected impact, before clattering down the freshly painted gray fire stairs. The heavy slug obliterated Mullaney's left shoulder, its momentum lifting the clerk up and back. Thomas Mullaney's awkward pirouette was arrested by the immovable concrete windowsill.

For the second time in a few moments, the bailiff lost his balance and rocked backward toward the gaping, open window. Losing his tussle with gravity, Mr. Chief Justice Thomas Mullaney disappeared from view without a sound. After what seemed like an eternity, his body crashed heavily into a heap of empty glass bottles in the interior courtyard far below.

With visible enjoyment, Abdul stomped heavily on Harry Cochrane's outstretched hand. The beefy Iraqi motioned the trio toward the apartment door with the barrel of a silver snub-nosed pistol.

"Drop gun or I shoot girl," Abdul ordered David, who tossed his Glock into a far corner without hesitation.

"I'm no girl, you miserable excuse for a human being!" Margaret Wilbur shrieked from her fetal position on the cold floor, oblivious to the danger surrounding her. She pushed Abdul's gun hand aside and punched him squarely in the crotch.

The Iraqi's dull moan of pain became an ear-piercing scream. Clutching at his left ankle, he dropped heavily to the concrete, writhing in agony in a small but growing puddle of blood. Standing behind Abdul on the fire stairs, two steps below where the drama was unfolding, Jock carefully inspected his shiny stiletto for damage, wiped it clean with an oily rag, and carefully inserted the weapon back into its sheath in the upper of his work boot. He looked up at Harry Cochrane expectantly.

"A little messy, but even someone that big can't get around very well if you sever his Achilles tendon," Harry's operative observed casually.

Harry Cochrane recovered first. "Let's see what happened to Rocco. I thought he was covering our backs. Jock, could you hand me my gun from the landing? David, get yours and watch this jerk."

Outside in the hall, he shook the groggy plumber.

"So, Rocco, what happened?" Harry asked.

"Feels like someone hit me behind the head wit a sledge hammah. Lemme at 'im!"

"No need, my friend. I think we're done here. Jock saved the day."

Harry helped the dazed Rocco Soldati to his unsteady feet.

"I'll tell you all about it while we're turning the big guy in to the police. Mullaney fell out the back window."

"No shit!"

Rocco winced as he explored the tender back of his swollen neck.

CLEANING UP

As the blue-and-white Hatzolah ambulance screamed away carrying the injured and fully restrained Abdul, its red lights flashing and siren honking, David and Maggie watched from the comfort of the deep leather seats of Harry's limo.

David reached over to gently touch the swollen purple bruise on Maggie's left temple and smoothed her rumpled chestnut bangs.

"I'd have given anything to have you safe—my life, all of my business. But it's finally over now. Harry's driver said the police we sent to Diether Kreuz's house in Mamaroneck found a couple of Abdul clones holding the good Doktor's wife and two daughters. I've thought for some time all the problems with our loan arrangements with NeuBank were not entirely of the Bank's doing. We should be able to get rid of the litigation without very much discussion or difficulty."

"Hold me close, David. I can't take any more of this," Maggie whispered.

"Clyde, could you please take us around to my place?" David asked. "Harry's going to be occupied for a while with NYPD paperwork. On the way home, we have just one small piece of unfinished business. I've got to report in," he said for Maggie's benefit.

The ebony limousine lumbered heavily around the corner of 59th Street into the clotting flow of evening traffic heading north on First Avenue.

David passed a finger through floating images of the "On" button of his cell phone and cautiously swiped in nine numbers, paused to listen for a short answering tone, and then tapped out four more digits.

Far away, in the basement of a building masquerading as a toxic industrial site on the snowy banks of the Pegel River, a high-speed computer generated a sound like the message signal on an answering machine. At the tone, David Garvey left his message.

"Standby to repel boarders," David enunciated carefully.

The waiting computer acknowledged his command with four short beeps.

"You really want to do that, David?" a sexy, female Finnish voice asked.

Even at the end of this road, Marja is still there, looking out for me, David thought to himself wistfully.

Lieutenant Garvey responded to her question with a single terse command: "Repel boarders!"

"What was that all about?" Maggie mumbled sleepily, snuggling even closer to him.

"Just some light housekeeping at the outpost in Königsberg. Nothing for you to worry about, my love."

David wrapped the overwrought woman tightly in both arms as they sped up the avenue through a haze of bright lights and frenzied traffic.

Marja already took care of it, David thought sadly to himself, a lump in his throat as he gazed wistfully into the distance.

Hours to the east, not yet light this late autumn morning, the two outer doors of the Fund's nerve center in Königsberg slid noiselessly shut. Heavy stainless steel bolts, carefully installed deep within the structure's internal iron girders by Marja and her construction crew as protection against this unlikely event, slid smoothly into place through their outer edges. Then all three hatch-shaped doors forming the only passages through the next security bulkhead inside the

Fund's European headquarters swung silently closed on well-oiled hinges, hermetically isolating its sensitive inner compartments from the rest of the building. Only someone listening very carefully would have heard the four dogs on each hatch-shaped door, their controls accessible only from outside surfaces, hum slightly as each tightened its thick, cast-iron panel against the gasket of its seat.

Deep inside the Königsberg outpost's inner core—its vault and document repository—three Iraqis in nondescript civilian clothes looked up from their tedious task of cataloguing the Fund's loans, mortgages and other financial assets to see a slatted steel sheet drop out of the ceiling, sliding noisily down a pair of tracks alongside the inner frame of the vault's only exit. Before they could reach it, their only escape route disappeared behind the rattling two-inch bulletproof, steel shield. One of the frightened men reached over to rap the metal barrier with his knuckles and then tried without success to lift it from the concrete floor. Even straining mightily, the three Iraqis couldn't budge the cork in David Garvey's extermination bottle.

"By the beard of Allah, what is happening, sir?" the most junior intruder looked quizzically at their team leader.

"Get back to work," the black-bearded sergeant directed gruffly. "We have much more to do before noon."

Inside the outpost's now airtight inner sanctum, its main security computer, in response to coded instructions written in a happier time by a radiant young Finnish woman against this dreadful possibility, directed a series of valves to click open. An entire bank of sixty-three carbon dioxide canisters hissed into the intake side of that sector of the outpost's ventilation system supplying the document storage rooms and its vault that guarded 1.4 billion dollars worth of loan collateral, a treasure trove that grew daily.

Six pairs of silently whirling fans swiftly dispersed the resulting clouds of the invisible and odorless gas into every nook and cranny of the heart of the European headquarters of the Königsberg Fund, now free of all living beings except for the Iraqi intruders. As the amount of carbon dioxide in the vault's atmosphere rapidly exceeded the level where humans could survive, the three Iraqis breathed faster and faster, their autonomous nervous systems trying desperately to save them from suffocation.

Just like we used to exterminate roaches and other vermin infesting the boats, David thought.

Soon, even the sound of breathing and fevered scratching on the slatted steel gate of the vault's execution chamber faded away.

Marja's lingering touch had purified David's prize as effectively as if she had personally strangled each of the intruders.

The outpost slept peacefully.

EPILOGUE

Tariq al-Tikriti looked dismally down the nearly deserted street from inside a dilapidated phone booth, torrents of rain pouring from the dark skies.

He gulped and stuck his finger into the floating holographic image of the last digit of a long number. A cadence of thrums was abruptly interrupted by a curt answer in Arabic.

"Yes?"

Tariq identified himself and meekly asked to be connected to the Exalted Ruler.

"You are late," the voice on the other end of the line thundered. "Give me news of the success of our operation!"

"Respected Uncle, there have been some slight delays, unforeseen difficulties . . ."

"No excuses! The embargo is strangling our people, your family. When will you deliver the assets of the Fund to our custody?"

"I'm working on it diligently at this very moment, dear Uncle. The goal is almost within our grasp. Please have an additional $5 million sent to the account in Luxembourg."

"You better not trifle with me, little nephew. That would be very bad for you and your mother and sisters."

Pulling a scrap of cellophane from his sodden trench coat pocket, Tariq began to crumple it noisily near the mouthpiece of the battered telephone.

"I'm having trouble hearing you . . . . Send the money . . . . I (crackle, crackle) can't . . . we will be succee—"

The young Iraqi passed a finger through the holographic image of the "disconnect" icon floating in the air, cutting the international connection.

He wearily replaced the handset on its hook and pulled the collar of his trench coat up around his neck.

A passing Royal Canadian Mounted Police van splashed muddy water on his brown leather hiking boots as he turned to trudge down the main street of Nanaimo, British Columbia, toward the ferry terminal's darkened bus station.

ABOUT THE AUTHOR

The author is a member of the New York Bar and has practiced international banking and commercial law in Manhattan for decades. A graduate of Yale College and Penn Law School, he lives in Fairfield County, Connecticut. He served as a commissioned officer in the US Atlantic Submarine Force.

"Doug McPheters does a fantastic job of providing the reader with a glimpse of what it would be like to fly a super-advanced airplane; his description of the Goshawk's maneuvering capability is very realistic and puts the reader in the cockpit with David Garvey."

Retired Air Force and commercial pilot

DIANA KLEBANOW

KLEBANOW